I0657987

Death in the Parsonage

Susan Spencer-Smith, M.S., M.Div., D.Min.

HOOPIE GIRL PRESS, INC.
Westerville, Ohio 43081
Weirton, West Virginia 26062

Death in the Parsonage © 2010 Susan Spencer-Smith

Manufactured in the United States of America

Distributed through Amazon.com

Cover design by Brion Sausser at Book Creatives

ISBN-13   978-0-9829763-0-2
ISBN-10   0-9829763-0-5

DEDICATION

For all the women pastors

APPRECIATION

I thank those congregations whose members have graciously informed my understanding of pastoral ministry and those professors who generously schooled me in theology, spirituality, pastoral care and church polity. Their wisdom is exceeded only by their patience.

I am also grateful to my husband, Grant Beamer, for his skillful and good-natured technical support, and to my sister, Roberta Taylor, for her steadfast encouragement and persnickety proofreading.

Susan Spencer-Smith
December 2010

"Let the cat wink, and let the mouse run." ~~ Proverb

CHAPTER ONE

Isabelle coiled the sleeping bag into a green lump and, because the bag had failed her, sat on the locust stump to pluck her hair and consider the problem.

The bedroll was clean. She saw to that every Sunday. But the thing was hot—steamily, itchily, feverishly hot. When the sun's rays clung to the pebbly creek bank long into the night, the bag bonded to her body like a sticky cocoon.

For each of eleven straight nights, since the real beginning of bug season, Isabelle had slept fewer than three hours. She needed at least five hours of sleep every day to stay alert and on top of her plan. She felt groggy and weak. She must, somehow and soon, find a safe place to sleep.

She blamed the spiders, ants and mosquitoes. They were loners, too, drawn like her to the shelter of these ancient woods and the pools and eddies of Muddy Creek. Her old insect welts—the ones that had come as she slept on a nest of white-pine needles—still oozed and crusted on her pale limbs.

Chemical bug repellents itched more than the bugs. She could have sneaked into Mr. and Mrs. K.'s barn to sleep with the cows and chickens. But inside held perils. Inside meant walls, lights, locks. Worst of all, inside meant feelings, words and actions that festered until the hurt came.

Outside, however, meant freedom, and Isabelle intended to keep hers.

Susan Spencer-Smith

"Such beginning, such end." ~~ Proverb

CHAPTER TWO

Tuesday, June 28, 2005

If the parsonage had been a personage, she would have been a bag lady.

Her face caved in like a crone's where deep-pitched roof met peeling boards. Two gables, one vertical and one horizontal, squinted hard in the solstice sun. Four tall, plain windows bared a gap-toothed smile.

The lady's neighbors—each more than a hundred yards away—kept their distance as if she stank. She wore a once-white coat of paint applied too sparingly. Sixteen severe stone steps zippered her down the hill. And she stuck out her tongue—a scaly vermilion door—at the world.

The new pastor, standing in the gravel driveway and fending off the sun's glare with a hand over her brow, wanted to stick out her own tongue in the bag lady's direction. But she would not do that, first because the bag lady was the parsonage provided by Glory Hallelujah Church for the comfort and care of its pastor, and second because the pastor should be grateful for it.

Annie Ido Scovill sighed and counted the steps again. She took three deep breaths, removed Fannie Fay from the backseat of the Volvo and turned to the man who had jumped down from the moving van.

"This way," she said. She forced herself to climb. Fannie Fay sensed tension and meowed in high pitch all the way up.

No one was at the door to greet them. But a tall cup of good joe was reception enough. Annie didn't know it wasn't Starbucks' best until she carried the big takeout bag into the house and it split open onto her jeans and the rug.

"What's that?" said the man, whose shirt pocket read *Jacinto*. "Lady, oh no, it looks like . . . oh, God . . . it . . . it's a cat all cut up."

Annie gasped. Bloody entrails, stinking and dark, lay at her feet. The severed head of a calico stared blindly out of the muck. The poor feline's front paws rose stiffly from the carcass.

Annie's heart sank. She felt vomit rising to her throat and looked away just in time to quell it.

The absence of greeting by an appointed church committee breached general etiquette. But the dead cat affronted her personally.

Apparently, someone had taken the trouble to learn that Annie Ido Scovill loved animals—dogs, horses, ducks, fish, hamsters—and that she most loved cats.

Annie resisted her first thought, that someone in Biddlebourne, West Virginia, didn't want her there, and her first emotion, a snarl of fear that grabbed her gut.

Instead, she swallowed the bile in her throat and forced a smile to her lips. "Looks like pranksters have been here."

But Jacinto frowned. "Hold it, guys," he shouted to the men who had begun hauling boxes off the van. He looked expectantly at Annie. Fannie Fay yowled in her carrier.

Annie's cell phone rang inside her purse, which she'd dropped onto the porch.

"Yes," she said, "you certainly can't come through with the floor this way. I'll only be a minute."

Jacinto and crew joked outside while Annie found the bathroom upstairs and secured Fannie Fay there. She went back downstairs and carried the gory mess to the back porch, then got on hands and knees to clean the blood, guts and feces off the rug. The job took all the tissue from the bathroom.

"All clear," she said to the men as she headed to the car for her overnight bag and Fannie Fay's supplies.

Fannie Fay squawked about her accommodations as Annie put on clean slacks in the bathroom. "Fannie Fay, Fannie Fay, Fannie Fay," Annie crooned while she freed her from the carrier and filled her dishes. "I can't let you out of the bathroom yet." Fannie Fay turned her back and hopped into the bathtub.

Death in the Parsonage

"Mind your business." ~~ U.S. Treasury Department

CHAPTER THREE

Isabelle yanked blond wisps out of the right side of her head until a male cardinal landed on a blackberry bush nearby and pecked a tiny berry.

Reminded of breakfast, Isabelle knelt at her luggage and dug out her food kit. It was plastic with a blue snap lid. Right after she got a check in the mail, the kit would hold crackers—oyster and Ritz, her favorites because they were round—peanut butter, raisins, canned tuna, bananas, beef jerky, oatmeal bars and good-to-go minestrone and chowder.

But today, four days before her next payment, the food kit contained only half a jug of water captured from the spring behind the old Grabathian orchard, a small bag of gnarly old apples from the Grabathian storage shed, four packs of Melba toast and a few ketchup and mayo packets.

She needed supplies. Counting on fingers, she figured she had to find four more breakfasts and four suppers before payday, lunches being both unnecessary and unaffordable. That meant breakfast today would be an apple and four Melba crackers—and, oh yes, blackberries. That was okay. She'd survived on less.

With her penknife she cored and pared the Stayman apple, careful to ream out the wormholes and insect whorls, and sliced it into perfect crescents that she laid out in a circle on the blue plastic lid. She lined up the crackers artfully inside the circle. When the cardinal flew off, she filled her hanky with berries and dotted the "apple pie" with them. At last she ate, smiling and rocking and thinking more about her problem.

Afterward, she scrubbed her face and hands at the creek and waded in to clean her feet. She had to hurry. There was much to do. With wet feet, she walked back to the hummock, pulled the binoculars out of her suitcase and went to her looking post on the locust stump.

"Home is home, be it ever so humble."
~~ Franklin P. Jones

CHAPTER FOUR

Annie quickly checked the rooms where the couch, dining table and bookcases would be placed. Neither the living room nor the dining room offered more than bare floors, ceilings and walls—all dirty. Everything about the lady was gray.

Back in Wheeling, a house like this was known as a railroader. You walked from porch to front room to dining room to kitchen. It was like going from corridor to coach to diner to sleeper on the Capitol Limited—if you didn't flunk algebra and miss the eighth-grade trip.

She stubbed her toes on a two-inch rise between the kitchen and dining room. This railroader, she concluded, had been built in stages. She would have to add a small incline to avoid further stubbings.

A porcelain sink with grooved drain board filled the wall under the kitchen window. The stove and refrigerator also sprang from the Ralph and Alice Kramden school of decorating. The linoleum was thin in the middle and curled at the edges like old oilcloth.

Jacinto called out from the dining room, "Missus, this bookcase don't work where you want it."

Annie turned to see that the top of the bookcase leaned precariously. "You must have set it on a grate or something."

"No, ma'am. This floor is sloping. I'd say about ten degrees. Look for yourself."

She stepped closer. He lifted the bookcase enough for her to understand that the floor, not the bookcase or anything under it, caused the crazy tilt.

"Where d'ya want it?" he asked.

"Try the middle of the room."

"If we put the bookcases in the middle, where do you want the table?"

She sighed. "Along the wall, I guess."

"Okay."

That afternoon Annie skipped lunch and went upstairs to tour the second floor. When she opened the bathroom door, Fannie Fay wound her big Maine coon cat's tail around Annie's right ankle and purred. Annie rubbed Fannie Fay's ears and looked around the room.

Annie was startled when her eyes lit on the dusty mirror over the sink. A cobweb had gotten tangled in her light brown hair, and the heat had splotched her rosy complexion. Her blouse bore bloodstains from the poor dead calico cat. Her metal-framed eyeglasses sat askew on her nose.

No time to freshen up now, Annie thought. She pumped the toilet handle three times, producing a sorry flush. Water like tincture of iodine hiccupped out when she wrenched the knob on the bathtub.

Three tiny bedrooms completed the second story. They all had carpet that was barnyard brown and dime thin. Doors were everywhere, many leading, Annie supposed, to puny closets that would hold not a fraction of their possessions.

Fannie Fay toured in her own way, sniffing corners and jumping at dust bunnies. Soon she grew bored and meowed so plaintively that Annie picked her up. But Fannie Fay jumped down, leaving a patch of long gray hair on Annie's sweltry skin, and ran to the attic door.

"No, Fannie Fay, we are not going up there. We will melt if we do."

But Fannie Fay cried and scratched the door and looked pitiful. So Annie trudged upward. The attic was so stifling that Annie thought she might faint. She deduced that if the house had any insulation, it was not tucked between the roof and the sagging plasterboard ceiling in the attic. There were no windows, though small louvers on the two short walls let in a few grudging rays of light.

Incredibly, closets abounded in the attic. Actually, they were cubbyholes. Someone had cleverly installed plywood between the floor and the middle of the angled walls. The result was a modified A-frame effect with storage in the legs of the A.

One cubbyhole door hung ajar. Annie pulled it open, hunkering to peer inside. She was gauging whether it would hold the Christmas trimmings when a whir of feathers smacked her in the face. She yelped and rocked back onto her derriere. The feathers made a run for her hair. She lifted her arms as a shield.

Frantic over the intrusion, a small bird whooped and looped in the top of the A. Feathers, fluff and dust whirled. Annie sneezed violently. Unable to stand, she scooted backward out of the cubbyhole. Fannie Fay pranced and pawed the air, desperate to catch the bird.

Annie stood and peered into the cubbyhole. She could barely make out a small table standing in the recess. It had one shallow drawer, the kind that holds TV magazines and nail clippers, and the drawer was hanging open. When she crept closer, she saw a mound of tattered paper in the drawer. Nearby the stiff pages of a book popped up. The bird, amazingly fierce for its size, swept past her and beaked a shred of paper out of the book.

Annie would have left the bird—she thought it was a house wren—to its nest but for a pang of conscience. She had treasured books since the day her mother put *Cinderella* in her grubby little hands. Though she did persistently and joyfully disassemble *Cinderella*, she owed much of what she was to books. That is why she shuffled to the little table and snatched the book.

The book was not a Bible, which Annie had thought it might be, or a *TV Guide*, which she supposed was a bible to some folks. It had a hard green cover and a label: *My Diary*.

She tucked the diary under one arm and Fannie Fay under the other. "I'll bring you something better for your nest," she told the wren.

The bird did not believe Annie and flew out one of the louvered vents to return, Annie supposed, with reinforcements.

~~0~~

Dear Diary,
Bedtime is awfal at our house. First Frankie and Sissie and me have to go and find our pjs. You never no where the dog drug them. The basmint or behind the cowch or under the table or any where he wants and he sleeps on them all day and gives them flees. I have flee bites on my ankles and all over my butt. Mommy says its from peeing the bed but I no its from flees.

I never no where im suppose to sleep. Sometimes with Sissie in her bed. Sometimes with mommy in her bed. The abslut worst thing is sleeping with mommy. Daddy never

sleeps with mommy any more. I hate sleeping with
mommy. She raps herself all around me. Puts her arms all
over the place and her legs on my bak. Shes hevy. Its hard
to breth when mommys legs are on me. The worst part is
she stinks like buze. She drinks all day and cant sleep at
night. So she raps her arms and legs around me and stinks
and talks. When she talks her breth smells bad like the cat
box. She talks all the time even in her sleep. She says mene
stuff like shes realy talking to me like you little basturd
you rooned my life and your nothing but trash and don't
pis on me you little monkee.

Some times I have to rock back and fourth to go to sleep.
That helps a lot. Or some times I have to pool my hair or
pool on my fingers to go to sleep. That helps me forget
mommy when my beds wet and I have to sleep with her.
And she hogs the blankits two.

Daddy says he wont waste no money on cole at night so
the house gets awfal cold. Colder when my beds wet or
mommy hogs the blankits. Then I have to get up erle and
find some close and make my lunch.

I almost always miss the buss and have to ask Misses G to
drive me to skul. She always says yes. I like riding to skul
with Misses G which is one good thing about not getting
enuf sleep. I realy realy like Misses G and she likes me. I
can tell because she asks me about my self and about my
family but never makes fun of me. She never makes me
cry. I figger daddy hates bedtime two.

Daddy dosnt sleep where most peple sleep. He sleeps in
the cole seller. I thot all dads sleep in the cole seller. But I
stayed all nite at Misses Gs house one time and Mister G
slept rite in the room with her. Geez. I was shoked when

he went right up the stares to go to bed. My dad has pink fiber glas lined up around the wall a matress on the floor and a candal stuck to a little table in there. Thats it. No lites or nothing. What on erth did he do that mommy makes him sleep in the cole seller. Every nite he starts calling to mommy from down there. Itll be in the middle of the nite. Wakes us all up. We never get good sleep always some thing going on. He starts screeming Vickie Vickie I love you Vickie. Mommy yells back shut up you shit head Im trying to sleep. Every stinking nite the same thing.

Some times he goes to the kichen and starts banging the end of the broom on the ceeling just to wake us up. Pound pound pound in the middle of the nite for a long time. What the heck is that about. So of corse the middle of the nite is when most of the fiting goes on. Around midnite becaws its when both hands of the clock are on the 12. Screeming beeting you name it. No sleep for me or Frankie or Sissie. Poor Frankie he failed skul three times. His techer wrote mommy a note and said Franklin Dwayne is not doing good and he will flunk if he dosnt do better. I saw the note on the table but mommy dosnt no I saw it.

"Necessity has no holiday." ~~ Proverb

CHAPTER FIVE

Isabelle alternately bit her nails and chewed the lining of her lips. What she'd just seen changed everything.

The field glasses now lay squarely in their nylon case inside the suitcase, which lay inside a double-duty garbage bag. Her kits—four of them, one each for food, cleanup, books and tools—were similarly tucked in and bound together by a hank of heavy twine.

Besides the four kits, she had a backpack. Because it contained her most valued possessions she usually looped it to her waist with two bicycle locks.

Now she knew the ugly story was true. That woman was in her house, Isabelle's house. With a zillion boxes and a cat. Isabelle recited the newspaper article from memory:

The Rev. Annie Ido Scovill, for nine years pastor of Christ Church in Chestnut City, has been named pastor of Glory Hallelujah Church in Biddlebourne as of July 1.

Pastor Scovil graduated from Sychar Theological Seminary and originated Seven Paths to Discipleship, a Christian development program.

She will succeed the Rev. Barry Woostine, who led the Glory Hallelujah congregation for twenty-six years until his untimely death in April at age 48.

Under Pastor Woostine's leadership, Glory Hallelujah Church grew in membership from 50 to 890. Pastor Woostine oversaw the establishment of Glory Hallelujah's popular Marriage and Family Day Ministries providing food, clothing, support and instruction in life skills.

Pastor Woostine's wife, Marcy, remains a member and teacher at Glory Hallelujah Church.

Pastor Scovill is a co-founder of the West Virginia Animal Rights Society. She enjoys cooking, crocheting, swimming and reading in her spare time.

Swimming. Isabelle wished this Scovill woman would swim out of Biddlebourne, to the Ohio River and beyond.

Never mind. She would overcome this problem as she had all the others—with ingenuity, planning and effort.

But first, although she was hardly hungry now, she must find food. She hadn't burnt many calories sitting on the locust log. And those apple slices had formed a big knot in her tummy. But she would have to eat before she unrolled the sleeping bag again for the night. Experience showed that food was found better before nightfall than after and that waking up ravenous had its own set of bad consequences.

She resolved to go for food right after regimen. "Three pieces, three pieces, three pieces," she recited as her hands deftly loosened knots and unsnapped clips. At last all her luggage—the suitcase, the set of four necessity kits and the backpack—rested uncovered and unlocked side by side. The garbage bags that usually encased them were spread in front of them.

Isabelle eyed the display from the north, south, east and west. Then she worked until exactly five feet of space stretched between each piece of luggage and each garbage bag was one foot away from its mate.

Kneeling, she opened the suitcase and slowly removed its contents. One at a time, she placed the items on the plastic. She turned the suitcase upside down and shook it hard. She checked every seam for bugs and dirt and brushed away specks of lint from the inside corners. She wiped the suitcase inside and out with a moist towelette.

Next she inspected her clothing. The undergarments must be free of stains, the socks smoothly paired, the knit tops unwrinkled, the shorts and slacks creased, the tennis shoes briskly white, the sweatshirts and sweatpants unsnagged. There must be five of everything. And everything must be clean and folded squarely.

Only one item failed inspection: The yellow blouse with rose-petal embroidery on the collar and cuffs had somehow acquired a tear on the hem. She scolded herself for carelessness and refolded the blouse into the top of the suitcase to be repaired on mending day.

When all the items were examined, counted and tucked back into the valise, Isabelle locked it, encased it in the black plastic and lined it up again with the other luggage.

The food kit held so little that she needed only a minute or two to remove the items, clean the container with a bleach-soaked wipe and return the meager victuals.

The tool kit was perfect already because Isabelle had spent an hour the evening before counting and polishing its inventory. And the book kit was empty, Isabelle having earlier offloaded its contents to a safe zone because of the weight factor.

But the cleanup kit was a different matter. She had recently shampooed her hair, shaved her legs, plucked her brows and performed all the other required chores, and her implements were soiled.

Chanting, "Toiletries, tools, tidies; toiletries, tools, tidies," Isabelle opened the cleanup kit and removed the bottles, jars and tools to the nearby plastic. When the kit had been emptied, she determined that it had developed no cracks or holes, cleaned it and put it back in place.

She shifted from her knees to her butt; the next part would take a while. First she checked whether each bottle and jar was no less than one-fourth filled. Shampoo, check. Toothpaste, check. Deodorant, check. Towelettes, low. Tanning lotion, check. Stain remover, check. Mouthwash, check. Foundation, check. Sunscreen, low. Bug spray, check. Blush, check. Swabs, check. Lipstick, check. Aspirin, check. Petroleum jelly, low. Soap, check.

On a notepad from the backpack she printed *TOWELETTES, SUNSCREEN, VASELINE.*

On the plastic bag she lined up the toiletries alphabetically—aspirin, blush, bug spray, deodorant, foundation, lipstick, mouthwash, petroleum jelly, shampoo, soap, stain remover, sunscreen, swabs, tanning lotion, toothpaste, towelettes. She took a bleach wipe to each bottle and jar, wiping the outside, the inside of the lid and the ridges where the lids attached. She used a new wipe for each container so that no ingredients mingled.

Now it was time to check tools. Out came shaver, tweezers, toothbrush, nail clips, nail file, comb, hair brush, clothing brush, utility brush, needle and thread, eyebrow pencil and shoe buffer. Isabelle hummed as she plucked wipes to rub every crevice and surface of the implements. After each one had been cleaned and checked for missing, bent or broken parts, she alphabetized the items on the plastic and smiled because none of them needed repaired, replaced or replenished.

At last she came to the tidies. *Toiletries, tools, tidies*, she sang while conducting regimen on the matches, scissors, hand broom, stapler, cellophane tape, envelopes, glue and batteries. They were disgustingly unalphabetized, but that could be fixed in minutes. Soon the tidies lay straight on the plastic and Isabelle was writing *STAPLES* on her list.

"You cannot unscramble eggs." ~~ Proverb

CHAPTER SIX

Annie's boss did not deliver the bad news until all the furniture was off the truck. She had just planted her backside on the swing and her feet on the cooler when he chugged onto the front porch, puffing and perspiring and smelling of Old Spice.

The air was thick with dust disturbed by the movers and with humidity just short of rain. Every bone in Annie's body ached. "Burl!" she said.

"Annie," he huffed.

She struggled to rise, but he waved her back. "Don't get up," he said. "I'll just have the coronary here and save the paramedics a trip inside the house. Those are killer stairs."

"I know. Sixteen of 'em." She had lugged eleven plants and three crates of Fannie Fay stuff up the steps. The movers had been gone less than an hour. Annie was reeling not just from her exertion but also from her realization about the condition of the house.

She dispensed with the usual rites of welcome for a visiting dignitary and pointed toward the crooked rows of bags, baskets and boxes crammed onto the porch.

The Reverend Burl Stout, superintendent of the district church and Annie's supervisor for the last seven years, dropped his rump onto a banana crate marked "Aunt Rose's antique china teacups—from England and Portugal." Dust to dust, Annie thought.

"How's it going?" he asked.

"Okay, I guess. Wanna buy a couch?" She pointed to the couch, the queen bed and G.P.'s rolltop desk bleaching in the sunlight of the side yard.

"Don't fit?"

"Don't fit."

Burl had his Indians ball cap in his hands and more sweat on his brow than any of the men who had just carried 12,540 pounds of household goods up sixteen steps—or 12,540 pounds minus a couch, a bed and a desk.

"Root beer?" she asked.

"Yes, thanks." He let out his breath as if he had been holding it under water. A tiny warning bell tinged in the reptilian region of Annie's brain.

"The ice is gone, but these aren't quite lukewarm yet," she said, moving her feet enough to lift the cooler lid and take out two cans of A&W. She handed one to Burl.

Annie popped her can open and waited while Burl tried to do the same. His fingers were slick with sweat. He needed three passes at the metal ring to tug it off. His brown boaters overflowed with sagging white socks. His red-and-white-striped tie dangled like a rayon necklace. The waistband of his pants rolled over his belt. He took a wide swipe of his face with his right shirtsleeve. To be fair, though, the day was hotter than Grandma's griddle at a pancake breakfast.

"Let's go in and turn on the air conditioner," Annie said, lifting her feet from the cooler.

"Don't bother."

"Why not? It must be ninety-eight out here."

One should always trust the brain. Reptiles haven't survived millennia on good looks alone.

"I forgot to mention a few things about the house," Burl said.

"I suppose you're referring to the original wiring and apathetic plumbing." Thirty-watters and plungers already led her shopping list.

"Well, not exactly."

"The slanting walls and sagging floors?"

"Uh . . ."

"Burl, tell me."

"Okay, okay. But you realize this house came to the church as a bequest. The congregation wants to make it right. I believe I made that clear when I introduced you to the committee."

"You did."

"And the trustees will be over tomorrow to see what you need."

Annie hadn't heard Burl pussyfoot like this since the Republicans asked to use Christ Church for a campaign rally.

The rusty chains of the swing screeched as Annie settled back. Crickets ticked like a hall clock. Someone up the road was trying to mow the yard before supper.

Burl took a swig of root beer and looked ruefully at the can. "I'm told the house is haunted," he said, "and I'm sorry to say there is no air conditioning."

~~0~~

Dear Diary,
We live in a four story house. Basmint living room level bedroom level and atick level. Mommy and daddy said we dint have enuf money so they made the atick level into a stoodeo partment. We rent it out some times. Last year we rented it out to 3 guys from the moorman church. They were very nice guys. Had on shirts and ties and pants all

the time even in the house! Daddy said nobody shud wear there tie in the house. Mommy said yes they shud and they got into a fite over it. Me and Frankie hid in the basmint under the pingpong table where its all a lot of dust and spider webs. Theres no bathroom in the atick level so they have to use ours. The 3 moorman guys dint stay that long. Maybe 3 weeks I think.

When skul started last year we rented the stoodeo out to a man and his wife. She was pregnint and let me tuch her belly. It was like tuching a big baloon filled with water. One day I was playing in the yard beside the house and I heard a terrible screeming. I ran over to the house and there was all kinds of comoshon. What happened was Alisha that was her name the pregnint lady was putting on make up and saw some thing black go back and fourth across the floor. Alisha and the husband left that same day.

Mommy says evul lives in that atick. I don't know about evul but I no lots of roches live in there. Lots of times when mommy and daddy fite I hide in the atick. I have lots of good hiding places. I have one speshul hiding place that Frankie and mommy and daddy and Sissie and nobody else nos about. When I go there I feel speshul and happy and get to lissen to music and not hear any fiting or cussing or yelling. I don't think I ever cried not one time in my speshul hiding place. Iv been getting into lots of truble for steeling things from the house for my speshul hiding place but Im not sorry. I no I shoulnt steel stuff from the house. I learned that in Sunday Skul. The part I hate is when Frankie sees me steel stuff and dosnt tell on me and daddy whips him because he says Frankie stole. Frankie gets into lots of truble becaws of me. Im sorry for that part.

"Clothe thee warm, eat little, drink enough, and thou shalt live." ~~ Proverb

CHAPTER SEVEN

Isabelle's small frame bowed slightly with the weight of the suitcase in her right hand, the four kits in her left hand and the backpack secured high over her shoulders. But she didn't mind carrying her things. They gave her freedom.

"Field, feathers, fat, Ford. Field, feathers, fat, Ford," Isabelle whispered as she walked toward the meadow where the sunflowers grew. Forty-five minutes later she was leaning against her tree. Its branches had feathery, ferny-looking leaves. But that wasn't the best part. The best part was that the tree had three lives—one for every thick, rough trunk that twisted from its base in the black earth up into its canopy of feathers. The three-trunk feather tree was so fat that Isabelle could hide behind it for hours without worrying. With her brown top and gray sweatpants, she even blended into the tree's colors.

She sat on her suitcase, holding the kits and backpack, and waited. She let her eyes rest on the rolling green hills that rose around her, first in deep greens, then higher in shadowed blues and then highest in smoky grays.

Nothing happened for almost an hour. Isabelle didn't own a watch but knew how to tell time in her mind by counting. Counting to one hundred as fast as she could equaled one minute. Therefore, counting to six thousand equaled one hour.

She was on 5,421 when the round little boy got off the bus and barreled onto the porch of the house. The Pinckney house. Isabelle rose because she knew that Mrs. P. would be busy with her round little boy for several hours now that he was home from summer school.

Nevertheless, Isabelle checked in every direction and especially studied the Pinckney barn. It was very old. It leaned so much that Isabelle knew it would fall down one day and she would have to find a new place.

But the Pinckney barn was okay for now. It would have been totally perfect if Mrs. P. didn't insist on keeping those chickens. The chickens ran all over the barn, pooping and scratching and clucking. Isabelle supposed Mrs. P. kept them because of the eggs.

Isabelle could understand why Mrs. P. wanted the eggs, but she couldn't understand why Mrs. P. didn't fetch the eggs at the same time every day. Some days she strolled to the barn and got eggs early—before lunch even. Other days she would appear at the barn when Isabelle thought everybody was eating supper, around six in the evening, judging from the slant of the sun and the number of cars that had returned to the driveways.

The chickens had often caused Isabelle to change her schedule. She disliked changing her schedule. Things should be done at the same time every day or . . . or . . . . She didn't complete the thought because it was too troubling.

But today Mrs. P. wouldn't be looking for eggs in the barn until the round little boy had been given his snack. Isabelle would have more than enough time.

Certain that no one was looking, she picked up her belongings and walked quietly to the barn, careful to zigzag so the grass would not become a path beneath her feet.

In the barn she looked around for signs of human life. The old horse collars still hung from the rafters. The tractor parts were still strewn on the workbench. The rusty milk pails still lay scattered inside a stall. The place still smelled of hay and manure.

And the old Ford still commanded the rear corner closest to the horse stalls, its blue fenders and white top as beautiful to Isabelle as when she was nine.

Mr. P. Senior had bought it secondhand. She supposed it now belonged to Mr. P. Junior like the house and the barn. It was really old, but she still appreciated the clean lines of the hood, the flare of the fenders and the smoothness of the upholstery. She peeked into the left back window and confirmed that the scuff mark was still on the back of the driver's seat—where she had accidentally placed it with her brown brogans many years earlier.

She stole to the square hickory pillar that stood in line with the east window—or window hole, since the glass was long gone—and noted that the chickens were roosting up in the loft. Good. They wouldn't set up a ruckus if she didn't work long or loud.

Satisfied that she was alone in the barn except for the damned cluckers, Isabelle went to the workbench and set her luggage on the plank floor. She lifted the kit bundle to the bench top and untied it. She put the tool kit in the center and the other three kits on the ends of the bench.

She opened her backpack, removed a coin purse and twisted it open. She sorted through the pennies, nickels and dimes until she found what she wanted. With it she unlocked the tool kit.

The small, rectangular case had once held Daddy's fishing tackle but now served Isabelle's purposes. Because everything must be lightweight, she had chosen Styrofoam—from a refrigerator box in Nashville—for the lining.

There were two layers of the polystyrene, each carved into a series of niches. In the customized niches of the top layer rested Isabelle's openers. Four picks with tips turned at varying angles. Five rectangles of hard plastic with thicknesses differing only by millimeters. Seventeen keys, each bearing the stamped imprint of a car line. And—her pride, her joy, her best trophies—seven skeleton keys.

The seven keys made her smile. They always made her smile. They were old friends, trusted and reliable, always ready to serve her. They made her feel like friends should—happy and safe.

But today she had little time for these friends. She turned to the car keys and checked the alphabetizing. Audi, Buick, Cadillac, Chevrolet, Dodge, Ford, Honda, Jaguar, Jeep, Lincoln, Mazda, Mitsubishi, Saab, Subaru, Suzuki, Toyota, Volkswagen.

Yes, she was free to proceed. From a pouch in her backpack she took a pair of thin rubber gloves. She pulled them over her hands and selected the Ford key. She went to the wide opening where the barn doors swung on corroded hinges and looked again to make absolutely, finally, completely certain that Mrs. P. hadn't parked the boy in front of the tube and headed out to pick up eggs.

She couldn't see inside the house but also didn't hear the television, which the round boy played way too loud. She was safe for now.

Quickly, she went to the Fairlane, inserted the key into the trunk lid, turned and pulled up. She looked earnestly into the cavity, enjoying the fact that a wide beam of light fell right into it through a hole in the barn roof. There wasn't much to choose from, but it would last until

Saturday, when she would make her way to the post office and pick up her payment.

Isabelle needed only a minute or two to take out one stack of Ritz crackers, the last flat can of sardines, three packets of squeezy cheese and half a dozen mini-boxes of raisins. The sardines would stink and draw flies, and the raisins would be as hard as creek pebbles by now, but she had no other reliable options.

She replaced the Ford key in the skeleton kit, replenished her food kit, put the gloves away and went to the barn door to check again. When she saw that both doors of the Pinckney house were closed and still did not hear the round little boy's pow-bam-bang cartoons, she slipped through the doorway and disappeared into the sunflower field.

Death in the Parsonage

"The bad gardener quarrels with his rake." ~~ Proverb

CHAPTER EIGHT

Wednesday, June 29

Annie's second day at 1010 Greenbriar Road started too soon. Mr. Gideon Pugh knocked on the back door at exactly 6:30 a.m. She was drowsing in a puddle of sweat atop an air mattress on the living room floor. An odor similar to that of a damp baby crib emerged from the stained turquoise broadloom beneath her.

She glanced at the travel clock and concluded there must be a fire or a death. She threw a robe over her T-shirt and shorts and ran to the door. The man standing there held a bucket of tomatoes and a plateful of frosted cinnamon rolls. He was short and grizzled, with white hair and sunburned face. He looked like the Santa Claus of Annie's childhood, and she liked him instantly despite his timing.

"I can come back later," he said, smiling with his whole face.

"I don't know who you are, but I'll take the tomatoes and rolls," she said. Annie could smell the cinnamon through the screen.

"Mr. Gideon Pugh, Pastor Ma'am. Head trustee over at the church."

"I'm glad you're here," she said.

Annie could not have meant it more. Only minutes earlier, she had been trying to get her bearings. In the state that is half sleeping and half waking, she had stood on a speck of an island in a sea with no shores. Burl Stout floated away on a rubber raft, paddling furiously with his hands. Her husband, friends and grandchildren frolicked in the cool water and waved for Annie to join them. But no matter how hard she willed her limbs to move, they would not.

"Nobody ever turned down Ma's sticky buns," he said.

Annie took a deep breath and said, "My nose tells me why. Come on in."

"You want me to bring in that sack, too?" he asked.

"What sack?"

He pointed to the corner of the porch where Annie had tossed the offending Starbucks bag the day before.

"Oh, that one. No, please leave it there," she said.

"I s'pose someone's left you some corn," he volunteered. "Early corn's been mighty good this year."

When Mr. Gideon Pugh learned that the bag contained not garden produce but animal remains, he was outraged. "Pastor Ma'am," he said, "you just wait till word gets out. Some little scoundrel's gonna get the whippin' of his life. Ma'll have his name before sundown. Just don't you worry."

He and Annie had a small set-to on the back porch. Mr. Gideon Pugh wanted to scald the hide of the juvenile delinquent or delinquents who had delivered the package to the new pastor's doorstep. Annie preferred a less intense, and less physical, response.

They compromised. Mr. Gideon Pugh would ask Mrs. Gideon Pugh to circulate discreet inquiries and report her findings. "You'll see," he said. "Ain't nobody or nothin' 'scapes Ma. You mind if I come in, Pastor Ma'am?"

"Of course not, Mr. Pugh." Annie stretched the door open. Mr. Gideon Pugh wiped his boots thoroughly on the mat and entered.

"I tried to reach you last night," she said as she put the sticky buns on the sink and took boxes off two chairs.

"I reckon you did, Pastor Ma'am. I'm awful sorry, but me and Ma spent the day looking after a new calf, and there ain't no phone in the barn."

"How's the calf?"

"He's fine, Pastor Ma'am, but Ma said to tell you she's awful sorry she wasn't here to greet you proper. She's so tired she'll probably sleep in till eight."

"I understand totally. I'm just glad the calf is okay," Annie said. Making a mental note that eight was late in Biddlebourne, she offered him a seat. He waited there while she rooted around upstairs for clean jeans, a fresh T-shirt and the white leather Minnetonka mocs.

When coffee was at last brewing, Annie fed Fannie Fay and cleared the table of dirty cups and phone books. Fannie Fay jumped to the tabletop and curled into her regular spot.

Annie pretended Fannie Fay had done something unusual. She picked up the cat and placed her on the floor. Fannie Fay methodically returned to her regular spot. Annie reached again for Fannie Fay. Fannie Fay narrowed her eyes and pointed her ears.

Mr. Gideon Pugh took in all the activity with a smile. "Pastor Ma'am, out here we're lucky if we can keep the goats out of the kitchen. A cat on the table ain't nothin' to worry about."

"I'm relieved to hear it," Annie said, "because Fannie Fay has claimed this table from the day we bought it."

With sticky buns, coffeepot and cat on the table, Mr. Gideon Pugh bowed his head and Annie gave thanks.

They took several bites before Annie said, "Thanks for coming by, Mr. Pugh. And please call me Annie Ido—or just Annie."

"Well, Pastor Ma'am, I heard you didn't have no husband. Me and Hermie—he's the church handyman, we call him Hermie the Handyman—reckoned to get over here and lend a hand with this place."

Maybe it was the sugar shock, the caffeine zap or both. Annie had her first laugh at the parsonage. But she had to explain.

"My husband's a major in the Air Force Reserve. He's serving . . . abroad. His unit received some special training after the 9/11 attack, and they were deployed earlier this year."

"Pastor, Ma'am, I appreciate all he's doin' for us over there. What kinda work does he do?"

"Well, he's a computer consultant in civilian life and works with intelligence in the Reserve."

Mr. Gideon Pugh nodded. "I served in the Korean War, Pastor Ma'am."

It was Annie's turn to nod. "And I thank you for that service."

There was a pause before Mr. Gideon Pugh went on. "So, I guess you and he ain't busted up after all."

"My goodness, no. What made you think so?"

"Hooboy. Pastor Ma'am, you know how folks work their mouths. All we heard from that district feller was your husband wasn't coming out here with you."

"Are you saying the congregation thinks we're divorced?"

"Pastor Ma'am, don't you fret. When I go home and tell Ma what you told me, everything'll be all right."

"The superintendent ought to come out and set things straight."

Now Mr. Gideon Pugh laughed. "I reckon he's got a lot more important things to look after. Ma'll take care of it."

This plan was not at all satisfactory to Annie. But before she could think how to tactfully say so, he said, "What's your mister's name?"

"G.P., for Granger Parker Scovill . . ."

"That's all I need to know," Mr. Gideon Pugh said. "Now about that couch you got settin' out in the side yard."

"Oh, dear," she said. "Several household items did not fit into the house, Mr. Pugh."

"Well, don't you fuss, Pastor Ma'am. We'll take care of that later this morning. For now, let's take a little walk through the house."

They started in the attic and ended in the basement. The lower they went, the worse it got. The tour was unlike Annie's of the day before. Then she had covered the more aesthetic points of the parsonage, such as torn wallpaper, missing stairs and bird nests. Now she and Mr. Gideon Pugh assessed the working, almost-working and not-for-years-working parts.

Mr. Gideon Pugh told Annie that the basement had been dug in 1842. The dirt floor "down there," which is what Mr. Gideon Pugh called the basement, had been packed into place with the iron shovels of pre-Civil War laborers.

The historical basement was dim and moldy. It was about fifteen feet wide and thirty feet long—the dimensions, Annie guessed, of the original house. It had stone walls four feet thick, a ceiling barely higher than her five feet six inches.

"Look at them walls," Mr. Gideon Pugh said. "They don't make 'em like that nowadays."

"You're right," she said. "By the way, who last lived in this house?"

"Vickie June Ransom, Pastor Ma'am. We always called her Vickie June Ransom even after she married Ernie Pargeon—he was a Pargeon from over Claypool. I guess her true name was Vickie June Pargeon. She died last year and left it to the church in her will."

"Was Vickie June a member of the church?"

"Funny thing. Visited a coupla times way back but left mad. Didn't even come to the rooster rodeos. It's a mystery why she gave it to the church. But she did, and she even left a little cash to spend on repairs."

"How much did she leave for repairs?"

"Oh, a little over five thousand."

Annie made a few mental calculations and deduced that five thousand dollars would not begin to bring the bag lady back to respectability.

The only light "down there" came from a bare bulb hanging from a thickly taped cord. Frankenstein's laboratory would have been more appealing, Annie opined silently. No matter, she thought. It is a poor preacher who blames her parsonage.

"Is the laundry equipment down here?" she asked.

Her guide didn't hear her. He had already opened the door to the first of three rooms and entered the gloom beyond.

"This is the coal cellar," he said. "Here's the bulb." Another freckle of light appeared.

Annie was amazed that electricity had made its way into the coal cellar. She was prepared to take Mr. Gideon Pugh's word on the coal cellar when he looked back and stepped aside. Peering in, she saw a row of ancient shovels hanging on thick wall pegs and a carpet of coal splinters on the floor.

The elemental smell of old dirt and compressed carbon reminded Annie of first and second grade, when school was heated by a fierce coal furnace tended by The Furnace Man.

"Dark," she managed.

"You'll get used to it. Just wait a minute."

Shortly, Annie beheld the furnace, a heavy-metal silo with ducts as big around as beach balls and duct joints the size of big packing boxes. Its iron door was a hungry black maw. Loose strips of shiny tape held it together.

"Is the house still heated by coal?" she asked.

"Yes, Pastor Ma'am. Sure is."

"I haven't seen a coal furnace in a long time."

"Still got plenty of 'em around here. Used to be several coal mines in this county. Closed now. Coal's pricey to transport, and the women complain a coal furnace is hard on the drapes and such."

Annie was sorrier than ever that the brown couch hadn't fit in the house. A good layer of coal dust would have obscured the spots where Fannie Fay filed her nails.

"Do you suppose one of the other doors leads to the laundry room" she asked.

"Didn't that district feller tell you we ain't got no washer and dryer yet?"

"It must have slipped his mind." Or perhaps the district man had thought it imprudent to bring up other missing amenities after delivering his news about the absent air conditioning.

"I'll just use the laundry over on North Avenue," she said. "I saw it on my way into town."

"Oh, the trustees had an emergency meeting in the parkin' lot Sunday after service. We voted to put in a brand-new washer and dryer. Comin' next week," he promised.

"Maybe we could set them up in the kitchen?"

"Shoot. Won't be no trouble 'tall gettin' 'em down here. You'll see."

"But I don't see any plumbing," she said.

"Over there by the water heater." He pointed to the corner opposite the furnace.

Annie made a quick decision. "Oh," she said, looking without seeing into the dank abyss. "Did the trustees happen to decide anything about air conditioning?"

Annie and the superintendent had not discussed air conditioning the day before. Shortly after pronouncing his awful news, Burl Stout had made an awkward exit. He flipped his ball cap onto his gray thatch, put the soda can on the porch railing and headed down the steps like a bird dog on point.

It wasn't that Annie expected the parsonage to present every possible comfort, beginning with air conditioning.

It was just that she had to fetch 12,540 pounds of household goods—minus the couch, queen bed and rolltop desk—from wherever they were to wherever they needed to be in a four-level house. She had to unpack every box, shift every piece of furniture, put up every picture, install every gadget, line up every book and hang every curtain—without air conditioning.

She had to do this in Biddlebourne, West Virginia, a Bible Belt town of twenty thousand souls, each of whom, Annie suspected, was certain that God intended all ministers of the Gospel to be males.

She had to do this while the Glory Hallelujah congregation conducted a massive building campaign, continued its extensive Marriage and Family Day ministries, and kept up with all the other ministries needful in a town far from major government resources.

And she had to do all of this while struggling through one of the hottest summers ever to sear the mid Atlantic.

"What?" Mr. Gideon Pugh shouted from the second side room.

"Did the trustees decide anything about air conditioning?" Annie yelled.

"Air conditioning? What for? You got at least twenty windows in this house."

"Mr. Pugh, can we talk?"

~~0~~

Dear Diary,

I hate dinner time two. Me and Frankie and Sissie all eat extremly fast. We have to eat and get out of the kichen fast. Daddy is always about to go off the deep end. Thats what mommy calls it when he screems at us and throws stuff. We always have to walk on egg shells. Thats something else mommy says. Its what she says when she means tiptoe here and wisper there and dont go where he is. I say that a lot, walking on egg shells, becaws its all me and Sissie and Frankie ever do. We cant tell what Daddy will do next. Weel be eating and all of a sudden he lifts up the end of the table and all the food slides on the floor. Its becaws he dosnt like what mommy cooked or whatever. If me or Frankie or Sissie dont get enuf to eat two bad. Yester day we were eating spageti and he picked up his plate and threw it aginst the wall. Spageti sliding down the wall plate broke all of us running from the table. He screemed come back here you little shits but we stayed in our rooms with the doors locked. Ha ha on him. Only he took it out on mommy. Something like that hapns almost every day.

Mommy tells the nabors I have nervus stomack. I don't have nervus stomak. What I have is nervus every thing becaws daddys mad every time we eat. Me and Frankie can eat a whole hamberger in about one minute. Sissie cant do it. She tries but throws up every time. Me and

Frankie can get out of the kichen in one minute. If I feel hungry later at night I sneek into the kichen when hes in bed and eat serial and milk and bananas. If theres any bananas usully not. Some times theres candy and I eat that. Mommy nos I eat the candy becaws my teeth rot out but it dosnt matter. Rotted teeth are better than an emtee stomack.

I cant think what makes daddy so mad. He says nonsense things to mommy her names Vickie June. He says whose he look like Vickie June whose he look like. And he points his fork at Frankie and says it again. Whose he look like Vickie June. Frankie looks like Frankie. Why does that make daddy so mad.

"Fear is a great inventor." ~~ Proverb

CHAPTER NINE

It was town day. Isabelle was excited but anxious. She would see people and feel more like the 27-year-old woman she was. But she couldn't let the people recognize her. That was difficult to begin with because of her appearance. She was a slight blonde with nearly white skin and big, brown eyes.

No matter what Isabelle did, people remembered her eyes. They said she had doe eyes. Or they said she had puppy eyes. She thought she had regular eyes, but people always remembered her eyes, and she had to deal with that.

The bigger problem was her voice. She spoke quietly, so quietly that people usually had to strain to hear her. She was afraid to raise her voice and had to fight every instinct to speak loudly, no matter what situation she was in or tried to imagine. When people concentrated on listening to her, they would look at her intently. And when they looked at her intently, they saw those big, brown eyes.

Nevertheless, Isabelle needed money and supplies. And the only way to get them was to disguise herself so thoroughly that the nosy postmaster and suspicious storekeeper would pay her no special attention.

She began the ritual, lining up her toiletries on the flat rock beside the elderberry bush near the creek bank. A fine row of yellow poplars blocked the view of anyone who might pass. Not many people passed the west branch of Muddy Creek anyway, since locals knew the east side supported a lot more muskie.

With all the items aligned on the rock, Isabelle got ready to wash. She didn't dare remove all her clothes, and she didn't want to get soap in the creek because of the fish and turtles. She had seen several stinkpot turtles just a few days earlier. So she filled her one-gallon plastic bag from the creek five times and dumped the water into a hollow pine stub lined with plastic grocery sacks.

Using bar soap, she bathed top to bottom, removing one piece of clothing at a time. The cool water felt good, and she lathered her arms and legs twice just to prolong the good feeling. She didn't need a towel after she rinsed. The warm air dried her skin practically on contact.

After removing the bags from the stump and laying them out to dry, Isabelle picked up the dreaded sunless tanning lotion. She slowly measured out a nickel-size circle of lotion and applied it to one leg from knee to toes. There was no mirror, so she took great care not to make streaks. She repeated the routine for her other leg, her arms, her face and her neck.

Isabelle hated using the lotion, not just because it cost twelve dollars but also because it was phony and prissy and came only in a heavy tube. But the lotion helped buy her freedom. It was worth all the costs.

The lotion needed to dry, so Isabelle sat motionless on the rock and counted to two thousand.

The next step in cleaning up was putting on the summer town clothes. Isabelle examined each item for rips or stains. "Blend, blend, blend," she repeated as she pulled at seams and held cloth up to sunlight even though she had checked the clothes recently.

Blend, blend, blend. Blend, blend, blend. Out here in the woods, Isabelle naturally blended in. The lean angles of her body and the drab colors of her clothes made her one with the branches, the soil and the tangles of vines and leaves.

It was harder to blend in when she went to town. Isabelle had spent an entire day at the Skyler County Fair the year before, splurging on fair food and taking note of what the young women wore. Afterward Isabelle had traveled to Wheeling and bought the jeans, T-shirt and sandals with Biddlebourne in mind.

The Levi's fit her body well but didn't bare her belly or outline her behind tightly enough to make men hoot.

The T-shirt advertised a band Isabelle had never heard and also fit her well. It was gray, because a white shirt would only have advertised her white skin, and made of thick cotton that did not delineate her small breasts.

The sandals, definitely not the kind Isabelle preferred, nevertheless were the kind that Biddlebourne girls preferred. They were made of thick black rubber with white stripes across the top, comfortable enough for short walks but given to sliding off her feet if she walked fast.

Never mind the sandals. Just wear them.

Isabelle didn't need much makeup because of the tan from the tube, but she did use an eyebrow pencil and a blush brush. She was careful to apply the colors sparingly. She wouldn't get to look into a mirror before others saw her.

Isabelle pulled her hair into a sloppy ponytail—another Biddlebourne practice—and stuck a Pittsburgh Pirates cap on her head, yanking the ponytail through the gap in back. She felt the tears start when she slipped the fake-leather belt through the loops on her jeans and fastened the special buckle. By the time she had inserted the little gold hearts into her earlobes, the tears were sliding down her cheeks. She slammed the palm of her hand across her face and wiped them away. Tears were for inside, not outside.

Isabelle put on the BluBlockers and took a deep breath. Morning light shot through the poplar leaves. She was ready to travel.

"It is well that war is so terrible, or we should get too fond of it." ~~ Robert E. Lee

CHAPTER TEN

Rule Number Three: No whining.

The official copy of "Annie and G.P.'s Five Rules for a Happy Marriage" rested in their safe deposit box at Mountaineer Bank with their marriage certificate, birth certificates, wills, insurance policies and Annie's passport.

They had, in fun, made up the rules on the second day of their marriage. They had sat on the porch of a cabin in Hocking Hills State Park on a glorious September morning. They promised each other they would never forget that morning or the five rules:

Number One: No secrets.

Number Two: No lying.

Number Three: No whining.

Number Four: No nagging.

Number Five: No sorrow borne alone.

Annie was coming close to breaking Number Five. However, she figured that if she did not give way on Number Three, she could hang in on Number Five.

Just as he had promised, G.P. called at 9 a.m. My steady, ready fellow, she thought.

"It's me," he said.

"How's it going?" G.P.'s unit had just moved—again.

"Lots to do. I'm busy."

"Are you okay?" she asked.

"That and more. I've been getting in more running, and the food is great."

G.P.'s unit had recently received a cook with Southern endorsements who hauled in gourmet cookware.

It was hard for Annie and G.P. to talk without mentioning where he and his intelligence unit were stationed and exactly what they were doing. But any discussion of G.P.'s location was forbidden.

"Fannie Fay says hello," Annie reported. Indeed, Fannie Fay was mewling soulfully from the kitchen table.

"Here. Talk to her," Annie said, lowering the receiver to Fannie Fay's right ear. The cat nuzzled the receiver. "She sends her love," Annie translated.

There came a pause in the conversation. They thought about things they had taken for granted until a force stronger than their own pulled them into its vortex. He remembered her soft smile. She remembered the glow of his black boots before he left their home in Chestnut City. The boots weren't shining now in the desert dust.

"What didn't fit?" he said finally.

"Oh, the couch, the queen bed and your rolltop desk."

"I hate not being there to help. What kind of shape is the house in?"

"Don't worry. The move went fine."

"What did you do with my desk and . . . what else was it . . . the couch?"

"And the queen bed. Mr. Gideon Pugh put the bed and desk in his barn. The couch is on the front porch here."

"Who's Gideon Pugh?"

"He prefers to be called Mr. Gideon Pugh as far as I can tell. Chairman of the church trustees. On the doorstep this morning at dawn. I was half asleep, but he charmed me with cinnamon rolls from his wife and tomatoes from his garden."

"So he put the furniture on his shoulder and carted it off?"

"Actually, Herman Hoobler helped him. Hermie the Handyman. Does odd jobs at the church and around town. Drives an old school bus full of tools and junk that he picks up to sell. Mr. Gideon Pugh and Hermie the Handyman put the furniture in the bus and took off about half an hour ago."

"What about their shoes?" he said with a laugh.

"Well, Mr. Gideon Pugh is practical and no-nonsense. Hermie the Handyman is frugal, matter-of-fact and hard-working. Birds of a feather are Mr. Gideon Pugh and Hermie the Handyman."

"How do you get that?"

"Oh, well-used work boots with good leather on Mr. Gideon Pugh and very old Nike knockoffs on Hermie."

G.P. laughed. "What possessed you to put the couch on the porch?" he asked.

"Everybody here has a couch on the porch."

"Be sure to cover it at night with that big yellow tarp."

"Okay," she said, thinking she might find the tarp by October.

"What about the patio set?" he asked.

"They don't have patios in Biddlebourne, but the wicker chairs and umbrella table look real nice on the back porch. The back porch is about the only spot that I've got arranged so far."

That reminded her of something. She took a big breath and considered how to say it.

"Maybe Hermie the Handyman will help you get the rest of the house in order," G.P. said. "You're preaching Sunday, aren't you?"

"Yes, but I think I can get most of the big boxes unpacked by Friday. Chloe and Daniella are coming for the weekend."

"What's the house like? Any surprises?" he asked.

"There was one strange little surprise on the doorstep when I arrived."

"What?"

"A Starbucks bag with a dead cat . . ."

"Uh-oh. What's going on, Annie? I don't like the sound of that."

"Oh, it was just a prank," she said, swallowing.

"Remember the toilet-paper trick those kids pulled at your first church assignment?"

The trees around that parsonage had looked like a tiered wedding cake. G.P. and Annie spent a day plucking tissue out of high branches. The trustees took a leaf blower to the lower limbs and had a private chat with the parents of one Teddy Paul Boyle. Teddy Paul wrote a note of apology to the Scovills in which he repented forever of his leadership of the "T.P. Gang."

Annie laughed and said, "Boy, do I remember. Kids have some weird ideas about welcoming the pastor."

She didn't tell G.P., just as she hadn't told Mr. Gideon Pugh, about the note in the bag with the cat remains, which had read, "Watch where you step, preacher."

"You didn't answer my question," he said.

"What question?"

"About the house."

She didn't want to answer the question. Any version of the truth would trouble G.P. "The house is interesting," she said at last.

"Go on."

"Oh, it needs some work here and there."

"Such as?"

"Such as new wiring and new plumbing, and the walls painted, and the carpet cleaned, and the holes in the wall patched, and the light fixtures updated, and a washer and dryer put in, and air conditioning installed. Just standard things for an old house."

All was silent.

"What are you sleeping on if you have our bed in storage?" he asked.

"The guest bed. It's quite comfy. Fannie Fay has claimed the windowsills already."

They sighed, almost in unison.

"What are you sleeping on?" she asked.

"A glorified bunk bed. But the mattress is okay."

"It's hard to believe that all six-feet-two, one hundred and ninety pounds of you fits on a military-issue bunk bed," Annie said.

"I'm so tired when I turn in that I could sleep standing up. The mattress doesn't make much difference."

"You'll fit right in at the parsonage if that's how you really feel," she said.

"I hate it that you have to handle the house alone."

"G.P., don't worry. Please don't worry. I'll worry if I think you're worrying. Mr. Gideon Pugh and Hermie the Handyman both pledged their help, and the church really does want to fix it up. It's no big deal. Just part of ministry."

"Speaking of which, what's your part in all of this?"

"Honestly, they don't expect me to lift a finger. The Ladies Aid Society is coming to clean, and their president, a very efficient woman named Edith Ann Smith, called today to synchronize cleaning supplies. But I told Mr. Gideon Pugh I'd do whatever I could to make the work go faster. I'm thinking of adding crown molding in the living room."

G.P. guffawed. "Do they know you're hammer-impaired?"

"No, and they'll never know since you're not here to hide the toolbox from me. Speaking of your absence, they all think you and I are divorced."

"What?"

"I'm not kidding. Apparently, Burl Stout told them I was coming here alone. One of Mr. Gideon Pugh's cousins used to go to the Chestnut City church, so she told him I was married when I was pastor there. The people here in Biddlebourne put two and two together, came up with nine, and that's how we got divorced."

"Sounds like Burl should set the record straight."

"Not according to Mr. Gideon Pugh. He's put Mrs. Pugh on it, and I'm starting to believe that by the time Sunday rolls around, everyone in Biddlebourne will know the real story."

"Incredible."

"Yes."

"When's your first day at the office," he asked.

"Since next Monday is the Fourth of July, I'll have a chance to take some boxes to the office."

"A lot of appointments lined up?"

"Not yet. But the congregation is eager to move on the new building."

"Scared?"

"Of the construction project?"

"Yes."

"No. Happy. Excited."

They were running out of small talk.

"I miss you," he said finally.

"I miss you, too."

"I just got your last letter. At least I think it's your last letter. Sometimes the later ones come before the earlier ones."

"Your mother says military mail delivery depends on whether it goes by boat or by plane."

"No mail comes here by boat," he said with a laugh. "That was World War II."

"I know, but Mom Scovill is convinced that's how it is. Should I keep sending letters? I'll have e-mail set up in a day or two."

"You don't have to send letters if they're a lot of trouble . . . ."

"No trouble at all."

"It's just that . . . letters are something to touch," he said slowly.

Annie heard him inhale deeply.

"Letters it is, then, sir." She could hear her own voice break and hoped he hadn't heard it, too.

"I have to go," he said.

"Okay. I love you."

"I love you."

She felt the heat of the sun's rising in the east windows of the living room. She also felt the heat of selfish guilt rising around the neck of her Michael Green T-shirt. She slept in an antebellum house while he slept in a bellum tent. There simply was no comparison.

Dear Diary,
Nitemares. I always have nitemares. Black demins in the house. Always in the house. I usully stand up to them and screem get out of my house or spirit be gone or dam you to hell. Mommy says dam you to hell all the time to daddy mostly but to me and Frankie and Sissie two. Mommys a wich anyway she says shes a wich. She says shes a practicing wich. And that she can conjer up what ever she wants and that is why me and Frankie and Sissie have to

mind her. I dont mind her eksep if I no shes watching I mind her very good. She says she conjered up a demin to get me at nite if I pee in the bed. I wish I could stop peeing in the bed but Im afraid to get out of bed to go to the bath room becaws the demin might get me. I tried to tell mommy I was afraid but she just said dam you to hell. Daddy gave me a liking with his belt for up setting mommy so I never will tell mommy again that the demins scare me. I just tell them to be gone or get out of my house.

Mommy said she will tech me how to be a wich. That on my 16 birth day I will be come a wich just like her. I don't want to be like mommy. Im afraid to tell her I don't want to be come a wich like her so I pray that god will keep me from be coming a wich.

Some thing reely scary hapned last week. Julie was spending the nite and we were sleeping up on the third floor so we coodnt here the fiting and cussing down stairs. We were laying in bed talking. All of a sudden we saw some thing black crawling across the floor. I figured it was mommy with one of her games becaws mommy tries to scare us like that some times. The black thing went slow up to the window. I started saying mommy cut it out and Julie stated saying yeh Misses Pargeon stop it we no its you. You could still see it moving. So we started screeming mommy and Misses Pargeon and please stop. Mommy yelled up from the first floor what the hell is going on up there? So it wasn't mommy after all. Julie and I promised each other never to sleep up there agin. Its evul evul evul. I cant get that nite out of my mind. I always think about it before I go to sleep and then I cant go to sleep. I miss a lot of skul becaws I cant go to sleep or if I can go to sleep I have the nitemares.

"No matter how many communes anybody invents, the family always creeps back." ~~ Margaret Mead

CHAPTER ELEVEN

Friday, July 1

Chloe arrived from Pittsburgh before dinner—hers, not Annie's.

"Ooooh, what a dump," she said as she sought a spot in the living room select enough to receive her Gucci travel case.

Annie was relieved by her sister's reaction to her new home. She had feared she would have to put Chloe up at the only motel in Biddlebourne—which she thought might have even fewer amenities than the parsonage—because Chloe had no patience with circumstances that did not bend to her will and comfort. When Chloe was pregnant with Daniella she had once entered a room where a floor fan oscillated and demanded, "Why is that fan not pointing at me?"

Besides being a wife, mother and sister, Chloe was an actress. Her uncanny knack for transforming herself into different persona, plus her uncanny knack for looking gorgeous in all climes and at all times, kept her as busy in stage plays, musicals and commercials as she wanted to be.

Chloe would say that Annie got Dad's brains, and Annie would say that Chloe got Mom's legs. Secretly, Annie knew her sister made better use of the glam gams than she would have under her preacher suits and pulpit robes.

"I had trouble finding you. You said the house with the couch on the porch, but every house has a couch on the porch," griped Chloe, who, as something of a local celebrity in Pittsburgh, was used to having the way cleared before her.

"I said the house with the *brown* couch under a *yellow* tarp on the porch," Annie replied.

Chloe blew out a breath of disgust and put her hands on her hips. "To think you've sunk to this. God, Annie, I do believe I saw a bird fly through that slot at the top of the house."

"A louvered vent. Yes. A pair of wrens lives in the attic."

"How do you know that?"

"I had a run-in with the mother bird. I stole her nesting supplies."

"What are you talking about?"

"I was in the attic looking for storage when I found the nest. She was using the pages of a little diary to make the nest, along with twigs and straw and the like."

"And you took the diary?"

"And gave her a ball of twine and a package of raffia in trade."

"Oh. Where's the diary?"

"I'm reading it. It's difficult material."

"Is it signed?"

"No, although she mentions some names."

"How do you know the writer's a she?"

"Just guessing. The handwriting looks girlish."

"Can I read it? Maybe there's some sexy stuff in it."

"Hm. It's confessional but definitely not sexy. I'd like to find the owner and give it back."

"Never mind," Chloe said. "Let's get back to the birds. Go up there with a broom and shoo them out. Then nail up something to the vent so they can't get in again. They might attack me while I'm sleeping."

"I don't think so. They can't get into the rest of the house from the attic. And Fannie Fay likes to sit at the window and watch them fly in and out. They're a family."

Chloe frowned, which indicated she was deeply peeved because, as Annie knew, Chloe did not ripple the smooth lines of her face unless she had an appreciative audience.

"Why are the birds so fascinated with this place?" Chloe demanded.

"Maybe it's the handy availability of fast food in the form of ants, wasps and flies."

"Uh-oh," Chloe said. "You mean they haven't exterminated this dump? I'm leaving right now if they haven't."

"I'm assured they have," Annie said, deciding not to mention that the pest control company had been to the house only the day before.

"What if they fly downstairs? What then?"

"The wasps or the birds?"

"The birds!"

"As I mentioned, I don't think they can," Annie said. "But if they do, I'll open the door and let them out. Where's Daniella?"

"The child?"

"Do we know another Daniella?"

"Perhaps you were referring to our grandmother, the redoubtable Daniella Loretta Young."

Oh no, not this again, Annie thought. "We don't have a grandmother named Daniella Loretta Young," she said.

"Oh, to be sure, my dear," Chloe said, "but today I'm in Loretta mode."

Annie sighed. She hated to ask, but there was no escape. "Loretta who?"

"Loretta Young, of course—a great lady of screens large and small."

"The one who came down the stairs in a big dress on that television show?"

"No, the one who dressed in magnificent gowns and carried herself regally down the spiral staircase as she made her entrance. Goodness, Annie, have you no sense of grandeur?"

"I think God has grandeur."

"No, no! Not God grandeur. Glamour grandeur. The kind that makes the head of everyone in a room turn when you arrive. The kind that makes men swoon when you let them bring you a drink."

"Swoon?"

"Yes. Swoon. Like this." Chloe backhanded her forehead and slumped onto the floor in an elegant heap of white linen and electric-blue silk. She was careful on the way down not to nick her Kenneth Cole pumps on the coffee table.

"No one around here swoons," Annie said. "But I think they do appreciate the grandeur of the land and the rhythms of life."

"That's not what I mean at all."

"You and I see the world through different eyes," Annie said.

"Oh, pish. To answer your question, my darling Daniella is on a dig in California."

"A dig? She's only seven years old."

"Yes, a dig! I saw it in a magazine called *Dig*. Did you know there was such a magazine?"

"No. Where did you see that?"

"Pediatrician's office. The dig is at the La Brea Tar Pits. Kids watch the diggers and do little digging jobs. They have a teacher there to explain everything, and there's a bone bin where they can touch stuff."

"So Bob is there with her?"

"Yes. At first he didn't want to go, but I asked my friend Glenn, who used to be a coach, and he told me about some football league on the West Coast that plays all summer. Bob couldn't book the flight fast enough."

"I never heard of such a league."

"Semipro. Not many teams yet. But you know how Bob is. He got tickets to some big match they're having and got all excited about it."

"What are they digging for?"

"What?"

"What are they digging for at the La Brea Tar Pits?"

"Oh, fossils and such."

"What kind of fossils?

"I don't know. I'll find out when my darling Daniella comes home and tells me what she dug up."

Realizing she had run smack-on to a wall of Chloe logic, Annie changed subjects. "What's your next show?"

"*Guys and Dolls* at the CLO," Chloe said with a big smile, pleased that the conversation had at last come back around to herself.

"I forget what the CLO is . . . ."

"Civic Light Opera. Pittsburgh Civic Light Opera. How many times must I tell you?"

"Oh, now I remember," Annie said. "What role do you have?"

Chloe—or Loretta—gave Annie her reproving look. "What role do you think? The lead, of course—Sarah Brown—the part that Jean Simmons played in the movie."

"Sorry, I forgot," Annie said. Chloe/Loretta liked to play the lead. She had recently said she would play only leads for maybe five more years, after which she would become a character actress. Annie was unsure how character actresses differed from lead actresses but sensed that a keen distinction between the two could be made by practitioners of the dramatic arts.

Annie knew only that if Chloe/Loretta did not receive a very large bouquet of red roses on opening night, hell would be paid by whoever was in charge of opening night.

The phone rang, and Annie moved toward the kitchen. "Walk around upstairs and give me some decorating ideas," she said as she picked up the black receiver.

"It's me, Shirley Burrows, call me Shirl," said the caller. She waited as if Annie would know why Shirley Burrows/call her Shirl had rung.

"Thanks for calling, Shirl," Annie said, groping for context. "Um . . . should we get together?"

"If you want to get paid," she said. Now she had Annie's attention.

"Oh, you're the treasurer," Annie said. "We met last week. I apologize for not remembering your name."

"That's okay. As long as I get *your* name straight on the forms, we'll be in business."

"I take it you have forms for me to sign."

"Sure do. I'll be right over."

Annie started to suggest that they meet at the church, but Shirl had already hung up.

"Are you off the phone yet?" Chloe called from the second floor. "Come up here. I want to show you something."

Chloe/Loretta was in the smallest room upstairs. "This must have been the radio room," she said.

"The radio room?"

"Yeah. Where the old-timers sat around looking at the radio while Glenn Miller played all those dreamy tunes."

"Oh, I get it. Now we have media rooms. Before that we had TV rooms, and before that they had radio rooms."

"Yep. Let's make it your music room. We can use your Mozart print, and your antique hymnals, and your beat-up music stand, and your piano . . . ."

"That's a laugh," Annie said. "The piano barely made it into the living room. No way will it fit up the stairs."

Chloe walked into the hall and looked over the staircase. "Okay. I have another idea. Let's paint the room the color of pearls for Glenn Miller's "String of Pearls" and put up the portrait of Mom and Dad at their wedding. It's from around then, nineteen forty . . . uh . . . ."

"Nineteen forty-eight," Annie said. "And that's a great idea. What about the bedrooms?"

"Oh, you mean tiny and tinier? Let's do one in red, white and blue for G.P. and you, and one in misty blue for a guest room."

"Why misty blue?"

"Because I look good in misty blue, of course."

"Oh." Annie could have argued until her face was misty blue, but it would have been useless. Instead she said, "Did you get up to the attic?"

"I certainly did not. Those birds might attack me. The dust might stir up my allergies. I can't risk anything this close to a new show. Besides, I need shrimp salad and bottled spring water for dinner. Light mayo and four multigrain crackers, please."

"How about some sweet tea, too?"

"Heavens, no. Bottled water only, please. I shall drink no water drawn directly from a country well."

Annie sighed and hoped the corner store had shrimp and bottled spring water.

"There's something I'd like to talk about after dinner," Annie said.

"What?"

"Something that was left on my doorstep the day I moved in here."

"Well, what was it, for heaven's sake?"

"I'd rather tell you after dinner," Annie said.

"Whatever. I hope it can wait. I need for you to help me study my lines after dinner. And of course I have to get to bed early—my beauty sleep, you know."

"Of course," Annie said.

~~0~~

Dear Diary,
I peed the bed again last night. I'm in third grade now. But I cant stop in time. Mommy sang the piddle song again this morning. Fatty fatty two by four coodnt get thru the bathroom door so she pidled on the floor. That dum song hurts my feelings. I tried hard not to cry but everybody laffed until I cried. Today she made daddy sing two and he dumped his joos on the floor and made me clene it up. I hate that song. Why cant I stop peeing in the bed? When I pee in the bed she makes me lay in it. Or go and get the itchy blankit out of the bottom dror of the buffay and rap myself up in it.

Id go up to the atick and sleep on the matress up there eksep theres a young lady living in the atick now. We must not have enuf money becaws mommy and daddy only let peeple sleep there when we dont have enuf money. The woman makes a lot of fuss overe stuff. Like if its storming shes afraid. If the lectric goes out shes afraid. If I drop a pan in the kichen when Im fixing dinner shes afraid. When some body nocks at the door and wants her shes afraid.

She probly did some thing bad the last place she lived. No body else wood let her live with them so we are the only ones who let her live with us. Shes afraid of stuff that aksully hapns and also stuff that dosnt hapn. She hears things that I don't hear and mommy dosnt hear and Sissie dosnt hear. Frankies gone most of the time. Like Sunday she said she heard voices in the atick closets. Daddy used some pli wood from the dump to make closets in the atick so we can store stuff up there. Her names Evelinn. Evelinn came down to the kichen rite at lunch time and said I cant consintrate becaws of the voices Evelinn goes to junyer collej. What voices mommy said. The voices in the closets Evelinn said. Mommy looked at Sissie and me and made a sour face. Ok Ill come up and chek she said. So we all went up to the atick. Mommy opened all the closet doors and or corse nobody was there. Evelinn said Im sure I heard peeple like soljers in a battle shouting and saying o god and like that.

Mommy put her arm around her and asked if she wanted to eat lunch with us. Later mommy said Evelinn is lone some. But Evelinn also imajuns seeing things not just hearing things. At lest 10 times she came down stairs screeming she saw a man in the atick. The last time I think it was the day before skul started Evelinn said theres a man in my room and mommy made sure daddy wasnt ratting around up there first then she told Evelinn your seeing things girl better better get your eyes cheked. Now Evelinn is so scared of every thing she sees and hears that she moved in with us. Sleeps in our bedroom with me and Sissie. Mommy says thats okay as long as Evelinn pays her rent. Mommy razed Evelinns rent when she started smooching her meals off us. This morning Evelinn said she went up to the atick to change out of her night gown and she saw a stranj man wearing a uniform and sitting on the steps crying. Stranj how Evelinn likes mommy. Stranj how Evelinn is scared to deth in our house but wont leave our house.

"A stumble may prevent a fall." ~~ Proverb

CHAPTER TWELVE

Saturday, July 2

Saturdays at noon were best. As a girl, Isabelle had longed to be at the Flix on Saturday to see the latest movie starring Sean Connery or Clint Eastwood. But no matter how much she cried or begged or promised, Mommy and Daddy hadn't let her go. They hadn't even let her go when she was old enough to babysit and pay for her own ticket and popcorn.

Now she had less interest in the movies. They weren't the same anymore. But she could use the Flix in another way.

Flix was the only theater in Biddlebourne and one of only two in the county. Young people who worked all week—as well as young families with kids in school—routinely went to the Saturday morning show at the Flix and stayed in town to shop and run errands.

Isabelle arrived at the Eighteenth Street gas station around eleven. She used most of her remaining change to buy a king-size Snickers at the counter and asked the cashier for the restroom key. The teenager handed Isabelle the key, which was tied with string to a wood paddle, without looking up from her magazine.

In the restroom Isabelle checked herself in the mirror and adjusted her cap and hair. She looked like half the women she had seen go into the Flix except that the others had dates or husbands.

Soon she was sitting in the little park by the courthouse, enjoying her candy bar and keeping watch. She made numerous trips to the tall waste can by the sign board in order to look in every direction. How lucky for her the courthouse was right in the middle of town.

Isabelle didn't see anybody who definitely could identify her, but she saw several questionables. One went into the nail salon, the others into the dog groomer's. Well, they would be no problem because Isabelle didn't do nails or dogs.

When the young people began leaving the Flix in small groups after the first show, she rose from the bench and strolled toward the post office. She hoped, hoped, hoped that several moviegoers would also go that way.

She wasn't disappointed. A family—mom, dad and four kids—trooped into the post office. The kids started fingering the collector prints and mail tubes while the parents went to buy stamps from a machine.

Isabelle hurried to the counter, smiling politely at the middle-aged man who was sorting papers. "Help you, ma'am?" he said.

"General delivery for Isabelle Watkins," she said.

"Sure thing." He went through a door behind him and returned with a handful of items. As he gave them to Isabelle, he looked past her to see what the kids were doing.

"Thanks," she said.

"I need to see ID."

"Of course," Isabelle replied, reaching for her purse.

The man barely glanced at her New York driver's license—in which she appeared unsmiling and white as paper. "Hey, don't touch the posters," he said to the children. Isabelle took her license, smiled and left without another word.

The easy part was over. Isabelle walked slowly along the sidewalk with others who had just left the Flix. Unfortunately, they were all singles or couples who had no children to draw attention from her.

She walked past the bank three times to find the most opportune moment. On her third pass she looked into the big front window and saw a short line of customers waiting for the next available teller. If she timed this just right . . .

Okay. Now. Isabelle smiled and held the door for a woman who was coming out of the bank. Eyeing the waiting line, she went to a writing counter and began opening her mail. There were only five pieces, all expected by Isabelle.

She opened the five envelopes, stalling. She signed the back of her check, which was written out to Isabelle E. Watkins in the amount of $1,200.00. She filled out a deposit slip and a withdrawal slip. Glancing again at the waiting line, she made her move, striding to the line to take her place behind a big man wearing the gray uniform of the Southern Electric Power Company. She looked at nothing, trying to seem both bored and patient.

"George, long time!" The man in front of her turned and looked toward the door, where another man in the same kind of uniform waved and grinned.

"Hey, Walter," said the man in front of her. The second man came to stand beside the first man, and they started yakking about power lines and union meetings.

A teller waved for the next customer, who walked to the window, leaving only George and Walter ahead of Isabelle. Isabelle cleared her throat. She couldn't let the line get out of order. She had to be second in line, not third.

After a long minute, the man named George turned to her and said, "Haven't seen my buddy Walter here in ages. Why don't you go ahead of us?"

"Oh, no, that's not necessary," Isabelle said.

"We insist, ma'am," the other man said.

And that was how Isabelle had to walk to the window when the next teller motioned. She dragged her feet and thought about running from the bank, but that would have caused too much commotion. No, she had to do this.

"How can I help you?"

Isabelle presented her check and banking slips. The teller, a man who seemed to be in his twenties, used an ink stamp on the bank of the check and began entering figures on an adding machine. "Isabelle Watkins. Isabelle Watkins," he said. "I haven't seen you in here before."

"Oh?" Isabelle said, instantly wary. "I don't come in very often."

The young man laughed and said, "In a town this little, I figure I see all our customers at one time or another. Where'd you go to school?"

Isabelle could divulge exactly nothing to the teller. But she couldn't act uppity, either. "Oh, I didn't go to school around here."

"That so?" he said, fixing his gaze on her face and stopping his work at the adding machine. "For a minute there, you looked like someone I knew in grade school. Her name was Isabelle, too."

This had gone way too far. Isabelle's heart was trying to leave her body. She had to remove herself from the bank. That would ruin her schedule and shopping for the day, but what alternative was there?

Suddenly, Isabelle looked to her right through the big front window and said, "My goodness, there's my sister now! I have to go. I'll come back later. Sorry for the inconvenience."

She snatched her papers and almost ran from the window. The teller called after her, "It won't take more than a couple of minutes . . . ," but Isabelle was out the door before he finished his sentence.

She waved an arm high above her head toward the opposite side of the street and trotted to the corner to cross. She was confused and upset. She completed her charade by going into Elderdon's Rexall and hanging around until she could walk out with a couple of women. She kept up a conversation with them about the weather as long as she was within view of the bank window. But as soon as they reached the next block, she said, "Have a good day" and walked on quickly.

She had to think. She didn't have time to go back to the woods and be back to town before the bank closed. She couldn't wait until next week to cash her check, now that the Scovill woman had arrived. So she went to the library and held a *Skyler County Sentinel* in front of her face for nearly an hour while she thought and got hold of herself.

When she left the library she had only fifteen minutes before the bank would close. She scuttled to the bank, looked in the window and saw, to her great relief, that the nibby young man was no longer working at the windows.

Isabelle completed her transactions without a hitch. The woman who waited on her had little interest in anything besides clocking out, since she looked at her watch three times while Isabelle stood in front of her. She tried to disguise her clock watching, but Isabelle saw it and liked it.

"Have a good evening," Isabelle said as she left. The woman smiled, bent and reached for the purse on the shelf under the counter.

Isabelle now liked banking at closing time better than banking at noon.

Think, think, think. Blend, blend, blend. Having gone without breakfast in anticipation of a big, delicious lunch at the Snacknmore, Isabelle was famished. Nervous frustration and fear had drained her. If she didn't eat soon, she would feel sick. She could not risk that. The first question they always asked in the emergency room was, "What's your name?"

Though Isabelle had never before taken two big risks in one day, she entered the Snacknmore in the middle of the afternoon. There would be no lunch or dinner crowd, if you could call fifteen or twenty people a crowd, to keep the waitress busy with requests for more coffee and napkins.

She decided to eat quickly—but not too quickly—and to keep her sunglasses on no matter how hard it might be to read the menu. She chose a seat with a full view of the door and a light fixture over the table.

The hamburger and fries were wonderful, wonderful, wonderful. Isabelle debated whether to order a piece of chocolate cake with ice cream—her favorite dessert, just like birthday cake. She was looking at the door, considering the cake and ice cream, when she saw him enter.

He was taller than he'd seemed behind the bank window, with brown hair and a few freckles. A memory lurched inside her. She put her face back in the menu and prayed he'd walk past her.

But he didn't. "Hey, Isabelle," he said, standing beside her table. "Did you catch up to your sister in time?"

"Oh. Yes, I did. She had to get going to . . . her dentist, though."

"Mind if I sit down?" he asked.

Panic marched through Isabelle, leaving behind a sweating scalp, rising gorge and turning stomach. She couldn't say no. Wait a minute. Yes, she could.

"Oh, sorry. I was just leaving," she said. No cake today, she thought wistfully.

"Do you like pecan pie?" he said.

"Yes." Oh, no. The truth had slipped out before she could stop it. Lying did not come as naturally to Isabelle as she needed it to.

"This place has the best pecan pie around. Let me buy you a piece." Without waiting for Isabelle's response he turned and shouted, "Hey, Irma, bring us two pieces of pecan, would ya?"

She was trapped. Inside. With someone who might know her. Isabelle struggled to keep her expression calm. Under the table top she pulled her fingers and cracked her knuckles. *What to do? What to do? Think, think, think.*

"My name's Larry," he said as he dropped into the chair across from Isabelle. "Where'd you say you went to school?"

"What year did you graduate?' Isabelle asked. Larry leaned in so he could hear her soft voice.

"Ninety-four," he answered.

"Skyler County High?" she asked in her loudest inside voice.

"Yes. Played baseball and wrestled. Too short for basketball. Too light for football."

Isabelle nodded as if she knew all about schoolboy sports. Her breaths came in jerks, and she had to lock her knees to keep from rocking back and forth in her seat.

"I see the Pirates are holding their own this year," she said, remembering a newspaper item she'd just read.

"Gotta step up that pitching, though," he said. "Olexis got a shoulder injury. Who knows for how long."

The waitress arrived with the pie. "You need coffee, Larry?" she asked, and Isabelle could see her wink at him. "Sure do," he said. "Just got off work and gotta fill up the tank."

"How 'bout you, Honey?" she said to Isabelle. Isabelle swallowed and said, "I'm okay with the water, thanks."

Isabelle ate the pie as fast as she could. It was tasty— not as tasty as chocolate cake with strawberry ice cream— and had the same crunchy texture it used to have at Mrs. W.'s house.

"Thanks for the pie. Gotta run," she said as she swallowed the last forkful. She picked up her meal check and purse and rose.

"Here. Let me buy your lunch," Larry said, reaching for the slip.

"Oh, heavens, no. I couldn't. But thanks," she said. He couldn't stop her from hurrying to the cash register, but he stood and walked beside her. "Would you like to go to a movie next Saturday, since that's your banking day anyway?" he said.

"I . . . I can't. I'm engaged," she blurted.

"I don't see any ring," he said with a grin. "I looked when you were at the bank."

"Well . . . we . . . the ring . . . We did earrings instead," she said, pointing to the gold hearts on her ears.

"It's just a movie. I won't bite," he said.

"Okay." Isabelle regretted the word the instant it escaped her lips. But she realized that lover boy wouldn't take no for an answer. *Damn, damn, damn.*

"Of one ill come many." ~~ Proverb

CHAPTER THIRTEEN

Isabelle's world was collapsing. That woman had moved into the house. Her cover in Biddlebourne was crumbling. She had very little food and dared not stay in town to buy groceries and other supplies. And now the sky had turned black and a hideous, hard rain pummeled her as she stood at the bus stop.

Isabelle had ducked into the shoe store after fleeing the restaurant and the man she thought of as Lurky Larry. She had paced the narrow aisles, pretending to look for a special pair of evening shoes. The saleswoman had let her roam for ten minutes before insisting on "helping," and Isabelle had to make another quick exit.

She needed time to think. She needed a place to think. Her hideaway in the woods was out of the question in this downpour. The Iuka bus rolled to a stop in front of her, and Isabelle gratefully boarded. "Stop fourteen," she told the driver, handing him her fare and stumbling to the back row.

Isabelle was the only passenger, and the driver kept looking at her in the rearview mirror. She must look awful, she thought, with her hair and clothes soaked and her sunglasses streaked.

"You all right, miss?" the driver said.

Isabelle forced a smile and a wave and said, "Oh, sure, but I got pretty wet." She took off her cap and shook out her hair for emphasis.

"What?" the driver said.

Isabelle thought of Biddlebourne Junior High volleyball practice and yelled, "I'm okay, but I sure am dripping!"

"Oh. Yeah, the highway's a mess," the driver said. "You have anybody picking you up at stop fourteen?"

Isabelle couldn't think yet, and before she could stop herself she said, "Uh, no." Oh, God, now what had she done? He knew she would be getting off the bus alone. What an idiot she was.

"Tell you what, why don't you stay on the bus till the rain stops? It won't hurt anything."

"Really?" Isabelle was so grateful—and relieved—that she cried. She knew how to cry silently, just as she knew how to walk silently, so the driver couldn't see the difference between tears and raindrops on her face.

"Yeah, sure. I got a daughter about your age. Wouldn't want her stranded in this weather."

"Thank you. Very much. I appreciate it," Isabelle said in her loudest voice. The driver nodded.

Okay, okay, okay. She had a place to think. Calm down, she told herself. *You can get around this. Lurky Larry doesn't have your address or a phone number. He can't find you. He can't find you. He can't find you. But he knows my name! He knows my name!*

The bus driver looked in the mirror at Isabelle several times, but she averted her eyes. Seeming to understand that Isabelle didn't feel talkative, he soon focused on driving the mud-slung highway that stretched into the countryside.

Isabelle stuck her damp hand into her jeans pocket and came out with the three pillowy, buttery mints she had received upon paying her check at the restaurant. They were delicious. But they weren't dinner. And they wouldn't be breakfast.

She was tired—no, exhausted. The uncertainty of the day and the uncertainty it cast on her future tightened like a noose around her psyche. She wanted to sit on Mrs. G.'s porch with a bowl of popcorn. She wanted to watch a Clint Eastwood movie in which the big, strong hero fought for her. She wanted to tell Frankie her problems. She wanted to be five years old again and start over. She wanted . . .

His hand wasn't rough, but it was annoying. She tried to shrug it off, but it only held on tighter and kept pushing her arm. She felt sick as her eyes opened and she looked up to see the bus driver's face looming over hers.

"Wake up, miss. My shift's over. It's the end of the line."

"Oh, I'm sorry. I fell asleep. I was so tired."

"That's okay. My girl does the same thing in front of the TV every night."

"Where are we?" Isabelle saw lights but didn't recognize her surroundings.

"We're at the bus depot in Spartansville," the man said.

"Oh, my goodness," she said. "I . . . I don't . . ."

"There's an all-night diner across the street and . . . and a motel on down . . . ."

For a moment Isabelle mistook the driver's intention. She grabbed her cap and purse, stood quickly and brushed past him.

"Hey, I just meant you might want to get some rest before you go home in the morning."

Isabelle turned and said slowly, "Oh. What time is it?"

"It's a little after nine," he said. "We ran late because of the rain. I guess it's all over now, though." He stooped to look out the back window and nodded.

"Thanks. I mean thank you for letting me ride . . . out the storm. I hope your daughter wasn't out in it."

The driver looked at her oddly and nodded again.

Isabelle walked to the front of the bus and turned to wave at the driver. "Bye. Thanks again."

She didn't waste one minute with indecision. She went to the Blue Bird Diner, ordered eggs and bacon and biscuits and chocolate milk to go and took the meal straight to the Starlight Motel, where she paid cash for one night.

The Starlight wasn't up-to-date on cable television and air conditioning, but it had a functioning shower and a double bed with a mattress that didn't sag in the middle. It also had a telephone. She was in heaven.

She hung her clothes carefully in the alcove and showered in warm water—with Jergens soap—until the skin of her thumbs started to pucker. She wrapped herself in the bedspread and sat on the edge of the bed to eat her feast. It had cooled considerably, but she didn't care. She ate every crumb and drank every drop before she leaned back and fell asleep with the TV on.

Sunday morning came fast. But Isabelle rose eagerly and discovered that her clothes had dried overnight. Of course she pressed them with the palms of her hands and checked them for tears and stains before putting them on. Checkout time was noon, so she went to the Blue Bird and had pancakes, sausage, scrambled eggs, toast, orange juice and coffee.

Back at the Twilight, she sat on the bed and turned on the television so she would know when it was 11:45 a.m. She had important matters to plan.

"With the trowel of patience we dig out the roots of truth." ~~ Proverb

CHAPTER FOURTEEN

They worked hard Saturday. Chloe, despite her disdain for manual labor, painted and papered the two bedrooms and the music room with help from the church ladies. It was the only job available, she said, that would not severely imperil her manicure.

In the morning Annie polished not her fingernails but her sermon. Next she unpacked boxes and found the Mozart print and the big lithograph of her parents so that Chloe could see them in the music room before going home.

Hermie the Handyman led the attack on the downstairs carpet, spreading goo over the offending spots, which put goo on every inch of rug. Walking through the house was like playing a ragged game of hopscotch. Hermie's sons—ages six, four and one—worked beside him, which generally put goo on every boy, too.

A team of scraper-wielding middle schoolers told Annie they were the Power Rangers Sunday School Class and tore into the wallpaper in the living room. The kids made a big mess but did a fine job. They giggled when Annie said the vibrations from their boom box could have shaken off the wallpaper.

In the afternoon Annie went to the hardware store, or the hardware shrine, for even Mr. Gideon Pugh raved about Vinny's All-American Store. Vinny's was said by one and all to have every nut, bolt and home-maintenance tool made on American soil in the last seventy-five years.

The outdoor temperature had moderated to an even ninety-two degrees by the time Annie got to Vinny's All-American. Customer cars bore tags from Pennsylvania and Ohio as well as West Virginia. The place was packed. People of all ages carried red mesh shopping sacks with the American flag embroidered on them or pushed red plastic carts bristling with rakes, fence posts and plumbing supplies.

The store was pure bedlam. Red-vested teenagers scurried among the shadowy aisles, pushing sliding ladders to retrieve goods on the higher shelves and running to the back room for special orders. The teen helpers shouted numbers and directions, customers compared the merits of garden trowels and garden claws, phones rang nonstop, the tinny bell over the door jingled, and three old-fashioned cash registers ka-chinged.

There was not a computer terminal in sight. There were no automatic doors. There were no closed-circuit cameras. A weathered sign read, "Made by Americans." But, Annie noted with disappointment, there was no sign to suggest where the how-to books written by Americans awaited. If there was method to the merchandising at Vinny's All-American, it was hidden under the goods.

Vinny's only apparent bow to technology was his cooling system. The air in the store was a heavenly, frosty sixty-five degrees by Annie's guess. She inhaled deeply and strolled.

It soon struck her how Vinny's All-American could carry a line of every nut, bolt and tool made in the United States since 1930. Earlier owners, upon failing to sell certain inventory, had simply layered new generations of hardware on top of old. The result was an intimidating collection of materiel dazzling in its disarray and inspiring in its diversity. It was a hardware hubbub of archeological potential—a scene worthy of a write-up in *Dig.*

The king of this chaos reigned behind a wood counter next to the entrance. The glass countertop was thick like a Coke bottle and scratched white with years of use. As he leaned authoritatively over the counter, his balding head reflected the fluorescent light. His tweedy-gray goatee pointed left and right when he instructed the young helpers.

Annie neared the throne and said, "Good afternoon. I'm looking for a book on how to install crown molding."

"Good afternoon, madam. Welcome to Vinny's All-American," said the oracle of hardware.

"Uh, thank you very much, sir." The last time she'd been called madam she'd ended up hearing a pitch from an encyclopedia salesman.

A red-vested boy stepped to the counter, obviously in want of information, but the proprietor told him, "Son, the pastor has come to call. I'll get to you shortly."

"How did you know I'm a pastor?" Annie asked with a smile.

"Your beauty and grace have been described to me. I would recognize you anywhere," he said. Annie laughed.

"Actually," she said, "I believe you have also been described to me, if you are Mr. Vinny Clark, that is."

"I am he indeed," said Vinny with a dip of the head. "Crown molding, is it, Pastor?"

"Yes."

"May I inquire whether you have done any carpentry?"

"Well, no, but I'm trying to learn."

"Excellent! I applaud your efforts," he said, "but it is possible crown molding will not make a suitable first project for you. Um . . . I do not wish to appear immodest, but I am myself an experienced wood craftsman. May I offer my services—free of charge, of course?"

"Oh, no, Mr. Clark . . ."

"Tut-tut. Vinny. Call me Vinny," he interjected.

"Thank you, Vinny. Please call me Annie Ido—or Annie. But as I was saying, I could not possibly impose on your good will. Besides, I really do want to learn."

"Hm," he said. He twisted the tip of his goatee between thumb and forefinger.

"Perhaps you have a beginner's instruction manual?" Annie said.

"I regret very much to say that we do not. You see, madam . . . uh . . . crown molding is not usually thought of as beginner's work."

"Oh," she said.

"But I have an idea," Vinny said. "Will you come with me please, dear lady?"

"Surely," she said.

Vinny limped toward a narrow aisle, almost disappearing before she heard him say, "This way, if you will, Annie."

She nearly ran to catch up. Then she almost bumped into him as he stopped short in front of a dusty display of paperback volumes that lay flat and obviously uncatalogued on a metal rack at the back of the store.

"Here we are," he said. He flipped several books out of his way and pulled out one titled *Series 101*. He opened the book, which was quite shopworn, and said, "As you see, here we have many projects suitable for the beginner. A small bookshelf, a napkin holder, a birdhouse. Yes, this will do nicely, I think."

Maybe a birdhouse—later, she thought. But for now she desired to install crown molding.

"Vinny," she began in her sweetest tone, "may I think about it?"

"Of course, of course. Please take this free of charge. If you use it, it will be payment enough to know that I have been of service to you." Oh, what a fine line it is between good manners and bad flattery, Annie thought.

There would be no refusing him. "Thank you, Vinny. I'm appreciative." She dropped the book into her red shopping bag.

"Please call upon me at any time, and my offer to help with the crown molding stands," he said as he gave a mock bow and offered his arm for the walk back to the doors.

"Vinny, your store is fascinating. I have several other home-improvement needs. If I may shop for a bit?"

"Indeed you may. Please let me know if I may be of any assistance whatsoever," he said before heading back to his command post at the entrance.

Chloe had ordered more paintbrushes because she could not possibly, no, not even wearing rubber gloves, be prevailed upon to wash used paintbrushes. Later Annie would salvage the used paintbrushes, but for now she had to buy new ones.

She walked the aisles slowly, savoring the cool, dry air. She dared not linger long, however, because Chloe needed the brushes and wanted to paint in the best light. Annie sighed and made her selections.

When she stood in the second lane to pay for her purchases, she glanced toward Vinny at the front counter. He was looking straight at her. And he wasn't smiling.

~~0~~

Death in the Parsonage

Dear Diary,
My brother Frankie gets the dirty end of it all. Its some
thing to do with daddy saying Vickie June whose he look
like Vickie June for gods sake whose he look like? I am
tall enuf now to look into the mere in the bathroom and I
look like mommy-blond hair and brown eyes and long
nose. Frankie dosnt look like mommy or daddy. Frankies
hair is brown and his eyes are blue and his nose is frekly.
The other brother and sister, the ones who dont live here
any more I cant remember what they look like. They dont
come to visit us and we dont go to visit them. Mommy says
there as good as dead but I no she dosnt mean it becaws
she only says it when daddys around and never when I ask
her by herself. When were by our selves she says they went
away becaws they had to and she misses them and why
dont I bring her a cup of tea.

I like getting tea for momy. Teas much much better for her
than the stuff in the bottles she has beside the bed and
under the sink. She use to keep the bottles in her closet
under a pile of dirty old jeans but I no every thing in every
closet in this house becaws the closets is where I hide
when mommy and daddy fite. I no every thing in every
closet. I no more than Frankie nos even if he is my big
brother.

Im starting to no why daddy treats him so bad. The other
day daddy tied Frankie to the front porch. In his under
ware. What did the nabors think. Forget that how the heck
did Frankie feel. I felt like I was dying every minut
Frankie was tied up out there. It was awfal cold. All
Frankie did was bring two sax of groceries up the hill.
Whats wrong with that. My hart almost broke. I went to
mommys room and said go untie Frankie off the porch hes
freezing to deth and she said I cant honey becaws daddyll

beat me if I do. Mommys a chiken shes afraid of daddy so afraid I thought Frankie was going to be killed. Mommy kills the kittens in the backyard and daddy kills Frankie in the front yard. How could Frankie just stand there in his under shirt and under pants and not even cry.

I no Frankies going to run away soon he dint tell me he wood but I wood if I was 15 years old and looked like a man. This kind of stuff is why peeple always say there goes those Pargeon kids like were dirty or some thing. Its always hanging over my head like big ugle rain clouds. I hate my life. Me and Frankies life is shitty but Frankies is worse than mine even. Mommys is shitty two. Going to church dosnt matter. God hates us anyhow.

Death in the Parsonage

"No rain dampens all." ~~ Proverb

CHAPTER FIFTEEN

With the TV on and the room key on the table beside her, Isabelle lay back on the pillows and luxuriated in the rain-free, bug-free, spy-free atmosphere.

Then, because she had eaten breakfast in her clothes, she took them off and examined them again for dirt and rips. She found one loose button and smiled.

But then she saw her naked body in the mirror over the dresser and was startled. She'd never had curves before, or maybe she'd never let herself look before. *Stop, stop, stop.* Sleeping naked had been a high indulgence—and a racy one, she thought. It made her remember Jerry Patrick Zingfarb in—where was it?—Denver. Or had it been Salt Lake City?

Get on with it, she told herself. Get on with it. So, using a small paper pad and pen from the desk drawer, she listed her categories of thought: *FOOD, PEOPLE, CLOTHES, PLACES, GOALS.*

She read her list aloud five times, to get in the swing of thinking, before noticing how wrong it was. She slapped herself twice on the arm, tore out the page and made new entries on another page: *CLOTHES, FOOD, GOALS, PEOPLE, PLACES.* God, how could she have gotten off course so quickly?

Never mind. You can do this. You just have to think it through.

CLOTHES. Mend blouse. Sew button on jeans. Wash underwear, socks, sweats and sleeping bag. Buy jacket (lightweight, tan).

FOOD. Peanut butter. Tuna. Cheese. Crackers. Oranges. Bananas. Jerky. Nuts. Raisins.

GOALS. Check out special place. New bank?

PEOPLE. Lurky Larry. The Scovill woman. The shoe clerk.

PLACES. Pinckney. Grabathian. Chordle. Lukett.

At the first commercial in the 11:30 a.m. TV program, Isabelle picked up her purse, the notepad and the key and left the room. She must hurry.

"Would you persuade, speak of interest, not reason."
~~ Proverb

CHAPTER SIXTEEN

Sunday, July 3

Annie woke up tired. The bag lady seemed tired, too, after enduring the procedures of the previous week. She also had house halitosis, exhaling the smells of cheap paint and archaic wallpaper paste. Annie vaguely recalled hearing that wallpaper paste had once been made from horse parts.

She made her favorite breakfast of buttermilk pancakes with fresh strawberries and followed that with half a pot of strong coffee. She felt much better by eight o'clock and went upstairs to finish dressing and see about Chloe.

"Aren't you coming to church?" Annie asked as she knocked on the door of the Misty Blue Room. "It's my first Sunday."

"What?" Chloe said from within.

"May I come in?"

"Enter."

"Are you coming to church?" Annie repeated.

"Oh, Annie, you know how I feel about church. And it's so hot and humid from all that rain yesterday. My complexion does not like this heat. I'm exhausted from my labors. Besides, your bathtub is out of order, and I just can't get ready without my Crabtree & Evelyn bubble bath."

Annie was disappointed. "Okay," she said, "but everyone will be let down not to meet you."

"Really?"

"Yes. Apparently, Shirl Burrows' brother-in-law's neighbor saw you in *Annie, Get Your Gun* in Philadelphia in ninety-eight."

"Ninety-nine."

"Yes, ninety-nine, and thought you were fab, and Shirl told him he could get your autograph if he came to church today."

"Well, I don't know. I did pack the peach shantung. And the big white straw hat with the little pink ribbons and bluish-green leaves. Tres chic."

"By all means, wear the peach silk. You are luminescent in it." Annie could not bring herself to offer that women in Biddlebourne, as far as she had observed, wore hats only for gardening.

Chloe beamed and turned a theatric profile while considering her options.

"The tub isn't broken," Annie added. "You just have to retract the little round gizmo to get the water started."

"Oh. That's good. What are you wearing?" Chloe asked, squinching her face as if dreading the answer.

"My navy-blue suit with a white blouse."

"What shoes?"

"Navy blue Nikes."

"Oh, Lord, you need help."

"No, I don't."

"I have a beautiful floral chiffon scarf that I got last year in Cozumel. I'll lend it to you."

"It would drag the floor when I kneel at the altar. Really, I don't need it."

"You are an embarrassment to me," Chloe said.

"I know."

"I still don't know whether I want to go. How many people will be there?"

"Oh, maybe four hundred or so. It's summer. Lots of folks are on vacation."

"Oh? That's a lot more than showed up at your last church."

"That is because the Biddlebourne congregation is much larger than the Chestnut City one."

"I don't get it. Biddlebourne seems so rinky-dink."

Annie stifled her pain at this unfair and untrue assessment. "Biddlebourne has fewer churches . . . ."

"That's another thing," Chloe said. "Why is the church called Glory Hallelujah and not Biddlebourne First or Second . . . or whatever it is."

"You of all people, Chloe Loretta, should not challenge an inconsistency in names. Glory Hallelujah is the name chosen by the congregation in 1935 at the founding. The people chose to praise God with that name."

"Oh," Chloe said with a yawn. Local history held little interest for Chloe, who continued, "Well, if I went to church, how would you introduce me?"

"I could introduce you as my sister, Chloe Dorsey, and suggest that people might recognize your stage name, Chloe McClelland. Or I can introduce you as Loretta Young."

"Speaking of which, you must introduce me as your *younger*, no, your *much younger* sister, Chloe Regina McClelland.

"For heaven's sake, Chloe, anyone can see you're younger than me."

"Hmph. How old are you now? Forty-something, right?"

"I'm 47. That is not a secret," Annie answered.

"What if people make the mistake of thinking we were born in the *same decade*? Where would that leave me?"

Annie looked at her watch. She needed to be at the church soon. "Where did you get the name Regina? This will be quite confusing to the people."

"I'm thinking of embellishing my stage name to Chloe Regina McClelland."

"What happened to Loretta?" Annie asked before she could stop herself.

"Loretta is merely a frame of mind," Chloe said, "whereas Regina is a state of being."

"Doesn't *regina* mean *queen*?" Annie asked, suddenly sensing Chloe's flow.

"Exactly," she said with royal diction.

"Of course," Annie said. "Chloe Regina McClelland it shall be."

"Well," Chloe said, pausing to consider the dramatic possibilities.

Annie knew her so well. "There's a grand staircase at this church—better to make your entrance. And I'll introduce you as my *baby* sister," she said.

She had her. Chloe got out of bed without another word.

Four hours later there was a sort of rear guard at the swinging back doors of the Glory Hallelujah main sanctuary. First were Mr. and Mrs. Gideon Pugh, followed by Pastor Annie Scovill, followed by Chloe Dorsey/Chloe Regina McClelland/Loretta Young. The first three of them did handshakes; the next three did autographs.

Some worshippers left by the side doors, avoiding the receiving line, Annie noted with disappointment. But most stood in line to greet the new pastor. As they filed past, Annie wondered what they thought of her sermon. She wondered whether they thought her outfit too conservative, even for Biddlebourne, although she was sure the lightweight wool was too hot for the first Sunday of July. She also wondered whether proper navy pumps would have made a better statement on her first Sunday in the pulpit. But it was better for Nikes to say, "Sensible and effective" than for pumps to say, "Stylish and hobbled."

Annie also wondered if anyone had actually noticed her apparel after they got an eyeful of her golden-haired, bronze-skinned sister in that shawl-collared peach shantung sheath, wide-brimmed hat and luminous pearl necklace and drop earrings.

Curiosity being the faith catalyst of the day, worshippers numbered nearly five hundred. No pew, not even the front rows, had gone unused, though Annie suspected several folks sat forward the better to see her sister than to hear the new pastor's sermon.

Chloe had sat on the left side of the very front pew, which drew attention enough, especially from the teenagers who had been sentenced to sit as a group in the second and third pews on that side. For added effect she fanned herself with the Cozumel scarf. Annie may have promised eternal life through Jesus Christ, but Chloe fanned a steady breeze of Eternity through the congregation.

She had kept right on fanning when near the end of the service Mrs. Gideon Pugh stood, smoothed her steel-gray hair, pulled down the hem of her flowered skirt and went to the lectern.

After reminding the congregation of her role as chairwoman of the pastoral liaison committee, she read a lengthy biography of the new pastor.

After her reading, Mrs. Gideon Pugh looked up, gazed sternly at the worshippers and said, "People, Pastor Annie is married to Mr. Major G.P. Scovill—that's short for Granger Parker—and he's serving us and our country overseas with the United States Air Force Reserve right now, and they have a son and a daughter-in-law and two granddaughters who live a ways from Biddlebourne, so let's be real hospitable to Pastor so's she doesn't miss her family too much."

Annie learned later that this was the longest church speech ever given by Mrs. Gideon Pugh. The effect on the congregation had been audible, visible and instant. Worshippers exchanged glances and exhaled that little "oh" that people say when they grasp an insight.

By 12:45 p.m. the church was quiet again save for the middler youth group whose thirty or forty members were running up and down the stairs and through the classrooms preparing for the big Bible quiz that afternoon. With their leaders, Annie shepherded them into the little chapel and prayed for good gamesmanship and lifelong learning. They bolted the instant she said amen.

"What a glorious morning," Chloe said as she and Annie stood in the vestibule.

"For you, obviously," Annie replied.

"Didn't you have a great time?" Chloe asked incredulously.

"You get opening-night jitters. I get first-Sunday jitters."

"I can't believe it. You didn't seem nervous at all."

"Maybe you didn't get all the acting genes in the family," Annie said. Their mother had starred in her senior class play, *Sis Perkins*.

Chloe laughed. "What do you think people were saying to me?"

"Oh, how gorgeous you are and how they want to see you in *Guys and Dolls* and . . . ."

"They were saying how much they liked your sermon," Chloe said, "and how you're a breath of fresh air, how you're a saint to carry on so well with your husband away."

"Really?"

"Really."

"Not one word about how sensational you look, and how talented you must be, and how did a brown-haired, almost chubby girl like me end up with a stunning sister like you?"

"A stunning, *much younger* sister, you mean?"

"Exactly," Annie said.

"Oh, there were a few words along those lines, but it was mostly Pastor Annie this and Pastor Annie that."

"Nobody wanted my autograph."

"But they all want you to be their pastor."

All of them except the several dozen who had left without shaking her hand. "You think so?"

"Trust me. I can read a crowd like you read a book."

Annie hadn't yet told Chloe about the "gift" she'd received on her doorstep the day she arrived at 1010 Greenbriar Road. "What if I treat you to grilled salmon at the Red Lobster in Spartansville for lunch?" Annie said in a costly fit of gratitude and relief.

"Sounds good. Let me stop at the house for my umbrella."

"Rain's over. There's not a cloud in the sky."

"That's right. I can't risk the sun. I must shelter my face. You know that."

"We won't be in the sun more than five minutes."

"Five minutes! Way too much. My tan is exactly where I want it. And I have no sunscreen on. Why is that? That is because you forced me to dress this morning as if we were evacuating the house in front of a tornado."

"You arrived at church after the service began. If I hadn't left directions beside the coffeepot, I'd have thought you were lost. It must have been ten after ten when you made your entrance," Annie protested. "You got up a little after eight!"

"My point exactly!"

Annie shook her head in resignation. But inside she was jubilant. She had made a good first impression—small thanks to her sermon and appearance, solid thanks to Chloe and Ma Pugh, and many thanks to her husband. And, oh yes, big thanks to God.

Annie was so full of herself that she apparently did not hear Ma Pugh call her name.

"Are you deaf, Annie?" Chloe said, swatting the air around Annie's left ear with her big hat.

"What?"

"Mrs. Pugh's been trying to get your attention."

Ma Pugh pulled lightly at Annie's sleeve. "Pastor Annie," she said, "I'd like a few words with you . . . privately."

"Certainly."

"Pastor, nobody I know gave you that . . . bag of stuff on your doorstep," Ma Pugh said when they were sitting in the Ladies Aid Parlor.

"It was a prank," Annie said. "Let's just forget it."

"There wasn't any message inside that bag, was there?"

Uh-oh, Annie thought. "As a matter of fact, Mrs. Pugh . . ."

"Call me Ma, Honey. Everybody does."

"Okay, Ma. Thank you. Actually, there was a rather juvenile comment in the bag. Somebody wrote, 'Watch where you step, preacher.'"

"In all my born days this has never happened in Biddlebourne," Ma Pugh said. "Why, the Presbyterians and the Lutherans and the Catholics has all got new pastors time to time and not one o' them has ever received such a thing."

"Not to argue, Ma, but were any of those pastors women?"

Ma paused and looked Annie straight in the eyes. "Oh, Honey, nobody would be rude enough to . . . . I know everybody in Biddlebourne and everybody knows me. I have quilting circle with Evajean Carmody and she's the head muckety at the Lutheran church, and I was in PTA for years with Mary Ellen Fletcher and she's the office lady at St. Gregory's and . . . ."

"Mrs. Pugh. Ma," Annie interjected, "I apologize for doubting you. I'll never do it again."

"That's okay, Honey," she said. "We're just getting to know each other. But now, back to that bag of business you got last week. I'd like to see that note, if you don't mind."

"I don't think it means anything."

"Pastor, I know what I'm doing. Do you still have the note?"

"Yes. It's at the parsonage."

"Pa and I'll be over this afternoon to pick it up."

Annie sighed. "Certainly," she said.

~~0~~

Dear Diary,
When no ones living up in the atick Sissie and me have
pajama partees up there. Im surprised mommy dosnt make
us stay away from up there. I cant understand why my
friends wont spend the nite but all of Sissies friends do.
Every one of them wants to spend the nite at our house. I
think its becaws they no its honted plus the fact mommy is
a wich.

A wile ago it was Sissies 13 birth day she had all her girl
frends spending the nite. Well gess what daddy did. Came
out of the basmint starck naked. Girls were screeming and
calling there parents. Went home rite then. My poor sister

was crying so mommy said Ernie whyd you do that to your dotter? And he just laffed and laffed and laffed. Mommy said Sissie was mortafide and daddy ruint her life now. I was in the living room when this hapned so I saw it all. Sissie thru the party food all over the kichen and that made mommy mad two. Sissie went to her room and slamed the door and I cood here her crying and calling daddy bad names and slaming the closet door agin and agin and agin. I cant understand how the closet door dint fall off its hinches. Mommy said to me go sleep with Sissie tonite and I said no I wont and I ran away to my speshul hiding place and dint come back until the next day. I dint take my bath that nite. I was afrade mommy would here the water and have a hissie all over again. So I just wet a wash rag and wiped myself all over with it. I dint pee in the bed that nite eather. When I got up the next day Sissie was all ready gone to skul and no body acted like any thing unusul hapned. I asked mommy who clened up the chips and pop and stuff that Sissie smashed all over the kichen and she said shut up you little dum-shit it ant your busness so I shut up. But I think mommy clened it all up. Daddy dint come to breakfast that day at lest while I was in the kichen so mommy and I sat at the table eating breakfast.

Mommy did some thing that day that never hapned befor she said sorry I called you dum-shit I dint mean it. I no I said. I hugged mommy so she woodnt feel so bad about Sissies party. The funny part is I havnt ever had a birth day party. Frankies older than me two but I don't think he ever had a party eather. I asked him if he ever had a birth day party and he shook his head and made a face like what, are you nuts. So I wont ever ask him agin. I no the answer.

"Fear is stronger than love." ~~ Proverb

CHAPTER SEVENTEEN

Isabelle's chest was the tower, and her heart was the big iron bell banging inside it. She was sopping with foul sweat and hunkering in a position that strained her thighs, knees and ankles.

The plan had been going swell. The embroidered blouse and the jeans were whole again, and the drying cycle was nearly done when she'd heard Mr. and Mrs. P. drive into the garage. There was no mistaking the grind of that automatic door. But Isabelle, fresh from a beautiful night of uninterrupted sleep at the Starlight, had been able to move fast.

She had turned off the dryer and stuffed everything, including the backpack and the bicycle locks, into the plastic bag. She hadn't turned on the light in the utility room to begin with, so there would be no flicker to warn Mr. and Mrs. P.

It usually took Mr. and Mrs. P. at least five minutes to make their way into the kitchen, but they would pass through the utility room, so Isabelle had to hurry. She whisked out the back door with her bag and was in the clear before she heard the second car door slam.

But wait! The detergent! What about the detergent? She never used Mrs. P.'s detergent but brought her own in a tiny cloth bag. She searched frantically in the big plastic bag but could not find the detergent. She had to go back.

She would have to punish herself severely for this failure, but that would be later. Right now she needed that detergent. The back door had locked behind her when she stole out, so she couldn't enter the house that way. Where? Where? Her thoughts raced through the house as she had stored it in her mind. Mental images of rooms flashed in and out.

After a long, long minute she knew what to do. She went to the window next to the utility room—what people called the powder room—and saw that it was cracked open a couple of inches. Without even checking for bugs and dirt on the sill, she tossed the plastic bag onto the grass, threw open the window and climbed in.

Within forty-five seconds she had the detergent and was back out the window. Mrs. P. wouldn't suspect a thing. Luck was with her after all.

But a new thought hit Isabelle. She couldn't sneak across either the back yard or the front yard now because Mrs. P would be in the kitchen making lunch and Mr. P would be in the living room watching sports.

So Isabelle had been forced to grab her bag and run under the front porch, where there were spiders and ants and—oh, God—mice. She knew those things for a fact. Therefore, when she had crab-walked to the deepest part under the porch, she had to hunker and not sit because if she sat she would wind up with ant bites on her back side—and mouse dung on her clothes.

The backs of her thighs burned as if she'd sprinted back to Biddlebourne rather than ridden the bus. Her ankles, contorted at an unnatural forty-five-degree angle, had gone numb. Isabelle counted to keep her mind off the agony and to estimate when lunch would be ready and Mr. P. would go from the front room to the kitchen to eat.

At 2,457 Mr. P. was stomping his feet and shouting at some coach, but Isabelle could smell hamburgers cooking. Her favorite. Oh, how she longed to knock on that back door and be invited to lunch. But that was impossible because of what had happened all those years ago.

Isabelle believed in her heart that Mrs. P.—and maybe even Mr. P.—would understand and forgive her. But nobody else would. Nobody else would look at her with a warm smile and say her name correctly and give her a hug and ask her to sit down.

Her heart thudded, her mouth watered, and her muscles seared until the count was 3,096, at which time Isabelle heard Mrs. P. call out, "Gideon, lunch!" Isabelle knew that Mr. P. would shout back, "Just a minute, dear," and that Mrs. P. would yell, "I'm sitting down! Come and eat, Gideon!"

All happened just as she remembered, giving Isabelle great and secret pleasure and distracting her from the pain. She was even more pleased when—at long-awaited last, at 4,254—Mr. P. took himself from the front room to the kitchen to join Mrs. P. for juicy, tasty hamburgers on big whole-wheat rolls that she'd raised on top of her stove and baked inside it.

Isabelle made for the oaks at the front of the house as soon as she heard Mr. P.'s chair scrape the pine-board floor. This was far enough for now, she thought. And she settled down to count to twelve thousand, after which both Mr. and Mrs. P. would be napping on the old poster bed with the circle-patterned quilt.

Death in the Parsonage

"Dead men tell no tales. ∼∼ American film cliché

CHAPTER EIGHTEEN

Chloe made a typically theatrical departure Sunday after lunch, carrying the luggage with which she had arrived as well as a shopping bag full of green beans, melons and other homegrown produce she had found time to purchase and which would benefit her figure, her complexion or both.

Chloe first called Shirl Burrows' brother-in-law's autograph-hungry neighbor and repeated the dates for the upcoming *Guys and Dolls* show in Pittsburgh, changed her traveling ensemble twice in response to steadily improving weather forecasts and telephoned several salons in search of a manicure appointment.

"A manicure couldn't wait until you got home? Not much is open around here on Sunday," Annie said.

"And then, pray tell, what would I do if I happened to meet a fan or a director or a prospective producer on my way home with my nails needing attention?" she said.

"How much does a manicure cost these days?" Annie asked.

"Oh, the kind I get costs fifty bucks minimum."

"Here," Annie said, taking some bills out of her purse and handing them to Chloe. "My thank-you for coming to help. Everything you did looks great."

That was true. Chloe—despite her disdain for manual labor—had painstakingly painted each of the three little rooms upstairs, allowing the church ladies to paint only the bigger, flatter areas while Chloe saw to the corners, the paper borders and other details. She had also single-handedly wallpapered the dining room. Annie loved the finely striped maroon, silver and navy paper. It was accented by a wide, high border of deep red roses and luxuriant gray-green foliage with silver streamers. It fit the old house and high ceilings perfectly.

"Thanks, love you, call me," Chloe said before spilling her luggage and herself into her canary-yellow Corvette and spinning out of the driveway.

She returned, however, a minute or two later and beeped the horn. Annie went to the porch and yelled, "What did you forget?"

"Let me take the bird girl's diary with me," she shouted back, "in case I have time to kill at the salon."

"No. I haven't finished it yet," Annie said. "I'm looking for clues so I can get it back to its owner."

Even from the porch Annie could see Chloe's disappointment. "Wait a minute," she said. Annie went inside, grabbed two devotional magazines from her desk and ran out to the driveway.

"Thanks," Chloe said as she received the reading material. In truth, Chloe usually read only her horoscope, her scripts and her darling Daniella's school papers. Devotionals were not high on her list or even on her list.

Annie had no evening sermon to prepare because Glory Hallelujah's Sunday night worship services would not resume until October, when the last of the apple crop had been harvested and sold, made into cider, mashed into applesauce or turned into animal feed.

She busied herself with box disposal, ironing, plant care and reading on the back porch. Around five o'clock she confirmed her 7 p.m. dinner with G.P.'s parents, Mary Jo and Parker Scovill. Perhaps, Annie thought, she would tell them later that today was a special anniversary for her.

Annie was sixteen, coming up on her junior year in high school, and G.P. was the new boy in the band—seventeen, dark-haired, tall, possessed of a mesmerizing smile and, it was said, a standout percussionist. Annie had already heard from Mary Louise, Rhonda and other agents that this G.P. Scovill was very cool, but when she saw him strapping that snare drum to his leg before marching practice in the summer of 1974, she was so shaken she nearly dropped her clarinet.

Annie had later wanted to say the rest was history, but love takes a smooth course neither in history nor in high school. She was too shy to say hello to G.P., and he was too surrounded by new friends and admirers to notice Annie. Finally, Mary Louise took pity on Annie, who was a mooning mess that summer. Mary Louise caused her brother Paul, a drum major in the band, to tip off G.P. to the fact that the quiet girl in the clarinet section thought he was cool.

G.P. understood even in high school that as a point of courtesy a gentleman acknowledged a lady's interest even though the gentleman had more exciting romantic prospects than a shy and studious clarinetist.

And so, on a balmy afternoon, after the first outdoor rehearsal on the first day of summer band camp at Badger Creek State Park, G.P. walked toward Annie as she put her clarinet in its case. He smiled and said, "Hi. I'm G.P."

"Hi. I'm Annie Ido, Annie." Was she smiling? Was her sweaty hair plastered to her sunburned face? If she arose from the folding metal chair, would the backs of her thighs stick to the seat? She stayed seated.

"Ido?"

"I say it like *I-dough*, not *I-do*, because it was my great-grandmother's name and that's how she said it. It's Irish," Annie answered, feeling foolish after her long and boring explanation.

"My name is Granger Parker, Granger after the great football player Red Grange and Parker after my dad. We just moved here from Indianapolis."

"I know. You're a very good drummer. The director's really glad you're here."

"Thanks. You're a very good clarinetist. I think you were the only one out of the whole reed section who was able to sight-read that last Sousa march today."

"I wasn't sight-reading. I played it last year with the community band," she explained. Another boring speech, she thought.

"Oh," he said. Annie could tell he was groping for a way to end the conversation civilly and go away, having done his gentlemanly duty. She felt heat rushing to her cheeks and said, "You were nice to say hello. I . . . I . . ."

"It was nice to meet you," he said. "Take care."

"Yes. You, too."

And G.P. walked back to rejoin his buddies in the boisterous drum section.

Band camp dragged by that year for Annie. Every day she argued with herself and with Rhonda and Mary Louise over whether she should go up to G.P. and say hello. Whatever she should have done or might have done, she was too shy to do anything. She was miserable, as concerned that G.P. might know how much she liked him as she was about his obvious delight in the attentions of other girls.

On the last evening of camp, Annie showered before dinner and put on a white blouse and a long, colorful skirt. Dinner that night was meatloaf, fried eggplant and canned green beans, one of her least favorite menus. Still hungry when she left the dining hall, she wandered along with her friends to the snack tent.

"Want half?" someone said, and Annie turned at the counter to see G.P. Scovill holding out half of a strawberry Popsicle and looking directly at her. Her tongue clove to the roof of her mouth, her heart attempted to leap out of her body, and the muscles in her knees melted. But in an adrenalin-enabled response she said, "Sure. Thank you."

"You're welcome. Want to go for a walk?"

She did if her legs would hold her up. Annie heard Rhonda and Mary Louise giggling, but what she later believed to have been a primal instinct for species continuation took over, and she mustered enough aplomb to say, "Uh-huh."

G.P.'s hand touched hers that night as he gave her the Popsicle.

Annie opened her eyes and pulled herself back to the present. She had work to do. She went upstairs and changed into jeans, a long-sleeved shirt of G.P.'s and her mission-trip work boots. She tied a bandana over her hair, took the big flashlight out of the kitchen drawer, got a pair of garden gloves from the back porch and went "down there."

Mrs. Gatwick, a homebound church member, was waiting for the coal that Annie would shovel out of the basement, coal that would never be used in this house that surely would receive a fine, new heating and air-conditioning system to cool the occupants of the house during the days and caress them during the nights.

The shovels hung awkwardly off huge square nails—railroad spikes, she supposed—that stuck out of the beams in the coal cellar. She propped the flashlight on a shelf, picked the shovel with the longest handle, snapped on the weary ceiling bulb and began to dig. Four of her sturdiest packing boxes, lightened of their household goods and reinforced with duct tape, awaited filling for their final use as coal bins to be taken to the Gatwick house.

The work hurt, but she grunted with satisfaction at each blunt thrust of the shovel. Soon, she hoped, she would be sleeping through every night, cool and dry.

When the sweat stung her eyes, she took a rag plug from a gas can and tied it around her head. When her fingers bled, she wiped them on her jeans. She dumped coal shards into the boxes and coal dust into the once-silver gift bag in which she had received her Mother's Day gift. *Mom's making good use of her gift, children. Thank you very much.*

At last, done with digging, she swapped shovel for broom and swept furiously. No stray pieces would trip the plumbers and other workers who would soon arrive. Finally, she dumped the last dust into the grimy gift bag and regarded the one remaining lump of debris.

Kneeling, she saw that it was embedded like time itself in the earthen floor. It peeked from the packed earth but would not budge. She jabbed it with the broom and whacked it with several shovels. It stayed put, stuck like tithes in a miser's purse.

She plodded upstairs and pulled the biggest butcher knife from the mahogany block—a wedding gift. Back in the cellar, squatting, she hacked until the sullen soil delivered a long, crusty artifact.

At last she had won. But not really. The coal that wouldn't budge wasn't coal. It wasn't a rock. It was almost surely a bone—a bone too long and sturdy to belong to a cat or a dog and entrenched too deeply to have been accidentally placed in the coal cellar.

The bone was shaped just like an arm bone, a humerus if she was not mistaken. Her butcher knife was ruined, so she rummaged in G.P.'s toolbox and borrowed a claw hammer and chisel. For more than an hour she squatted, sweated, chipped and clawed.

When she had freed all the remains from their rigid grave, she crawled to a crumbling wall and put her back to it. Once, such a riddle would have amused her. But not now, not here.

Suddenly, she remembered. She wiped the face of her Timex. Seven-thirty. She had to make up an excuse to tell Mary Jo and Parker. Then she had to figure out who was buried in the basement of the preacher's house. Then she had to figure out how to hide it all from the boy who had become the man she loved.

Dear Diary,
Mommy has sugar dibeatus realy bad. Some times she goes into sugar shok. She lays on the floor and has sezures. I sit on her stomak while Frankie or Sisie put a spoon of sugar down her throte. I can remember when I was 5 mommy had a sugar sezure on valntines day. The ambulunce from the fyunral home came to our house on valntines day and took mommy to the hospital but she came home the same night. Since then I think mommys gone to the hospital in the ambulunce almost every week only its not realy an ambulunce it's the big black car they take the dead peeple in to the cemetary. I hate seeing that car. It never comes in the day time. Always at night. The middle of the night. Usully they take mommy but some times they take daddy when hes dizzy or throwing up two much. The one driving it is always that creepy Mister Lawson. When mommy goes in the fyunral car at night shes sick from drinking buze plus doing stuff. One time when she was drinking her buze she put her arm threw the up stairs window. Blood every where. She went to the

hospital in the black fyunral car and came home the next morning like nothing even hapned. Another time mommy put her arm threw the ringer on the washing masheen. She broke her arm and they put a cast on her arm at the hospital. She came right home and took the cast off. Threw it on the back porch. It was on the back porch more than a year. I no becaws it was there for two 4th of Julys. Another time she put her hed threw the wall in the dining room. They never fixed the hole its still there.

"He that corrects not small faults, will not control great ones." ~~ Proverb

CHAPTER NINETEEN

Monday, July 4

Isabelle awoke cranky because it was backpack day. Yes, she had to get up and do regimen, but, no, she wasn't happy about it. This was because Saturday's rain had left the woods boggier than usual, forcing her to sleep in the limestone cave on Sunday night. Sleeping in the cave meant keeping watch for ratsnakes and bats, which did not take to human company. Thus, sleeping in the cave meant not sleeping, or not sleeping much. Isabelle couldn't remember whether she'd slept at all, which signaled to her that she should be extra careful today about everything.

She needed daylight and reasonably dry ground for regimen. Therefore, regimen needed done in the cave, and it needed done early while the sun beamed into the cave on the slant. This meant that breakfast and bathing, which always came first, must happen efficiently.

Although Isabelle loved efficiency almost as much as she loved anonymity, breakfast and bathing were two of her Permitted Pleasures—the precious PPs. They should be planned and savored, embellished and prolonged.

Hurrying breakfast and bathing only deepened the despond that had settled upon her.

The cave was still dim, but Isabelle knew daylight had come because she heard the *fee-bee* of the chickadees. Their song made her resolve to soldier on. Disengaging the food kit and laying a clean dishcloth in front of her—after all, she had done laundry yesterday and could enjoy at least the tablecloth part of a hurried breakfast—Isabelle chose a protein, a starch and a fruit: cheese, crackers and raisins.

Isabelle took a minute to eye the breakfast spread and to reflect on mixed blessings. Mrs. G. had spoken often of mixed blessings, and Isabelle had struggled to understand. Were mixed blessings like salad mix—some red cabbage and some light green lettuce and some dark green romaine? Were mixed blessings like cookie dough—a blend of flour and sugar and butter and baking powder and vanilla? Or were mixed blessings like the sixth-grade mixers in which Isabelle stood alone while boys picked the other girls for square dancing?

In the Dallas incident, Isabelle had gained insight into mixed blessings when Jake L. gave her a job without a background check and afterward came to her room wanting unspeakable things. She'd had to rid herself of Jake L.

Her learning had continued at the San Diego airport when she'd lost her ID and frantically backtracked until she found it—and four twenty-dollar bills—in the trash can of the restroom.

Mixed blessings, mixed blessings, mixed blessings. Isabelle thought about Lurky Larry and the bad rain on Saturday, which had sent her unexpectedly to Spartansville but which had also brought her a night's sleep in a real bed and a shopping trip to a big store where nobody looked twice at her.

With her selections lined up one-two-three, Isabelle ate and watched. Squirrels and chipmunks rarely ventured into the cave, and she wouldn't have minded if they did, but the bigger animals demanded constant vigilance. She chewed her bites twenty-seven times each and made sure no crumbs fell on the earth.

She drank exactly eight ounces of bottled water before tidying the food kit and making it travel-ready again. Carrying all her luggage, she walked to the stream and bathed as best she could in the creek's roiled waters.

Isabelle transported herself and her possessions back into the cave and set the backpack in front of her. She would not kneel and remind her poor legs of yesterday's adventure—another mixed blessing. So she sat on the powdery soil, unzipped all seven compartments of the pack and put its contents on the clear plastic bag that had been folded atop them.

These items were the best remnants of her past, and none should ever touch dirt or be touched by hands other than Isabelle's. If any single item fell into the possession of someone else, Isabelle's life could tip and submerge like a wood boat with a hole in its bottom.

Remembering the good parts of her life was important to Isabelle, which was why backpack regimen should be done in a way that allowed her to touch the good parts while thinking of them.

Yes, I'll be okay. Yes, I'll be okay. Yes, I'll be okay. The array before her grew as she had grown. The baby spoon only four inches long. Two red barrettes. A cracked photo of three children standing on a porch and peering earnestly into the camera lens. A penknife. A sport wristband. A movie ticket stub. The binoculars. A colorful paper fan. A thimble. A black velveteen bag containing her paper work. A green velveteen bag containing money.

A red velveteen bag containing toiletries. An empty brown leatherette purse with a long shoulder strap.

Working fast, Isabelle checked, dusted, numbered, reread for the thousandth time and straightened. From the black bag she extracted two passports and two driver's licenses, a birth certificate that had been folded many times, a diary with a clasp, a worn and laminated Social Security card, an electric bill for 1010 Greenbriar Rd., Biddlebourne, W.Va., and a small box holding paper, pen and pencil.

Out of the red bag came a washcloth and toothbrush, the rubber gloves, a small plastic tub of baking soda, a small plastic bottle of aspirin and cartons of tampons and sanitary napkins. The green bag yielded a wallet, a coin purse, a plastic pencil case and a checkbook. Isabelle counted everything, including eleven tampons and $165 in cash. She sharpened the pencil with the penknife. She shined the spoon, hair clasps and binoculars. She put on the wristband for a moment. She wiped the purse inside and out.

The items were put away now. Regimen was over. And, yes, Isabelle was emotionally exhausted, but, no, she had not cried once. It was a mixed blessing.

"If the facts don't fit the theory, change the facts."
~~ Albert Einstein

CHAPTER TWENTY

Tuesday, July 5

Annie did double devotions before driving to the church. She arrived at 8:30 a.m. and continued relaying boxes into the office. She'd moved in most of her boxes on the Fourth while other church staff had a vacation day.

Trudy Bigler, church secretary, was due at nine, according to Shirl Burrows. When Trudy hadn't arrived by 9:45, Annie shelved her plan for a 10 a.m. staff meeting and called Hermie the Handyman to say they would meet at 11 a.m. instead.

She arranged drop-ins with the publisher of the *Skyler County Sentinel*, the manager of radio station WVCO, the staff chaplain at Unified Memorial Hospital and the directors of Biddlebourne's two funeral homes. She arranged to visit Marcy Woostine, the former pastor's wife, to whom the congregation had sold the previous parsonage upon Pastor Woostine's untimely death.

She copied the pages of the church directory at twenty-five percent reduction, punched holes in the pages and added them to her day book. While she had the day book out, she tried to make a list of things to buy in town, but looking at black on white only aggravated her headache.

She sat at her desk staring at the boxes that needed unpacked, finally propping her chin on her hands and letting her brain throb. She closed her eyes and tried to pray away the pain, but it pounded, pounded, pounded.

"Oh, Pastor, I'm so sorry to be late, and on your first day and everything . . . ."

Annie opened her eyes and looked up. A young woman wearing shorts, tank top and a blush stood before her. Trudy. "What happened? Are you all right?" she asked.

"Oh, yes. I'm perfectly fine. I . . ."

"Yes?"

"I slept in. I was out late, and I forgot to set the clock, and it was past nine when I woke up, and I had to go to Elderdon's and get Grandma's medicine before I came to work, and . . . ."

"It's okay," Annie assured her. "Did you get my message about the staff meeting at ten o'clock?"

"Yes. I'm sorry."

"It's all right. I called Hermie and told him we could meet at eleven. We can get back to the ten-o'clock schedule next week."

Trudy looked even more embarrassed.

"Will ten o'clock work for you?" Annie asked.

"Yes, ma'am," she began, and Annie knew she wouldn't like what was coming because it was rarely fun when they called you ma'am.

"Yes, ma'am," Trudy started over, "but once in a while I need to spell Mom on Tuesday mornings when the sitter doesn't show up on time."

"I understand," Annie said, though she didn't. Not yet. "We'll work it out."

The phone rang. Trudy hurried to answer. "Hello. This is the church. I mean this is Glory Hallelujah Church. I mean good morning Glory Hallelujah Church may I help you?"

Trudy reddened again, listened thoughtfully and said to Annie, "It's for you."

Annie stepped back into her inner office and picked up the phone.

"Annie, I just called to wish you well on your first day in the office. But if you want me to, I'll come over there and start training that girl this afternoon," said the caller. It was Marilyn Caperton, church secretary superior, typist terrific, office manager most meritorious.

"Marilyn, how good it is to hear your voice. I suppose you have already tabulated the Sunday offering and attendance."

"Of course," she said, "and had staff meeting with your successor, the Reverend Jeremiah Pennington."

Annie and Jerry had been seminary classmates, he a shining star of systematic theology and she a lesser star of practical theology.

"How did that go?"

"Fine. I think he will catch on quickly to how I do things."

"You are unconcerned, of course, with how he might prefer to do things?"

"He will save a great deal of time if he does things my way."

Annie knew from years of sometimes painful experience that this was true and likely to remain so as long as Marilyn remained at Christ Church.

"Perhaps you will be lenient, as you were with me, and let him think that you are handling one or two matters according to his ideas."

"We shall see," Marilyn said. Poor Jerry, Annie thought. All the systematic theology in the world could not save him now.

"Seriously," Marilyn went on, "that girl who answered the phone needs help. I can be over there by three o'clock and start teaching her the proper procedures."

"Let me think about it."

"Very well. Pastor Pennington is buzzing. I must go." And Marilyn clicked off. She would enhance Jerry's ministry at the Chestnut City church, as she had Annie's own, if he would let her. Indeed, they would see.

Through the doorway Annie saw that Herman Hoobler—Hermie the Handyman—had walked in with his oldest boy, Seth.

Seth went straight to a desk where a vintage typewriter sat, tucked into its platen a piece of paper from the trash basket and began typing as if he had crucial correspondence to produce. He seemed considerably more efficient than the secretary.

"Have a good time with Carl last night?" Hermie asked Trudy. She nodded. Her brown ponytail and gold hoop earrings bobbed.

Annie walked back into the secretary's office and saw Hermie wink at Trudy. "Good morning, Hermie. Thanks for your flexibility about the meeting. I hope you weren't inconvenienced."

"Heck, no," he said. "I always got me something to do. Ain't none of it goes much by the clock."

The staff meeting should have been called a half-staff meeting. The little session took on a trying tempo all its own. Annie had prepared a list of questions for Trudy, who knew the answers to none of them. Hermie pitched in with some useful information, however. Around 11:20, when Shirl Burrows came in, Annie ended the meeting and said they would meet again the next Monday. Trudy gave her an apprehensive glance. "Or whenever we can work it out," Annie added.

"Brought the mail," Shirl said as soon as Trudy and Hermie had beat a dual retreat from Annie's office. Shirl put a grungy mailbag in the middle of her desk. It bulged with perhaps ten pounds of envelopes, cards and catalogs.

"I'll have Trudy go through this," Annie said.

"Best not." Shirl ran a hand through her wavy, graying hair and adjusted her rock-band T-shirt.

"Oh?"

"Not if you want to keep track of things."

"Shirl, do you mean Trudy is not well organized?"

"I wouldn't say it exactly that way, but yeah. She has a heart of gold, though."

Annie didn't know what to say. Shirl evidently took that as her cue and summarized Trudy's situation. She was a high school senior, smart as a whip and lived with her mother, Blanche, her bedridden grandmother, Earladean, and her five-year-old twin brothers, Barry and Garry. Her father, George Bigler, had died of emphysema two years earlier after a long career as a coal miner. The family scraped to get by, and the congregation did its part by employing the bright but disorganized Trudy as church secretary. Trudy worked around her school schedule. Annie wondered what that would mean for the church office come September.

"She speaks Spanish and French," Shirl said.

"But can she file reports in English?" Annie asked, only half facetiously.

"Probably not. And, one more thing, I guess you'll find out anyway."

"What's that?" Annie said.

"Trudy's dating Carl Hoobler. He's 28, and her mom doesn't like it one bit!"

Annie nodded and said, "I see."

Shirl showed no signs of departing. "You gonna open this mail?"

"I have a few other things to do," Annie began, but Shirl had already dipped into the bag and seemed to be pawing for something in particular.

"Do you pick it up every day?" Annie asked.

"Yep. Sure do. They call me Mail Call Shirl. That way I'm sure to get the church bills. Gotta get the bills paid, heh heh heh." She tossed circulars and catalogs into the wastebasket beside Annie's desk.

"Ah, here it is," she said finally, gingerly turning over a purple envelope and snapping it onto the blotter in front of Annie.

"What is it?"

"Looks some different from the usual mail."

Indeed, the envelope did not look like the regular glut of printed products received almost daily at a church—mailings from district and regional headquarters, ads for church supplies, occasional offerings sent by vacationing or otherwise absent members, newsletters from other churches, magazines touting ways to boost attendance and offerings, and the inevitable and usually useless catalogs.

This envelope had no return address and, even more strangely, no postmark. It seemed to have jumped into the mail stream by some nonstandard route. It was addressed to Annie in—of all things—cut-out magazine letters. *REVERND SCOVULL* was the sum total of the address.

"Odd," Annie said.

"I'll say." Shirl waited. Clearly, she wanted Annie to open the envelope in her presence. Just as certainly, Annie wanted to open it in private. The contents could be a personal matter pertaining to a parishioner.

The purple envelope lay like a land mine on the blotter.

This is silly, Annie thought. Picking up scissors, she cut a thin strip off one end of the envelope and withdrew a page of lined notebook paper, the kind school kids use, and saw on it a sentence of sorts, also spelled in letters from a slick magazine: *YOU BEEN WARNED.*

"Let me see that," Shirl demanded. Annie handed it to her.

"Ella Mae Pugh told me about that delivery you got your first day. Now this is going too far. I'm taking this straight over to her house."

"Why?"

"Because she and Gideon between them know everybody in the county, and nobody 'fessed up to that sack of dead cat you got last week, that's why. They got six kids of their own, you know, and whoever isn't their kids or their kids' kids is their kids' friends. A stranger's behind this, and that's got us worried. We're gonna nip this baloney in the butt, that's why."

Annie considered mentioning the message in the Starbucks bag but realized Ma Pugh would do that. Annie didn't even think about sharing news of the bones in the parsonage basement with Shirl. She would be brave and professional and mature, even though she was beginning to feel insecure about life in Biddlebourne.

"This is absolutely unbelievable, just unbelievable," Shirl said, stuffing the envelope and note into her jeans pocket and turning to go. "By the way, I'll be giving you a town tour tomorrow afternoon. I'll pick you up here about two."

No choice in activity or schedule was offered. None was asked, for Marilyn had trained Annie well.

"Will you let me know what happens? With the letter?" Annie asked.

"Everybody will know what happens."

~~0~~

Dear Diary,
I'm not dum and I'm not dirty. I no Im not dum but
mommy calls me little dum-shit. She says shes just joking
but I cant beleve that. She dosnt call Sissie dum-shit
maybe becaws Sissies always at Jonies house. I wish I had
a good friend like Jonie but the kids wont play with me so
much. Say Im playing in the yard and a kid comes into my
yard there mother starts yelling rite away come home
come home so nobody stays in my yard very long. And if I
go in the kids yard same thing the mother yelling you have
to go home now. I wish I had even one kid to play with. I
no its not becaws Im dum becaws Im not dum! And its not
becaws I smell becaws it use to be but now I take a bath
every nite. Daddy use to yell up stares don't use so much
water your using up all the water for the close. But I lock
the bath room door and take my bath. He dosnt yell any
more about the water. I saw on TV where you lite candals
and put them around in the bath room for relacksashun
which is what I do. Mommy wood have a fit if she nu but I
sneek the candals out of the buffay drawer when shes not
looking and hide them in my dresser under my old under
ware that dosnt fit any more.

I love relaksing in the bath tub with the candals lited
around me. What the hell are you doing in there Frankie
will shout outside the bath room I gotta go. Two bad I say
go in the woods. After I started taking my bath at nite it
helped me sleep some times. I still have nitemares and
mommy and daddy still fite and cuss and throw stuff at
nite but some times I can go to sleep. This week I dint pee
in the bed one time. Good for me! I hate skul tho. All the
kids make fun of me and Frankie but not Sissie becaws
Sissie always spends the nite with Jonie and dresses at her
house and looks okay when she gets to skul. Me and
Frankie don't look ok. I herd my techer tell the principull

that Im like an orfin. Our close are always rinkled becaws mommy wont let me use the iron and I sneeked and tried to use it on my own but I burned my self and am afrad to try any more.

Mommy dosnt do the londry at our house daddy does it. I do not no why mommy dosnt do the londry like all the other moms but she just screems at daddy go down there you old fool and wash the close and he dos it. The washing masheen is in the basmint. When my dad washes the close he uses an old q stik to adgitat them while they are washing. He dosnt hang them on the close line like the good nabor ladis do but he just throws them across the line he dosnt use the close pins or any thing. Some times the close blow off the line when its windy outside and get dirt and bugs on them one time a worm was in my jeens.

When the close are dry he throws them on the old day bed down in the basmint. Its realy not a day bed its just an old matress with a ping pong thing on top of it we just call it the day bed becaws I saw that on TV on Giding Lite. Any way me and Frankie have to go the basmint and go fishing for our close to ware every morning. Under ware pajamas shirts its all on the day bed well maybe on the day bed becaws some times theres no close at all on the day bed just a towl or an old sheet. Some times I have to wear the same under ware a hole week. When I grow up Im going to be like Misses W and wash my close in a otomatic masheen and put stuff that smells like pine trees in the masheen and dry them in the masheen with the little sheets of paper that smell good and iron every thing the socks and the under ware and the blouses and the pajamas. Ill ware clean under ware every day when I gro up and have five blouses and five pars of jeens and five pars of shoes.

Death in the Parsonage

"Half the truth is often a whole lie." ~~ Proverb

CHAPTER TWENTY-ONE

The matter of Lurky Larry troubled Isabelle. Yes, it was flattering that a man wanted to go with her to the Flix, but, no, it was foolish for her to think a man wanted her for herself. Lurky Larry's overture had not come close to being a mixed blessing; it was an overture not to be repeated.

Isabelle had felt infinitely perkier after backpack regimen Monday morning. She had enjoyed the rest of the holiday swimming in an isolated pond, eating an entire watermelon from the Smith farm, playing with a collie puppy and reading a book beside the locust stump. She didn't get to watch *The Price Is Right*, however, because the Lemasters were off work on the Fourth of July.

Now she was rested and ready. On this Tuesday she had a goal to accomplish. She checked her written goal sheet to be sure. Yes, there it was in black and white: *Take care of Larry.*

Isabelle had been planning the completion of this goal from the moment she'd written it. She had conceived the scheme, outlined its parts, envisioned its execution and fantasized its results. She need not think again until her goal was accomplished, so it would not matter if the next several hours presented surprises.

Isabelle visited the Pinckney barn and emerged in gray knit skirt, blue knit shirt, black flat shoes and, as always, the sunglasses. She had covered her hair with a jaunty blue-and-yellow scarf and carried her backpack. She'd rather have taken only her purse, but the backpack held materials she might need.

Soon she sat erect in the bank manager's guest chair, smiling and looking directly at him. He was a tall, balding man wearing a three-piece charcoal-gray suit and a starched white shirt. Small framed photos of a neat woman and three neat children faced him from a corner of his desk, which was otherwise free of personal objects. Isabelle would have acted differently if he'd been the sport jacket, loafers and sports cars kind of bank manager. Either way, she knew what to do.

"Um, this is a matter of some delicacy," she said, looking him in the eyes before dropping her gaze. The nameplate on his desk read *Graham Millard.*

"Of course," he said. "I can promise you the utmost discretion."

Excellent. "I . . . I was in the bank Saturday . . . ," she said, making no effort to raise her tone above her natural near-whisper.

"Yes?"

"Um . . . oh, this is upsetting . . . ."

The manager leaned in and nodded solemnly.

"I am afraid," she said, "that one of your employees has behaved inappropriately."

The manager sat up straight and adjusted his tie. His face flushed, and Isabelle recognized the reaction of a typical low-level supervisor.

"I . . . I don't want to get anyone in trouble," she said softly.

"Oh, no, of course not," he said. "May I know what happened?"

"Really . . . it was nothing very serious, but it was disconcerting, and I do hope it won't happen again."

"I'll see that it doesn't. Please go on."

"It's just that an employee with *Larry* on his name tag followed me to a restaurant and made advances that I did not welcome."

The manager examined Isabelle's face, and she shook her head just a bit to rue the misadventures of a maiden in distress. Taking a deep breath, she continued, "I was quite surprised to see him approach me as I dined. I was so taken aback that I agreed to go out with him just to make him desist in his persuasions."

The manager wore an expression of uncertainty. Isabelle went on, "I would hate to have to pull my account from your bank. You have otherwise provided excellent service."

"I see. Uh, Miss Watkins, would you excuse me a moment?"

"Yes, of course. But you won't bring him in, will you? I would wish not to see him . . . again."

"Oh, no. Naturally not. I'll be back in a moment. Please make yourself comfortable."

Isabelle did not relax while the manager was out. He was gone nearly five minutes, by the fake-gold clock on the shelf behind his desk.

When the manager returned with a file folder, he placed it on his tidy desk and opened it. "Now, Miss Watkins, I see that you have been with us for . . . oh, for six years . . . and that you . . . ."

"Yes?" Isabelle said softly.

The manager turned over several sheets of paper. Isabelle knew what he wanted and waited patiently while he searched. "And I see that you hold . . . sixteen certificates of deposit . . . and two money-market accounts

. . . and that you maintain a Freedom Flyer checking account with a balance of . . . ."

"Yes, Mr. Millard?"

"Eighty-nine thousand, four hundred twelve dollars and twenty-five cents."

"Actually, as I mentioned, I made transactions Saturday. That balance is ninety thousand, four hundred twelve dollars and twenty-five cents."

"As you see, Mr. Millard, my investments are designed to provide me a modest monthly income. Of course, other banks could provide that service . . . ."

Only then did Mr. Millard return Isabelle's full gaze. He snapped the folder shut and said, "I see. Miss Watkins, you have my personal assurance that you will not be bothered by Larry again at this institution."

"Thank you, Mr. Millard. I'm so glad we could clear this up."

Because she had not required herself to think while she was in the bank, Isabelle did not realize until she left that in completing one goal she had also erased the necessity of another goal. Now she would not have to get a new bank.

"Misfortune is not what which can be avoided, but that which cannot." ~~ Chinese proverb

CHAPTER TWENTY-TWO

Annie fell into a self-pitying funk late Tuesday morning. She knew better but asked Trudy to get the district superintendent on the phone.

"Is he at that office in Lemleyville?" she asked.

"Yes."

Oh, dear. Trudy seemed unsure of the location of the district office. That was bad. Or was that good? Maybe, Annie thought, she could avoid the annual avalanche of paperwork generated by the district office if the church secretary did not know where the office was. But the district nevertheless knew where the church—and Annie Ido Scovill—were. Oh, well.

"He's on line two," Trudy yelled through the open door. Annie yanked the phone to her ear and greeted her boss.

"Burl, you let the people out here think G.P. and I are divorced, and you sent me to live in a house hot enough to grow bananas. What were you thinking?"

"Good morning, Annie," he said. "I thought you might call."

"You confused the congregation . . . ." Annie wasn't done, but Burl broke in.

"Listen," he said, "I already got an earful from Mrs. Pugh about the divorce thing, and all I can say is that I was misunderstood. I told the committee you would be moving into the house alone, and I thought they had read your profile where it says G.P. is on military duty. I'm sorry about all this."

Now what could she do if Burl insisted on being courteous and apologetic? He was taking the wind right out of her sails of righteous indignation. Annie had once preached a sermon about what to do when bad things are nobody's fault. Now she had a dose of her own theology.

"Okay. I understand," she said. "Mrs. Pugh has pretty much taken care of this over here, too. But you should have let me know the parsonage was in such sad shape before I got here. I could have prepared better."

"I didn't know about it until the day before you moved in. I tried to call you at the Chestnut City parsonage, but I guess you were out partying."

"A farewell picnic."

"Right."

"Why didn't you leave a message?"

"I tried to reach you until nine that evening. Will you please tell me what you could have done to prepare at nine o'clock the night before you moved?"

Annie thought. Hard. For the sake of her rapidly waning indignation she had to think of something she could have done in advance to lessen the pain of moving into 1010 Greenbriar Road.

"I could have borrowed fans from members of the Chestnut City congregation." There. Point made.

"I agree you could have done that. Again, I am truly sorry. If it gives you any comfort, Mrs. Pugh scolded me roundly."

"I admit I should not find comfort in that . . . ." Annie couldn't go on because she found it hard to talk while laughing.

"Annie, how is G.P. getting along?" Burl asked.

"He's okay."

"I hope you're okay, too. Are you?"

"Well, Burl, now that you mention it, I have been stung twice by wasps that apparently survived the work of the exterminators."

"I am truly sorry for that. I do apologize."

"And there is enough mold in the basement to produce penicillin for the populations of India and China."

"I did not realize how bad it was. I regret this very much."

"The toilet needs the application of an industrial-strength plunger each and every day. The house is so misaligned that not one of the inside doors will close all the way. No room has lighting fixtures capable of emitting more than sixty watts."

There was a loaded pause before Burl said, slowly, "Annie these things are unacceptable. Give the word, and we will move you into a home more suitable for the work we are asking you to do."

The cat carcass, the threat letters and the bones made a jerky newsreel in Annie's head. If she so much as mentioned any of them to Burl, he would have her out of the parsonage—and maybe out of Biddlebourne—before another Sunday rolled around.

But that would not do. The cat corpse and notes surely were the mischief of persistent but misguided pranksters, and the bones had been in the basement long before news of the "lady preacher" was announced.

People in Biddlebourne only imagined that Annie could not see their sideways glances and hear what they called her in the stores and in the church parking lot.

Among other things, some of the people resented her driving that "foreign-made junk." They didn't know the car had once belonged to Annie's beloved Aunt Esther. She would tell them about the car when the time was right, but the bones in the basement were a much more present danger to her ministry.

Annie was too experienced to be dislodged by such nonsense. Further, no male pastor would cut and run under the same circumstances, and she hated the thought of boxing up her household again so soon. Besides all that, there was G.P.

"Are you still there?" Burl asked.

"Still here. I'm thinking."

"Oh."

"You asked if I was okay."

"That's what I asked."

"Here is my answer: In spite of everything, I am okay."

"Is that your final answer?"

"That is my final answer today."

"Fair enough. Has the church received you well?"

"Generally, yes, though I had a weird welcome— probably from a jokester." She had to speak of the cat remains for the simple reason that the Pughs and other church folks knew about them, and Burl would think it odd if she didn't also remark on the incident.

"How's that?"

"Oh, just a little bag of stuff left on the porch. Nothing to worry about. But I have something else to ask. What did you mean about the parsonage being haunted?"

Annie could hear Burl sucking air between his front teeth and scratching his chin.

"Mrs. Pugh did say something about finding a culprit. Anyway, I'll tell you what I know about the house, but it's not much. And the word *haunted* is definitely too strong."

Annie waited.

"A woman who identified herself only as Minnie called me the day before you arrived in Biddlebourne and said she wanted to talk about the Greenbriar Road parsonage I don't have any idea how accurate her statements were, although I realize that she was right about the lack of air conditioning in the house."

"What did she talk about besides air conditioning?"

"She had some crazy story that the house has ghosts."

"Go on."

"She said the neighbors had reported unexplained goings-on at the house for years and that after Mrs. Pargeon died her family tried to sell the house but nobody would buy it because of the gossip."

"What?" The trustees told me the house was given to the church in Mrs. Pargeon's will!"

"It was, but the family contested the will and got control of the house. They did try to sell it but got no takers, I presume because of its condition and the so-called ghosts there."

"It is in bad shape. But haunted? That's ridiculous. There are no ghosts in the house—just a family of nesting birds in the attic."

Annie fiddled with her pen on the desk, tapping out an impatient rhythm.

"Of course there are no ghosts," Burl went on. "I gave the suggestion no credence when this Minnie called, and I give it no credence now. I only mentioned it to you because I thought you should realize there was a stigma attached to the house."

"This might explain something I've been wondering about."

"What's that?"

"I've wondered why a family with no connection to the congregation would donate the house, even if it is in deplorable condition. I suppose that when no buyer could be found, the heirs gave the house back to the church and thus gained at least a tax deduction for the charitable contribution."

"You may very well have hit the nail on the head."

Annie continued, "And a church would be the type of owner least likely to fear or even acknowledge talk of ghosts."

"Again, I agree. Also, considering what we now know to be the extraordinarily poor condition of the house, the family likely had to get rid of it any way they could. None of them wanted to live in a rundown house, and a renovation would have been costly and might not have led to a sale anyway because of the ghost nonsense. I'm sure the Glory Hallelujah trustees have come to a similar conclusion."

"Yes, yes . . . so, then, I am living in a very old, inadequately maintained, non-air-conditioned, unpopular and possibly haunted house. Would that sum it up?"

"According to Minnie."

"All right. I stand advised."

"Let me repeat," he said. "If the house is truly unmanageable, I will encourage the congregation to find more suitable housing for you."

Annie pondered briefly. She truly did not want to organize 12,000-plus pounds of possessions now, and the congregation had promised to improve the house. But the deciding factor was G.P. He would be anxious if she had to move their household twice in one month—or even in one year—without his help. And he would be crazed if he found out their home housed a dead body.

"I'll stay put for now," she said.

"Let me know if you change your mind."

"You can be certain that I will. And, Burl . . ."

"Yes?"

"I am enjoying the assignment at Glory Hallelujah.

There are challenges, but the congregation is eager to build. It's an exciting place to be."

"We have confidence in you."

Would that everyone in Biddlebourne felt that way.

"Thanks. See you at the district cookout. August twenty-seventh, right?"

"Right."

"My best to Shelby."

"My regards to G.P."

Annie hung up wondering whether G.P., upon receiving Burl's warm regards, would hasten to inquire what topic had prompted her conversation with the superintendent in the first place.

~~0~~

Dear Diary,

Nabors. We have some good nabors and some bad nabors. The bad ones make it worse and the good ones make it better. Once the nabors across the street invited my brother Frankie to go to the Dary Queen with them not me and Sissie just Frankie but thats ok becaws they do not have any dotters just sons. They keep there house real nice and there car real nice. They have lots of flowers in the yard and on the porch. I think you have to be a little rich to have a nice house and a nice car and flowers on the porch. Anyway they went to the Dary Queen and got there ice creem. Well the nabors sons got theres but they dint get any ice creem for Frankie. How mean is that. Sissie says our family has a stickma. A stickma is a bad thing that sticks to you so people don't like you or want to be around you. The nabors said they were afraid Frankie wood drip ice creem in there fancy car and he shood just be glad he got to ride in there car.

Me and Sissie are the only ones nice to Frankie all the time. Well mommys nice to Frankie when daddys not around but she dosnt have to do with Frankie when daddys around becaws it makes daddy sooooo mad! May be Frankie has a girl frend I think becaws I no he sneeks out at nite. I woodnt tell on him for any thing and nether wood Sissie but I don't know if she nos about him sneeking out.

Some of the good nabors are Misses G and Misses W and Misses L. They ask me over and give me good things to eat and let me wach any thing I want on TV even cartoons. If daddy nu I was going to the good nabors to eat and wach TV he wood get very mad and probly give me a liking with his belt.

I never had a boy frend. Sissie says Im too yung but if I had a boy frend I cood go to his house two and eat what I want and wach TV. And o yes Misses G washes my close when I visit her she says she likes to wash close so I ware her big shaneel robe while she washes my close and I eat potata chips and wach TV in the living room. She dosnt care if any chips get down in the couch. What a good nabor.

But we have other nabors two who want to save me. They are Misses and Mister P. I dont like the dad as much as I like Mister G but hey hes better than my dad. Misses and Mister P have a lot of children. Misses P is bisy all the time with the children but she always has time for me two. Iv been eating breakfast lunch and dinner over there a lot. Before this mommy would get mad and yell at nabors who tried to save me but now she aks like nothing unusal is hapning. Misses P NEVER says a bad word about my family. She let sme sleep at there house two no matter what day it is even Saturday nite before Sunday skul. She makes snikerdodles just for me but I always share with there kids.

The only thing Msses P dosnt like is when I run away to one of my speshul hiding places. Some times I cant be around people becaws things are bothering me and I want to cry or shout or write in my diary. I borrow stuff from home but never from Misses Ps house and go to my speshul hiding place in the woods and make stu. Im a pretty good cook now even daddy says so but he still throws food off the table some times nothing will ever stop him from throwing food off the table I think. My stu that I make in my speshul hiding place in the woods is more like soop. Its better than mommys cooking but worse than Misses Ps cooking also worse than Misses Gs cooking.

Misses P wont let her kids go any where with me tho. I dont know why but I dont care becaws she likes me so much even if Mister P calls my house hell house. He knows a lot of people in town and I guess he knows a lot of things arent right in our house. Not just my parents but the demins and wiches and gosts. Misses P said last night she was sure she sees stranj things in the windows of our house every once in a wile. But im not scared in my house of what I cant see. Im scared of the peeple I can see.

Death in the Parsonage

"One cannot put back the clock." ~~ Proverb

CHAPTER TWENTY-THREE

Isabelle celebrated her double victory at the bank by lunching at the Mug, an eatery with fare so fine the oak benches had been rubbed concave by the solid behinds of loyal patrons. Isabelle melted into the midday crowd. Although she had to sit at the counter with her back to the door, she didn't mind because it also put her back to the other customers.

"Smothered steak, mashed potatoes, green beans 'n ham, salad, chocolate cake and a Coke," Isabelle murmured to the waitress with *Jean* stitched on her uniform.

"Good choice, Sweetie," Jean said. She walked to the ancient eight-burner stove and began dishing up Isabelle's lunch. "How's your brother?" Jean asked as she spooned thick, red-eye gravy over the potatoes.

Isabelle was sure she'd misunderstood. She'd been daydreaming about Lurky Larry's dismissal from the bank. "Pardon?" she said.

"I was just wondering about your brother. Haven't seen either of you in, Lordie, must be going on ten years," Jean said.

The panic became a monster. It tore at Isabelle's chest and gripped her throat. She gulped air and tried to think.

But she couldn't think. This wasn't a thinking place or a thinking time. And she couldn't just tear out of the restaurant and run down the road. Oh, God!

Jean put the food in front of Isabelle and smiled. "Aren't you the Henley girl from Markburg?" she asked.

"Oh. Oh, no. I'm not," Isabelle said, and a hideous giggle gushed from her. "You must have me confused with someone else."

"I could have sworn . . . ," Jean said. "But now that I see you up close again, I guess you aren't who I thought you were. But you sure do look like Flora Henley. Must be the sunglasses. Ha! That's one on me."

Isabelle needed to calm down. She needed to cut off conversation with the waitress. She needed to create a thinking mode. So, as casually as she could, she reached into her backpack and took out a Jane Austen. *I'll be okay. I'll be okay. I'll be okay.*

Isabelle knew that books were one of the most effective conversation killers—almost as effective as pretended stuttering or pretended craziness or pretended drunkenness. She gave the waitress her biggest smile and turned to *Pride and Prejudice*.

So when the waitress, who had returned to refill her Coke, said, "I've got it now. You're Allison Billett," Isabelle pretended to be engrossed in her book.

Sneaking back into the woods late that afternoon, Isabelle knew time had come to go to ground. She had barely survived the bank incident, the Snacknmore incident and the Mug incident. Things were coming to a head. She had to think—for a long time. She had to go to her most special place and pull herself through the thinking knot. There could be no distractions, no close calls, no chance of recognition.

"We are the church. The church meets. Therefore, we meet." ~~ Pastor Annie Ido Scovill

CHAPTER TWENTY-FOUR

Exactly one week after moving to Biddlebourne, on the evening of her first, flustered day at the church office, Annie met with the full board of trustees of Glory Hallelujah Church.

Her anxiety level was in the red zone for two reasons, only one of which was the fact that the air conditioning of the parsonage depended on the vote of the board. Much more pressing was the body in the basement.

They met in the biggest church room, which was the youth room, in the coolest part of the building, which was the lower level. Still, the air hung heavy with heat and charcoal smoke from neighborhood grills. The concrete walls, painted lime green by enterprising youth, sweated like the trustees and the pastor.

Mr. Gideon Pugh presided. A platter of Ma's snickerdoodles rested in the middle of the hand-hewn oak conference table, and a cooler jammed full of drinks sat at Annie's feet because she was, after all, the pastor.

Annie was pleasantly surprised by the lack of nonsense at the beginning of the meeting. Mr. Gideon Pugh was a down-to-business kind of man.

"Pastor Ma'am," he said after the opening prayer, "I'm much pleased to report that the trustees of Glory Hallelujah Church has raised $176,000.02 since the year of 1990, that the young people of the church has pitched in $814.39 from car washes and the rooster rodeo and a bunch of other jobs they done, and the Ladies Aid has pledged an even $25,000 from their bake sales and cookbooks and such. We got a whole lot of folks comin' out here to Biddlebourne to give their kids a good country upbringin'. We figure the good Lord is tellin' us to add on here at the church, and we're tellin' you we got $201,814.41 to do it with. Now what do you think of that?"

Annie was thinking that Burl Stout had been right about one thing—and just one thing—when he called on her to come to Biddlebourne: A rare opportunity for the church truly was at hand.

"Your vision and work are outstanding, Mr. Pugh. I'm excited about what you've done here. I say let's keep going until the job is done! With God's help we can do it!"

All around the table—at all nine places—there were nods of agreement and expressions of determination. Not one trustee looked away or crossed the arms or appeared otherwise to be sulking. Annie was heartened by this stunning display of church unity. In that instant, as she looked around the table and felt a tingle running up her backbone, she knew they were experiencing one of those rare times when God breaks in on what humans have wrought and works something of God's own.

"Friends," she said, "your vision is extraordinary. May I offer a prayer of thanks?"

"That would hit the spot," Mr. Gideon Pugh said.

A minute later Annie posed a question. "Just out of curiosity," she said, "how much of the trustees' funds came from the sale of the former parsonage?"

"Bern," the chairman said, looking to the bearded man who had the big, blue ledger on the table in front of him.

"Bern Schilling, Pastor. I'm the board treasurer," he said, opening the book. "That amount was, let's see here, exactly $81,431. That's after paying our share of the closing costs and the real estate man's commission."

There was a noticeable shift of bodies and feet around the table. Mr. Gideon Pugh said, "Now, folks, we went all through that. Jake Fetterson earned that commission fair and square. He worked like a field mule getting the papers lined up. Don't let's begrudge the man his bread 'n' butter."

The woman sitting on Gideon Pugh's left—Annie thought her name was Thelma—frowned and sat up as if she were going to speak. But in the tense silence of the moment she instead took a deep breath and clamped her jaws shut.

Gideon Pugh was a church leader in more ways than one, Annie realized, when with a deftness that she was coming to expect in him he said, "You know what, Pastor Ma'am? We forgot to introduce ourselves to you, though I 'spect most of us were in service Sunday. Folks, let's go around the table and say our names and a little about ourselves. Thelma, start us out."

The woman's brow eased a bit. She turned to Annie and said, "I'm Thelma Blivins. I've been around here going on forty years. I was here when we put on the chapel and when we built the picnic grove. And now I guess I'm gonna build again. I run Blivins Stone Works over by Gooseneck. My husband ran the company till he died, and now I run it."

Annie had met Thelma early Sunday morning when the Ladies Aid Society descended upon her in the church office before worship. They were glad Glory Hallelujah had finally got itself a woman pastor, and it had been about time for a change, and would she care to come to the next Ladies' Night Out? Annie said she would, and they had left pleased.

"Hello again, Thelma," Annie said. Thelma winked at Annie, a behavior the pastor saw so seldom that she first thought it to be a tic.

On they went around the table, stopping at all nine places. Annie jotted names and notes in her day book, and the trustees squirmed as they gave their impromptu speeches. Annie was interested most in Minnie Glendenning. "Herbalist, bowler, painter, chemist, done everything," Minnie rattled off.

Annie circled Minnie's name and next to it wrote, "Garden gal—called Burl about house?"

When Vinny Clark introduced himself, Annie said, "It's good to see you again, Vinny."

"Likewise, Annie. You got that crown molding up yet?" A titter here and a smirk there told Annie that Vinny had already shared the lowlights of her Saturday shopping trip.

"I am as surprised to see you here as you were surprised by my carpentry plans," she said. "I did not realize you were a church trustee."

"I'm pleased to serve, ma'am."

They came back around to Mr. Gideon Pugh.

"Well, Pastor Ma'am, you and me's already met. But I got to speak my piece since I made the others do it. Me and Ma been runnin' cattle thirty-four years on the farm, plus we got a little craft business that Ma does to keep herself out of mischief. We got six kids, all gone from home as far as me and Ma are concerned but who keep comin' back from time to time. I reckon you'll meet up with the whole clan sooner or later.

"Now, then, that's done," he went on. In the scramble to provide coherent self-introductions, everyone including Thelma had forgotten the real estate commission.

The chairman pulled them back to business. "Pastor Ma'am, we got a building plan of sorts lined up. It's not final or anything. We'd appreciate you lookin' it over and tellin' us what you think by next Monday night."

"Of course," Annie said. "But I do have another question."

"Yes, ma'am?"

She cleared her throat. This was a delicate matter. "What is a rooster rodeo?"

Several trustees looked sideways at each other. To their credit, they did not actually snicker. Thelma Blivins spoke up. "It's a carnival, only country style. The kids—most of the kids are in 4-H, you know—come and show their pets and their project livestock. That way they get in some practice for the county fair, and they sell concessions, and the dads put on a tractor pull, and the moms put on a bake sale. You know . . ."

"That's a new one on me," Annie said. "When's the next rooster rodeo?" I'd like to make some of my peach pies for the bake sale."

Turning on the oven would transform the parsonage into a three-story slow cooker. No matter. It was a good cause, and making peach pies was one of Annie's favorite culinary projects.

Thelma said, "That would be appreciated. The next one is July thirtieth." Annie hurried to put the date on her calendar.

"That's right," Calvin McAleer said. "Jen's getting Harvey all primped up for it."

"Harvey?" Annie said.

"Her American fuzzy lop. A real show-stopper."

"Calvin, I'm thinking real hard about what a fuzzy lop might be, but I just can't come up with anything."

Calvin laughed. "Oh. Right. A lop's a rabbit breed with long ears. Jen's won three county ribbons already. Her mother and I think she'll place at the state fair this year."

"You must be very proud of her. Is it all right if I stop by to visit Jen and Harvey this week?"

"We'd be honored."

There was a smile or two now around the table that hadn't been there before. Annie had passed another test.

"All right, then, let's talk on that parsonage," Gideon Pugh put in. "Folks, we got our hands full over there. The pastor and I have made up a list of what needs doin'. I got these copies here for you to look at."

He passed papers around the table, and eight heads bent to read. It took a while because there were thirty-three items on the list.

"I had no idea it was this bad," Bailey Haines said.

"Me neither," said Minnie the Garden Gal Glendenning. "I knew we shouldn't have sold the other parsonage just because someone gave their old rattletrap house to the church."

"Now, Minnie," Gideon Pugh said. "In case you don't remember, we had a lot of work over the years on the other parsonage, too. We owed it to Marcy to offer her the house. Besides, this one we got now has a much stronger foundation. Why, it's got foundation stones four feet thick!"

"Doesn't mean much if the rest of it's falling down," Minnie said.

Bailey Haines spoke. "My concern is that with the church expansion going on, we'll be stretched mighty thin doing all this work at the same time over at the parsonage."

"I been thinkin' 'bout that," Gideon Pugh said. "I'm thinkin' that maybe we ought to get contractors to do the big jobs at the parsonage so's we ourselves can concentrate on the church. What do you say?"

"Are you talking about hiring strangers?" Minnie Glendenning asked. "I'm not in favor of that."

"Not exactly," Gideon Pugh said. "We'd need a heating man and a structure man and maybe a plumber, but Dwayne Cushing's a general contractor and can give us some good names to start with."

"Who's Dwayne Cushing?" Minnie asked.

"You mean to tell me you ain't met Dwayne Cushing yet, Minnie?" Gideon Pugh said. "Him and his family joined the church, oh, must be two years ago."

"No, Gideon, I have not met Dwayne Cushing."

For the first time that evening Gideon Pugh appeared flustered. He looked around the table at the other trustees, from whence came no help.

"What if we ask Dwayne Cushing to come to the meeting next Monday night and tell us a little about his business?" Annie suggested, treading where no angel would have.

"That sounds all right, I suppose. But that doesn't obligate us to hire him or any of his people," Minnie said.

Annie looked at Gideon Pugh. "Course not," he said. "But you know what, Minnie? You just gave me a good idea."

He turned to face the table at large and said, "Everybody, do me this. Write down on that piece of paper I gave you the names of any good plumbers, or electricians, or house fixers, or furnace people you done business with over the last four or five years or so. Everybody got a pencil?"

Gideon Pugh is a genius, she thought. Annie watched as the trustees jotted the names of their favorite residential tradespeople. Gideon Pugh then read the names aloud and helped the trustees pick the top two in each category.

Even Minnie seemed okay with Gideon Pugh's plan, especially when her favorite plumber somehow wound up at the top of his group. Annie noticed that Dwayne Cushing also made the final list.

"Mind you, now, Gideon," Minnie said at last. "We're not cutting into the church expansion money to pay for the parsonage repairs."

Bern Schilling cleared his throat. Everybody looked his way. Clearly, he was offended.

"Minnie, that would amount to the mixing of funds as well as misappropriation of designated funds," Bern said. "It will not be entertained, let alone tolerated. You know perfectly well that we have $18,347.57—not one penny more and not one penny less—in the parsonage maintenance fund, for you see that balance on the fiscal report I have distributed this evening. Not a cent of the parsonage maintenance fund shall be spent elsewhere, and not a cent of the church building fund shall be spent elsewhere."

Minnie did not look even mildly chastened.

"Well, then," Gideon Pugh said, "why don't I call up these furnace men—let's see, Frankie Conaway and Howard Leasure—and get estimates on installin' a new furnace and air conditioner so's we can get the pastor some cool air? I figure that's the best place to start."

"How much?" Minnie asked.

"We won't know till Frankie and Howard do some figurin', but I supposed we're talkin' several thousand," Gideon Pugh said.

"What's wrong? All the windows painted shut over there?" Minnie asked.

"Well, matter of fact, Minnie, most of the windows seem to be trackin' okay. But the pastor here, she's more of a city gal, and I seen for myself how she's about to burn up in the parsonage. She ain't used to this heat." As Gideon Pugh spoke, rain began splatting on the sheet-metal protectors over the windows.

The trustees thought again. Annie prayed silently, fervently.

"Every single one of us has air conditioning at home, including you, Minnie," said Thelma Blivins.

"All in favor of starting with a furnace and air conditionin' at the parsonage, say yes," Gideon Pugh proclaimed. The chorus of yeses was the best music Annie had ever heard. She had no intention of souring the song with questions about a body in her basement.

~~0~~

Dear Diary,

Daddy is not alowed to go any where in the house eksep the first floor and the basmint. Hes not allowed in the living room eather. When he waches TV he has to stand in the door way of the living room. Some times he sits in his chair in the door way but he never sits in the living room. Its very werd I no this for sure becaws at Misses Gs house Mister G sits in the living room. I cant remember why daddy isn't allowed to wach TV in the living room. Some thing about his behavyer Sissie says. I ask her all the time about it but she always just says its his behavyer. Mommys the one who wont let daddy be in the living room but I no better than to ask her how come. Shed just call me dum-shit.

I don't see what daddy does all day long. Mommy says hes worth less and never goes to work but I no he goes to work some times sweeping the floor at Belwix store. He told me he likes that job becaws no body bothers him there but I think he likes it becaws he can sneek his buze into the store at nite and take a drink when he wants to. I dont want to be like daddy eather becaws he dosnt have any frends not even mommy is his frend. I want to be his frend but he looks at me werd like Im a kid from another planet. When he does that and I feel like crying I just go in and take my bath with the speshul candals or go hide in one of my speshul places. I have lots of fun stuff in my hiding places so I can be there all day and all nite and hardly even no what time it is—flashlites and maches and blankits and Cambell soup and pop and candy for sure my diary, every thing I need.

"To me the meanest flower that blows can give/Thoughts that do often lie too deep for tears."
~~ William Wordsworth

CHAPTER TWENTY-FIVE

Isabelle waited until the sun went down and the lights went out in the house. The occupant, she knew, kept unpredictable hours. Sometimes it was lights out around nine, other times not until nearly midnight. That was one more thing to dislike about the Scovill woman.

Neither did Isabelle enjoy the thistles in the woods where she had to kneel so she could remain unseen while she calculated the sun's position. She was glad when sunset arrived and gladder when the lamp in the living room went out. She shifted her luggage and her legs and got ready to sprint.

But she had to wait much longer. The bedroom light was on when a star or two began shining in the northern sky. And the light was still on when Isabelle startled out of an awkward sleep a good while afterward. She yawned and stood to stretch. Neighbors could not see her in the blackness now. And she watched with relief as the window in what used to be her bedroom went dark.

Isabelle groaned with fatigue. Recent incidents had sapped her energy, and the weather had caused her two bad nights in the cave. Besides her physical weariness,

Isabelle was experiencing the kind of emotional pain that could lead to mistakes—awful mistakes that would dictate another move. She had promised herself there would be no more moves. She could not take another move. She could not run again.

And so, if Isabelle could not obtain an unrestricted period of thinking time, all would be lost. Everything—everything important to Isabelle—depended on gaining access to her most special thinking place. She had prepared the best she could, selecting the right key from the skeleton kit and placing it—along with a clean hand towel—in the littlest pouch of her backpack. She'd eaten that big lunch at the Mug but had not eaten dinner. That was fine. She would eat as soon as she got to her special thinking place.

Fast, fifty, floor, flap. Fast, fifty, floor, flap. She made herself as small as she could with the luggage in hand, looked in every direction, waited while a truck passed in front of the house, and speed-walked fifty paces to the back door.

She checked all around her again because it was possible to detect shapes and movements even in the darkness. All was clear. With the key in her right hand, she covered her left hand with the towel and twisted the doorknob. The door opened. *So the Scovill woman does not lock her doors.* Isabelle returned the key to her backpack.

Isabelle entered the kitchen. Only a ticking clock cut the silence. She stood like a statue for a count of 200. Then she inched toward the pantry one slow, soundless step at a time, hugging her luggage close to avoid contact with a table, chair or box.

When she reached the pantry door, Isabelle froze and counted again to 200. Her breathing was almost under control when she heard noises on the stairs and sensed a dark flash near her feet. She involuntarily dropped everything—the suitcase, the kit bundle and the towel. They fell in slow motion. Every thunk on the linoleum sounded like a thunderclap to Isabelle.

She sank to the floor and forced herself to inhale through her nose and exhale through her mouth. Her heart thrummed and her limbs quaked. She closed her eyes and clenched her teeth to await the inevitable discovery.

An eternity passed. She estimated she could get out of the house in thirty seconds. She began concocting a story to tell the Scovill woman. She steadied her breathing. At last she slowly opened her eyes, straining to see what had run past her. When she felt a furry swipe against her ankle, she realized it was the Scovill woman's silly cat.

Then she heard what she'd hoped not to hear. "Fannie Fay, what are you doing down there?" came the voice from upstairs, followed by footsteps. The form leapt from the floor beside Isabelle and flew again, this time moving toward the dining room. Isabelle held her breath to keep from screaming.

"There you are. What did you do downstairs? I heard a big thump." Isabelle trembled. Her legs hurt from her crouch, and her lungs hurt from not breathing. She counted to ten before she rose and expelled breath at the same time. A bedroom door closed upstairs.

The alarm was over—for now. Isabelle quickly took a carton from one of the stacks and placed it on the floor so the Scovill woman would think the cat had knocked it over. Then she used her towel to open the pantry door. She stepped inside, bent to lift the rectangle of vinyl that lay on the floor and pulled open the wooden door underneath it. In twenty seconds she was safe and secure in her most special hiding place of all.

Death in the Parsonage

"Love is sweet, but tastes best with bread." ~~ Yiddish proverb

CHAPTER TWENTY-SIX

Wednesday, July 6

E-mail to G.P. – 1 a.m.

Dearest Husband,

I can't sleep because I've not yet gotten used to the sounds the house makes, but Fannie Fay is sawing cat logs beside me with one paw on the mouse pad as I type.

I can smell the honeysuckle and hear the summer night through the open windows—cars going by, MTV turned up high next door at the Wilsons (teenagers), someone putting out the trash. Hermie the Handyman carried our trash to the curb yesterday. He says he always does that for the pastor, but I wonder if it's a "habit" he started this week.

It rained again tonight. I was reminded of our trip to Blackwater Falls in the summer of '86 and how we made love in our room at the lodge with the windows open after it rained. It was the Fourth of July, wasn't it? I remember because you said something about fireworks indoors and outdoors.

Chloe left Sunday. She said I wanted to make every room look like a library. I said she wanted every room to look like a scene from "South Pacific." I hope you'll like our compromises.

Wrens are hatching a brood in the attic. They chirp all day and flap all night. Chloe stuffed underwear around the attic door and said it was her or them. She said they walked around on the floor of the attic at night and kept her awake. Only Chloe could hear bird footsteps.

Shall we get two twin beds for our bedroom since the queen bedsprings wouldn't fit up the stairs? Or maybe a king mattress with two twin springs? It will be a tight fit either way. Our bedroom is 12 feet by 12 feet.

The granddaughters send their love as well as the artwork attached. That's you on the left and Analeise and Brooke on the right with hearts flying out of their heads in your direction. I told Analeise that you wear desert fatigues. She calls them "feebs." Please note that she put seven stars on your collar. You are now the highest-ranking officer in the Air Force Reserve. Congratulations, my love. Since you have received a raise in pay, send me $500 or so for the new beds (ha ha—just kidding—the bank account is holding up fine).

We're moving at full gallop on the parsonage renovation. The church ladies have scrubbed everything from top to bottom—floors, walls, cupboards, fixtures. Hermie the Handyman cleaned the carpets.

The second-floor rooms are painted (thanks to Chloe), and she wallpapered the dining room. About that crown molding—I came away as good as empty-handed when I tried to get an instruction manual at a place called Vinny's All-American Store. I'll have to look for a manual at the home center in Spartansville when I can get there.

I'm already super busy at church. The building project is moving along. We're interviewing architects and bearing down on the building fund. Lots of opinions are floating around on building style, but the congregation wants very much to build.

Shirl Burrows, she's the church treasurer and they call her Mail Call Shirl, brings mail and news every day. She told me that Vinny Clark, who runs Vinny's All-American, used to have a huge retail territory selling vacuum cleaners to hotels and schools until he had a freak accident. The warehouse man was on break, and Vinny grabbed the keys to a forklift so he could get a delivery van loaded. Well, he didn't shut the motor off when he left the forklift, and it went out of control and pinned him against a wall. Both his legs were broken, and one of them never healed. He still walks with a limp. Shirl says he never got over it.

Well, after the trustees meeting last night, Vinny asked again if I want him to put up crown molding in the house. I'm tempted to accept his offer, but just for the living room. Chloe put a beautiful paper border in the dining room, and I wouldn't want to change it. But if Vinny does any carpentry for us, shouldn't we pay him? What do you think?

The new washer and dryer are here (in the basement), but the plumbing isn't hooked up yet. The bug man sprayed again—all but the attic. I asked him not to disturb the wrens. The man said the insecticide wouldn't hurt Fannie Fay. Fannie Fay loves the windowsills and open air, so she'll have to adapt when the air conditioning comes.

Friday a flooring contractor is coming to see about leveling the floors.

Speaking of Friday, that's my day off. I plan to do the wash (if the machine is hooked up). I already cleaned up the coal from the floor. There were about 20 pounds of it that I'll take to Mrs. Gatwick, one of the widows of the church. She says she's heated her house with coal all her life and doesn't intend to change now.

Hermie the Handyman also mowed the grass. I tried to give him $20, but he wouldn't take it. We'll give him a nice Christmas check. I'm running your truck every other day like you said. It's started okay each time. You have a bunch of mail, but most of it looks like junk. Do you want me to open the stuff from the Pasadena High School alums? Several of your computer magazines are expiring. Shall I renew them? Your Mom and Dad watch CNN for hours every day hoping to get a glimpse of you. I was supposed to have dinner with them Sunday, but something came up and we had to reschedule.

I'm praying for you every day and thinking of you every night. Don't worry about anything. All is well with me except that I miss you. I'll e-mail soon. I send my love.

Annie Ido

~~0~~

Dear Diary,
I don't under stand why we have to go to Church. I mean
every Sunday its Sunday skul and Church. Mommy and
Daddy never go but they make me and Frankie and Sissie
go only Frankie sneeks out thru the back door of the
Church basmint. Me and Sissie never tell on him tho
because he gets the worst part of every thing and needs to
get away when he can. Daddy wont go to Church but he
reads his Bible all the time I mean all the time. He can
even say Bible sentences without looking. When hes mad
about some thing and not drunk yet he says Bible
sentences to win the argyoument. Mommy calls him a
hippocrit when he says Bible sentences. Well I said
Mommy and Daddy never go but Mommy use to go only

*she wood be drunk. Gees and those women call them
selves Christuns. They wood say look at that drunk woman
and her kids SITTING UP IN FRONT like we dint have
the rite to sit in the front of the Church.*

*That's why me and Frankie and Sissie have manners
because of Church. Boy some of those Church Ladies
realy give you the evul eye if you don't say mam and sir
and thank you and please. Daddy says manners are very
important. That is funny because Mommy says his
manners are atroshus.*

*I shoodnt lie not all the Church Ladies are stuck on
manners and stuff like that. Some of them are very nice
and give you books and candy and hug you and fix your
hair and ask if you want to have lunch at there house. I
always say yes to lunch because theres no lunch at our
house on Saturday or Sunday just because me and Frankie
and Sissie are home from skul. Mommy says fix your own
lunch you lazy bums. Sissie leeves the house to go to her
girl frends and Frankie sneeks out his bedroom window
on Saturday without even coming down stairs first. I don't
have any frends house to go to and Im afraid to jump out
my bedroom window its on the second floor so on
Saturday I go down and fix sereal for my lunch and on
Sunday I say yes when one of the nice ladies asks if I want
lunch. Some times we go to a restront and some times we
go to the ladies house. I like the lunch at the restront best
you can have a cheeseberger and french fries and a milk
shake and cake all you have to do is order it. The hard
part is you have to mind your ps and qs at the restront. Sit
up strait and cant let your elbows be on the table and have
to say thank you EVERY time the watress gives you some
thing and have to talk to the lady and her husband and the
other kids two. Sissie gives me the evul eye if I don't do it*

rite. Too bad Frankie misses the nice lunches at the restront. It makes me tired to be good all the time but the lunch is deleshus. It wood be wonderful if the Church Ladies gave me lunch on Saturday two.

"Far from home, near thy harm." ~~ Proverb

CHAPTER TWENTY-SEVEN

Isabelle dared not hum, but she smiled as she gently set down the suitcase, the kit set and her backpack in her most special hiding place. She scooted two feet to her right, placed her right hand on the wall and felt her way until she touched a smooth cord. She followed it to the prongs at its end, lifted her arm just above her head and plugged in the work light that had once belonged to her father.

The light was weak but soothing to Isabelle. Tears of gratitude filled her eyes as she examined the place that had saved her life and her soul. It was three feet high, five feet wide and fifteen feet long. The walls were plywood, the same kind of plywood her daddy had used to build closets in the attic. Though warped and unpainted, these walls were beautiful to Isabelle, for they had been the only ears that always listened in her darkest years.

The bottom of the special hiding place was also plywood, but it was strong and sturdy enough to hold Isabelle and everything she had brought here over the years. Nothing had changed since her last visit. The fan, the blankets, the stuffed animals, the canned and packaged food, the bottled water, the hotplate, the magazines, the books, the radio, even the emergency toilet jug were all there, lined up neat and clean and calm for her personal, undisturbed use and enjoyment.

She spread two blankets for a bed because she had dropped off her sleeping bag at the Pinckney barn that afternoon. She debated turning on the fan, but the night outside was cool and the house would lose heat fast. Isabelle reflected smugly that she knew this for a fact, so she decided to save the fan for really hot days and nights and also not to turn on the hotplate unless it was absolutely necessary.

She unpacked, which is what she called removing the items from the suitcase and kits and piling them neatly along the west plywood wall. She didn't need to change clothes, she confirmed to herself, because she'd had the foresight to wear thin cotton slacks and a light top for this homecoming. She enjoyed a bag of delicious potato chips and a can of cling peaches. Things were going quite well now that she was in her special place, as she had expected and known they would.

She gathered Snookums into her arms, lay on the blankets and—with only a sigh between her and the Permitted Pleasure of a full night's sleep—closed her eyes.

"He that has no shame, has no conscience." ~~ Proverb

CHAPTER TWENTY-EIGHT

As invited—or as directed—Annie met Shirl in the church lot Wednesday afternoon.

"Get in," Shirl said. Annie did. The heat index in Biddlebourne was 108 degrees. In her polyester skirt and blouse, Annie felt like a hot casserole bundled in plastic wrap. Annie's outstanding shoe collection was going largely to waste in Biddlebourne. But that was only because she had not yet racked and color-coded the fifty-seven pairs of shoes she owned.

No matter, she thought. The Hush Puppies were holding up just fine. In point of fact, her tour guide, Ms. Shirl Burrows, a.k.a. Mail Call Shirl, was her commanding self shod in Hush Puppies, the pair of which Annie fixed her gaze upon as soon as she entered the 1977 Cadillac Fleetwood.

"Nice shoes," Annie said, pointing to the pond-green suedes.

"Nice shoes," Shirl said, pointing to Annie's purple suedes.

At that moment, each knew they would be friends.

It was a whirlwind cruise that Shirl had in mind. With the Caddie's air turned to the max in concession to the heat of the day and the windows powered all the way down in concession to her nonsmoking passenger, Shirl chain-puffed Camels and horn-honked cars and cows for three hours. She was the imperious captain of her four-wheeled ship, and Annie was its wide-eye crew.

Thus they sailed the streets of Biddlebourne and shore-hopped at exotic and eccentric ports of call. They visited Darrell Kelley's Read All About It, a newsstand of prodigious media where Darrell himself produced a copy of the Wheeling *Intelligencer* upon request, and the Bow-Kay, where owner Kay Schumann gave Annie a spray of vase roses in welcome but only because, Shirl said, Kay wanted to keep doing altar business with the church. Another stop was Greens on Green Street, whose owners, Bub and Gwen Greenaway, gave Annie a coupon for a free sprig of mistletoe come Christmas season.

"What about the police station and the social service agencies and places like that?" Annie asked Shirl after they left Greens on Green Street.

"Oh, you won't have any trouble finding them on your own. I'm taking you to the interesting places," Shirl said with a wave of the hand and a flick of the cigarette. Ash fell to the floor, adding to the pyre already formed there from cigarette packaging, greasy food containers and junk mail addressed to the church.

"What's your definition of *interesting?*"

"Let me see," Shirl said. "Interesting. That would be where my friends and relatives work, plus the stores where I like to shop and the restaurants where I like to eat."

Annie laughed. Shirl kept on driving and smoking and honking.

Shirl saved her most interesting stop for last in their marathon of visits. Around five o'clock they were on the outskirts of Biddlebourne. The Fleetwood, the springs of which were well past prime, bobbed into a berth next to small outbuilding.

No. On second look, Annie realized it was a mailbox as big as a refrigerator. It was covered in grapevines except for the door, about one foot square at waist level, which bore hand printing:

This is a Mailbox.
Not a Trashcan.
No Junk Mail!
I Mean It.
Minnie

"Well stated," Annie said, pointing to the mail receptacle.

"Yeah," Shirl said, flicking more cigarette residue onto the floorboard.

"Are you going to build a fire right here in the car for your own junk mail?" Annie asked.

"Maybe. Let's go in and give Minnie some hell."

"What?!"

"Just kidding, heh heh heh. Come on. I'm thirsty."

Shirl got out and slammed the door behind her, hauling her big yellow purse over her left shoulder and tucking her cigarettes into her right rear jeans pocket.

"You're not locking the car?"

"Nah. Let 'em steal it. I could use the insurance money."

Annie hastily followed Shirl, who walked confidently into the well-tended yard and stomped up to the front door. She pounded only once on the door, which was opened immediately by Minnie the Garden Gal Glendenning. She was a wiry woman with wizened face and wrinkled skin.

"Shirl Baby!"

"Minnie Girl!"

The two hugged as if they had not seen each other in years, though they had both been in worship Sunday morning, Shirl the treasurer in the back section of the left pews and Minnie the trustee in the back section of the middle pews. Church officers got dibs on the back seats.

"Well, here she is," Shirl said to Minnie as if she were showing off a new appliance.

"So I see," Minnie said.

All sorts of thoughts flitted through Annie's head. Minnie hadn't wanted to air-condition the parsonage. Minnie had feared church funds would be used for parsonage repairs. Minnie had given Mr. Gideon Pugh a hard time about employing contractors for the parsonage renovation. Minnie had griped to the other trustees about the condition of the former and current parsonages. Minnie no doubt had been the one who had called Burl Stout to report the "haunting" of Annie's home on Greenbriar Road.

Red flags. Big red flags. Big, billowing red flags with sparklers unfurled in Annie's mind as she wondered whether Minnie had also been the one who'd led the unwelcome wagon to Annie's doorstep the previous week.

"How's she doing?" Minnie asked as if Annie were not in the room. An even bigger, redder flag wrapped itself around Annie like a misbegotten funeral pall.

"She's all right," Shirl said.

"Really?" Minnie said.

"Really."

"Well, then, let's have some special iced tea," Minnie replied.

"Great," said Shirl.

Annie soon learned that special iced tea was a product of Minnie's herb garden and her years of study in the arcane arts of plant medicine. The pastor had quaffed a whoppingly tall tumbler of special iced tea before Minnie turned to Shirl and said, with a cackle, "She likes it. Shall we tell her what's in it?"

Shirl said, "Heh, heh, heh. I s'pose so."

By then Annie didn't care so much that the drink was liberally laced with rum. "Whew, that does go down good on a hot day," she said.

Minnie grinned and said, "Would you like to see the garden?"

They walked and talked in the garden for nearly an hour. Annie heard about the healing properties of mint and the wooing properties of catnip. She saw bees hovering over the fragrant flowers and birds splashing in an emperor's array of bathing basins. She was told how Minnie had learned to till her garden by hand one tiny plot at a time until it looked like a handsome and carefully made quilt full of of colors and textures and meanings.

And Annie heard about the Greenbriar Road house. Not a lot, for when the conversation turned to the wasps that lodged with her in the parsonage, Minnie said, "I can help you with the wasps but not with other things in that house."

"What other things?" Annie said.

But Minnie would not answer. She looked at Shirl, who looked back at her, but neither said a word.

Minnie escorted Annie and Mail Call Shirl to the Cadillac. Annie couldn't hear what they whispered beside the mail hut as she climbed in. She slept during the ride back to the strange little house she shared with cat, birds, wasps and ghosts.

Dear Diary,
Chrismas is tuff. Mommy and Daddy drink our Chrismas
that's what Sissie says. O we have a Chrismas tree tho.
Frankie hauls it up the hill from town. Puts a rope around
his chest and on the other end of the rope he ties up the
trunk of the tree. Id say its 2 miles up the hill from town.

Frankies strong. Just pulls it up the hill and dumps it on the porch. Me and Sissie set it up and deckrate it wich we love to do. Theres about 20 boxes of Chrismas deckrashuns in the atick. We sit for ours up there and sort them out and fix the lites and untangle the little silver strands from before. We don't dare ask for any money to buy new things but that's ok because the old things are still pretty and shiny. I make hot choclate and Sissie makes rice crispy squares and we deckrate the tree.

Since Daddys not allowed in the living room its okay to deckrate the Chrismas tree in there. Yesterday Mommy came in while me and Sissie deckrated the tree and told us when she was our age she got new dresses and shoes all the time and went to dances and partees. I don't know how to dance but dancing dosnt mean any thing to me because I don't have a boy frend but Sissie for sure has a boy frend and nos how to dance. Mommy even ate a rice crispy square and said mmm-deleshus. The Chrismas tree is pretty with angel on top ornaments all over with the little silver strands all over that and 40 or 50 twinkel lites. I hope we leave the Chrismas tree up a long long time.

I don't know wether well have any packages under the tree because Daddy says Chrismas is non sense but Mommy disagrees with daddy on that. Well see. I got Mommy a locket with a peace of my hair in it to ware around her neck if shell ware it. I got Daddy a belt becaws he won a belt buckle at that place up the road. I got Frankie a com because hes always coming his hair. I cant decide what to get Sissie theres so much she likes.It will l have to be some thing small because Iv spent almost all of my birth day money from Misses G al ready. I didn't buy any thing for me but maybe Mommy will get me some thing. Misses G always gets me some thing.

"No matter how long the night, the day is sure to come." ~~ Congolese proverb

CHAPTER TWENTY-NINE

Wednesday was the first day in thirty-six that Isabelle enjoyed the peace of her most special place. It had been necessary to vacate her special place in May as soon as she'd read the article about the Scovill woman in the newspaper, which had said only when she would start being the pastor and not when she would move into the house.

It was just as well, Isabelle thought, because it had been a hot summer so far, and though her special place afforded her many comforts, it could get steamy. Isabelle often wondered whether she had any sweat glands because she couldn't remember sweating. Just the same, she had been in the special hiding place many times as a child on days—and nights—when she felt as if her very brain was on fire. That's why she had the fan, the water and the towels.

The fan did help, but she could not withstand hard summer heat in the special place without respite, so she listened carefully for signals Wednesday morning. Signals would tell her when the Scovill woman awakened, when she took her bath, when she ate and even when she went to the bathroom.

Isabelle heard the toilet flushing very early, signaling that the Scovill woman was an early riser. Isabelle had already suspected this, having seen her arrive at the church early Monday and Tuesday. Just the same, Isabelle knew enough to wait.

The signals kept coming. Footsteps on the stairs, a television turned on to a talk station, the refrigerator door opening and closing, that stupid cat meowing and the woman talking to it, the box being thumped back onto the stack from which Isabelle had taken it.

The back door slammed and Isabelle sat up expectantly. But it soon slammed again, and Isabelle realized the woman must have fetched her newspapers off the grass and returned to the kitchen. There followed what was for Isabelle a very long period of silence. Was the woman praying? Reading? Thinking? Eating?

Whatever the woman did, it lasted a long time. Isabelle's tummy was grumbling by the time she heard the final slam of the back door. She estimated the time at eight in the morning.

Isabelle cleaned her face, hands and feet with a moist towelette and ate canned pears and a package of cheese and crackers. Now she felt rested, clean, safe—even energized. Now she could take back from the Scovill woman what was rightfully her own.

"Of two evils choose the less." ~~ Advice traceable to Aristotle

CHAPTER THIRTY

Thursday, July 7

"Annie, what's wrong with you?"

Her good friend Gloriana Jamieson, she of the beautiful soul and wheelchair-bound body, had just come home from a date. It was rare enough for a single woman pastor to go out on a date, but it was even rarer for Gloriana. In normal circumstances Annie would have proceeded at once to the topic of the date, but this was not a normal circumstance.

"I found a body in the basement of the parsonage."

"A body? Like the Kiwanis uses at Halloween?"

"No. A real skeleton. Real human bones."

"Are you sure?"

"Yes. You know how G.P.'s dad talks about cases and osteology and bones and bodies. Like that."

"Oh my! Shall I come over?"

"Oh, no. You must be tired after your date. I'm just . . . unnerved."

"Who wouldn't be? When did you find these bones?"

"Sunday."

"Sunday!? And you waited four days to call me?"

"Glori, I guess I was in denial. I was kind of paralyzed on the Fourth. I didn't even go to the fireworks. I had an awful day Tuesday at the office, and a meeting with the trustees, and yesterday a tour of the town, and I . . . I just wanted to forget the bones."

"For heaven's sake, Annie. That's pitiful. What are you going to do?"

"That's why I'm calling you. What do you think I should do? I suppose I should call the authorities, but it would lead to a big investigation and waste a lot of time and hold up the air conditioning and . . . ."

"I believe you just answered your own question," Gloriana said. "Call the police. Or call the sheriff. Take your pick."

"But it would really, really upset G.P."

"Annie, you can't seriously be considering not calling the cops."

"Well, I could just rebury the bones. They've been down there a lot of years. Let them rest in peace, so to speak."

"You're still in denial, Annie. Or maybe you've moved on to another form of avoidance. You are not thinking clearly, of that I am sure. Have you been sleeping well?"

"Oh, Glori, it's been awful. It's so hot in the house that my clothes stick to me. I can't catch my breath. I haven't slept all night since I got here. There's so much to do."

"Annie, stop right there! You are under a great deal of duress. Do you realize that?"

"I suppose I do. I miss G.P. so much. I can't talk with anybody . . . ."

"You can talk with me."

"Of course. I didn't mean that. But you have plenty to do already. The ministry. All those weddings this year. And how many has it been, five or six funerals in the last month?"

"I'm all right, perfectly all right. It's you I'm worried about. Who's helping you at the parsonage?"

"The contractors are here day and night working on the place. I can't argue with that."

"It sounds as if you never have any privacy—any time to yourself when you can unwind with a good book or a funny TV show."

"I suppose not."

"How is your devotional life?"

"Okay, I guess. I get up early every day and read scriptures and pray before it's terribly hot in the house. And of course my church office is air-conditioned."

"But you can't live in your church office, Annie."

"No, of course not." .

"Call the cops today and get those bones out of the house. You don't need the extra stress."

"All right. Okay. I suppose so," Annie said. "But . . . but . . . Anyway, how did the date go?"

"I don't want to talk about it."

"A jerk?"

"No, the opposite."

"That scares you, doesn't it?"

There was no answer. "Is that why you won't talk about it?" Annie continued.

Finally, Gloriana spoke. "It scares me more when it's a nice guy than it does when it's a jerk. You know why."

Indeed, Annie knew that Gloriana—a gorgeous redhead with a trim figure and hazel eyes—flinched when she met a decent man. It meant she couldn't blame the path of their relationship on him but must deal with him squarely and allow him to deal squarely with her and her so-called handicap.

"I understand," Annie said. "Call me tomorrow."

Gloriana said she would, and Annie put in her next call.

When Chloe answered, Annie asked, "Did you meet a fan or a producer on the way home?"

"For your information, an entire family recognized me in Weirton at dinner."

"So you took the Ohio River route then? I don't know why you do that. It takes much longer than the interstates."

"I do that because it's more scenic, and more people know who I am. Anyway, why are you calling?"

"Uh, just wanted to see how your trip went," Annie said.

"No, you didn't call me for that. You never call to ask about my trips. Why did you really call?" Chloe demanded.

"Um . . . I . . . uh."

"What's going on? I spent all day shopping. Now I need to steam my complexion. I need a bath. And I need my sleep tonight because Bob and my darling Daniella are due home tomorrow."

Annie inhaled, exhaled. "I dug out the coal in the coal cellar Sunday night, and there was a set of human bones in the ground under the coal, and that is why I'm calling you."

That stopped Chloe. She clicked her new nails on the telephone receiver. It was a rhythm Annie remembered from many meals in their childhood home when Chloe had eaten her 250 calories and strummed the table until receiving permission to leave.

"Are you still there?" Annie asked.

"You need to move out of that hell hole," Chloe said. "Get that boss guy of yours to find you a better place. Earl, or whatever his name is."

"It's Burl. But moving isn't as easy as you seem to think, and I don't want to worry G.P., and I still have to deal with these bones. Give me some good ideas."

"Some good ideas besides calling up your father-in-law or that trustee person or the police?"

"Yes, some good ideas other than those."

"And they say you're the level-headed sister in this family," Chloe griped.

"Those bones could ruin everything I am trying to do in Biddlebourne," Annie grieved. "Those bones will take attention away from the church expansion and the parsonage renovation and my visitation schedule and everything else."

"Do you have any idea whose bones they might be?" Chloe asked.

"How could I know that?" Annie said.

"I thought you liked all those detective shows. You brag that you can figure out who the killers are before any of the detectives."

"Do not!"

"Do too!"

"That's not the point. I have no idea who was buried in the basement. Oh, this kind of thing would just upset G.P. too much."

"Here's an idea," Chloe said. "Wait twenty-four hours before you do anything about the bones. I know you pray about this and about that and about everything. Pray about the bones and see what happens."

It was the best idea Annie had heard yet. She was sorry she hadn't thought of it first.

~~0~~

Dear Diary,
Frends are good. If you have any. Its funny about Frankie.
He dosnt have boy frends but he has a girl frend. Shes
byootiful. I saw them at the shopngo when Mommy sent
me to get her cigarets. He pretended he dint no me and I

pretended I dint no him but I went behind the deturchent shelf and wached when they cheked out. Long silky black hair and finger nails out to there with pink polish. I thot he had a girl frend because he sneeks out with his hair comed and smelling good. But it was for sure when I heard Mommy screeming Frankie you stay away from that slut you hear me. Its funny that Mommy treats Frankie like dirt but is mad that the girl frend isn't good enuf for him.

Mommy says Im still too yung to have a boy frend but Sissie says Im not too yung. I woodnt care about a boy frend Id just like to have any frend. Secretly I think Mommys jelus of Frankie and dosnt want him to have any frends but her. Misses G told me her husband is her frend! I cant imajun that. They hold hands and kiss and she gave him the last bite of her fried chiken at the restront Sunday after Church. Mommy and Daddy only give each other cigarets or buze.

I use to have girl frends but not any more. They told me they coodnt hang around me any more. I kept asking them what was wrong finly they told me. Mommy went to Sallys house one night. Sally and Bernadet lived next door to each other. When Mommy got there she had Sallys mother call Bernadets mother over. My Mom was bad drunk. She told them there dotters were sluts. I dint no what a slut is but Sally told me a slut is a girl who dosnt respect her self. After my mom said Sally and Bernadet are sluts they woodnt spend the night at my house and dint ask me to there house any more. There mothers are nice tho they don't get mad at me because of Mommy. There like moms to me. They took me under there wings and teach me many good things about life. I wish Sally and Bernadet were my frends but there moms are my frends. Nobody is my girl frend any more.

"In a cat's eye, all things belong to cats." ~~ English proverb

CHAPTER THIRTY-ONE

Isabelle was ready to sortie upstairs, having taken an entire day to prepare. She turned out the work light, knelt under the entrance and pushed up. The board gave way and lifted, along with the remnant of linoleum that covered it. Isabelle kept pushing until the entrance was clear. She stood on her suitcase for extra height so she could half jump and half pull herself out of the hiding place.

She wasn't prepared for what awaited her. When Isabelle rose above the floor, she looked straight into the teeth of Fannie Fay, who had opened her mouth and raised her voice in alarm at the sight of a human emerging from nowhere.

Fannie Fay yowled and Isabelle cringed. This cat was straight from hell, as far as she was concerned. It would not shut up, its high yowls turning into fevered, continuous squawks. Isabelle figured the cat would only keep on yowling unless she did something. But what could she do to shut it up?

She pulled herself the rest of the way out of the hiding place and crawled out of the pantry. She could not risk anyone looking in the windows and seeing her. She crawled to several lower cupboards, but they held only cooking utensils, potatoes and onions. She crawled to a pile of boxes to see what they contained but couldn't decipher the writing on them. Then, with her knees beginning to prickle, she got to the refrigerator. The cat shut up and came to join her at the refrigerator door.

"So you like to eat, huh?" Isabelle whispered. The cat peered inside the refrigerator. "Well, then, let's see." Soon the cat purred as it devoured the dollop of cottage cheese that Isabelle had tipped onto the floor.

Isabelle sat back and leaned against the sink watching the cat finish the food. The cat looked at her, and Isabelle gave it another helping of cottage cheese. The cat licked it off the floor in a few seconds. Good grief, the thing could put away the food. Isabelle giggled softly. "You can't have any more. She'll know if too much is missing."

The cat looked at Isabelle with an expression that made Isabelle giggle again. "Okay. If you won't give me away, I'll get you some treats now and then. Deal?"

Fannie Fay did not understand the words but knew a potential playmate when she saw one and sidled up to Isabelle. Isabelle held out a hand and Fannie Fay nuzzled it. Isabelle got the hint and scratched the cat behind the ears. Fannie Fay purred again as Isabelle rubbed her head.

Isabelle could not push her luck. She dared not roam the house until she could handle the cat better. Mommy and Daddy had said pets were filthy beasts. She crawled to the refrigerator, took the plastic bag from her pocket, rose on her knees and removed a dozen ice cubes from the freezer. She tied off the bag, closed the freezer and crawled back to the pantry. She dropped quietly into her hiding place, letting the floorboard and linoleum fall in place behind her. Fannie Cat stretched out on the linoleum and resumed purring.

"A lie is an abomination unto the Lord and a very present help in trouble." ~~ Adlai Stevenson

CHAPTER THIRTY-TWO

Friday, July 8

Annie had barely slept Thursday night, the comfort of the Misty Blue Room and the welcome coolness of the night notwithstanding. She tossed and prayed. Fannie Fay paced on her abdomen before running downstairs.

Annie had to tell someone—other than her friend and her sister—about the bones. It had to be someone who was official in a low-key way, someone who would know what to do but would not overreact. And it should be tomorrow, her day off, when she would not need to have office hours.

She ticked off the possibilities. Burl Stout? No, no, no. He would declare the house inhabitable and order the church to move her into another abode. She would be unable to conceal any of it from G.P., who would fret himself sick. Plus, she would have to pack and unpack all over again.

Shirl Burrows? Heavens, no. Mail Call Shirl was the next best thing to a local radio station.

Nor could Annie confide in her father-in-law, the redoubtable Dr. Park Scovill, retired chief pathologist of Spartansville Unified Memorial Hospital. He could be counted on to respond with scientific objectivity. But he could not be counted on to keep quiet. Nope, not Dad Scovill.

What about one of her brothers? No, she decided quickly. They had their own lives in faraway states. It would be selfish to involve them in this little problem.

Mr. Gideon Pugh? He had a trustee-related interest in the house and a long history in Biddlebourne. He also had demonstrated prudence in delicate matters.

But still, she thought as Fannie Fay rattled her bowl in the kitchen for breakfast, Mr. Gideon Pugh belonged to the American Legion, and he ran up the American flag on his porch and even on his truck. Would he put civic concerns ahead of Annie's wifely concerns? Better not to chance it.

Stumped, Annie heaved out of bed, showered and put on a lightweight jumper, flowered blouse and the blue Propet sandals. She breakfasted on cantaloupe, toast and cottage cheese. Fannie Fay had cottage cheese with a side of kibbles.

Annie performed her regular morning tasks, then set about her day-off chores. She sorted mail, made a grocery list, called her mother-in-law to offer another nonspecific apology for Sunday night and was assured no offense had been taken. Checking her e-mails, she was relieved to learn that the floor man could not visit the parsonage until the next week.

Annie loaded the four coal boxes into G.P.'s truck, Friday being a run-the-truck-and-rev-the-battery day, and forced herself to do her to-dos.

She soothed herself with a strawberry milkshake on the way to the home center in Spartansville. It was a milkshake that she vowed to walk off that very day. She was thunderstruck at the home store by the crown-molding directions that she read in a book on a shelf—a nicely supplied and happily arranged shelf at the front of the store. She put the book back on the shelf and left. There would be no corner turns, blade tilt settings or miter tables for Pastor Scovill.

She went to Mrs. Gatwick's house and carried the coal to her basement. Mrs. Gatwick gave Annie a beautiful watermelon from her garden. Annie bought groceries and picked up dry cleaning in Biddlebourne and went to the bank. She noted with consternation that the bank seemed understaffed. Then, to her horror, she came within a mouse whisker of dinging the truck bumper on a bank sign.

She revisited all the places Shirl had taken her, saying hello and trying to remember names. She walked to Hinkle's Office Emporium and ordered sticky address labels for G.P. and herself.

And she still did not know what to do about the bones in the basement.

The phone was ringing at the parsonage as she struggled through the back door. Her feet hurt, her head hurt, and she had seven heavy sacks of supplies to carry up the sixteen stairs from the truck. But she answered the phone.

"Hi, Annie. It's me."

"G.P.! I hadn't thought you would call. I was going to e-mail you again tonight. It's so good to hear your voice."

"Yours, too. I have to make it short, though."

"Okay. Are you all right?"

"Yep, sure am. What's new there?"

Annie took a deep, deep breath and let her head hang into the phone. She and G.P. had never kept personal things from each other—even the bad stuff. She knew that he would eventually hear about the bones, but she wanted that to be after he was home—home alive.

"You received the e-mail I sent on, oh, what day was it, early Wednesday, I think?"

"Got it, and I see you've been busy. "Too bad you couldn't make it to Mom and Dad's Sunday night."

"Oh, Sweetie. There was a counseling crisis." She closed her eyes and sank into a chair at the kitchen table, letting her purse, keys and the first bag of groceries slide to the floor.

"A counseling crisis already? You have hit the ground running. I hope you were able to help."

"Oh, yes. I think so."

"Good. Did they hook up the washer and dryer yet?"

"What?"

"The washer and dryer. You said they might install them by Friday."

"Right. Right. No, they're not hooked up yet. There's kind of a mess in the basement."

"Sure. I can only imagine. Is it terribly inconvenient?"

"No, not really. People are coming in and out of the house to do the work, but the alternative would be far worse."

"I was thinking about the beds."

"What about the beds?"

"Don't you remember?" he said. "You asked whether to get two twins or a king for our bedroom."

"Oh, sure, now I remember."

"You should probably get two twin box springs with a king mattress. The mattress will be flexible enough to go up the stairs, and of course twin springs will fit, too, won't they?"

"Definitely," she said. "I guess that's settled."

"Were you really kidding about sending money? I checked to make sure my checks are going in."

"Oh, dear, I'm sorry, G.P. Of course the bank account is fine. I'm fine. The church is fine. Everything is fine."

The silence of long marriages filled the phone line. Annie tried to concentrate, to say something light, to say something about anything except the bones in the basement.

"Well, then, I guess I should go," he said.

"I love you and miss you."

"Ditto. Annie, are you sure you're okay?"

"Absolutely," she said perkily.

"You don't have to send me air-mails. I'll settle for e-mails, and they're quicker for you," he suggested.

Annie thought. "I like writing the letters. I'll send both kinds. Okay?"

"Yes. I'll be home in eighty-four days if all goes well."

"I pray every day that it does."

Annie hung up and looked at the fallen groceries, hoping she had convinced G.P. that all was well on her side of the ocean.

~~0~~

Dear Diary,

Frankie got food poizning yesterday. He was vomiting bad. Mommy was some where getting relijus pictures for my grand mother. Daddy wasnt home when Frankie started puking but Daddy came home and saw him. He rubbed Frankies face in the vomit I don't know why. Mommy came home and said Ernie you son of a bich I cant go any where for a fu ours with out you doing some thing to him. Rubbed Frankies face in the puke. I wanted to screem stop it hes sick but I no better. I stayed up at the top of the steps where I cood see but Daddy coodnt see me. Frankie saw me and never said one word to me when he came up stairs just went in the bath room and stayed a real long time then came out and sneeked out his window. I think he went to see his girl frend but he nos Ill never tell

*on him. When Mommy came up and said wherve you been
I said taking a nap on my bed. She looked over at the bed
wich was all rumpled up and went out of the room.*

*That reminds me once we were eating dinner and
Frankies frend just nocked on the front door. Mommy said
Frankie duck because Daddy threw a bowl of chilly at
Frankies head. Almost hit him two. Frankie ran out of the
house yelling lets go, dint even grab his coat and it was in
Janyoury.*

"Know thyself." ~~ Proverb

CHAPTER THIRTY-THREE

Isabelle had been going to sleep early so she could be fresh to follow the Scovill woman's activities each morning. It was just as well, she thought as she ate pears and cheese early Friday, because the woman made virtually no noise in the evening that signaled clearly what she was doing. This meant that Isabelle must also maintain PQ, which stood for Perfect Quiet. It was a habit she had learned well in her childhood and which came to her now as second nature.

Isabelle smiled and hummed several bars of the Mr. Clean jingle as she reflected on her ability to maintain PQ. Frankie never, ever had been able to do PQ, and Mommy had never asked Sissie to do PQ. But Isabelle, being the youngest, had been required to do PQ often while the man visited Mommy. Because Isabelle was light on her feet she had, in fact, become so good at PQ that she could walk in PQ anywhere in the house—and see in PQ anything she wanted to see.

Isabelle was further pleased when the Scovill woman seemed to do on this morning exactly what she had done on the other mornings. She made the same sounds in approximately the same order, down to talking to the cat and going out to pick up the newspapers off the driveway.

This made Isabelle's work much easier because it removed the distraction of worrying about discovery.

Discovery was her greatest fear. She had many fears. She feared never having a home again. She feared never having a family again. She feared never having a friend again. She feared the legal consequences of her past actions and decisions.

But most of all—more than all the other fears combined—Isabelle feared discovery. As long as the people of Biddlebourne did not recognize her, as long as people did not connect her to her family, as long as nothing about her years away was discovered, she was as safe from recriminations as a newborn child.

In returning to Biddlebourne, she had taken the first impossible step in facing her fears. She had thought she could begin over, just as if she had gone away and endured a long labor that birthed a new Isabelle.

But that was not to be. When she had stepped off the bus at the Skyler County Courthouse, she quickly smelled the sweet alfalfa in one breath and lied to the lunch-counter lady with her next.

And soon, with an anguish so visceral it seemed to twist itself around her bowels, she had realized several things. First, she realized that returning to the place was one thing but that returning to the people was another. When she went to Mrs. R. or Mrs. P.'s door, she couldn't make herself knock. She wanted them to throw open those doors and welcome her like a long-lost child. But she was afraid that even they would greet her with cold looks and cutting words, that they might even call the sheriff.

She had come to realize, too, that the very sights, sounds and smells she had so longed to experience again awakened feelings of such intense loneliness that they nearly suffocated her.

Hearing the "noon o'clock" whistle at the grain mill reminded her that no one ever wanted to eat lunch with her. Seeing the blinking neon lights at the drugstore reminded her that the only boy who ever treated her to a soda had been her brother. Smelling the Irish soda bread at the Kearns Bakery reminded her that other kids ran from the store when they saw her come in with Vickie June or Ernie Pargeon.

And she realized, finally, that her life—and, indeed, her soul—had been cleaved in two. She was twenty-seven years old and had run away from Biddlebourne shortly after her thirteenth birthday. Half of her was the Isabelle of Biddlebourne, and half was the Isabelle of Indianapolis, Chicago, Denver, Dallas, Las Vegas, Los Angeles and points abroad.

Half of her listened to her parents, admired her sister and protected her brother. The other half took counsel from no one but herself and a few trusted, paid advisors. Half of her believed she could grow up to do and be whatever she dreamed, and the other half knew she was nobody and nothing.

All those realities were the reason Isabelle needed to think. She needed to stop being two people—innocent child and fearful adult. She wanted to be the best of both Isabelles, unbroken, unafraid, unscorned. She wanted to live happily in the home that rightfully belonged to her. That meant she had, among other things, to get rid of the Scovill woman. She needed a plan that was brilliant—doable, effective and absolutely untraceable to her.

Isabelle had already decided, as the product of several carefully planned and executed thinking sessions in May and June, on the name of her plan: Born Again in Biddlebourne. She had thought three weeks about the words *born again* because the other preacher at Glory Hallelujah Church—Pastor Woostine, whom she had liked a lot—talked about being born again in a way Isabelle had not understood.

But when Isabelle thought about *born again*, she thought about coming into the world again as the daughter of parents other than Vickie June and Ernie Pargeon. She thought about living in a house where the dad and mom slept in the same room, even in the same bed, and where the children all had their own clean, dry beds.

She thought about playing dolls with other little girls and jumping rope and crawdadding in the creek and picking berries with siblings and cousins. About going to school in clean checkered dresses with matching bows in her hair and shining shoes on her feet. About shopping with her mom for party outfits and watching her brother play baseball. About playing the piano at recitals and learning how to ride a horse. About helping her grandmothers make quilts and apple butter and potato salad for family picnics.

There was only one place on Earth where Isabelle could be born again in the way she wanted. That place was 1010 Greenbriar Road, Biddlebourne, West Virginia. She had tested this theory in more than a dozen cities over the last fourteen years, hoping each time she pulled up stakes that the next place would be the one where she could be new.

But no matter how big the locale, how beautiful, how friendly or how sunny, it had not generated in Isabelle the ability to free herself of the emotional and psychological baggage that weighed her down.

She knew that she would have to let herself be discovered in order to overcome her fear of discovery. If she did not let herself be known again in Biddlebourne, she could never surmount all the other fears and accomplish her goals. It was a circular problem that had confounded her for months.

This conundrum—this tangle of fact and fear, this compound of pain and guilt, this cancer of obsession and alienation—ruled Isabelle's life. It formed the box in which she allowed herself to live. It was why she at once hated and loved the box of plywood that formed her special hiding place. It was why she had to stay in her special hiding place until her plan was as perfect as a full moon in October.

Death in the Parsonage

"A still tongue makes a wise head." ~~ Ancient proverb

CHAPTER THIRTY-FOUR

Sunday, July 10

Considering the tension Annie took with her into the pulpit, her second sermon at Glory Hallelujah Church was received surprisingly well. It had also been received well six years earlier at Christ Church.

As Annie led worship, she felt as if every prayer and scripture aimed itself at her. She had to tell. She had to report the bones. She had to free herself of the solitary responsibility for the obviously human skeleton lying in a black Glad bag in the coal cellar at home. She had to focus on the tasks of ministry. Preaching fresh sermons. Teaching. Visiting. Leading. Not digging. Not hiding. Not lying. Not worrying.

After worship, many people stopped to inquire about G.P. and the house. She assured them that G.P. was safe so far, though she was unsure of that moment by moment, and that the scheduling and presence of workers in the house were no problem to her, though to some extent they were.

The questions brought another problem to Annie. What if any of the several workers who were being dispatched to the parsonage went to the coal cellar and opened the bone bag? Further, since the hookup of the washer and dryer was now set for Wednesday, workers would definitely be in the basement then.

Annie concluded that she had to either give up the bones or hide the bones better. She was so preoccupied she nearly missed Ma Pugh's whispered words as the ushers began counting the offering and turning off the lights.

"Pastor," Ma said in a low tone.

"Yes, Ma? How are you?"

"Fine as buttermilk biscuits. Listen now. I looked into that . . . delivery you got at your house your first day."

"What did you discover?"

"First I thought it was one of those Bascombes from over Selby—a bad bunch all of them and the dad in jail and the mom working at the Watering Hole and the other kind of place, too, if you get my drift."

"I see."

"But it wasn't them. I'm sure 'cause Shirl found out the whole clan of em's hied off to North Carolina or Georgia or somewhere down south—to start a new line of mischief making, you ask me."

"I see."

"And I put the question to my boy Glenn and his boy Keith, but they swear it wasn't any of the kids from around here. Keith said he'd have sure heard it bragged about over at the pool hall—I hate it that Glenn and Dorinda let him go there but they won't, absolutely won't, serve beer to minors at the pool hall, so I guess I have to accept it—but nobody has said a thing about gettin' one over on the new preacher. Me and Pa just can't figure it out."

Annie imagined police coming to the parsonage to question her and search the premises. "Mrs. Pugh, perhaps we ought to forget it. Even if you have not found the likely culprit, doesn't it still seem to have been a prank?"

Ma Pugh looked doubtful. "Pastor, I'd let it go except for one thing."

"What's that?"

"Shirl showed me that purple letter you got. The bag of cat pieces was bad enough, but that letter was downright threatening. As chairlady of the committee, I don't think I can let it go. We ought to report it to the police."

Cat guts. Threats. Bones. Police. Life was thornier by the day in Biddlebourne.

Annie couldn't persuade Ma Pugh not to stop at the police station on the way home, so she went to her office to console herself. Soon the building was quiet, the ushers having refined and reduced their counting routine to exactly twenty-five minutes, and the youth having taken summer break from Bible quizzing.

Annie felt lonely. She wanted to go home and eat leftovers with G.P. She even wanted to go out and spend too much on seafood with Chloe.

She checked her day book. Although she'd been in Biddlebourne less than two weeks, it already brimmed with meeting dates, planning notes and lists. They had discipleship classes, Bible studies, an evangelism campaign, a fund-raising campaign, an advertising campaign, men's groups, women's groups, teen groups, kids' groups, vacation Bible school, the varied Marriage and Family Day ministries every week, and an array of fellowship events and service activities that kept Trudy busy ten hours a week just printing up fliers, minutes and bulletins. Annie thanked God that Trudy had managed to learn the location of the print button on the Sharp copier.

Annie had also booked two weddings and begun making rounds to members' homes. She planned to cover one alphabet letter every two weeks. She had eight more days, including Sunday but not including Friday, to visit the final thirteen A-families listed in the church directory.

Annie next made a to-do list for the week and a to-do list for Monday. She allowed herself a bit of self-satisfaction as she reflected on her emerging routine. Up at 6:30. Shower and dress. Devotions. Breakfast. Write to G.P. Read the *Skyler County Sentinel*, *The Intelligencer* and *USA Today*. Walk 20 minutes. At the office by 8:30. Work until 5 or 5:30. Dinner. Meetings or visits until 8:30 or 9 p.m.

No such routine pertained to Sundays, of course, and Annie, a creature born and bred of self-discipline, felt more loose-ended, disorganized and worried than she ever had before.

She took the cell phone out of her purse and called Chloe.

Chloe's response was exasperated. "You simply cannot be serious. I thought you'd have this all taken care of by now!"

"I am very serious," Annie said. Chloe made one of those exaggerated *tsks* that meant the discussion was not about her, her career or her clothing but must nevertheless be pursued for some undeniable reason. The phone line augmented the *tsk* nicely.

"Good Lord, Annie. I don't know much about the law, but isn't it illegal not to report the discovery of human remains?"

"I am choosing to regard the bones in the basement as a grave upon which I inadvertently stumbled."

"Malarkey!"

"Not if you consider the age of this house and the fact that the cellar floor is made of dirt. It is entirely possible that the bones were interred there by an early resident during the mid-1800s. Perhaps there was a death in the family while the Civil War was raging, and the family had no choice but to bury the body in the house."

"As if there was no dirt anywhere in the county except the basement of that house?"

"No, as if there was no absolutely safe place in town to bury a loved one, no preacher to conduct the service, no money to buy or build a coffin and maybe even no family or friends around to grieve."

"You could get into trouble if you keep the bones under wraps. I just know it."

"All I am really suggesting is that I will not report the bones until G.P. gets home."

"This is all about G.P., isn't it?"

Annie gulped. "He's worried already about stuff around the house. He called the other day to ask about the washer and dryer and the beds and other things. I couldn't forgive myself if I let one more thing—especially a weird thing like a skeleton in the house—trouble him while he's away. You know how he is. He worries when he can't act on things."

"I know. I know. Still . . ."

"As soon as he comes home, I'll show him the bones and we'll go to the authorities together. The bones have obviously been there many years. What are a few more months?"

"You sound like you're trying to convince me, but you're really trying to convince yourself."

Annie paused. "Okay. You're right. But I know I have to wait until G.P. is home to report the bones."

"You have to do what you have to do," Chloe said with a noisy sigh.

"Meanwhile, I can at least make some discreet inquiries. Maybe I can have the whole puzzle solved by the time he's back. I'll say, 'Look, G.P. I found some bones downstairs and asked around, and it turns out they are the bones of a Confederate soldier who was injured, and he sought shelter in this house, and the owners were sympathetic and hid him and when he died of his injuries they buried him quietly in the basement.'"

"Uh-huh."

"Maybe that is a bit much. I imagine there is some equally innocuous explanation."

"Whatever. Gotta go. I'm late for my sauna and massage."

Annie marveled silently at the services available in a big city on Sunday and said, "Oh, okay. Thanks for helping me make up my mind."

"I didn't change your mind one little bit. Don't blame me when you get arrested for breaking whatever law it is you are breaking—that you are breaking at this very minute!"

"As usual, you are overdramatizing," Annie said.

"And you, sister dear, are sidestepping," Chloe said. They both hung up.

Annie tried to reach Gloriana, but there was no answer at her parsonage. Of course not. Gloriana was doubtless visiting her flock on Sunday afternoon, as Annie knew she should also have been.

Dear Diary,
I cant remembr when the other man started coming to the house. The other man and his wife use to be best frends with mommy and daddy. The other man and his wife live rite here in town. He never talks to me but he comes to the house all the time now always when daddys at work or at the bars. Mommy use to make me and Frankie and Sissie go up stairs when the other man came but Frankies usully out of the house now eksep for sleeping and Sissies most

of the time at her girl frends house. Only I don't have any place else to go I mean no girl frends or boy frends only Misses Gs house or another nabors house. I cant go there all the time because that makes mommy real mad she says the nabors shood but out of our familys bisness.

Anyway when the other man comes mommy makes me go up stairs. I like it when the other man comes to the house becaws mommy's real nice to me and gives me cookies if theres any in the kichen and lets me take an extra bath with her bubble sope. When I was little she made me stand between the piano and the wall when the other man came to the house. I gess she dint want me to be roming the house by myself when I was little. I hated standing between the piano and the wall. My legs got so tired because the other man stayed a long time. Frankie and Sissie wood be in skul but I wood be at home because I was two little for skul. I had to wate and wate for them to be done with there time. Some times my legs hurt so bad I wood put one arm aganst one wall and one arm on the piano and let my legs dangl to give them rest. I use to think it was ours and ours that he stayed when I had to stand between the wall and the piano. Mommy says he is her frend and they like to talk to gether. I think they do some other stuff two but that's jus a gess.

Death in the Parsonage

"A hedge between keeps friendship green." ~~ Proverb

CHAPTER THIRTY-FIVE

Normally, Isabelle would not brook a Permitted Pleasure during thinking mode. But the special hiding place had become intolerably warm.

Nearly two decades earlier she had built the special place. She had sought no help and received no help. She had discovered the original hidey-hole on her own one day at age six while maintaining Perfect Quiet in the pantry during a visit by her mother's man friend. She had stolen the plywood from her dad's stash, and he in his drunken stupors had never noticed the loss. She had borrowed his tools and used them without knowing their names and, in some cases, their intended functions. She had enhanced the original cubbyhole when she'd been alone in the house or when her mother was too drunk or hung over to keep tabs on Isabelle.

It had taken a whole winter of sneaking around to finish her special hiding place. She had to pound with the hammer when nobody else was home or when Vickie June and Ernie were passed out drunk. Those were the only times Isabelle considered their drinking to be beneficial.

After pounding the big nails into the plywood deep enough to make the boards stay in place, she had brought in personal supplies. At first she hadn't known how to string an extension cord and needed a flashlight and lots of batteries, all of which she stole from Vinny's All-American. She brought in blankets from the buffet chest in the dining room because she was sure her mother opened those drawers only if Isabelle wet the bed, and Isabelle had taught herself not to wet the bed so that her mother would quit opening the buffet drawers.

The snacks had been tricky. Sissie and Frankie had treasured their chips and candy on the rare occasions when their parents got them at the grocery store, so Isabelle learned to take the things they didn't like. That's how she'd come to stash jars of olives, bags of stale vanilla wafers and packets of pickle loaf in her special place.

Before long she'd become adept at taking more than she needed at meals—when there were meals—and placing the extra in her pockets or underpants. She also had all the snacks that people gave her at church and that Mrs. G. and Mrs. P. gave her.

Isabelle had thought and thought about why the cubbyhole had been there under the pantry in the first place. It wasn't until she had American history in fourth grade that she figured the spot might have been used in the Underground Railroad. She had remained interested in the Underground Railroad, because she felt an affinity with the people who had risked their lives to escape cruelty and also because she learned and admired some of the methods they had used to avoid detection.

Through the worst years her special place had saved her sanity and, once, her life. She remembered not a single moment of discomfort in her special place from childhood, but now each passing hour brought more physical misery. The heat built up during the days much more than she remembered. The fan helped a little, as did the ice cubes she routinely sneaked out of the refrigerator upstairs, but Isabelle still suffered.

It was the thinking. Playing games and reading forbidden magazines in the special place had been happy pastimes, but thinking through her troubles was work. And work took energy. And expending energy heated up her body.

The hiding place had become so hot that Isabelle actually began to sweat. At first she thought the moisture on her arms was simply the residue of ice she'd rubbed on herself. But when she wiped those droplets away, more popped up on her arms, her neck, her face and even on her knees.

Isabelle tried lying perfectly still. She tried thinking of snow slopes in Denver. She tried drinking more liquids. But by dawn on her fifth day in the hidey-hole Isabelle was exhausted from the combination of mental exercise and high temperatures.

Isabelle was so intensely uncomfortable she could scarcely think, which she realized defeated her entire purpose in being there. However, Isabelle was not too worried. She told herself she could leave her special hiding place any time she wanted. She also told herself she would likewise be hot outdoors.

But there was some good news. The Scovill woman continued her habits. She rattled the door knobs, turned water on and off, walked down the stairs, opened and closed the refrigerator and cupboard doors and talked to the cat in very much the same sequence every morning. The woman's noontime habits were less predictable, as she had come home for lunch only three days out of the last six.

But this was Sunday morning, which Isabelle knew would be different. The Scovill woman had to be at the church until at least noon. Now Isabelle had a prime opportunity. She stood to push on the trap door above her, but it resisted.

At first she thought the Scovill woman had put boxes or bags on the pantry floor, but she decided that would have made it impossible for the preacher to reach any of the pantry shelves. Isabelle pushed again . . . and heard a shrill *meoowwwrr*.

Isabelle smiled and pushed until the linoleum slid off the other side. When she rose out of the hole, she saw Fannie Fay cowering against the wall.

"Here, kitty kitty," she said, but the cat didn't budge. Isabelle crab-walked to the refrigerator, opened it and spotted a package of deli turkey slices. She gave the cat one piece. Fannie Fay gobbled and asked for more by meowing and smiling at Isabelle. "Okay, just one more," Isabelle said.

With Fannie Fay at her heels, Isabelle went upstairs to check out the bedrooms. The tiny one Frankie had slept in looked altogether different. The wallpaper was gone, replaced with pearly gray paint. Isabelle thought it was beautiful and wished her mother had let her paint the house. The marks inside the closet reminded Isabelle that Frankie had been four feet six inches tall at age twelve, and Isabelle had to wipe tears from her eyes.

She glanced into the bedroom she and Sissie had shared. It was blue now. She couldn't remember what color it had been those many years earlier, and when she looked inside the closet she found no height marks for either herself or Sissie. She'd known she wouldn't. There was a double bed covered by a quilt. Isabelle looked closer, saw the tiny, even stitches and knew the quilt was handmade.

The last bedroom, the one in which her mother had slept, now had white walls and red trim on the window. This should be the Scovill woman's bedroom, but there was no bed. However, there was a dresser and a rocking chair. There was a jewelry box on the dresser, and the closet was full of women's and men's clothes and shoes. This confused Isabelle, who definitely had not seen a man arrive and stay at 1010 Greenbriar Road.

Isabelle opened the jewelry box and poked around. She found nothing of high value except a pair of ruby earrings. She tried them on and looked in the mirror. She was shocked at her damp, straggly hair and flushed face and quickly removed the earrings.

Isabelle opened the top drawers of the dresser and saw plain white underpants and bras in tidy stacks, as well as makeup containers, handkerchiefs, buttons and polished rocks. At the very bottom of the middle drawer she found a tarnished watch. She put it to her ear and heard ticking.

For nearly five minutes Isabelle debated with herself. If she took the watch, the Scovill woman might raise an alarm. But it would be very difficult for anyone to tie Isabelle to the watch, and the Scovill woman most likely would think she had misplaced it—if she noted its absence at all. On the other hand, if Isabelle took the watch she would have the luxury of knowing the time—all the time. She could time the Scovill woman's movements and be absolutely certain what to expect next in the house.

She could have purchased a watch—no, a hundred watches—anytime she wanted, but time was a fickle friend and she had a love-hate relationship with timepieces. Her mother had often shouted at Isabelle, "When the hell is my lunch going to be ready?" or "How long can it take you to walk to the store and back? Where did you sneak to?"

Over the years Isabelle had learned to tell time in ways that were comfortable and convenient for herself—without sticking to the exact minutes and hours ticked off on a clock or watch—but things were different now. The Scovill woman's habits needed to be carefully noted so that Isabelle could gain respite from the heat—and later from the cold—with security.

Isabelle put the watch on her right wrist, then on her left wrist. It hung loosely, and she turned her arm this way and that to admire it. She smiled into the mirror, holding her wrist next to her face, before closing the dresser drawer and making her way to the bathroom.

She had just flushed the toilet when she heard the back screen door slam. She recognized the slam. She went to PQ mode, stopping in her tracks and quieting her breathing. Fannie Fay meowed and looked at Isabelle. Isabelle made no motions, spoke no words. Fannie Fay left the bathroom.

Soon Isabelle heard a child's voice. "Look, Dad, there's Fannie Fay. Can I play with the cat, Dad?"

A man said, "Okay, but only for a minute. We have to fix that pipe and go pick up your mom for church."

What pipe? Kitchen pipe or bathroom pipe? Or basement laundry pipe? Isabelle heard the man and boy walking and laughing and knew she had to act fast. With no more than twenty light footsteps she was in the woman's closet, observing strict PQ and standing behind several long plastic clothing bags.

She was sweating from anxiety and gagging from the noxious odor of the plastic. She had to pee despite having just used the bathroom. Stress had always done that to her. Footsteps on the stairway and into the bathroom told her she'd vacated that room in the nick of time.

In misery, Isabelle waited.

"Advice is a stranger; if welcome he stays for the night; if not welcome he returns home the same day." ~~ African proverb

CHAPTER THIRTY-SIX

Monday, July 11

If Annie's first try at a staff meeting had disappointed her, the second attempt dismayed her.

When she arrived at the church at 8:42 a.m., she found Hermie the Handyman and his boy Seth bordering the front sidewalk with impatiens. They chatted a few moments, covering the obligatory topics of the morning's weather and the weekend's trash strewn by passers-by.

The answering machine at Trudy's workstation was blinking brightly with a big, red *12* when Annie entered the office. Theorizing that emergency callers would have reached her at home or on her cell phone, she decided to let Trudy pick up the messages upon her arrival, which Annie optimistically expected around nine.

Once again Annie's trust in human nature was dashed, for at 9:30 Trudy hadn't come in or called. When ten o'clock came, bringing in the slightly damp Hermie the Handyman as well as the budding typist Seth, Annie called Trudy's home and learned from her Grandmother Earladean's caregiver that Trudy was on her way to work.

"When did she leave the house, if you know?" Annie asked.

"Oh, I'm sorry. She was already gone when I got here at eight," said the caregiver, whose voice Annie vaguely recognized.

Annie's schedule for the day was jammed. She was to meet with Mr. Gideon Pugh and arrange a time for people to restore the woodwork and doors, people to replace missing ceramic tiles in the bathroom and people to make another pass at the nests that had been built cannily by the wasps in the ceiling and cubbyholes of the third floor.

Not only that, but Annie needed to finish the A-families, start an honest-to-goodness new sermon for the following Sunday, meet with one of the two design semifinalists for the church expansion and call on Ed Gregorsky's aging, nonmember mother in a hospital fifty miles away. And, oh yes, she was expected to meet with the church trustees at seven in the evening.

"Hermie," she began, but Hermie was ahead of her.

"I heard," he said. "The meetin's been changed to eleven. No problem. Me and Seth'll go pick up some stuff we left at the parsonage by accident."

"Would you like to borrow my keys?" Annie asked, heading for her own office.

"Nah, don't need to. I got my own set," he said as he motioned for Seth to follow.

"Oh, okay," Annie said. She made a mental note to inquire why Mr. Gideon Pugh had breached protocol by distributing parsonage keys without consulting the resident pastor.

She went to the answering machine, picked up a notepad and pen and punched the button under the *12*. She had written off two hang-ups and one oh-never-mind and was jotting the names of Sunday's flower donors when Seth burst back in.

"The cops! The cops!" he said, pointing out the window to the circular driveway where a Skyler Police Department cruiser, lights flashing, had stopped. Two young officers walked toward the church.

Oh, no, they know about the bones! She frantically looked for the on/off button to stop the mechanical voice on the machine as it measured off another message, but she couldn't find it. At that moment the phone rang and Shirl Burrows appeared beside Annie, as if from nowhere. Shirl simultaneously pressed an unseen switch to turn off the answering machine, picked up the phone, ground out her cigarette on the notepad and dropped the daily mailbag on the floor.

"Yeah," she said to the caller. She listened a couple of seconds and said, "That's fine. Just bring 'em to the church office, heh heh heh."

"Shirl, where did you come from?" Annie croaked.

"From the dark side of the moon, see?" she said, pointing to the front of her T-shirt, which bore the words *Moon Mad Mama* and showed a woman who looked remarkably like Shirl baying in the direction of a sickly-green moon.

Annie didn't have time to ask more because the police were already in the office, hats in hand, and the shorter one was saying, "We're looking for Pastor Scovill."

"I'm Pastor Scovill."

"We're following up on a report made by Ella Mae Pugh," the officer continued. "May we meet somewhere privately?"

"Certainly," Annie said, moving toward her office despite the tremor in her legs.

"I'll come along, too, if you don't mind. I was the one who discovered the letter," Shirl said, preceding Annie and the officers into the pastor's inner office and sitting at the small conference table.

Forty-five minutes later, Annie was convinced of several things. One was that Shirl Burrows was a handy person to have around because she had calmly and clearly answered most of the officers' questions about the previous week's threat letter.

A second thing was that she, Annie, must act soon on the bones in the parsonage basement or become a nail-biting, tongue-twisted mess.

Her third conclusion was that Trudy Bigler was going to get the Marilyn Caperton fast-track course on church secretarying because when the officers left Annie's office Trudy was just setting down her lunch sack and purse. Her hair was wet, and her face shone without makeup.

The officers left as they had arrived, quickly and with lights flashing red, blue and white. Threats against a preacher were serious business in Biddlebourne.

"Is everything okay?" Hermie the Handyman asked Annie. He and Seth apparently had returned from the parsonage and planted themselves in Trudy's office but had been unable to hear the conversion through the pastor's door.

Trudy slid into the armless chair behind her desk and began shuffling papers.

"Everything's fine," Annie assured Hermie, but he clearly did not intend to accept so brief an explanation. Nor would he have to, for Shirl piped up. "Nothin' to get your drawers puckered over. Just a little love note for the pastor," she said, whacking Annie on the back and guffawing.

Hermie smiled at Annie and took Seth by the hand. He could wait for the details, which Shirl would tell to all by noon. Father and son left hand in hand to return to the joys of lawn care.

"Shirl, may I have a word with you in my office before you go?" Annie said, pointing to her door and nodding formally.

"Yeah, sure," Shirl said, taking the hint and moving toward Annie's office.

"I'll be right in, Shirl," said Annie as she turned to Trudy. "Are you all right?" she asked.

"Yes, ma'am, I'm fine. I . . . I apologize for being late."

"Trudy, tell me something."

"Yes, ma'am?"

"Are you late for your classes at Skyler High School?"

"No, ma'am. I've only missed three days of school in the last five years, and I was only late twice—once when we forgot to set the clocks ahead in April and once when I had to walk on account of missing the bus."

"I'm only asking because I very much need your help in the office. Why are you usually late for your job here?"

Annie wasn't prepared for Trudy to burst into tears, which she did, but Annie was prepared for excuses, which Trudy did not give.

"I'm sorry," said the tardy Trudy. Tears streamed through her thick eyelashes, ran over her apple cheeks and pooled at the corners of her mouth.

"I know you're sorry, and I accept that apology, but if there is a consistent reason you cannot be here at nine o'clock, I need to know it so that we can work out a better schedule for you."

"I'm so tired when the alarm goes off at seven," she said, reaching for a tissue.

Annie added numbers quickly, looked again at Trudy's hair and said, "Are you staying out late with Carl every night?"

A fresh stream of tears sprouted. "Well . . ."

"Trudy, are you having a sexual relationship with Carl?"

Now the tears became a torrent. Trudy folded her arms on the desk and dropped her head into the nest that they made on the blotter. Her words were incoherent, but Annie thought she said, "Oh, God, how did you know?"

"Trudy, you should talk with your mother about this," Annie said. She was thinking that Trudy was almost an adult and that perhaps even the pastor had no right to ask such personal questions. But she also was thinking how naïve Trudy was, how Carl Hoobler was ignoring the law, and how Trudy was in her pastoral care because she and her family belonged to the church.

Trudy nodded without lifting her head and said, "But I can't tell her. She'll be so mad at me."

"What if I come over to your house around six tonight?"

"But Mom will be there then."

"I know."

"I don't think I can tell her," Trudy said, finally lifting her puffy face.

"That's your choice. But you and I will talk either way because you're taking risks, probably more risks than you realize."

"Oh . . ."

"I'll be there at six, and if you decide you don't want to talk to your mom yet, we'll just go to Elderdon's and talk over a cold drink. How about that?"

"Really?"

"Really."

"Okay."

"Meanwhile," Annie went on, "I'll ask Marilyn Caperton to come in several afternoons a week to share some tips of the trade with you."

"Who's Marilyn Capperton?"

"Marilyn Caperton. She's a very experienced church secretary. I think you'll like her, and she'll teach you a lot."

"Okay. I guess I could use some help."

"That's all settled then."

Trudy blew her nose and wiped her eyes. "I'd better start in," she said, turning to the answering machine and picking up the notepad on which Shirl had recently quenched her cigarette.

Annie returned to her inner office, shut the door and said, "Shirl, I need some information."

Mail Call Shirl didn't blink before replying. "What do you need?"

"I need to know why people say the parsonage is haunted."

"Why? You been hearin' bumps in the night, heh, heh, heh?"

"Actually, the house does seem to groan and cough at night. But what I wonder is whether there's a connection between this silly ghost thing and the cat remains and purple letter."

"Hm." Shirl looked straight at Annie and pressed her lips together. After a long interval she said, "We don't know that the cat thing and the letter are hooked up, let alone whether they have something to do with bullshit about ghosts in the house—sorry about that word, it just slipped out, heh, heh, heh."

"I understand. So they're just nonsense, then, the stories about ghosts?"

"Well, I don't know . . . ."

"Shirl, this is a problem, perhaps not a big one, but if people start to think the church is tied in with ghosts or scandal or anything like that, it could seriously hurt the church's growth and building plans."

Shirl squinted as if trying to see the future. At last she spoke. "Yeah, I'll do some research. Nobody or nothin' is gonna hold up the building campaign."

"My feelings exactly," Annie said.

When Shirl had assured Annie that the day's mail held no threat letters—she had inspected everything—she left to do her research, and Annie leaned into Trudy's office to say, "Will you hold my calls for fifteen minutes?"

Trudy nodded and peered at her watch.

Annie sat in her chair. She put her favorite Bible and her day book on the desk in front of her. She bowed her head, breathed deeply and prayed. It was not an elegant prayer. It was angry and frightened. She told God how little she deserved the extra mess that had marked her arrival in Biddlebourne. She told God she did not have time to do all that God was asking her to do. She told God it was unfair for her husband, at his age, to be in a war zone, even as a noncombatant gatherer of intelligence. She told God how offended she was by the carcass on her doorstep and threat in the mail. She told God how confused she was by her discovery of a skeleton in the parsonage that should have been her haven of solace and base of service. She told God how all the predicaments in which she found herself were totally God's fault.

Having cleared the air, Annie called Mr. Gideon Pugh, Mrs. Marilyn Caperton, Mrs. Mary Jo Scovill, the architectural firms of Limon & Ernst and Silvio Guattieri, and Pizza Hut's delivery line.

Not long afterward Annie, Hermie, Trudy and Seth were enjoying a piping-hot, deep-crust pie with all available toppings except pineapple, chicken and anchovies. They sat around the old typing table in Trudy's office. Seth typed a bunch of capital *S*s on the typewriter, recycling paper out of Trudy's waste basket. Hermie said that despite the break in the weather it was still too hot in the middle of the day to plant more flowers. Trudy said that her grandmother had tried to get up by herself in the middle of the night and bumped her shin on the bedside table.

"Speaking of bumps in the night," Annie said, "I heard the funniest thing about the parsonage the other day."

"Oh? What?" Trudy said.

"I heard that it was haunted. Isn't that funny?"

Seth, having conquered the letter *S,* was concentrating on *E.* Hermie got out his pocketknife and commenced to cut the seams of the pizza box so that it would fit into the recycling bin behind the church.

"Look at the time," Trudy exclaimed. I have to get back to work!"

"Have you heard anything about ghosts at the parsonage, Trudy?" Annie persisted.

Trudy shook her head as she reshuffled Sunday's attendance sheets. Hermie took the flattened box in one hand and Seth's hand in the other and said, "We gotta be gittin' home. Bethie's cannin' today. Seth here, he strings the beans, and I scald the jars."

"Be careful, then," Annie said, acknowledging that lunchtime was over and that it was over because she had brought up the subject of Glory Hallelujah Church's haunted parsonage.

Later that afternoon Annie saw two A-families on her way out of town to visit Clara Gregorsky and another A-family on her way back from the hospital. At 6:10 p.m. she arrived at the Bigler residence. She was met at the door by Trudy and her mother. "I told her," Trudy said. She sucked in a hollow, shaky breath.

Annie waited for Blanche to comment. Her body seemed bent at the waist, and she twisted a stringy wad of tissue.

"It's my fault," Blanche said. Annie waited for Blanche to continue, but she appeared unable to do so.

"May I come in?"

"Of course." Annie entered the living room of the small duplex apartment. The twins, Barry and Garry, were on the floor pummeling each other and tossing the TV controller back and forth. Earladean lay on her hospital bed in the tiny dining room.

Blanche sent the boys to the basement to play. The three of them—Trudy, Blanche and Annie—had a long discussion. Blanche was devastated by Trudy's news of her relationship with the much older Carl Hoobler, and Trudy was devastated by her mother's response to the news. Annie listened at length to their frustrations after the death of George, Blanche's husband and Trudy's father.

They had become isolated from each other after George's death, Blanche struggling to take care of Earladean and the twins, and Trudy struggling to make straight As in school and keep up with her job at the church. Their lives were burdened by much labor and many responsibilities.

They agreed to talk again the following week, and when Annie left around eight o'clock, both mother and daughter had dried their tears. But, Annie thought, the real work had only begun.

The trustees were waiting for the pastor at the church. They filled her in on their progress—emphasizing that the washer and dryer would be installed Wednesday in the parsonage—and she filled them in on her work with the house and the church building campaign. Several minor matters, including building rental rates for weddings, were handled quickly, and they adjourned around nine.

At home Annie fetched the wretched bone bag from the basement and stowed it in the closet of the USA Room. She took a cheese-and-tomato sandwich and a glass of iced tea to the computer in the dining room and started her work.

She hadn't been sitting in front of the computer more than five minutes when she heard a knock on the front door. She hurried to open the door and turn on the porch light. Vinny Clark stood before her with tool kit in hand.

"I came to see about that crown molding, ma'am," he said with a bright smile.

"Oh. Uh, that's very kind of you, Vinny. Actually, I'm still working . . . in my office . . . the dining room . . . ."

"I'll just be a minute," he said as he opened the screen door and entered the living room.

"Really, Vinny, I appreciate your visit, but another time would . . ."

"I'll be out of your hair in a wink," he said. "Just gotta check first to see if there's any wood I can use."

Annie froze as Vinny Clark strode toward the basement door.

Dear Diary,
My favorite nabor of all time is Misses G. She and Mister G call me there little chicade. They are very welthy with a nice house fancy yard and other stuff. I stay with them when Mommy goes to the hospital. Mommy says she cant leve us with daddy because he forgets were there. This year right after skul started I went to stay there. Frankies staying with the coch and his wife. I don't know there name it starts with a c or a k. Mommy says Misses G has moshenal problems now and takes medicine. Who cares. Shes nice to me. Mommy also says Misses G is difernt. Im so glad Misses G is difernt that's why shes nice to me. I am the prinses at Misses and Mister Gs house. She says Im like a grand dotter. Shes trying to save me from stuff. I

herd her tell Mister G yesterday. She gets up realy erly
and reads or paints prety picturs. Some times she wakes
me up around 3 in the morning and says do you want to
make cookies. I always want to make cookies and she lets
me eat all I want some times a whole pan of them and she
lets me put nuts and razins and lots of chocklat chips in
them. This is a hole lot better than what hapns at my
house at 3 in the morning. When its dinner time Misses G
says what does my little chicade want for dinner and I can
say hambergers and french fris. That's what I usully want,
some times five days in a row. Misses G dosnt care if its
10 days in a row she fixes hambergers and french fris. She
has a big freezer in her basmint that is full of hambergers
and french fris. She lets me pick were I want to sleep two.
She has twin beds in her bedroom. She tells Mister G to go
in the gest room and sleep and he does because its going
to be just us girls in the bedroom. She dosnt make even
one sound when she sleeps can you imajun that. She sets
my hair in her curlers in the morning and I look realy cute
for school. Some times we sleep up stairs in her dotters
twin beds her dotters gone away to college and never
comes to see Misses G. I can wach TV whenever I want.

Misses G also can so very good. She makes close and sock
pupets for me. And she has a porch swing out back. I can
swing when ever I want and Misses G swings with me and
tells me stories and lets me tell stories. She laffs at the
right places and never makes fun of my stories or me.
Some times I swing for ours. Misses G dosnt care she just
pops her head from the back door and says how are you
doing my little chicade. The only thing not ok is that
Misses G dosnt want to share me with the kids. I have new
frends now in the forth grade. They like me and I go to
there houses some times but they never come to mine.
When they come down and ask if I can come and play with

them she always says no. I don't realy mind. After all I am the prinses.

Frankie stayed with Misses and Mister G about one week when he was just born. Frankies 3 years older than me. It was before I was born and Misses G went over to our house and it was erly in the morning. My mom was having her morning cup of win and Misses G cheked on my brother and he had diper rash and she just took him home. Her house is spotless no junk or dirt any where in it not even the basmint. When I grow up my house is going to be spotless two. O and Misses G is a good Church lady. She prays every night. And now I pray every night two. O how I love Misses G. She always tells me Im byootiful never stupid and ugly. Shes my angel from heven. God sent her just for me.

Death in the Parsonage

"The way to be safe is never to be secure." ~~ Proverb

CHAPTER THIRTY-SEVEN

Tuesday, July 12

Isabelle lay on the quilt in the blue bedroom. After all, it had been her bedroom before and should be her bedroom now. She liked the pretty designs on the quilt and did not wear her shoes on the bed. Fannie Fay rested beside her, and Isabelle gave her tidbits of deli ham.

It was a relief to be out of the hidey-hole, but it was an unprecedented relief to be out of the hidey-hole and lying on the Scovill woman's bed, keeping track of the time with the Scovill woman's watch, playing with the Scovill woman's cat and enjoying slightly cooler weather. She had to admit the Scovill woman's house was peaceful.

All of that would make it only slightly harder for Isabelle to rid herself of the Scovill woman. Isabelle wanted only what was due her. With the breeze blowing through the sheer white curtains and the cat purring on the other pillow, Isabelle resumed her thinking project.

After the close call of Sunday with the man and the boy who had nearly found her in the bedroom, Isabelle had realized the house was hers every morning—with limitations. The Scovill woman never came back to the house in the morning, though she did sometimes come back for lunch and had come back once in the late afternoon before going out again.

The workers were a different matter. The man with the little boy had arrived several times with a key to let in men who checked various things or performed various repairs. They did not go upstairs, though they left quite a mess in the basement. The preponderance of problems obviously lay in the basement and kitchen. So, she concluded, if she stayed on the bedroom level—and that's where the bathroom was anyway—she was safe. And if the man and boy—or any of the workers, for that matter—made for the blue bedroom, she'd have plenty of time to smooth out the quilt and squeeze into the closet behind the clothes.

Isabelle's enjoyment of the Scovill woman's unintended hospitality extended to meals. Isabelle took just enough spaghetti or baked beans or cole slaw to assuage her hunger but not enough to cause suspicion.

Isabelle knew she was risking discovery, but the risks were calculated and she was skilled at calculating those risks. With no worries about the heat or food, she could complete Born Again in Biddlebourne with all her wits about her, which would yield the highest percentage of success.

She had completed her plan. It was printed in capital letters with black ink in her notebook. Although she had produced very little of it the first couple of days in her special hidey-hole—the place being extraordinarily hot— she had found the peace of the blue bedroom so remarkable that the plan had come together quickly after she'd been nearly scared to death by the man who looked at the bathroom pipes.

"That just goes to show you," Isabelle remarked to the cat, "what a difference a house makes." The cat gave her a skeptical look, and Isabelle explained, "When you have a happy place in which to work, the work becomes fun. It makes you glad to be alive. It gives you a purpose. It's worth the risk."

This did not come as news to Fannie Cat, who had never lived anywhere but happy places, and she yawned. But Isabelle went on, "I'm sorry you and the woman will have to go, but, you see, the house belongs to me. It was my parents' a long time ago. They paid off the mortgage. I don't know how they did it, what with Daddy drinking up so much of the money. I think maybe Grandma and Grandpa Pargeon helped them with money. Anyway, if I knew where Sissie and Frankie were, I'd share it with them, but only them. I can't share it with strangers."

Isabelle's head was on the notebook. Actually, her head was on the pillow, but the notebook was under the pillow, the better for her to absorb and remember the details of the plan.

She was practicing reciting to herself what she had to do. That way she would have total command of the plan, she would be highly unlikely to forget even the smallest nuance of it, and she would eventually be able to destroy the notebook page on which it was written so that no one could ever connect her to the outcome. She took a deep breath and began.

Plan name: Born Again in Biddlebourne.

Parts of plan: One, clear the way. Two, claim property. Three, renovate and move into house. Four, find Frankie and Sissie. Five, contact L.A. lawyer. Six, meet with Denver police.

Major elements of part one: Fix Isabelle Watkins. Fix Annie Scovill . . .

So relaxed was Isabelle that she fell asleep on the quilt on the bed in the blue bedroom. Fannie Fay fell asleep, too, and there slumbered the cat and the squatter until the preacher returned.

Death in the Parsonage

"It is not work that kills, but worry." ~~ Proverb

CHAPTER THIRTY-EIGHT

Wednesday, July 13

Fannie Fay awakened Annie by squawking into her right ear. The computer monitor next to Annie's head had defaulted to screen-saver mode. At first Annie thought the sounds and images belonged to her hideous dream—of a skeleton with its hands around her neck.

Annie checked the time. Eight-thirty. She was running late, very late. She had a lot to do that day and two hours fewer than usual in which to do it. She gave Fannie Fay her breakfast, showered and dressed, stuffed books and papers into her case and arrived at the church office at 9:32 a.m.

"Good morning, Pastor," Trudy said as Annie dragged through the outer office on the way to her own. "I sorted yesterday's mail and put your messages in that basket by the door." She pointed to the square white receptacle she had nailed to the doorframe.

"Thanks" was all Annie could utter as she turned on her computer and got ready to work. Her skull ached for want of sleep. Her eyes burned. Her hair hung damp and stringy from the shower. She had not eaten breakfast and had forgotten to bring lunch. She had skipped her morning devotions, newspapers, walk and letter to G.P. This was not going to be her best sermon.

Annie was grateful Trudy was able to handle the morning's callers, and by the time she stepped away from her sermon outline at 11:05 there were seven blue message slips waiting for her in her new message basket.

Trudy eyed the pastor nervously. Annie was not too tired to realize that Monday evening's meeting with Trudy and her mother had placed their relationship on a different footing from that of secretary and supervisor. Now Annie knew some of the most intimate details of Trudy's life, and Trudy's demeanor told her she was unsure what that meant for her office role.

"Trudy, I very much appreciate your dealing with all the calls this morning," Annie said. "I guess I am jammed today on my work."

"You're welcome," Trudy said. "I don't know what to say about the other night . . . ."

"There's no need to say anything," Annie responded. "What we discussed is confidential, and we won't talk about those matters here unless you want to."

"But are you disappointed in me?" Trudy asked. The frightened little girl was speaking for the troubled teenager. Annie wanted to hug her and and soothe her. But such actions would constitute unprofessional behavior, so Annie said, "Trudy, I think you acted with great courage and responsibility in telling your mother about your relationship with Carl. It isn't too late for you to change the nature of your friendship with him—or your friendship with your mother."

"I know. I'm trying," Trudy said.

"Good. I know," Annie said. "And on another subject, I think you have the stuff to make a top-notch secretary. I hope what you learn on the job here will help you one day in your career."

"I want to be a teacher," Trudy said, looking at her desk blotter.

"You will make a wonderful teacher," Annie said. "Speaking of teaching, Marilyn will be here today at two-thirty to go over some things with you."

"Great! I want to learn."

"I know that. Marilyn will help us a lot. For now, I need to get back to the sermon. I'll be in my office most of the afternoon."

"Okay."

Annie bent again over her commentaries and notes. But soon Trudy knocked and said, "Pastor, it's the technician calling from the parsonage. Can you take the call?"

The technician had news and a question. A pipe had burst when he turned the water back on after the washer installation. What did Annie want to do with her belongings that had gotten wet?

"Where did the pipe break?" she asked.

"Behind the sink in the bathroom," he said. Hermie the Handyman and Mr. Gideon Pugh had been suspicious of that very pipe, and Hermie had been to the house Sunday to determine what parts were needed to replace it.

"Is the bathroom flooded?"

"Well, it was, but I found a mop and got most of the water off the floor."

"Is that the only area that was damaged?"

"I put the bath mat and the hamper in the tub. But I didn't check the other side of the wall. What's back there?"

"That's a bedroom closet," Annie said, thinking instantly and fearfully of the bone bag she had recently placed there.

"I'll go check it for damage," he said.

"No!" Annie shouted. "I mean, I'll be right over. I should make a report to the trustees as soon as possible."

In only eight minutes Annie raced back to the parsonage and ran up to the USA Room. She was more than shocked—she was aghast—to find a stranger standing at the bedroom window.

"Oh, hi," the woman said. "You must be Pastor Scovill."

Annie gulped air and swallowed spit. *How in the world? Who was this?* She made her face smile. She put a hand on her chest and said, "Whew, I shouldn't take those stairs at a run. Yes, I'm Annie Scovill, but who are you?"

The woman gestured toward the window and said, "I'm just here to measure for the new drapes." She wrote something in a notebook and snapped it shut. "That will do it. Thanks very much."

Before Annie could move or speak again, the woman was out the door, with Fannie Fay at her heels.

What's happening? The trustees haven't said a word about new drapes. Anyway, the Ladies Aid Society would make them. How did that woman get in here? She didn't tell me her name . . . or the name of her company . . . or leave a card.

Annie sat on the rocker to calm her nerves but quickly remembered she had to rescue the bones from the closet. She opened the door to paw past the clothing and boxes. She saw that a little water had seeped through the wall and that the closet would have to dry out. But there was no major damage to the closet and certainly none to the bone bag that she could see.

Still, it had been a close call. Custody of human remains was not to be taken lightly, Annie reminded herself as she returned to the rocking chair to decide where to put the bones. She had to think quickly because the technician was downstairs, eager to write *installation completed* on his work order and get to his next appointment.

Annie chose the one level of the house where there was no plumbing. She climbed to the third floor, keeping her head low as she reached the top of the stairs in the event birds, wasps or any other creatures mistook her for a pecking post. She stashed the bone bag in the same storage area from which she had retrieved the little green diary and said a satisfied "There" before hurrying downstairs.

The installer, whom Annie had barely kept from following her into the bedroom to check the closet, was finishing his work in the basement. "I'm real sorry, ma'am," he said. "This kind of thing sometimes happens in these older houses." He looked with raw disdain at the old pipes and wiring in the shallow draft of the ceiling.

"If I were you," he continued, "I'd get new plumbing right away before any more pipes bust."

"I'll certainly take that under advisement," she said. Annie was exhausted, hungry and anxious. She was more than curious about the "drapery measuring." She needed answers, the sooner the better.

"The company can't be responsible for the water damage since it was caused by the existing plumbing," he went on, clearly bent on removing himself and his employer from liability.

"Of course, of course," she agreed, willing to promise anything if only he would leave.

"Okay, then, sign here," he allowed finally. "If I can use your phone, I'll just call the dispatcher and let him know I'm on my way to the next job right after lunch. This one took much longer than I expected," he said with one last dollop of repressed indignation at the behavior of the parsonage plumbing.

"Oh, yes, help yourself," she said, hoping desperately that he had shed all his disappointment. But no. He leaned on the new dryer and gazed disconsolately at Annie.

"Would you like a sandwich and a can of root beer—to go?" she asked, at last sensing his intention.

"Well, now, I wouldn't want to put you out any, but I did miss my lunch hour."

"No trouble at all," she said. They went up the kitchen, where Annie, with great speed, prepared two sandwiches. Ben, which he said was his name as she slapped turkey onto rye, vanished as soon as his lunch was in hand.

Annie felt sick from strain and sleeplessness. She called Trudy and said she would be out of the office the rest of the afternoon. Trudy was organizing her desk to impress Marilyn and sounded relieved that Annie would be absent as they worked.

Annie made a salad of romaine lettuce and tomato, afterward sitting at the kitchen table with her rabbit lunch and a large mug of black coffee. The house was warm but not miserably so, and she managed to relax a little in spite of her fears and fatigue.

Her gaze drifted to a stack of dish towels on the table. She took the towels, intending to put them in a drawer, and noticed the little green diary under the pile. When had she left it there? She couldn't remember.

Annie absentmindedly picked up the diary and riffled its bird-pecked pages, wondering again how it had ended up in an abandoned end table in an abandoned attic. She turned to the back inside cover and saw, in the sunshine streaming through the window, a sentence she had not previously noticed. *This is the story of B.P.—for my eyes only.*

Annie smiled at the secrecy that had attended the writer's words. She looked again to make sure she'd seen the initials correctly. Yes, she was right. She wondered where B.P. was now. Whoever and wherever she was, her *P* likely stood for *Pargeon*, the name of the family who lived last in the house.

She flipped to her bookmark and began reading another chapter from the life of an abused and desperately lonely child. Despite the coffee and the intensity of B.P.'s entries, she fought drowsiness.

Annie was awakened by the phone, her head on the table where it had dropped as she read the diary. She answered with a cloudy "Hullo."

The woman said, "What's wrong with you? You don't sound normal."

"Who's calling, please?" Annie responded.

"It's your sister, Chloe, you dummy," the woman said. "You sound like you have a cold."

"Not a cold. I was napping."

"What!?"

"Napping."

"I have never, in all my life, seen you napping. Are you sick?"

"No, just tired."

"What are you so tired from?"

"Research."

"What kind of research?"

"Research into the burial of human remains."

"That's why I'm calling. You have me worried. Which is causing stress lines on my forehead. I suppose you have not yet reported the bones to the sheriff, or the constable or whoever is in charge of law enforcement in the country."

"No, but I found out some things."

"Like what?"

"Like a death certificate, or something similar, has to be filed for every death in West Virginia."

"Okay. That makes sense. What else?"

"Every death has to be reported to a registrar of vital statistics for that county."

"What county are you in?"

"Skyler."

"Annie, you are exasperating me. I can feel the grooves growing in my forehead as we speak. I think we both know that a death certificate has to be issued and a death reported to somebody at some office. I can't wait to hear how you will use that information to avoid reporting the bones."

"You are so suspicious. I don't want to *avoid* reporting the bones. I just want to *delay* reporting the bones."

"Until G.P. comes home, right?"

"Exactly. Meanwhile, I can do a little more digging— ha ha, get it?—and try to come up with the cause of death."

"You can't handle this by yourself, Annie. It's time-consuming. It's probably illegal. It might even be dangerous. And you are destroying my concentration!"

"What do you mean by *dangerous*?"

"I can't believe how naïve you are. The body may have resulted from a murder, for all you know."

"And I can't believe how dramatic you are. I'm sure there is some perfectly natural explanation for the bones. And I intend to find it.

"Don't say I didn't warn you."

~~0~~

Dear Diary,
Another time mommy went to the hospital rite after she tried to deliver puppies in the middle of the nite only there werent any puppies. I was sleeping in Sissies bed becaws I peed in my bed again and dint want to tell mommy. Well mommy came in the room and turned on the lite. I woke up out of a ded sleep so did Sissie. Sissie said what the hecks going on mom. Mommy was so drunk she coodnt stand up. Mommy grabbed the shaneel bed spread off

Sissies bed and spred it on the floor. Sissie said o no mom not again. Mommy sat down on the floor next to the bed spred and said there now lady lets have those puppies every things going to be all rite. I looked at Sissie and Sissie wispered to me moms delivering puppies. I wispered back there aren't any puppies are you blind. Sissie said shh. So Mommy handed one puppie to me and another one to Sissie only there werent any puppies. Thats all rite lady thats all rite she kept saying. We use to have a dog named lady. I dont know what ever hapned to lady becaws she dis appered a couple summers ago when she was pregnint. Rub the puppies rub them mommy yelled so me and Sissie pretended to rub the puppies. Frankie woke up from all the noise and came in the bedroom and had a fit. He tried to make mommy stop delivering the puppies but Sissie said shut up and go along with her. But Frankie called some body and they came to take mommy to the hospital. Funny I never been to the hospital not even to a doctor. I dont hardly ever get sick and if I get sick I go see Misses G or Misses P.

Death in the Parsonage

"The birth of what's dead is the birth of what's living."
~~ Arlo Guthrie

CHAPTER THIRTY-NINE

Old Isabelle was dying.

She had begun expiring an hour ago when she calmly extricated herself from a difficult situation with the Scovill woman. How fitting, new Isabelle thought, that her rebirth had begun in the very home that she had occupied in her former life.

Crouching among the thorny shrubs in the woods behind the parsonage, Isabelle exulted not only upon being reborn but also upon being reborn so naturally, so efficiently that is seemed . . . predestined. Yes, it was definitely predestined, a mixed blessing of such magnitude that it threw new light on her tortured past.

It was the old Isabelle who had suffered in the house; the new Isabelle would thrive there. The old Isabelle had run away; the new Isabelle had returned. The old Isabelle had feared the entire world; the new Isabelle feared nothing, not even the Scovill woman who had taken over her house. The old Isabelle was a person to whom bad things happened; the new Isabelle was a person who made things happen.

It had all happened, she thought joyfully, in one surprising instant. One moment she was quaking in fear of being found out. The next moment she was confidently facing the Scovill woman. It proved that—no matter what her parents had insisted years earlier—she was smart, resourceful, competent and as good as anyone else.

It didn't matter that she must now wait until nightfall to go back inside. She stacked chunks of moss on a low log and sat to make herself a ball of nature while she tarried and considered.

She reviewed the mixed blessing of the hidey-hole. For seven days and eight nights she had lasted in the plywood retreat without her presence once being detected by the droves of maintenance, repair and installation people who tramped above and below.

However, the plywood box no longer met her needs. She had outgrown all of it—the size of it, the closeness of it, the darkness of it, the unrelenting loneliness of it. Soon she would forever give up her most special hiding place, but she would not cry as she had those many years ago.

When the Scovill woman's watch showed it was midnight, Isabelle used the moonlight to creep back into the parsonage. She dreamed untroubled dreams and awakened at nine o'clock. At the refrigerator she ate meatballs with the cat. Upstairs she helped herself to a mirror from the Scovill woman's bathroom vanity and a pair of deep-red sandals from her bedroom closet.

A faint breeze bearing the scent of alfalfa met the new Isabelle when she walked out the front door of 1010 Greenbriar Road.

"Though a lie be swift, the truth overtakes it." ~~
Proverb

CHAPTER FORTY

Thursday, July 14

E-mail to G.P. 1:15 a.m.

Hi, Honey! Thanks for your e-mails. I'm not deleting them—I've been reading them over and over again. It was wonderful to hear your voice last week. I had SUCH a busy day! I took that coal to Mrs. Gatwick. And I ran your truck. And I ordered the envelope labels for both of us. And you were SOOO right about the crown molding! I saw a book in Spartansville and have since repented of any desire to mold crowns!

Whew! Lots of things are going on at the church. The only thing in summer recess is the Youth Bible Quiz Team. The building project is barreling ahead. I've talked with one of the two potential architects. The trustees have narrowed their selection to two firms and want me to recommend the "winner." Both appear to be solid with lots of experience. One of them has done more church construction, so I think that one will be my choice.

Marilyn Caperton sends her regards, as do Burl Stout and your parents (who assure me that they are NOT watching CNN 24/7). I hope they can come to dinner on the 29th. I want to make up for missing dinner over there last week. I signed up to make baked goods for the Rooster Rodeo on the 30th, so I'll make enough for the dinner, too.

You will get a kick out of the Rooster Rodeo next year. As far as I can tell it's a cross between a carnival, a county fair and a tractor pull. Everybody around here is excited about it. I guess I am, too. I'll send you a box of the more sturdy delicacies from the Rooster Rodeo. I hope they arrive in edible condition!

I went shopping for the king mattress and twin box springs. Found a good sale. They will be delivered Friday. I ordered a very-firm mattress—same as our last one. If you don't want very-firm, let me know right away, okay? I can call the delivery number and have them change the mattress if necessary.

The laundry appliances are installed in the basement. Yeah! There was a minor problem with the installation, but everything's okay.

Marilyn is working with Trudy (the church secretary) to bring her up to speed at the office.

I am finished prepping my Sunday sermon and am glad to have it ready.

Daniella is driving Chloe and Bob crazy trying to figure out what kind of bone she dug up at the La Brea Tar Pits in California. That's where Daniella and Bob were while Chloe was here helping me with the house.

Well, I should go check on Fannie Fay. I'm okay. Everything is okay. Don't worry. See you in 78 days! I love you!!! Hugs & kisses, Annie Ido.

Annie hit the send button, shut off the computer, picked up the little green diary from the kitchen table and headed upstairs. She fast-tracked her preparations for bed and was stretched out in one of G.P.s T-shirts on the guest mattress by 2 a.m., with a fan throwing a breeze in her direction and Fannie Fay gazing at her from the windowsill. Before turning the light out, she forced herself to read another entry in the life of "B.P.," not realizing that its contents, coupled with repeated nights of no sleep or little sleep, would set her up for yet another nightmare peopled by strange beings and troubled by even stranger doings.

Annie was resting on a park bench, reading a newspaper and drinking from a cup. G.P. was running nearby on the grass with a kite, trying to get it to catch a wind gust and go aloft. The day was warm and breezy, but Annie was aware of impending rain. The undersides of the tree leaves were turning up, making silver-green dots in the moody sky. G.P. asked Annie if she wanted to go home, but she didn't want to stop what she was doing. She insisted on reading the newspaper even as G.P. packed up. She would not heed his pleas to run with him to the car. The rain began coming down, and she sat on the bench, soon soaked to the skin. Children pointed at her and laughed as they ran past Annie to shelter. They were all wearing pajamas. Still she sat glued to the bench. A group of workers arrived and, despite the rain, set up a backhoe and unpacked tools. They began hammering and drilling and digging and dumping dirt into containers. G. P. was honking the car horn furiously, but Annie did not get up from the bench. The work crew pointed the backhoe toward the bench and scooped her and the bench up together in one swift mouthful of the claw. She couldn't breathe because of the dirt. She was dragged along with her feet dangling. She lost sight of the sky. She could no longer hear the car horn. Even the children's taunts faded away.

Annie awakened drenched in sweat. Disoriented, she spent several agonizing moments thinking the backhoe was in the house—in the attic above her—before she got command of her senses and realized she had been dreaming.

Fannie Fay, in one of those eerie behaviors that pets exhibit when their world tilts, also seemed spooked. She began mewling on her windowsill, then left the sill and went to the door, all of which Annie saw by the pale light of the half moon. Fannie Fay soon stopped squealing, however, and began hissing. In full and sibilant voice, Fannie Fay fled down the stairs.

"No, Fannie Fay. Come here," Annie called. But Fannie Fay, who had never before rejected a spot on a bed, ignored Annie and continued carrying on so loudly that Annie got out of bed and went to fetch her.

"What's wrong?" Annie asked. Fannie Fay paced in front of the pantry door. Annie opened the pantry door. Fannie Fay pawed at the floor and screeched. Annie was perplexed because Fannie Fay usually reserved this sort of behavior for the vet who inoculated her.

Annie saw what had grabbed Fannie Fay's attention. She bent and picked up a foil packet of tuna that had fallen to the floor. "Oh, all right. I am such a pushover," she said. Annie opened the pouch and dumped it into Fannie Fay's bowl. Fannie Fay looked pleadingly at Annie until the fishy aroma hit her nostrils. She could not resist and fell to the food with abandon.

Annie waited while Fannie Fay finished the tuna. She carried the cat back upstairs and dropped her gently on the pillow beside her own. This was a location to which Fannie Cat was quite partial. However, the cat arched her back, walked haughtily across Annie's midsection and returned to the bedroom door. She balled herself up and dropped to the floor. And that was that.

"Fine, then," Annie said. It was shortly after five in the morning. Dreading what she might dream if she slept again, she left her bed, performed the morning routine that always before had brought her comfort and headed to the church.

~~0~~

Dear Diary,
Last week me and Frankie were staying with grandma,
daddys mother. Frankie was standing at the bottom of the
steps looking at himself in the merer that was on the closet
door. He said to grandma dont I look nice and she said no
your ugly and stupid and youll never be handsum like your
brother. I think I know now why daddys always saying
whose Frankie look like for gods sake Vickie June whose
he look like. I think me and Frankie belong to the other
man and Sissie and our older brother belong to daddy.
Our older brother stays with grandma becaws she loves
him and dosnt love me and Frankie. Well Frankie called
grandma bad names when she said that mean stuff to him
and he went out and got in her car. I ran out to the porch
and she came right after Frankie and stuck her arm in the
car window with the enjine going. Frankie rolled up the
window on her arm and draged her to the end of the drive
way. Then he unrolled the window and let her lose and
drove away. She never liked Frankie but I think she likes
me becaws she dosnt know that daddys not my daddy.

Death in the Parsonage

"You can't put new wine into old bottles." ~~ Proverb

CHAPTER FORTY-ONE

Grable Wade had met a thousand Isabelles. Each wanted a shiny little car, but Grable didn't go near the key hooks until he asked that most crucial question.

"How would you be paying, Miss . . .Miss . . .?"

"Watkins. Isabelle Watkins. I'll pay cash if you have what I want. And your name?"

"Grable Wade, ma'am, and I'm pleased to assist you. Our featured vehicle today is the taupe-colored Taurus. See it over there, the one with the big star on the windshield, next to the red truck?" He jingled a sparkly key ring in front of Isabelle.

"No, thanks. I'll test-drive the truck first and that red SUV parked beside the service door second."

Grable, hungry for the $500 bonus that would go to the seller of the Taurus, said, "The little tan number parks like a dream . . . and it's easy for little ladies to handle."

"The truck keys, please," Isabelle said.

"Of course, ma'am. But I'm afraid the SUV is being driven this week by the service manager."

"Good. You can get the keys from him while I take the truck out."

Less than an hour later Isabelle backed onto State Route 2 in a brilliant-red heavy-duty truck with four-wheel drive. In her purse were the title to the truck and a coupon for $50 in gas or services from Ricky's Shell. She drove to Ricky's, where she demanded that Ricky himself adjust the clutch and where she pumped $43 in gas and bagged $7 in Snickers and Cokes.

Her next destination was the row of boutiques on the south side of Spartansville where her best-dressed classmates had shopped years earlier. Pleased to find the shops augmented by new establishments catering to petite women, she stopped at every store. She moved through the aisles of merchandise, first calling upon salesladies to carry her choices to the dressing rooms and later requiring them to fetch different sizes and colors while she rested in the little leather chairs.

The salesladies, recognizing an authentic spree, offered shades to please Isabelle's eye and textures to please her touch. She responded graciously, choosing only what enhanced her small, neat frame and deftly refusing those items that did not. Thusly Isabelle outfitted herself in the finest slacks, jeans, jackets, blouses, skirts, dresses, accessories, hosiery and undergarments—*more than* five of every kind.

Isabelle paid cash at each store, thanked each phalanx of salesladies for their assistance and tidily stacked her purchases in the cab of her truck until there was no room for anything else in the truck but herself.

Tired, hungry and happy, Isabelle drove to the Blue Bird Restaurant and ordered meatloaf, mac and cheese, chunky applesauce, biscuits and butterscotch pie. She drank grape soda pop—the Blue Bird was the only Nehi source in the area—and ordered chocolate cake to go.

At the Twilight Motel she slept like the newborn that she was.

"Calamity is the touchstone of a brave mind." ~~
Proverb

CHAPTER FORTY-TWO

Annie tried. Really. When she called G.P.'s parents with her dinner invitation, she tried to spill her story to Dad Scovill. He was a man of science. He loved her. He treated her as if she were his own daughter.

However, the eminent Dr. Parker Scovill was also a fastidious practitioner of the arcane art of Going By The Book. Having served twenty-three years as chief pathologist at Spartansville Unified Memorial Hospital, he knew every federal, state and county law, guideline, suggestion and possibility regarding the disposition of human remains.

Of course, Annie admitted to herself that the task of working out the provenance of the bones was beyond her experience. Dad Scovill could tell her exactly how to determine the age and gender of the bones and probably a good deal more. However, she fretted, he was more likely to send her posthaste to the nearest law enforcers.

And, she further reasoned, even if she managed to fabricate a story that made the whole situation seem plausible but hypothetical, he would be suspicious. He would insist upon coming to the house. She would be forced to empty the bone bag in his presence, possibly upon the dining table, aaugh, and he would pause only long enough to lecture her sternly before telephoning township, county and state officials. He would turn her over to the merciless grasp of law enforcement officers, who would whisk her away from the parsonage to an "interview room." Ha! She was not a neophyte. This interview room would be a minimally disguised holding cell. Her name would be placed on a police report. A *Sentinel* reporter would pick up the report from the police blotter. Her name and mug would appear in the newspaper, probably on page one, and anybody and everybody would talk about her and the bones to anybody and everybody else, including some cousin or neighbor or high school classmate who would, in turn, mention the matter to a sister-in-law or great-nephew, who would just happen to be serving in G.P.'s unit, and she would have a puzzled, worried, distressed husband in no time.

And if the ubiquitous great-nephews of the world did not snitch her out to G.P., of course Parker or Mary Jo Scovill would do so themselves. G.P.'s parents believed in writing "the little details of everyday life" in their letters to G.P. They didn't do e-mail, of course, having worked in that unenlightened cusp of time between Univax and Pentium.

To Annie's possible credit, she did practice telling Dad Scovill some version of the actual truth about the bones. She practiced the words to herself several times, each time adding what she considered to be clever embellishments as to why G.P. did not need to know about the bones.

For instance, "Hi, Dad, I was sweeping up the basement floor and found some bones that the cat dragged in. I was just thinking that I would practice my osteology skills and try to figure out how old these bones are. G.P. will be so surprised when I tell him Fannie Fay's latest escapade. Where would I find such a reference book?"

Or, "Hi, Dad. I was reading up on archeology digs in the Holy Land, and I sure would like to know more about how they determine the age and sex of human bones. Where would I look up that kind of thing?"

In the end, she demonstrated her ingenuity by saying, "Well, Dad, it sure will be good to see you and Mom. We'll have burgers, baked bones, cole slaw and peach pie. How's that?"

He said, "Pretty good, except hold the baked bones. Your mother-in-law's already got me on calcium supplements."

"Oh," she said weakly, "Oh, ha, ha, ha. I meant baked beans. Gotta go. See you soon."

Annie went over material for Sunday's worship bulletin, handled a couple of reports, wrote notes to worship visitors and had generally cleared her in-basket of its administrative chores by the time Trudy arrived, on time.

"How did it go with Marilyn?" she inquired.

"She's awesome," Trudy said.

Annie laughed and said, "You are a believer, too, then?"

"She showed me how to change an address in all the computer files by just making the correction in one place, and how to use the fax machine, and where to go for the best deals on office supplies, and . . . ."

"She is a marvel," Annie allowed. "I'm very pleased that you apparently have learned so many useful things so quickly. Is Marilyn coming back this week?"

"Yes, ma'am, on Friday. We're going to go to lunch, I mean if that's all right with you."

"Of course. It's my day off, but it won't hurt a thing for you to let the machine take messages while you're out."

"We're going to that little place on Doud Street. We're going to have scones."

"Wonderful!" Annie exclaimed. "Do you need anything before I leave on some errands?"

"No, I don't think so. Is it okay if I call you on your cell phone if anything comes up?"

"Of course."

"Okay. I have to get to work," Trudy said. "I'm updating the member addresses for a new directory. Marilyn showed me how."

"Great," Annie said. Hallelujah, she thought.

Annie picked up her purse and organizer and went to her car, which had not yet lost its overnight coat of dew. She had left a window open to keep the interior from combusting. That's how she knew even before opening the door that she had received another unwanted visit.

A gagging reek swelled from the interior of the venerable Volvo. From a distance of four or five feet, Annie peered inside. There on the front seats, the front floorboards, the dashboard, the center console and on the steering wheel, lay dozens of dead chickens. Their heads hung limply and awkwardly from stiff bodies, and their feathers were congealed and yellowed, as if they had been glued on with ancient mucilage. The chickens surely were long dead, for they stank abominably, worse than anything Annie had ever before smelled, worse than the nasty delivery on her first day in Biddlebourne and much worse than the vilest thing she had ever dissected with the help of Huey Householder in high school biology. They stank so bad that she threw up.

"Now, now, Pastor Ma'am, don't you worry," Ma Pugh said, patting first Annie's back and then her hand. She had left a pile of quilt pieces unsewn in her craft room in order to pick Annie up at the Biddlebourne police station, where Annie had made her report.

"I'm all right now, Ma. I was just surprised."

"I bet you were. Me and Pa were, too. We just can't figure out who's doing these things. Never seen anything like it before."

Then, with a meaningful look, Ma Pugh added, "Me and Pa don't think you're safe at the parsonage."

"Because of a few dead chickens?"

"Honey, somebody don't like you. It's not kids. At least I don't think it's kids. That leaves grownups. Grownups have got cars and—I hate to say it—weapons and such, and if they can sneak into your car, they can sneak into your house."

"I hardly think so," Annie said. "There are good locks on the doors."

"But I know you been sleepin' with the windows open until the air conditionin' is put in," Ma said.

"Yes, that's true, but if I run away, whoever's doing these things will think they've cornered me. That wouldn't be good for the church or for me."

Then Ma had another thought. "You got another car to drive?"

"I have my husband's pickup truck."

"Well, then, you're all set until you get your car back," she said.

"I suppose so," Annie said.

"Don't like to drive the truck, hey?" she said knowingly.

"Oh no, it's not that. I drive it every other day to keep the battery charged while G.P. is away. It's just that . . ."

Ma Pugh looked at Annie expectantly and said, "Oh, I see. You don't get near the gas mileage on the truck as on the car."

"Well, Ma," Annie said, "I suppose the gas mileage is similar in the two vehicles. But G.P., uh, he thinks of the truck as a special possession."

"He don't want you to drive it," Ma Pugh said flatly.

"Oh, of course he doesn't mind my driving it. He certainly wouldn't want me to be without transportation. But he says I don't shift the gears right. He says I should double-clutch. I have never gotten the hang of double-clutching. And once when I was driving it, I had a little accident and one of the taillights got broken. He tried not to make a big deal of it, but he was quite upset."

"I see, I see," Ma Pugh said. Annie figured that with several sons and many grandsons, she probably did understand the bond between a man and his machine.

"I think I have an idea," Ma Pugh said. "You got that fancy travel phone of yours on you?"

"Yes, right here." Annie reached for her cell phone.

Before Annie knew what Ma Pugh was doing and could stop her from doing it, the woman had called Hermie the Handyman and arranged for the pastor to drive his old school bus while her car was being checked out and cleaned up. It turned out that the Hooblers had a Ford van and wouldn't mind making do with it for a while, especially since the kids were on vacation from baseball, soccer and basketball.

"Gears in that old thing is loose as a goose," proclaimed Ma Pugh, proud of her quick-thinking arrangement. "You won't have to double-clutch, might not even have to clutch at all," she opined.

"How can I ever thank you?" said her lips. "Oh, help me, Lord," said her heart.

"Pshaw, it's nothing. Don't even think about it," she said. "Now that's figured out, let's talk a little bit about those dead chickens. You should have called me soon's you seen 'em," she scolded.

"You're right. I wasn't thinking clearly."

"Well, I'd a been addlepated myself if it'd happened to me. But now what are the police gonna do?"

"They've impounded the car to go over it for evidence. Fingerprints, that kind of thing."

"They got any idea who would do such a thing?"

"Not so far as I know," Annie said, "although they mentioned that some people named Pinckney are missing a couple dozen chickens."

Ma Pugh's face clouded. "Hm. Did they figure the chickens and the cat parts and the letter is all tied up together somehow?"

"The sergeant said he was going to read the report that the officers made Monday."

"Uh-huh. Now listen, Pastor, like I was sayin' before, I'm surer than ever you ought to come stay with me and Pa a while. It's our bounden duty to look after you, especially as the mister's away and you got no family 'tall 'round here.

"I mean, land sakes, you all alone over at that parsonage and with all that construction going on over there. Me and Pa's thinking' you ought to come and stay with us a while."

"Oh no, I couldn't," Annie said. A spear of panic stabbed her chest.

"Wouldn't be a bit of trouble," she said. "You could have Junie's old room."

"Oh no, I really couldn't," Annie repeated. "I have my own fix-up projects going on at the house, and I have Fannie Fay, and she doesn't change locations well, and all my clothes and shoes and everything are at the house."

"Wouldn't take Pa and Hermie half an hour to bring over what you need, and that cat o' yours will get along just fine with Mister Whiskers."

"I'll think about it, okay?" Annie said. The panic inside her was rising to her throat. She was about to choke. "Well, I've got to get on the road," she said, trying to close the conversation. "Will you drive me over to the Hooblers?"

"Be glad to. Then I'll come back here and have a little talk with the sergeant. Lessee, that'd be Sergeant Boo Dillon, I think."

"Yes. Do you know every member of the police department?"

"Oh, I doubt it. But Boo used to play basketball in the back yard with our second boy. Harry. Harry lives over in Ohio now. Got a big house and all."

"Oh . . . wonderful."

Hermie met them in the yard and solemnly handed over the bus keys.

"I'm real sorry about that chicken mess," he offered.

"Oh, that's all right. Just a prank," Annie said unsteadily.

"I don't think so," Ma Pugh said, continuing, "Hermie, your insurance will cover the pastor, right?"

"Sure will. Insurance card's in the box beside the driver's seat."

"The bus isn't all filled up with junk, is it?" she asked, suddenly suspicious.

"Took it all out soon's you called," he said.

"Well, then, Pastor Ma'am, you're all set to go," Ma Pugh said.

"What kind of gas does it take?" Annie asked.

"Plain old regular," Hermie said. "This kind o' bus, it's not finicky."

"I can't thank you enough, Hermie. I'll get it back to you as soon as humanly possible." She meant that. She really did.

"No hurry. You just use it as long as you need it," Hermie said.

Hermie instructed her on the operation of the bus, which wasn't much different from G.P.'s truck, only bigger—much bigger—and when she got in and closed the door with the hand crank, she felt only slightly sick.

Annie called Trudy on her cell phone as she drove to Vinny's All-American Hardware. No emergencies at the church. Good. At Vinny's she purchased shims for the bookcases, more bug spray for the wasps, a bigger plunger for the toilet and digging implements.

The hospitable proprietor himself rang up her purchases, for which business he thanked her profusely and quizzed her roundly. "Why do you need a pickax?"

"Vinny, I live in a house that has some rather unusual structural problems."

"Pastor, we trustees ought to be taking care of all that. No need for you to trouble your pretty little head."

Annie smiled despite her disgust at his sexist flattery and said, "Of course the trustees are working very hard, but I feel it is my responsibility to do all I can, too."

He pointed to the pickax on the counter and said, "So I see. Digging a new sewer line, are you?" Perhaps his question was playful, but his tone was not.

"No, but there are several placements that need dislodged," she said as she rummaged for her billfold.

He squinted as if trying to picture placements that might need dislodging. She pulled out a wad of bills and said, "I have exact cash. That's sixty-two dollars and eighteen cents, right?"

He glanced at the faded display window of the old cash register and said, "Yes, ma'am, but the church ought to pay for the tools if they're needed for the parsonage."

"Well, G.P. likes to buy his own tools—he's kind of funny that way."

"That right?"

"Thank you very much," she said. "I don't need a bag. Have a good day, Vinny." She dropped the spray and shims into her purse and tucked the plunger under her left arm and the pickax under her right arm.

"What'd you say you needed that pickax for?" he repeated. But by then Annie was far enough away to pretend she hadn't heard the question.

As Annie placed her purchases on the first row of seats in the old bus, she congratulated herself on deflecting Vinny's curiosity even as she realized she had left her sales slip on the counter. She started the engine and sped away.

She went to the Biddlebourne branch of the Skyler County Library, looked through the electronic card catalog and left with a well-used copy of *Human Osteology: A Clinical Guide.* Annie returned to the church office, met with a young couple for prenuptial counseling, made telephone calls and answered questions from Trudy and visitors. On the outside she was calm and efficient. But her insides twisted like a bride's handkerchief.

"I'm leaving now," Trudy said a little after four.

"Okay," Annie said. "See you tomorrow."

"Before I go, here's a message I took while you were over at the . . . police station," she said, handing Annie a blue slip with a big *G* on it.

"That's okay, Trudy. We can talk about the police station. It was just a silly kid's stunt."

"That's not what I heard," she said.

"What did you hear?"

"Oh, not much, Pastor Annie. Hermie told Carl he was lending you Old Yeller—that's what he calls that rattletrap of a bus—and Carl called me up about some things, and he just said you'd be driving Old Yeller for a while, that's all."

That wasn't all. Annie knew it. But she needed to focus on other things at the moment. "What about the message?" she asked.

"Some woman called. I can't exactly remember her name." Trudy wore a guilty blush.

"That's okay, Trudy. Did she leave a message?"

"She said her name was Glorious or something like that," she said.

"I think I know who it was. The message?"

"She just said you know her and please to call her."

"I will do that."

"Do you want me to get her on the phone for you?"

"I can do it. You've put in a good day already. Thanks a lot."

"You're welcome."

Annie called Gloriana. "How about dinner?"

"That would be great," Gloriana responded. "As a matter of fact, I have a whole chicken thawing out. It was in the freezer only eight or nine months."

"Sorry, Glori, but I can't do chicken today. I'll bring some takeout ribs if that's okay with you."

~~0~~

Dear Diary,
My grand father died last week. Had a bad heart. And gaul blatter trouble. I never saw him much because my older brother and sister lived with those grandparents and mommy and daddy don't take us there. Well, hardly ever. The phone rang and I heard daddy start cussing and yelling oh my god oh my god. Mommy started screaming. I don't know why mommy started screaming because my dads parents never got along with mommy. Anyway it seems grand pa died in his bed with grand ma right there beside him! The funeral was Saturday. Very sad. After the funeral we all went to grand ma's house and the neighbors brought food and pop and cakes and cookies. I ate all I wanted and nobody stopped me. So did Frankie.

But Sissie only ate one sandwich and went upstairs. After we got home mommy told Frankie to go to grand mas house and get her caseroll dish because she forgot it there. This is so weerd. Grand ma lives a block from us. Frankie opened the front door and there standing on the steps going up was our grand father. Imagine. We just had his funeral and there he was. Another time at my grand parents Frankie was sleeping and something slowly pulled the blankets off him. No one was there when he woke up and looked around. Lots of things like that happen at grand mas house.

"Fate is nonawareness." ~~ Jan Kott

CHAPTER FORTY-THREE

Isabelle came out of the bank Thursday morning with a smile on her face and $1,500 in her purse, enough to rent and supply a nice studio apartment until she moved back to Greenbriar Road for good.

During a breakfast of waffles, bacon and coffee at the Snacknmore, Isabelle scanned the *Skyler County Sentinel* for apartments. She chose one close to the bakery, which was her favorite store in Biddlebourne, and went to make arrangements for the 2-rm 1st fl util furn vgc.

As custom demanded, the landlord begin by saying, "Your people from around here? I'm new here myself, but . . ."

"They used to be. My name is Isabelle Watkins. May I pay in cash, or do you prefer a check?"

"Uh, cash works."

"Fine. That's $250 for the first month, $250 for the last month and $100 for the cleaning deposit?" She handed the man a fistful of fifties, which he counted quickly. "Sorry, miss, I gotta check. Ya' know?"

"Perfectly all right. I'd like a receipt, please."

"Oh, yeah. You bet." He handed her a pale yellow half-page and two keys.

"I'll be moving in immediately," Isabelle said.

"Uh, you have a job around here?"

"I am currently self-employed. My work is quiet, and I do not drink or smoke."

"Oh. Okay."

"My clothing is in the truck. Do you mind helping me carry it in? I want to see about household items today."

"Well," he said, looking out the window at the gleaming truck and back at Isabelle in her designer jeans and coppery top. He also took in the expensive red leather sandals and genuine turquoise bracelet.

Isabelle took off her sunglasses, looked straight at him with her big, brown eyes and smiled.

"Glad to help," he said.

"One God, no more, but friends good store." ~~
Proverb

CHAPTER FORTY-FOUR

The ribs were wonderful, falling off the bones and dripping with sweet, tangy sauce. They ate on Gloriana's screened-in back porch.

"You are a nervous wreck," Gloriana said flatly after they had followed the ribs and corn with a pint apiece of fudge-mallow ice cream.

Gloriana and Annie had been in seminary together, had kept in touch wherever they were pastoring, and had weathered together many ups and downs of doctrine, debt and decision. Outside of family, they were each other's closest friends.

"Glori," Annie began.

"Chickens notwithstanding, you're worried about the bones."

"Yes."

"In your mind, you are weighing two important but competing ends."

"Yes."

"On the one hand, you want to turn those darned bones over to the right authorities and be done with it."

"Yes."

"But on the other hand, you fear that doing so could unleash a flood of notoriety, even scandal, which could tarnish the church's reputation, divert the energy of the church from the important business of expansion, and simultaneously induce great alarm and frustration in G.P. with regard to your well-being."

That was it in a nutshell. Annie said so.

Someone else might have lectured Annie on the inadequacies of her thinking, on how her actions could be construed as obstructing justice, on how her presumptions could be far off-base, on how the Biddlebourn congregation had sufficient steadiness to weather such difficulties, on how G.P. Scovill knew well that his wife's vocation held a wide variety of distressing elements, on how law enforcers had ways to handle the bones, on the fact that God would devise the best resolution to the situation if only Pastor Annie Scovill would leave everything in God's care.

But Gloriana was her best friend.

"What can I do to help?" she said.

Annie showed her what she had brought and told her what she wanted to do.

Gloriana threw her fudge-mallow carton into a trash can fifteen feet away, slapped the sides of her wheelchair with both hands and said, "I'm in."

"Thank you," Annie said, and they calmly regarded each other. It was one of those little moments in life they would remember long after the clock had ticked it away.

But the moment passed. "I have to stop at the hardware store on the way home. I'll see you around nine," Annie said.

"Okay."

"But before I go, I have a couple quick questions on a pastoral matter. Are you still a child advocate for the county court?"

"Yep. I keep an eye on a couple cases at a time and testify once in a while."

"I thought so. What makes child abuse happen?"

"Good heavens, there are a hundred things that can lead to child abuse. The books say that almost all parents who abuse their children were abused themselves in some way as a child."

"But things like drug addiction and alcoholism in the parent can also contribute to child abuse. That's still true, isn't it?"

"You know it is. Why are you asking these things?"

"I ran across some disturbing information recently. I'm not sure what it means, but I think I have a responsibility to follow through."

"In addition to everything else you are doing?"

"Yes, I guess so."

Gloriana nodded and paused a moment. Finally she asked, "Am I correct to think that you have mentioned none of these problems about bones and child abuse to Burl?"

"You are correct in thinking that."

"Annie, he's a good superintendent. He could help."

"Again, you are correct, but he's already talking about moving me out of the parsonage. It wouldn't take much for him to force a move to another house. I don't think I could do another move right now."

"I see your point. See you later."

~~0~~

Dear Diary,
Every weekend when the weather is nice daddy makes me and Frankie and Sissie pick dandylions out of the yard. We all sit on the ground with a spoon digging out the dandylions. Some times when he isn't looking we just

snap them off. Its the wrong thing to do becaws the
dandylions come back the next week and then hes really
mad becaws we cheated. Even if its 90 degrees outside us
kids are out there digging away at the dandylions. Daddy
does it becaws he wants to be the boss. He cant be
mommys boss she wont let him but were just kids and cant
stop him from bossing us. Also daddy dosnt want to be
blamed if things go wrong so he bosses us all the time so
things are right. But his idea of right isnt my idea of right.
Daddy dosnt like being blamed. Mommy blamed him when
my little brother Jeffie died. Jeffie was only 2 years old.
He had asma and daddy woodnt go and get his medicine
at the drug store he said Jeffie didn't need it and mommy
shood go her self if she wanted the medicine so dam bad.
But Jeffie died. Mommy called the big black funeral car
and it came but Jeffie died on the way to the hospital.
Mommy said daddy killed Jeffie but daddy said a very bad
word and went down to his room in the basement. The
doctor put mommy in the sickiatrick ward for three days
when Jeffie died becaws she said she wood kill herself. I
don't know if she reely tried to kill herself. She dint go to
Jeffies funeral. They put Jeffies coffin in the same big
black funeral car as he rode in to the hospital. I always
pull the dandylions when daddy says to even if I just snap
some of them off becaws I don't want daddy to let me die
if I ever get sick.

"Tell the truth/But tell it slant." ~~ Emily Dickinson

CHAPTER FORTY-FIVE

Isabelle enjoyed the Flix matinee and a late lunch of salmon and fresh fruit at the Belwix Department Store tearoom. She strolled through the store afterward, selecting items to be delivered to her new apartment. She went to Elderdon's and purchased tissue in designer boxes and to the Bow-Kay for a luxuriant philodendron in a gold pot. At the post office she picked up her mail.

Because Belwix did not carry cast-iron cookware and Isabelle preferred to cook steaks and chicken breasts on cast iron, she stopped at Vinny's All-American. She was checking the contents of her shopping cart against her list when she heard a familiar voice.

"Hello. Are you here to buy drapery hardware?"

Isabelle's heartbeat quickened, flashing heat to her chest and brow. She had only a split second to marshal her thoughts. Taking a deep breath and gripping the cart, she turned and said, "Why, Mrs. Scovill. It's good to see you!"

The woman smiled and looked at Isabelle with a question in her eyes.

Isabelle turned on the same smile she had given the landlord. The woman only continued gazing at her.

"What a coincidence to run into you," Isabelle said. "I *am* looking for curtain rods. Which do you like best, gold, silver or nickel?"

The woman glanced at the skillet and carving knife in Isabelle's cart and said, "Nickel."

As Isabelle wrote *nickel* on her list she felt the Scovill woman looking her up and down. "If you'll excuse me, I'll check out those brushed-nickel brackets right now."

Before the Scovill woman returned to her shopping, she nodded, smiled and said, "Certainly. And by the way, I like your footwear."

"The best fish swim near the bottom." ~~ Proverb

CHAPTER FORTY-SIX

Gloriana arrived at the parsonage a little after nine Thursday night. She brought the crutches that she had used, with difficulty, before doctors assigned her to the wheelchair. Laboriously, painfully, she ascended the front steps.

Annie fetched Glori's wheelchair out of her minivan and carried it up the steps behind her. They stopped in the kitchen long enough to eat sandwiches and wipe the sweat from their faces.

They reversed the process. Annie carried the wheelchair down the basement steps in front of her, and Gloriana went down carefully on the crutches. Annie set the wheelchair on the packed earth floor, and Gloriana almost fell into it, breathing heavily.

But Gloriana made no complaint. "Where's the stuff?" she said.

"Here's the book," Annie said. "I have to go get the rest." She climbed back up the stairs, made sure the doors of the house were locked, went to the attic for the bones and carried them to the basement. She pulled the pickax from behind the coal furnace and leaned on it while Gloriana opened the book.

"Spread the bones out on the laundry table for me," she said. Annie complied, gently placing each porous piece on the old Ping-Pong table she'd found behind the furnace when she stowed the ax there.

"Is this all the light there is?" Gloriana asked, pointing to the miserable bulb overhead.

"No. I got this out of Old Yeller." Annie produced a big work light on a heavy orange cord.

"I'm afraid to ask what you mean by Old Yeller," Gloriana said.

Annie laughed. "Didn't you see the school bus in the driveway?"

"Yes, I did," Gloriana said, "and I assumed that it is a church vehicle for the transportation of children to Sunday school."

"It's a long story, but the bottom line is that Old Yeller is my current ride. I drove it to your place yesterday, but you were out back and didn't see it."

"I guess not. But what happened to the Volvo?"

"Well, Old Yeller is the transportation arranged for me by the church after the incident with the dead chickens."

"Couldn't you drive G.P.'s truck for a while?"

"Yes, but there were complications. I'll fill in the details later. For now, we've got a lot to do down here."

Gloriana took a deep breath. "Agreed. Let's dig."

Annie put on her garden gloves and lined up six heavy-duty garbage bags by the wall in the central part of the basement. She laid into the earthen floor. She swung the ax again and again, each time loosening a tiny bit of stubborn dirt. Every two feet she dug a narrow hole about six inches deep. She was perspiring like an athlete within minutes. She ran upstairs and came back down with a towel and a six-pack of Mountain Dews. She dug more holes and collected more dirt on top of the garbage bags. Annie swilled two Dews. Gloriana declined.

Annie went into the coal cellar, put down two more garbage bags and dug again. She hacked at and around the place where she had found the bones. Her hands became blistered inside the gloves. Her back hurt from the manual labor. Her head pounded from tension and fatigue. But she didn't quit until the job was done.

Annie sat on the floor beside Gloriana and said, "I found two things. What did you find?"

"I have finished my task," Gloriana said. She would have said more, but they were startled by shouting and pounding above them.

"What's that?" Gloriana asked.

"Sounds like someone at the door."

"It's late. Maybe an emergency. You'd better go and see."

"Oh, my goodness, look at me, I'm a mess. I can't go to the door this way. I look like a middle-aged mud urchin."

"Don't worry. It's probably just a trustee wanting to check on something."

"Oh no, that would be awful!" Annie said. "They're scheduled to do a whole bunch of stuff tomorrow all over the house, including the basement. They can't come down here now!"

"Be calm. Maybe it's somebody bringing you garden produce. I could use some green beans if that's what they have."

"Glori! How can you talk about green beans? I've made a mess of the basement. I've made a mess of myself. What will I tell them?"

The incessant pounding upstairs got louder. "That you've been working in the basement," Gloriana replied. "Now go. Here, see. I've got my cell phone out of my pocket. If anything at all goes wrong, just stomp on the floor hard and I'll call 911. Okay?"

"Okay," Annie said, sprinting up the steps as the noise persisted.

"What in the hell took you so long?" said the angry voice as Annie peeked out the window to the front porch. There, in all her splendor, stood Chloe Dorsey, or Chloe McClelland, or Chloe Regina McClelland. Whatever her name was that evening, the woman rapping on the door was Annie's sister, star of stages large and small.

"What are you doing here?" Annie yelled through the window.

"Let me in! What's wrong with you?"

"Oh, you scared me," Annie said, unbolting the door.

"That's hardly the welcome I imagined," Chloe said as she billowed through the doorway with her handbag and suitcase. When she got a full look at Annie, she said, "Oh, my God! There's dirt all over you. What have you been doing? Digging ditches? If I were you, I would simply draw the line about this parsonage renovation. You should not have to handle earth-moving implements. Not for one minute!"

"This is not a very good time for a visit," Annie said. Chloe put on her annoyed face because Chloe visited whom she wished when she wished, and persons thusly blessed were expected to show proper gratitude.

"Whatever do you mean? It's an excellent time. The director's uncle died in Sheboygan or Shewaukee or some such place in Michigan, and I have the weekend off from rehearsals. I have come to continue helping you with this dreadful excuse for a house. But first, please fix grilled salmon and a salad for my dinner."

"I can't grill salmon right now," Annie said. "I am quite busy in the basement. Come with me and I'll show you."

"I will not descend to the labyrinth below," Chloe intoned.

"What's that? A line from Shakespeare?"

"Hmph."

"I guarantee that if you will lower yourself to the bowels of the building, you will be amazed and amused," Annie said.

"First, I must put on my muck-about shoes."

"That's the smartest thing you've said since you arrived. It is earthy in the basement."

Chloe rummaged in her suitcase and pulled out a pair of pink kidskin sling-backs. She took off the leopard-print stilettos in which she had arrived, wrapped each one in a thick sheaf of white tissue paper and placed them carefully inside the suitcase. She slipped on the sling-backs, stomped on the floor to make sure her silk slacks were once again hanging evenly and said, "Okay. I'm ready."

"Those are your muck-abouts?" Annie asked, pointing to the two-inch heels on Chloe's shoes.

"Why, yes. There's a tiny tear in the heel of the right one. See it? These aren't good for anything but mucking about, that's for sure."

"What do you know about mucking about?"

"I just called 911," Gloriana called up from the basement.

"Oh, no!" Annie cried. She ran to the top of the basement stairs and yelled down, "Uncall them, Glori. Quickly! It's just Chloe. We don't need the cops!"

"Why did you stomp on the floor then?" Gloriana yelled back.

"I didn't. Chloe did."

"Who's Chloe?"

"My sister. You met her at my brother's wedding. Don't you remember?"

"Yes, I remember now. But why did Chloe stomp?"

"Glori, call them off quickly, please!"

"All right. I'll try. But I think they're already on their way."

"Glori, I have to hide the bones!" Annie shrieked.

"What? You still have those bones?" Chloe exclaimed. "I'd think you would have turned them over by now to . . . to somebody responsible!"

"It's a long story," Annie said with exasperation. "Just stay here, would you please?" Annie pointed to the recliner in the living room. "Or, better yet, thaw out your salmon and start your salad."

"Very well, but I am not going to bed until I hear the whole story," Chloe said, gliding off in her muck-abouts toward the kitchen.

Annie and Gloriana had a devil of a time convincing Sergeant Boo Dillon that 911 had been called in error. By the time he arrived Annie had helped Gloriana up the basement steps and they were sitting in the living room with iced tea, which Chloe had actually made with her own hands and brought to them as a small concession to the gravity of the situation.

Gloriana explained what had happened, to wit, her cell phone, which she kept set to call 911 automatically because of her physical condition, fell out of her pocket, and when she picked it up she accidentally hit auto-dial.

"I see, ma'am," Boo said, "but why did you tell the dispatcher there was trouble here at the parsonage?"

Gloriana smiled winningly. "Oh, no, Sergeant. I was merely saying there was trouble with my telephone. I am so very sorry for the inconvenience. May I make a small donation to the police family fund as a gesture of contrition?"

"That's not necessary, ma'am. Only if you want to."

The sergeant left with a nice check, a big paper cupful of sweet tea and a slightly perplexed expression. His last comment as Annie opened the door was, "All I can say,

Reverend, is I've seen more of you in a week than I've seen of all the other preachers in town all year."

Annie forced a smile. "Ha ha. I'll try to stay clear of the law from here on out." Boo grinned and tipped his cap as he left.

"I cannot stand this one minute more. What is going on?" Chloe said. Annie shushed her and held her finger to her lips until they heard the door of the police cruiser slam.

"Come downstairs," Annie said, locking the door and drawing the curtains.

"I'll stay up here, if you don't mind," Gloriana said. "But bring up the book and my notes, will you?"

"Of course," Annie said, and Chloe trailed her across the dining room and kitchen and down the basement stairs.

"Watch your head," Annie said needlessly as she turned to see Chloe taking the steps one by one with head lowered to protect her hairdo.

Annie took her to the table where she had laid out her finds of the evening. "Look at these," she said.

"Why are you displaying a grimy belt buckle and a clump of dirt as if they were museum pieces?" Chloe said.

"Don't you get it? This belt buckle and this wedding ring," Annie said as she tapped the dirtball on the table to reveal a metal circle, "belong to the bones."

"And . . .?" Chloe pressed.

"I dug up the basement floor to look for more clues to the identity of the bones," Annie said. "And I found the belt buckle and the ring."

"Now I know why you look like an army private in swamp training," Chloe said. "But seriously, don't you think you've carried this far enough? You were scared to death when that policeman showed up tonight."

"That was just a fluke. Glori and I have this under control," Annie said.

"You are unquestionably the most stubborn person on the planet."

"Persistence makes perfect," Annie said.

"Practice makes perfect," Chloe said. "Persistence makes problems."

"Tennessee Williams?"

"Annie, how could you do this to yourself?" Chloe wailed. "You've just started a new assignment. You have this horrible house to pull together. You have a church wing to build. You're here alone, and you've got yourself all wound up over a bunch of bones. I will make one more attempt—and, believe me, this is my last attempt, for you are wearying me—to induce you to turn over those bones to . . . people. Please!"

"I didn't want to tell you this, but I think there's a very troubled young woman who desperately cares about these bones. I can't tell you any more right now, but it's important that I protect her . . . and these bones . . . for now. She has been so hurt in . . . in Biddlebourne. She cannot bear one more hurt."

Chloe dropped her head and sighed hard. When she looked up she said, "I have half a notion to e-mail G.P. and tell him what's going on so he will talk some sense into you. I know you would listen to him!"

Annie was so pained by Chloe's threat that she could not speak for several long seconds. Finally she said, "First, you can't seriously believe that I am the kind of woman who does what her husband tells her to do.

"Second, it will take Gloriana and me a week at most to get to the bottom of the bones, so to speak. My intentions are honest even if my methods are unsophisticated. G.P. will worry excessively if you tell him. And if he is worried and distracted while he works in the field, there's just that much more likelihood he'll make a mistake or get hurt himself. All I want is my husband back in one piece. I will thank you very much not to mention the bones to him, or to anyone else."

Chloe exhaled another signature sigh of disgust. For good measure, she rolled her eyes so dramatically that even in the dimness Annie caught the effect. Nevertheless, Annie could tell that Chloe was coming around. But she needed a clincher.

"And perhaps if you will hold your tongue on this matter, I will organize a nice motorcade of fans to come over and see you in *Guys and Dolls* at the CLU."

"CLO. Civic Light Opera. How many times must I repeat that?" Chloe corrected. "How many cars?"

"Oh, at least half a dozen."

"With signs?"

"Big signs with your name on them," Annie promised.

"Will the people bring me flowers?"

"I shall see that they do."

"Will they applaud wildly for me?"

"I will encourage that, as well as much shouting of 'Brava, brava!'"

"Well, all right then, but make it ten cars. What can I do to help in the next three days?"

"First, help me put these in a safe place," Annie said, opening the door of the furnace and extracting the precious bag of bones.

"You've been storing the bones in a garbage bag in the furnace?"

"No, I just shoved them in here before the police came. I couldn't risk their being seen, could I?"

Chloe laughed. It was not her professional stage laugh. It was the laugh of her childhood, unrehearsed and unrefined. She laughed so hard she made Annie laugh.

"I have to admit," Chloe said, "that this is more interesting than laying tiles, which, if I remember correctly, is what I did when you moved into the parsonage over at Chestnut City."

"So you did," Annie said. "You were a blushing bride of two months, and while Bob was at summer training camp you spent a week with G.P. and me, planting flowers and laying tiles and hanging pictures."

From the door at the top of the stairs they heard Gloriana ask, "What's so funny down there?"

"I remember," Chloe said.

"I appreciated it very much," Annie said.

"I know."

Annie shouted up to Gloriana, "We're just enjoying the humor of the situation."

Annie said to Chloe, "I'm thinking of hiding the bones somewhere outside the house. I've had several close calls already. An installation man the other day . . . and the police sergeant tonight . . ."

"Stop, stop! I believe you," Chloe said. "Do you have a rented storage unit yet?"

"No, and I really can't rent one because Mr. Gideon Pugh and his wife would hear about it and wonder why I hadn't stored these other things in their barn."

"What do you mean by *other things*?"

"Don't you remember? G.P.'s desk and the queen bed are in the Pughs' barn."

"Oh, yes, I do remember now. "How about hiding the bones at Gloriana's parsonage?"

"I couldn't ask her to do that. She already lied to the police tonight for me. Which reminds me, let's go upstairs and finish our conversation there."

"Okay." They took the bone bag, Gloriana's research materials and Annie's archeological finds up the stairs. Annie made a quick second trip for the wheelchair.

Upstairs they sat up late as Annie filled in Chloe and Gloriana on her recent experiences with cat remains, threat mail and stinking chickens. They adjusted their plan to include Chloe. At a quarter past one, they accompanied Gloriana to her ride, Chloe retired to the Misty Blue Room with a fan and a bowl of ice, and Annie got out the air mattress and went to the USA Room. Fannie Fay walked between the pantry door and Annie's bedroom door, plaintively meowing all the while.

Downstairs, lying on a blanket from Ernie Pargeon's Army days, Isabelle pondered the day's events and conversations.

Dear Diary,
This is the hardest part to write even to you diary. Its the worst thing that ever hapned to me. One day when I was about 5 or 6 years old it was report card day which is the worst day in the world at our house. Frankie was getting the stuffing beat out of him I mean reely reely bad. I was standing on the steps going up stairs and screeming mommy make daddy stop. Please please please. I begged and begged. Frankie wood have been 8 or 9 becaws hes 3 years older than me. I was crying crying crying screeming screeming. My dad just kept beating Frankie with that dam belt. Mommy told me to get my ass up stairs becaws if my dad saw me or heard me I would be next. So I went up stairs until it was all over. Frankies screems were so horrible. My poor poor brother. He goes thru hell. I love him so much.

Death in the Parsonage

"He who rouses a sleeping tiger exposes himself to danger." ~~ Chinese proverb

CHAPTER FORTY-SEVEN

Friday, July 15

Annie needed time to fill the holes in the basement floor and get the bones out of the house before the various service people arrived. She arose at 5:30 a.m., labored mightily in the basement for more than two hours, showered and headed for Chestnut City.

Chloe was on the front porch, obviously waiting for her, when Annie returned and parked Old Yeller in the driveway. "They're already in the basement installing the floor jacks," Chloe said as her sister climbed the front steps. "How did it go in Chestnut City?"

"No problems," Annie said. "The, ahem, valuables are well stored in a safe deposit box at our old bank. I had to get the biggest box they have." She didn't mention the pang of remorse that had struck her as she walked past the box where she and G.P. once kept their Five Rules for a Happy Marriage. But G.P. would understand when he came home and she explained everything. He really would.

"Are you all set?" Annie asked Chloe.

"Yes," she said in a hushed tone. "I'll go to the main library in Wheeling. I'll call you on your cell phone if I find anything really good."

"Remember, Glori said the bones probably belong to an adult male."

"Just refresh me a bit. She determined this how?"

"You heard her last night," Annie remonstrated. "She looked up the length and thickness of the leg bones in the book."

"Oh, yes. Right," Chloe said. "So I am looking for anything about a man who went missing around Biddlebourne from . . . when?"

"No more than thirty years ago," Annie said.

"How can we be sure of that?"

"The Pargeons had a flood in the basement around 1976."

"What does that have to do with the bones?" Chloe asked.

"I'm just guessing, but the old water heater went out around then, and by some crazy coincidence there was a water line break at the same time, and the basement was flooded."

"How do you know that?" Chloe asked.

Annie was growing impatient. "The church trustees told me. The Pargeons made a big point of saying the water heater was ONLY twenty-eight years old when they turned over the keys to the church."

"But I still don't see how that ties in," Chloe complained.

"I can't be sure, but I'm thinking they never would have let the water-heater installer, not to mention the city water department, mess around in the basement if they had known there was a body buried there. And a flood would have brought a body to the surface."

"Oh," said Chloe with sudden understanding. "So if there was a flood there in '76, the body landed there after that?"

"That's my theory."

"Okay," Chloe said. "I'll search back thirty-five years, just to be safe. When do I have to be back?"

"No later than five-thirty," Annie said. "Ladies Aid Night Out starts at six-thirty. We can't be late."

"I think I'll wear my beige linen pantsuit with the cocoa silk top," Chloe said.

"Fine, fine. I'm wearing black polyester slacks and a white cotton top."

"Oh dear," Chloe said. "I didn't realize they still made polyester."

"It doesn't matter. What matters is that you and I meet Glori back here after dinner to go over all the clues together."

"Check. Should we synchronize our watches?" she said mischievously. They laughed.

Chloe had already driven away in her Corvette when Mr. Gideon Pugh arrived. The yellow Corvette and the yellow school bus sitting side by side in the yard had made quite the sight. Annie was sorry Mr. Gideon Pugh had missed it.

"I s'pose the joist crew's already downstairs," Gideon Pugh said when Annie joined him on the front porch.

"Yes, I believe so. I just returned from an errand, and my sister let them in to get started," Annie said.

"Oh, Miss Chloe's here from Pittsburgh then?"

"Yes. She came to give me a hand with . . . things."

"Bless her heart," he said.

"Indeed."

"Well, Pastor Ma'am, I figure I'd better stick around to keep an eye on things. The fumigators is coming again. Sorry about those pesky wasps. I hope this time does it."

"I trust that it will. And Mr. Pugh, would you mind directing the furniture delivery when it arrives?"

"You gettin' a new couch?"

"No, new beds. Twin box springs and a king mattress. Will you let the men in and show them to the master bedroom, please?"

"The master bedroom?" he said.

"The one closest to the bathroom," she explained.

"Oh, the *master* bedroom," he said. "Sure will. Just leave everything to me. I reckon you got a lot to do on your day off."

"I certainly do," Annie said. He did not know the half of it.

Annie turned to leave, but Mr. Gideon Pugh stopped her. "Ma says she means it. You ought to come and stay at the house a while. Won't take us no time to tote your clothes and cat and . . . what-not over there. There's something mighty strange going on around here."

Annie hesitated. Had he noticed her early departure with the bone bag? Her expression must have shown her concern, for Mr. Gideon Pugh added quickly, "Course, the house is lookin' better 'n' better every day." He looked around, admiring the wallpaper, paint and clean windows. "Ain't no place like home."

"My feelings precisely," Annie said.

Annie drove away in Old Yeller. Many residents waved at her as she drove, and she guessed they thought they were waving at Hermie Hoobler. He was a popular fellow around the town. Tongues were wagging, of that she was sure, but perhaps the townspeople would think her a trouper for trying out this particular set of wheels.

She got to the Parkersburg antique mall just after noon, had a sinful lunch of greasy beef burritos in the food court and took her treasures around to the vendors.

The dealers were talkative, and Annie had what she needed within a couple of hours. When she returned at the parsonage Chloe was dressed for dinner and sitting at the dining table touching up her manicure.

Annie called to Fannie Fay, who came in from the kitchen and wrapped herself around her right ankle.

"She sits by that pantry door day and night," Chloe noted. "Don't you feed her enough?"

"Of course I do. But she knows the tuna is in there."

"I think she's bored," Chloe said. "Why don't you let her play in the attic?"

"I haven't let her go up there because of the wasps," Annie said. "If this fumigation works and the wasps are gone for good, Fannie Fay can play in the attic all day long."

"Mr. Pugh said to tell you that they knocked down some more wasp nests in the attic, plus they sprayed some stuff around," Chloe reported.

"Good," Annie said. "Did the beds come?"

"I didn't ask. I forgot about them. He also said he had to speak with you about the renovation."

"Oh? We talk about the renovation almost every day. I'll give him a call in the morning. I'm going up for a shower right now. I'll be back down in twenty minutes or so."

"Twenty minutes!?" Chloe said with alarm. "You can get ready in twenty minutes?"

"It's a gift," Annie said and ran up the steps to her bedroom, where, just as she'd hoped, the new mattress rested in plastic-covered glory on the double twin springs. There were even ten or twelve inches of space around the beds in which, if she and G.P. walked sideways, they could stand to make up the bed and get in and out of it.

Chloe and Annie rode to Ladies' Night Out in Chloe's car, Chloe having laughed derisively when Annie suggested they travel in Old Yeller.

"You didn't tell me it was going to be Mexican," Chloe complained as they parked at Elmer's South of the Border on Second Street.

"What's wrong with Mexican?" Annie asked.

"Calories!" she retorted, patting a hip for emphasis.

"Just eat a salad then," Annie said.

"Tsk."

"I already had Mexican food once today," Annie noted.

"Then just have a salad," Chloe mocked.

"Tsk," Annie replied.

Members and guests of the Ladies Aid Society filled the banquet room of Elmer's. They oohed and aahed over Chloe's ensemble and said nothing about Annie's. The pastor knew she would have received compliments if she had been able to wear her ruby sandals.

While the others talked of clothes and families, Annie pulled Shirl Burrows aside and asked what she had discovered about the purported haunting of 1010 Greenbriar Road.

"Minnie and I got an earful for you," Shirl said. "Sit with us tonight, and we'll fill you in. We already fixed the place cards so's you and your sister are next to us."

"Uh, why thank you," Annie said, unsure about the ethics of moving name cards until she saw other women also switching cards. It was a game of musical chairs in which everyone played the piano.

Annie asked, "You and Minnie do not mind if Chloe gets, uh, an earful, too, do you?"

"Heck, no," Shirl said, slapping Annie on the back and shouting to the assemblage. "Everybody, listen up, the preacher's gonna pray so we can get our orders in. Reverend?"

Annie did as bidden, and the ladies quickly found their seats to tend to the serious matter of choosing entrees. Pitchers of tea and coffee, and pictures of children and grandchildren, soon flowed in all directions.

Minnie started. "I don't want you to get your drawers in a knot, so I'll fill you in a little on the hauntin' over at Old Lady Pargeon's house."

"People called the former resident Old Lady Pargeon?" Annie asked.

"Yep. Sure did," Shirl said. "The kids did, anyway. Said she spooked them. Said they saw dead animals at her place and heard all kinds of screamin' comin' from the house."

Minnie nodded sagely. "There's more to it than that, Shirl. That's just a bunch of kid talk. I got some real facts because I know Mizz Pargeon used witches' brews!"

Chloe's eyes got bigger, and her right hand went to her mouth. Annie gulped and said, "I'm sure you're just using a popular expression, Minnie."

"Oh, no," Minnie said. "I mean it. She was a real witch. I know it. I know it because she bought her potion-making mixtures from me!"

Annie and Chloe traded astonished looks. "That's why I didn't want to tell you about it before," Minnie confessed to Annie. "I figured you'd run me out of the church."

"Of course not," Annie said. "But I don't understand what you mean, Minnie."

"It's like this," Minnie said, leaning over the table conspiratorially. Shirl nodded and leaned in, too.

Just then Ma Pugh, vice president of the Ladies Aid, stood and said, "All right, ladies, it's time to see who the winners are." The other ladies cheered and picked up their place cards. Annie and Chloe hastened to do the same.

Ma Pugh began calling out numbers, and ladies began calling out, "Here." Each time someone yelled, everyone applauded and Mary Ellen Brinkman handed the winner a prize.

Annie expected first, second and third places to be rewarded. But Ma Pugh called numbers until every lady, including the pastor and her sister, had the pleasure of responding, "Here."

The tabletops had been cluttered to begin with, what with purses and pictures and drinks and baskets of tortilla chips and sombrero party favors provided by Ma Pugh strewn about. But after all the prize flowers and prize vases and prize stationery and prize candles were awarded, the place looked like tag day at the dollar store.

Annie was relieved when the prizes had all been handed out. Dinner would soon be on its way, and she and Chloe and could get back to the scoop on the haunted house with Shirl and Minnie. But, as if on cue, the ladies immediately began swapping their prizes. In some locales this might have been thought of as unseemly, since every prizewinner had just expressed heartfelt delight over her winnings. But this was the Glory Hallelujah Ladies Aid Night Out, and custom prevailed.

So Annie reluctantly traded her purple bud vase for a box of get-well cards bearing pictures of sunflowers. She had liked the purple bud vase, actually, but was pleased again when she traded with Shirl for a cat calendar.

Trading proceeded until salads were delivered. The prizes were dropped like so many hot coals, signaling the start of the food-comparison portion of the party.

"I knew I should have ordered guacamole," Thelma Blivins lamented as she tasted the stuff on Blaney Wilkins' plate.

"What do you think is in that fajita besides beef?" Margie Vinacore asked.

If the place had been a hangar, ear protectors would have been provided. Several times Minnie said, "As I was saying about Mizz Pargeon . . . ." But each time Annie had to respond, "What? I can't hear you."

When the party broke up at the stroke of eight o'clock—because children had to be put to bed and non-cooking husbands fed—it was clear that Annie and Chloe would have to wait to hear the full skinny on Old Lady Pargeon and her witches' brews.

Gloriana was waiting for them at the parsonage. They got down to details as soon as Annie and Chloe hopped into Gloriana's car.

"What did you find out?" Annie asked Gloriana.

"I called everybody we talked about last night—my friend in the sheriff's department, my cousin who's been with the Biddlebourne police since eighty-two, even that guy Phil I used to date who runs that convenience store up on Route 2. But nobody remembers anything about a man from Biddlebourne who was reported missing in the last twenty or thirty years."

"What about previous pastors at the neighbor churches?" Chloe asked. "Pastors hear about EVERYTHING that's going on, don't they?"

"Sometimes pastors are the last to know," Gloriana said with a smile, "especially things that a family wants kept secret. I did call two previous pastors of other churches in Biddlebourne, John Goodpenny and Marvin Ang. They both said about the same thing, that they never heard of any unsolved missing-person cases here."

"Oh, darn," Chloe said. "Annie, what did you find out? You were so mysterious on the way to the restaurant. Is it something big?"

Annie withdrew the belt buckle and wedding ring from her purse and held them in her palm. "This belt buckle

was made in Cincinnati by the Piletson Company! What
do you think of that?"

"Impressive!" Gloriana said. "Did you find out how old
it is?"

"Old, maybe thirty years old."

"Which means exactly what in terms of our research?"
Chloe asked.

They all sat looking at the Ziplocked belt buckle.

"Okay. For one thing, I learned that this design is
unique," Annie said, pointing to the outline of a truck on
the buckle.

"A truck! Now that is rare," Chloe said.

"Not just any truck. A beer truck," Annie said.

"Aha! Even more rare!" Chloe rejoined.

"Annie, did they say that emblem holds special
significance?" Gloriana asked.

"That's what I'm trying to tell you. Back in the '80s
Piletson held a series of bar contests and gave these
buckles as prizes. See here? There's a bottle opener on the
back. The buckles were made only for those contests."

"So this Piletson made beer as well as belt buckles?"
Chloe asked.

"Haven't you ever heard of Piletson Pilsener?"

"You know that alcohol dries my complexion!"

"Oh, I know Piletson well!" Gloriana pitched in. "It
was my drink of choice in college."

"You're kidding!" Annie said.

"I sowed lots of wild oats back then," Gloriana said.
She straightened her back and asked, "How many of these
buckles were made?"

"Maybe a couple thousand," Annie said.

"A lot of buckles," mused Chloe.

"I know, but people tend to remember that kind of
thing," Annie said. "I'm thinking that if I ask around—
discreetly, of course—I will hear about people in

Biddlebourne who won these Piletson buckles at a bar contest."

"It's worth a shot," Gloriana said. "What about the wedding ring?"

"I took it to three different jewelry dealers, and they all said about the same thing."

"Which was?" Chloe prompted.

"That it's a cheap, ten-karat wedding band, the kind available at novelty or similar stores."

"I take it there is no engraving on the ring," Gloriana said.

"Correct.," Annie said.

"Looks like a dead-end," Gloriana concluded. "Chloe, what did you find?"

"Same as you," she said. "Nothing. No adult males have been reported missing from the Biddlebourne area for thirty years."

"That only means Mister Bones wasn't reported missing around here. Maybe he was killed somewhere else or just plain died somewhere else and was brought to the house to be buried," Annie said.

"It was a very shallow burial, if that's what it was," Chloe observed.

"That's true," Gloriana said. "And that makes me think it was done either hastily or with the expectation that the body would never be found."

"Yes. I see your point," Annie said. "So if the perpetrator thought he or she was safe from discovery, they had a very believable story in hand as to why the dead man was no longer around."

"Or maybe he was not from around Biddlebourne," Chloe said. "Maybe he was a transient who had the misfortune of visiting the house and never left."

"*Arsenic and Old Lace*, right?" Annie said.

"Maybe."

"Wouldn't there have been an awful smell from the body?" Gloriana asked.

"Yes, there would have been," Annie answered. "Wait a minute. Is it possible that Mrs. Pargeon used her notoriety as a so-called witch to keep people away from the house? Or that she used herbal concoctions to stop the odor?"

"Hm," Chloe said.

"Could be," Gloriana said.

Chloe said, "Maybe Old Lady Pargeon put a witchy spell on him and killed him."

Annie sighed. "You don't seriously believe the witch story, do you?"

"Not exactly," Chloe said, "but it is kind of fascinating."

"What is?" Gloriana demanded to know.

Annie and Chloe filled her in quickly on what Minnie and Shirl had begun to tell them at Elmer's.

"So, let's summarize what we have learned so far," Annie said.

"The bones belong to a man," Chloe said.

"That man loved Piletson beer," Gloriana said.

"That man was married," Annie said.

"To a cheap wife," Chloe added.

"The bones probably were buried in the basement after 1980," Annie said.

They lapsed into silence.

"So what we've got is not much," Gloriana concluded. Annie and Chloe nodded.

"What's next?" Chloe said.

"I'll inquire about beer-drinking contests," Annie said.

"I'll expand my search for missing persons to the whole state or, better yet, to the region—Indiana, Kentucky, Michigan and the rest of West Virginia," Chloe said. "I'll go back to the library tomorrow."

"I'll go over the bones again to look for signs of foul play," Gloriana said bravely. "I'm getting on to this forensic business."

Annie said, "I'll have the bones at your house by noon tomorrow."

~~0~~

Dear Diary,
I dont have a good time with all the nabors tho. Like the ones who live five houses down. I use to play with the dotter in there back yard never in mine. One day she crossed the line into my yard. Her mom must have been waching her becaws she had to go home and I was never allowed in there yard again. The dotter told me it had some thing to do with my mom and dad like I had to confess or some thing. I cant ever keep a frend. I can get a frend but I cant keep a frend. I just want some body to be my frend some body my age not the nabor ladies age. Some of the nice nabor ladies show me many good things to do and tell me Im a prinses but there not my age and dont play games and hide and seek and monoply and stuff like that.

Death in the Parsonage

"Write down the thoughts of the moment. Those that come unsought for are commonly the most valuable." ~~ Francis Bacon

CHAPTER FORTY-EIGHT

Isabelle lay on her new bed, under her new appliquéd coverlet, in her new studio apartment. The new television set showed the program she had selected with her new control gadget. Her new pale-yellow towels hung next to her new pale-yellow hand towels and washcloths. Her new toiletries, groceries and other supplies rested neatly in the cupboards and niches of the apartment.

She should have been happy, relaxed, clear-minded. She had carefully worked her way up to actually spending time in the apartment. She had not entirely quit her most special hiding place. She had merely left it temporarily to take her rebirth in manageable stages.

In so doing, she had heard and seen things that surprised her. That shocked her. That . . . that . . . moved her. How could the Scovill woman know as much about Isabelle as she seemed to know? How could the Scovill woman, knowing what she knew, choose not to hate Isabelle? Had the Scovill woman simply gone to the police station and told them about Isabelle after their meeting at Vinny's? Apparently not, for everyone had seen her coming and going in the new red truck and could easily locate her through the purchases she had made.

Something very, very strange was going on. Isabelle took out her planning pad and wrote. She had to figure this out before she returned to her most special hiding place for the very last time.

"Belief is better than investigation." ~~ Proverb

CHAPTER FORTY-NINE

Saturday, July 16

In the morning Annie celebrated the completion of her visits to all the A-families in the congregation. They had eggs benedict, or in Chloe's case egg benedict, with cantaloupe and coffee on the porch, or in Chloe's case the veranda.

"I need to get my eyes checked next week," Chloe said.

"Oh?" Annie said. "Are you finally going to get bifocals?"

A freezing glare served as Chloe's answer.

"Sorry," Annie said. "I forgot that your eyes are not subject to the same vagaries as those of us mortals."

"Tsk."

"Seriously, though, are you having trouble reading? In your line of work that could be a difficulty."

"Of course I'm not having trouble reading," Chloe said. "But, Lordie, my eyes must be playing tricks on me."

"How so?"

"I could swear I had the border on the dining room wallpaper aligned just . . . just so. But last night when I was at the dining table doing my nails, several of the intersections seemed askew."

"Oh, no!" Annie said, reaching for her cell phone on the table.

"It's not that bad," Chloe said quickly. "Perhaps it was just the dim light . . . or my imagination. You're taking it much too seriously. Don't worry."

Annie shook her head and held up her left forefinger as she punched in numbers on the phone with her right thumb. "I'm not worried about your eyes," she said as she waited for Mr. or Mrs. Pugh to answer.

Chloe took on a hurt expression, but Annie stabbed another piece of melon and put in on Chloe's plate while mouthing the words "Fifteen calories." Chloe smiled and cut off a small piece.

Mr. Gideon Pugh answered. "Annie Scovill here," the pastor said.

"Yes, Pastor Ma'am, I wanted to talk to you about the leveling joists. The fellers put 'em up in the basement yesterday, just like we agreed, but there's a bit of bad news, I'm 'fraid."

"I think I may know what it is," Annie said. "Are the jacks lifting up the floors and affecting the walls upstairs, including the wallpaper that was just applied?"

"Can't get one past you, Pastor Ma'am," he said.

"I have to admit that I didn't notice a thing, Mr. Pugh," Annie said. "My sister, however, did."

"I'm awful sorry," he said.

"That's quite all right. We had to correct the sagging floors and walls, and the wallpapering can be redone."

"I called Justine and Bern and Thelma and Minnie— and, oh, as many of the trustees as I could get on a Friday night—and we already made the plan to pay for new wallpaperin' out of the Pargeon money. We want to apologize to Miss Chloe, too, for she did most o' that paperin' with her own two hands."

"I'm sure she will understand. None of us could have guessed what the floor raising would do to the wallpaper."

"We'll have somebody over there real soon to fix it," Mr. Gideon Pugh promised.

"No need to hurry," Annie assured him, eager to keep more workers—and their observant eyes—out of the parsonage.

"It sure ain't an emergency, but if you come on over to the house and stay a while, we can have the furnace put in the same day as the wallpaperin' is fixed and several other things gets done," he said. "You won't have to put up with the noise or the dust or the paste or anything like that."

With the bones out of the house, Annie truly was torn. She wanted the air conditioning as soon as possible. She wanted the wallpaper corrected and the floors straightened and the insects removed and the plumbing repaired as soon as possible. She wanted Fannie Fay to play in the attic and not pace anxiously all day. But most of all she wanted no disruption to be so evident that G.P. could find out about it and lose his concentration. And in less than eighty days he would be home if Annie focused.

"Was that what you wanted to talk with me about? Chloe said you asked to speak with me."

"Just the wallpaper and . . . a couple other little things. Have you thought any more about moving in with Ma and me for a while? Ma just won't let me alone on this," he said. When Ma Pugh got hold of an idea, she was like a church treasurer with the money sack. There was no letting go.

Annie sighed. "Mr. Pugh, I really think that I will be at my best professionally if I remain in my own home—even with the workers coming and going."

"It's not the workers Ma's so upset about," he continued. "It's them dad-blamed surprises you been gettin' that's got her riled. Says she couldn't forgive herself if somethin' awful happened to you over at the parsonage. You're all by yourself over there."

Annie caught the dread in his voice. But this was rural West Virginia, for heaven's sake. Soon enough the source of the silly little pranks would come to light. Meanwhile, for reasons with which neither Mr. nor Mrs. Pugh would agree, Annie would remain in her home.

"At least I'm not alone here while Chloe's staying," Annie said. "I'll talk it over with my husband, though." That seemed to satisfy Mr. Gideon Pugh, if not Mrs. Gideon Pugh, but he had one more point to bring up.

"Pastor Ma'am," he began, and she gritted her teeth, "I'm just wonderin' about the basement."

Be cool. Be cool. "What about the basement?"

"You said the hookup man had problems with the water line, and we had Earl Blankenship come and fix that, but you didn't say nothin' about them holes in the basement floor. Did the appliance man dig them up?" he asked.

She was caught! What could she say? And she thought she had covered the holes so well!

"Holes in the basement floor," Annie said, trying to make her words sound like neither exclamation nor question. But she heard her voice cracking. And she felt her heart pounding.

"Yes, ma'am, Pastor Ma'am," he replied. "Earl told Minnie there was a bunch of mole hills down there, and when Minnie asked him to say more, he told her there were more'n two dozen spots where it looked like someone had been diggin' for gold. Ha ha ha. But I seen the holes for myself yesterday."

"I don't think there's any gold in the basement. Ha ha," Annie said as she struggled to think of a plausible excuse.

"Pastor Ma'am, we gotta be sure on this before we bring in the new furnace," he said.

Oh, no. Now the digging could delay the air conditioning.

Chloe, meanwhile, having guessed the subject of their conversation, was going through her own distressing emotions. First, she looked surprised. Then she looked startled. Then she looked alarmed.

Mr. Gideon Pugh must have taken Annie's hesitation for what it was. "However," he continued, "I s'pose I could call up the appliance company and ask what the heck happened down there."

"Oh, no. Don't do that!" Annie said quickly.

"Us trustees ought to get to the bottom o' this," he said. "You know how those pesky wasps has hung around. I'm wonderin' now if badgers or—heaven help us—skunks has found a way into the basement. Doors been open a lot with the people comin' and goin'. Critters can gum up a new furnace in no time."

"Mr. Pugh, I think my cat has done some digging in the basement lately."

"Oh, surely not."

Chloe slapped her forehead—lightly so as not to disturb her makeup but still pointedly enough to show Annie what she thought of her tack on the basement holes.

"Uh, well, you know how cats love to dig," Annie said, making a face in Chloe's direction to indicate she was doing the best she could in a difficult situation.

"Well, I know how Grady—that's our old barn cat— dug up Ma's cucumber garden one year and, boy, Ma's never forgive him yet."

"Uh-huh," Annie said, "and I have changed the location of her litter box several times since we moved in, what with the water break in the bathroom and everything . . . ." She held her breath as she finished the sentence.

"Sure, I guess a cat that was determined . . ."

Just then in the background, Annie heard Ma Pugh say, "Gideon, I'm waiting."

"Comin', Ma," he said. "Sorry, Pastor Ma'am, but I promised Ma I'd go with her to the flea market today. She says she needs some peaches—like we ain't got fruit by the barrels around here already."

"Gideon!" Annie heard once more.

"That's quite all right, Mr. Pugh," Annie said. "I'll see you both Sunday morning."

"Yes, ma'am," he said.

Chloe was practically apoplectic.

"Are you out of your mind?" she said. "A brigade of backhoes couldn't have dug that many holes in the basement, let alone your poor little Fannie Fay!"

"That was all I could think of at the moment," Annie wailed.

"Aahh," Chloe moaned.

"Okay. What would you have said?"

"Never mind. But about the wallpaper now, I am only slightly disappointed by the news about the floor jacks. I've been thinking I should have gone a shade lighter on the border anyway. I'll pick up some samples while I'm out."

"I'll see you at dinner," Annie said. She drove full speed to Chestnut City, removed from the safe deposit box what she had put in the day before and took it to Gloriana's parsonage.

~~0~~

Dear Diary,
Im suppose to turn into a witch when Im 16. I gess theres going to be some kind of ceremony. I dont know whats going to happen any more now that daddy ran away. Mommy says he left town with some no good huzzie named

Susan Spencer-Smith

*Wilma. I never heard of Wilma before. I asked mommy
how she knew the name of the woman and she threw a
whiskee bottle at me and swore and screamed and
screamed and screamed. Im never going to ask again.
Sissies gone two. She went to live with our cousins over in
Claypool. I met the cousins a couple times around
Christmas and I dont like them at all. They eat chicken
legs and throw the bones on the floor. Disgusting. Even
more disgusting than my house. And my cousin Sheree
made fun of me the whole time we were there the last time
because I said I was going to become a witch. You are an
ignorant little nobody from hicks ville she said like she is
so uppity with her hair going all over and her fancy skirts
and boots. Clothes don't mean any thing. I know Im a
good person no matter what clothes Im wearing. Im awful
nervous now that daddy is gone. One minute I think
mommys glad hes gone and the next minute I think shes
not. The other man, her boyfriend, comes to the house
almost every day now. He never sees me but I see him.
Some times I watch them in the living room until they go
to mommys bedroom. I know what they do in there
because Sissie told me. Im so nervous that I pull my hair
out of my head. I have a bald place on the right side of my
head. About as big as a 50 cent peace. No witch. No hair.
No nothing for me.*

Death in the Parsonage

"He that nothing questions, nothing learns." ~~
Proverb

CHAPTER FIFTY

"Minnie says Miz Pargeon would come to the house and buy herbs for spells and such," Shirl reported. It was late Saturday morning, and Annie was listening intently in her church office to a fuller report on the late, unlamented Old Lady Pargeon.

"How did Minnie know the herbs were for spells? Couldn't they have been for rheumatism or asthma or some other malady?"

"She was all the time askin' Minnie for weird herbs, like white willow and ginkgo and stinging nettle," Shirl said.

"Isn't white willow used for headaches?"

"Maybe, but it's also used for voodoo spells," Shirl said.

"However do you know that?"

"Minnie says so, and I read it myself in a book," Shirl replied.

"Shirl, that seems farfetched to me."

"Old Lady Pargeon also kept Minnie hoppin' to get her stinging nettle!" Shirl said, "And everybody knows stinging nettle hurts people."

"Still . . . I don't know," Annie said. "Mrs. Pargeon probably had chilblains or some such ailment that responded to herbal treatment."

"Then why did people hear moaning coming from that house all hours of the day and night?" Shirl demanded. "Old Lady Pargeon was doin' her spells. Everybody knew it. And that place is haunted. There's been all kinds of unexplained goings-on over there."

"Give me a for-instance."

"Okay. For instance," she began, "after Old Lady Pargeon died, people would see faint lights on over at the house, sometimes for hours at a time, but when they went to investigate, nobody was there."

"Moonlight and shadows," Annie said.

"Huh-uh. When people went to look into it, they would find doors ajar and light cords swinging, especially in that damned, er, excuse me, darned basement!"

"Wind and uneven walls and floors," Annie said.

"Once, Hermie the Handyman even found tracks in the dust in the attic, and before you say it was critters, I'll tell you that the footprints looked like sneakers. What do you think of that?"

"Curious kids."

"Okay. The neighbors, the Wilsons have teenagers, you know them . . . ."

"We've met, and the kids brought over squash last week," Annie said.

"The Wilsons—and there's no better Christians around than them, even if they are Lutherans—the Wilsons declare, I mean declare, that they heard clankin' and bangin' over at the parsonage all last summer."

"Let's see. Mrs. Pargeon had died by then, and the house was going through probate, right?"

"Right, but the point is, it was not occupied!" Shirl said impatiently. "It was spirits come back from the dead, dragging chains around—or something like that."

"I doubt it," Annie said.

"You don't believe in ghosts at all, do you?"

"Only the Holy Ghost," Annie said. Both laughed.

"Anyhow, whether you believe it was ghosts or not, there's been a steady stream of stories comin' out of the Pargeon house. A whole lot of nothing good has gone on over there."

"Shirl, tell me something else, would you?"

"What?"

"Why did the church accept the house as a parsonage when it has such a . . . such a questionable background?"

"Well, I'm not a trustee, but . . ."

"Yes?"

Shirl hesitated, looked out the window and took several deep breaths. "The long and short of it? It was a good way to get a new parsonage cheap after we sold the other one to Marcy, and it gave us a leg up on the building fund."

"But didn't the trustees realize that church rules do not permit proceeds of a parsonage sale to be reinvested in anything other than another parsonage?" Annie asked.

"Oh, yeah, they knew it, all right," she said, "but that's just the point, 'cause that rule's only good when there's no other parsonage, and when we got the house on Greenbriar Road, we could use the money we got from the old parsonage for the church building campaign."

"Okay, Shirl," Annie said. "I have one last question."

"Go ahead."

"Do you know anyone around Biddlebourne who wears a belt buckle with a Piletson Beer truck on it?'

"Why would you wanna know a thing like that? Don't tell me you're into beer junk!"

"No, not exactly. It's for a . . . church project I'm working on."

"I hope you're not gonna give out beer belt buckles to the youth. On the other hand, maybe the Glory Boys wouldn't mind gettin' a Pillie buckle."

"Pillie buckle?"

"Oh, yeah. Lots of people 'round here got 'em back in the seventies—or was it the eighties? That was when they quit servin' liquor at the pool hall and a coupla restaurants got the idea they'd pick up the business and put in bars. There was a big stink about the liquor licenses. Four or five places had to duke it out over two licenses that the state said they'd give out. Anyway, you got a Pillie buckle for winnin' at darts, and a Pillie buckle for winnin' a dance contest. You got a Pillie buckle for doin' almost anything at any bar."

"So a lot of them are floating around . . . so to say?"

"Ha. That's a good one, Pastor. Yeah, I s'pose so."

"Do you remember anyone in particular actually wearing a Pillie buckle?"

"Shoot, you saw 'em all over town for a while, but I guess most folks got tired of 'em. You gotta admit, it ain't much of a fashion statement."

"Shirl, who are the drinkingest folks around here?"

Shirl shot Annie a bemused look. "Okay, I get why you might wanna know who's on the up end of a bottle more than other people. Well, the Bascombes, I figure, put away more Johnny Walker per man and woman than any other family in the county till they got run out by their landlord."

"Who hung around with the Bascombes?"

"Oh, nobody from the church, if that's what you're after."

"Oh no, that's not what I'm thinking," Annie said quickly. "I, uh, am just wondering whether drinking is much of a . . . social problem in Biddlebourne."

"Oh, sure. I get it. The Timberlake bunch—live out on Bimming Hill—never turned down a drink. Some of the Hooblers tilt the bottle a lot, too, if you get my drift. Not Hermie, though. The worst woman drunk we ever had in Biddlebourne was Old Lady Pargeon. And, my God, she was nasty when she was plastered. Her and her old man would get cross-eyed drunk and yell and curse and bust up furniture and call the kids names. It was ugly. The Wilsons must 'o called the cops a dozen times, Vickie June and Ernie got so stinkin' loud."

"You've been very helpful," Annie said.

"Well, if that's all your social research for today, I'm gonna go home and hose off the car. Rained like hell on the way to my brother's place in Cincinnati the other day. Got mud up to the door handles. See you tomorrow."

"Thanks again," Annie said as Shirl left to coddle her Caddie.

Annie finished her preparations for Sunday worship and hurried home for a quick lunch. She had just kicked off her shoes and dropped her purse on the kitchen table when the phone rang.

"Hi, Honey!" G.P.'s voice brought tears to her eyes. She missed him so much. She missed him in so many ways she couldn't count them. Sometimes she wished he were not so competent and reliable because the Air Force Reserve would not need him as much as she did.

They talked for a long time—about the new furniture, about Fannie Fay, about his family and hers and theirs, about missing each other. Her stomach grumbled, but she forgot about lunch.

"I heard something crazy yesterday," he said.

"What's that?" Annie asked.

"One of my buddies with the Forty-First said his wife's nephew saw you driving a school bus around Biddlebourne."

Alarm! Red flag! Peril!

"Oh, that," she said, taking a deep breath. "There was a little trouble with the Volvo, and Hermie the Handyman lent me Old Yeller—that's the bus—to use for my errands until the Volvo's back in service."

"What happened to the Volvo?"

"Dead chickens," she said.

"You ran over some chickens?"

"No, they found me."

"I'm not following you, Annie."

"Oh, G.P." This was a moment of truth, she knew, that would have long consequences. To tell the truth, the whole truth, and nothing but the truth—or to tell the truth, part of the truth, and nothing more than a little truth—that was the question.

Annie made her decision. "When I was coming out of the office one day this week, I found a whole bunch of dead chickens in the car. Boy, did they ever stink!" she said with a giggle.

"Dead chickens," he mused. "I don't get it. Is that the Biddlebourne notion of initiating a new preacher? I have to say I don't find it amusing."

"I filed a police report, and they're keeping the car to look for any useful evidence, and that's why I'm driving Old Yeller for now. It's really kind of adventurous."

"I'll bet," he said. "But Annie, I don't understand. Why aren't you driving the truck if the Volvo's at the police station?"

"Oh, I wouldn't want to get any dents or dings in your truck. When you get home, I want it to be just the way you left it."

"I trust you to drive it," he said.

"I know you do, but Ma Pugh seemed so pleased to have come up with the Old Yeller option that I took her up on it. You're not upset about this, are you?"

"No . . . ," he said, but she thought he was.

He added, "Are you upset about driving an old bus?"

"Oh, these things are to be expected," she said. "Lots of adjustments needed, several mixed signals, a snag here and there, but I'm making the best of it. For the most part I feel as if I'm making headway."

He let out a long, slow breath, a mixed sound of concern and curiosity that she had heard hundreds of times.

"I did promise Mr. and Mrs. Pugh that I would talk with you about a related matter, though."

"What's that?"

"Oh, it's just that they have an exaggerated view of the dead-chicken incident and think I ought to move into their house temporarily, because of the dead chickens and because of all the house renovation . . . and what-not . . . and I've told them several times already that it would be difficult for me to work well if I had to factor in another move so soon after the last, and Fannie Fay is used to the house, and I do have my own fix-up plans here that I want to proceed with, and, anyway, I said I would talk it over with you, but I've already decided I'm not moving in with the Pughs."

"If you've already made that decision, why are you discussing it with me?" His tone had turned from cautious to weary.

"Oh, I'm sorry, G.P. Of course I want your opinion on it. What is your opinion on it?"

He was not fooled. "My opinion—my useless opinion—is that if two people who have lived in the community for decades think there is sufficient danger for you to stay with them for a while, you should take their advice."

"But, Honey," she began.

"Never mind, Annie. I know you too well. You'll do what you plan to do, and nothing I say from here will change your mind. Just be careful, okay?"

"I'm always careful."

"I've gotta go." His voice was sadder than Annie had ever heard it.

"Okay. I love you," she said.

"I know that you do. But I don't think you know how much you mean to me." He ended the connection before she could respond.

Suddenly Annie hurt all over. She called Fannie Fay, took her to the back porch, sat at the table and wept quietly. It was only early afternoon, but already she had held awkward conversations with Mr. Gideon Pugh, Shirl Burrows and G.P. She had not told G.P. the entire truth, she had ignored the counsel of people who wanted only to help and support her, and she had involved her sister and dearest friend in her bone-hiding shenanigans.

Fannie Fay purred contentedly on Annie's lap despite her owner's errors. That was another thing. She had been ignoring her loyal little pet, the pet that sat patiently by the door waiting for her return each evening, the cat that greeted her each morning with cat talk and purred beside her elbow on the table while she drank coffee.

She was spending more time on the bones than she should, thus denying the congregation her full attention. Furthermore, she had not informed her superintendent about all the unpleasant incidents that had occurred. One or two little difficulties upon arrival were predictable, but three nasty incidents made a pattern, and Burl would certainly act on the pattern formed by the cat guts, the threat letter and the dead chickens if he knew of them or, really, when he knew of them. He would find out eventually. Of that she was sure.

Guilt poured over Annie's bruised soul like saltwater on an open wound.

~~0~~

Dear Diary,
I know why daddy always screamed at Frankie. He doesn't belong to my dad and daddy knows it. I think I don't belong to my dad either. It's like my mom and dad had two sets of kids, the good kids and the bad kids. My older sister and brother who live with grandma now are the good ones. They belong to dad. Me and Frankie are the bad ones but Frankie's worst of all. I'm not sure about Sissie. That's why daddy would always sit at the dinner table and say to Frankie who do you look like? I didn't know about this until we had sex in health class and now I know every thing that happens between a man and a woman. I think daddy knows that Frankie belongs to moms lover and not to him. I don't think he suspects I belong to the other man too. I think I belong to the other man because when daddy used to scream at Frankie for not looking like him mommy would look at me like to change the subject and say doesn't she look like Alma? Alma is daddys mother the one who takes care of my older brother and sister all by herself now that grand pa died with his heart. I hate it when mommy says I look like Grandma Alma because mommy hates Grandma Alma. I don't hate Grandma Alma. But I just wish she would take me to live with her like my older brother and sister. That's why I think I belong to the other man because Grandma Alma won't take me in and mommy always changes the subject so daddy won't think I look like the other man too. Mommy knows that if daddy suspects he'll beat on me the

way he used to beat on Frankie before Frankie went to stay most of the time with the coach and before daddy ran away with Wilma. Frankie is getting along a lot better at the coaches house now than he ever did at home. Mommy calls the coaches house and asks to talk to Frankie but they always say hes not there or taking a shower or mowing the yard.

"You have to dig deep to bury your Daddy." ~~ Gypsy proverb

CHAPTER FIFTY-ONE

Minnie Glendenning beckoned. Annie followed her to the back porch, and they sat in a canopied swing.

"I thought you would come today," Minnie said, offering iced tea from a side table. Soft sunlight dappled the herb and flower garden.

Annie shook her head. "Why?"

"We didn't get to finish our conversation last night," Minnie said.

"Minnie, I'm confused about the parsonage . . . about the things people say have gone on there."

"I know."

"You do?"

"I've watched you since you came. You're a determined lady, I'll give you that. "

"Thank you, Minnie. Maybe I am determined, but I'm also becoming frightened. So many things are happening."

"You're not used to living alone, are you?"

Annie looked past Minnie at the firethorn bushes that outlined the garden—big, wildly gyrating branches of vibrant red that invited hummingbirds—and remembered her mother's pyracantha bushes. She burst into tears.

Minnie, who seemed not at all alarmed, pulled a tissue from her pocket and handed it to Annie silently.

Annie sniffled and said, "Minnie, do you have any children?"

"Yes, but we . . . we're not in touch."

"I'm sorry to hear that," Annie said, but Minnie waved a hand to dismiss the topic.

"That's what's so hard for me," Annie said. "I've promised to serve the church wherever I am called, but the church is a long way from my family."

"What about your parents?" she asked.

Fresh tears brimmed up and spilled out. "My parents are gone . . . ."

"Were they good parents?" Minnie asked.

"Yes, very good."

"I don't know which is harder—when the parents are good or when they're not," Minnie said.

Annie understood that children hurt when they lost their parents no matter what kind of life they led. "Sometimes I feel like an orphan," Annie said.

Minnie only nodded.

"It would help me a lot to know more about the parsonage," Annie said. "Odd things seem to crop up all the time there."

Minnie crossed her arms over her painter's smock and said, "That house has been doomed for as many years as I can count."

"Please tell me about Mrs. Pargeon's herbs."

"Like I was sayin' last night, before all that other stuff got started at Ladies' Night Out, Old Lady Pargeon was a witch, sure as I'm a bowler."

Annie blew her nose and laughed. "I guess I wouldn't put witchery in the same alley as bowling. What did Mrs. Pargeon buy from you?"

"Oh, lots and lots of things over the years," Minnie said mysteriously.

"Can you remember anything in particular?"

"Well, the thing that blew my gasket was she was always after me for stinging nettle. It's not a bad remedy for arthritis, but you have to flail yourself with it to get the good out of it."

"No kidding?"

"Oh, I know some folks'll make it into a tea, but Old Lady Pargeon, she got it from me by the hank, and, well, there's some hard ways nettle's used."

"What kind of hard ways?"

"For childbirth and hemorrhoids—stuff like that," Minnie said.

"But what's so awful about that?"

"I never knew exactly what she was gonna do with my herbs. I tried not to sell her the kind that can cause hurt, but Old Lady Pargeon woulda burned down my house if I didn't sell to her."

"What else did she buy from you?" Annie asked.

Minnie took a long draft of special iced tea and twisted the hem of the smock. Her cheeks reddened, and Annie wondered whether this came from rum or embarrassment.

"I sold her comfrey, and they say that's bad for the liver. It's got some good applications, too, and I wouldn't have got so suspicious except she was always asking me about a couple o' other remedies that's just plain poisonous, no matter how you chop 'em or cook 'em."

"What poisonous herbs are you talking about?"

"Mandrake . . . and vervain . . . and henbane. Why, those are some of the most toxic herbs ever harvested. It was almost as if she was trying to poison someone to death."

"Minnie, do you really think Mrs. Pargeon was poisoning people?"

"I don't have proof, mind you, but there's been rumors. For one, I never did believe that story she told about old Ernie goin' off with another woman."

"Ernie was her husband, right?"

"Ain't nobody told you yet about old Ernie?" Minnie said, apparently astounded.

"I guess not. Please do tell."

"Well, Ernie was Old Lady Pargeon's husband. He went missing from work. Didn't show up for more'n a week—not that a drunk like him ever was reliable on the job to begin with. The boss went to the house lookin' for him, and Old Lady Pargeon said he'd hightailed to Montana with his girlfriend."

"And you did not believe that story?"

"Huh-uh. Not for a minute."

"Why not?"

"Pastor, this stuff is in the way of gossip, and I wouldn't want you to think I'd ever gossip."

"Of course not, Minnie. But I am interested in the background of the people in this community."

"Since you put it that way, I guess it is local history, kind of. Well, I never believed that story about Montana and the girlfriend and all. And neither did Shirl, by the way. First, because Ernie couldn't get . . . wasn't able . . . uh, you know, he couldn't do his husbandly duty."

"I think I understand," Annie said. "Is that why you think he didn't have a girlfriend?"

"Pastor, I don't think Ernie Pargeon coulda' had a girlfriend because there's no way people around here wouldn't a known about it."

"It is a close-knit community," Annie observed, which was her way of acknowledging that everybody knew everybody else's business in Biddlebourne.

"So then, as far as you know, Ernie Pargeon disappeared, and the reason given by Mrs. Pargeon for his disappearance seemed inadequate?" Annie asked.

"Yes."

"Minnie, was there a police investigation into Mr. Pargeon's disappearance?"

"Nope."

"How can you be sure?"

Minnie regarded Annie the way a mother regards a toddler, with a mixture of indulgence and patience. Finally she said, "Pastor, if Shirl don't know about a police investigation in Biddlebourne, and I don't know about a police investigation, it just flat-out didn't happen."

Annie laughed with Minnie and nodded to signal understanding. "Okay then. I believe you. But I'm very curious about something."

"What?"

"Minnie, do you think Mrs. Pargeon poisoned her husband to death?"

Minnie peered into the distance, then focused closer on Annie's face as if she were seeing her with new eyes. She flattened her hands on her knees. "I reckon she might have," she said. "But I'm just an old woman with a garden full of weeds. What do I know?"

"There's something else I'd like to know."

"Might as well ask. Cat's out of the bag now—no pun intended, Pastor," Minnie said with a grimace.

"When did Mr. Pargeon go missing?"

"Oh, about 1990."

"You seem sure of that."

"I remember it 'cause the census people were coming around that year and Gordie Hagendorn—he was goin' house to house for the census—got all bent out o' shape when Old Lady Pargeon said there was only one person living in the house."

"And Gordie expected her to say there were two, a wife and a husband?"

"No. Gordie expected her to say there was five: her, her husband and their three kids."

"Do you remember the children's names?"

"Course I do. I'm not in my dotage yet."

"I'm sorry, I didn't mean . . ."

But Minnie interrupted. "They called the boy Frankie and the girls Sissie and Izzie."

"Lizzie?"

"No. Izzie. Poor little thing. She hated bein' called Izzie. Old Lady Pargeon never dressed her nice or took her anywhere. I 'spect she never fed her much, either. She was skinny as a stick in winter. Nose always runnin'. I gave her more than one hot meal, mind you, but I never let on to anyone that I did 'cause Old Lady Pargeon woulda beat the tar out of the little girl . . . said no kid of hers would beg from the neighbors. That woman was one hell of an excuse for a mother, and nobody but nobody around here grieved her death."

A wave of cold shock hit Annie. "Was the child's name Isabelle?"

"Isabelle Marie Pargeon. That was her name. I know because she told me so herself one afternoon whilst we were sittin' right here on the porch, rockin' in the breeze and eatin' chocolate ice cream. She looked up at me with those big brown eyes and said, 'My real name is Isabelle Marie Pargeon.' I remember it like it was yesterday. And she said, 'But you can call me Belle.' I almost cried. She didn't have nothin' of her own except her name, and her nickname was always our little secret."

They sat silently for a minute while Minnie regained her composure.

"Whatever happened to Isabelle?" Annie asked.

"Disappeared. Just like her dad. One day she was in school, seventh or eighth grade, I think, and the next day she wasn't. The principal herself come to the Pargeons' house to see what happened. I know because my nephew Jasper—he's a mailman, you know—he had that route back then."

"What did Jasper see at the Pargeons?"

Minnie sniffled. "He didn't exactly see it. But when he was puttin' the mail in the box on the front porch he couldn't help hearin' the principal—I can't think of her name right now, but it'll come to me—ask about Isabelle, and Old Lady Pargon shoutin' at the principal to get the hell off her property, and her kids had gone to live with relatives, and good riddance to the little bastards. I'm sorry, but that's what she said. She called her own children little bastards. She was a hateful, evil woman. She's probably the one hauntin' the parsonage. Can't get any peace. Don't deserve any peace, you ask me."

"Minnie, I can't tell you how much you've helped me understand . . . things at the parsonage."

Minnie seemed overcome by the memories their conversation had evoked, and Annie was ashamed for causing her pain. But Minnie's recollections were God's answer to her recent, very fervent prayers.

Annie reached over to put her arm around Minnie, who wiped her eyes with the smock and said, "Look at me. Light's almost gone." She jumped up from the swing, went to an easel in the corner of the porch and picked up a paint palette.

"I'll be on my way," Annie said, but Minnie had already begun swirling vibrant colors on the canvas as if she could paint away the past.

Annie was elated, for the mystery of the bones was solved. Surely they were the remains of the late Mr. Ernie Pargeon, the boozing, boasting, missing husband of Mrs.

Vickie June Pargeon. Annie could get back to her
ministry. She could laugh with Ma and Pa Pugh over the
"cat holes" in the basement. She could relieve her friend
Gloriana of the burdensome possession of the bones. She
could e-mail G.P. and tell him the story of the bones, and
he would be relieved. She could, finally, to her sister's
complete satisfaction and relief, turn the bones over to the
proper authorities, carefully phrasing her report with
regard to time.

"I'll let myself out," Annie said. She tiptoed through
the kitchen and living room. When she got behind the
wheel of Old Yeller, she began humming *One Fine Day*.

Dear Diary,
When I wrote about going to our cusins place in Claypool
it made me remember one time we went to see the other
cusins in Pensilvanya. We spent a whole day there. We
were driving back daddy was driving and suddenly for no
reason he reached to the back seat and started punching
my brother Frankie in the head and body all over. Again
and again and again even while he was driving. Mommy
said for gods sake you jak ass leave him alone youll kill us
all. But daddy kept hollering he dont look like none of his
cousins eather Vickie none of them. Every thing about our
house was like the war until daddy left. I used to watch TV
about the Vetnam war every day. It used to be a battle
field here two in the car and in the house and in the yard
and in skul and in church. Funny thing is my oldest
brother the one who looks like daddy and who use to live
with grandma is in the army in the real Vetnam war thats
why I watch the war on TV every night mommy prays and
crys all the time for him. Now shes always drunk morning
noon and night, especially night.

"Fear has magnifying eyes." ~~ Proverb

CHAPTER FIFTY-TWO

Chloe stood on the front porch with her hands on her hips as Annie approached the parsonage. "Get up here quickly," she yelled.

"What's going on?" Annie demanded when she got to the top of the stone stairs.

"The police brought back your car," Chloe said.

"So I saw," Annie said. "Is that why I just ran up the steps and will soon need oxygen?"

"No, no. That Mrs. Pugh just called and said she and her husband were coming over tonight to look at the holes in the basement floor. I knew we couldn't let them do that. Annie, why did you dig all those holes anyway? Couldn't you have just dug around where the coal was and left well enough alone?"

"No, I couldn't," Annie said. "I dug the holes to look for other clues and . . . as a kind of random sampling to be sure there weren't other skeletons down there, to be sure it wasn't some kind of mass burial ground."

"Oh."

"What did you tell the Pughs?" Annie asked as they made their way to the dining table.

"That we were going out to dinner and would be back late, and you would speak with them tomorrow afternoon, after church."

Annie thought fast. She could tell the Pughs about the bones tonight, for she knew whose they were. The disclosure would surely solve a local riddle going back more than a dozen years. But even if Annie knew whose bones she had found, she did not know how they got to the basement. And, so intimate were the details revealed by Isabelle Pargeon in the little green diary, that Annie felt she knew the child and wanted to protect her. What had happened to Isabelle, or Belle, as she preferred to be called? What had happened to Frankie and Sissie? Had Vickie June or any of the children had a part in Ernie's death?

She had only half a minute to make her decision. Chloe was tapping her fingernails on her alligator handbag.

Finally Annie said, "Thank you. I guess that means we have to hotfoot out of here for dinner and stay out until quite late. Otherwise, the Pughs might just 'happen to drive by' and we'll have to take them downstairs and tell all."

"What have I told you all along?" Chloe said. "Didn't I say you should have given the bones up as soon as you found them? Didn't I? Now look at the mess we're in. I can feel the worry lines forming on my face. And by the way, you have a batch of other phone messages on your machine."

"I have a lot to tell you," Annie said, ignoring Chloe's tirade. "But for now I'll check my messages and get ready to go. I'll call Glori on the way to see if we can pick her up for dinner. I'll fill you both in on what I know. You can drive."

"I hate worrying. I shall have to get facial injections after this."

Desperate enough to spend money, Annie asked, "Would a lobster salad calm your nerves?"

"Perhaps, if accompanied by chilled white wine and a light lemon mousse," she said, checking her makeup in the compact from her purse.

"Okay," Annie said.

"Okay," Chloe said.

As it turned out, Annie felt guilty enough to treat both Gloriana and Chloe to lobster dinners at Bells Inn, an upscale restaurant on the shore of a lake formed by a dam.

"I brought my printouts from the library," Chloe said when they had ordered their "hospitality drinks," the freebies offered by the management to whet their palates for more costly fare.

"No need," Annie said. And she proceeded to tell them about Mr. Ernie Pargeon, husband unapparent of the late Mrs. Vickie June Pargeon.

Chloe and Gloriana were transfixed and relieved by Annie's patchwork story of Ernie Pargeon's disappearance.

"I can spend more time with the living now," Gloriana said. "Those bones were creepy."

"I'll pick them up tonight when we drop you off at home," Annie promised.

"I found not one promising lead at the library," Chloe stated.

The waiter arrived with their Mermaid of the Mist, Dam Slam and Lady in the Lake, the last of which was chilled white wine embellished with two candied cherries. When they saw the size and not-so-subtle placement of the two cherries in Chloe's drink, they had a fit of laughter.

"Shhh, people are starting to look at us," Gloriana said.

"They are?" Chloe replied. She straightened her back, tossed her hair off her forehead and looked around with a portrait smile.

"I doubt anybody here recognizes you, if that's what you're thinking," Annie told her. "Seriously, Pittsburgh is way too far for most people around here to go for a show."

"You forget, sister dear, that I have appeared in no fewer than seven regionally aired television advertisements for Novack Chevrolet, the Ohio Valley's leading provider of high-quality, high-value family transportation."

"Really? Wow!" said Gloriana.

"Please, Glori, don't encourage her," Annie pleaded.

The waiter had borne their sidebar stoically but now said, "Ladies, perhaps you are ready to order?"

After they ordered, they toasted the closure of the "Case of the Parsonage Bones," as Chloe dubbed it.

"Just one thing still bothers me about the bones," Gloriana said.

"What's that?" Annie said.

"Well, clearly Mr. Pargeon was a heavy drinker. And clearly he and Mrs. Pargeon had a poor marriage, but what if she really did poison him?"

"Don't you see?" Annie said. "It doesn't matter now if she did. Mrs. Pargeon is dead. A crime can't be prosecuted without a suspect."

"What if the kids helped her kill him and they are implicated somehow?" Gloriana pressed.

"What if they did?" Annie said. "The kids are nowhere to be found, and at this point I cannot imagine that there is sufficient evidence to make any sort of case. Besides, everybody in Biddlebourne knows that Ernie Pargeon was a falling-down drunk. Everybody will assume that he failed to survive his last drinking binge."

Even as she spoke, Annie's fears about Isabelle multiplied. It was as if Isabelle "Belle" Pargeon had confided all her troubles to Annie. She felt human concern, as well as pastoral concern, for the little girl of

1010 Greenbriar Road. Isabelle's secrets had become Annie's secrets. Chloe and Gloriana's ties to the bones were broken, but Annie's certainly were not.

Further, Annie knew, it mattered a great deal whether Isabelle Pargeon was connected to her father's death because Isabelle Pargeon was alive and in Biddlebourne.

Annie was startled to hear Chloe asking, "But why didn't Mrs. Pargeon report his death?"

"Who knows?" Annie said. "My guess is that she was too drunk to think straight or that she killed him. Either way, it's all moot now."

It was well past the Pughs' bedtime when Annie and Chloe got back to the parsonage. Annie took the bones out of the Corvette and stashed them in the first relatively safe place she spied.

As Annie closed the top of the piano, Chloe admired herself in the mirror on the dining room wall. "Now my complexion can return to its naturally radiant state."

Before they slept, Chloe agreed to attend worship the next morning, not so much to hear another of Annie's sparkling sermons as to provide moral support when her sister told the Pughs about the bones.

The night was heavy with humidity. Chloe grumbled as she fetched ice and fan for the Misty Blue Room. Annie had no complaints as she prepared to sleep in pillow-top comfort on the new king-size bed in the USA Room. Fannie Fay paced, which behavior Annie took to be her way of stalking the bird family in the attic.

Annie flipped her bedside light on and picked up Belle Pargeon's little green diary. She prayed for her husband, her children, her grandchildren and Isabelle Marie Pargeon. Then she turned to page seventy-two.

~~0~~

Dear Diary,
We have dogs and cats at our house. Mommy says now
that daddys gone and Im in sixth grade and old enough to
feed them and clean up after them we can have dogs and
cats because there better company than daddy was. It
makes me sad she says it but I like the dogs and cats. Only
problem is they have to be shot sooner or later. Mommy
says oh the dog has rabies we have to shoot it or the cat
has fleas we have to shoot it. Then Frankie gets one of his
buddies and takes the shotgun out of the cabinet in the
basement where daddy kept it and goes to the dump and
shoots the cat or dog in the head. Sometimes I don't even
see them go to the dump and there's another hill of dirt in
the back yard where they buried the cat or the dog or the
puppies or kittens. Isnt that nice. Frankie told me this
morning that we use to have a maid when I was a baby. I
cant imagine that because mommy and daddy always say
were poor and dont have any money. Then Frankie told
me why. Because daddy broke mom's arm and leg and she
couldn't do anything so he got her a maid so he wouldn't
have to do anything. Now Im the maid. I do all the cooking
and cleaning and laundry. It makes me really tired but at
least we have clean clothes and some thing to eat. Mommy
complains about what I make. Hamburgers and french
fries are still my favorite and thats what I make but
mommy wants roast and I dont know how to make it. Mrs.
P. showed me how she makes roast but I didn't write it
down and can't remember it now. I know you start with a
big piece of meat. Thats all I remember.

"He that is down needs fear no fall." ~~ John Bunyan

CHAPTER FIFTY-THREE

Sunday, July 17

The explosion was thunderous. G.P. stumbled out of the smoke and saluted the madcap men who scurried all over the scene. Sulfurous fumes singed Annie's nostrils. Fannie Fay hissed and arched and paced. Gloriana waved at them and walked without crutches into the clearing beyond the flames. Great-Grandmother Annie Ido Stealey mopped her face with a big, white muslin apron and called Annie in for blackberry pie. Mr. Gideon Pugh put a ladder to the side of the house and shouted incoherently into one window after another. Chloe carried, on her back, a mirror as big as a grandfather clock.

Annie's eardrums ached and her breathing stalled. Sweat soaked her nightgown. She struggled to free herself from the vise. Instinctively, she reached for Fannie Fay on the bed beside her. Fannie Fay was not there.

Annie turned toward the bedside clock. The dial glowed dimly. It was three in the morning. She willed her eyes to open. She must find Fannie Fay. She must get a glass of water.

Soon Annie's mind began to clear, but the room remained shrouded. Gray moonbeams haloed the room.

She could see the air—wispy and diaphanous like a gauze shroud. How odd.

She got out of bed and turned on the ceiling light. The moonbeams disappeared, but the smoke remained. The odor remained. The heat remained.

Later, Annie did not recall calling 911 and getting Chloe and Fannie Fay out of the house. She didn't recall how long it took two fire trucks, an ambulance and three police cruisers to arrive. She didn't recall who called Mr. Gideon Pugh or any of the other church trustees who parked in the Wilsons' driveway and stood silently at the edge of the parsonage property. And she didn't know how dozens of people got to the parsonage so quickly with blankets, food, first aid and pole lights.

"Pastor Ma'am," Mr. Gideon Pugh said, "are you sure you and Miss Chloe are okay?"

Annie, Chloe and Mr. Gideon Pugh were standing in a huddle by the mailbox, watching hundreds of gallons of water being pumped into and onto the parsonage even though the fire seemed to have ebbed.

Annie nodded. Chloe nodded. Fannie Fay buried her head in the collar of Annie's robe.

"You folks was the only ones in there?" he asked.

"Oh, yes. We were out late and dropped a friend off before we came home," Annie said.

"Okay. Just wanted to be sure."

"I don't know what happened," Annie said. "We were sleeping. I remember dreaming about an explosion. Did you hear anything, Chloe?"

"Of course not," she said. "I was using my earplugs to cover the chirping of those dreadful birds in the attic."

"Frank—Frank Zellerman, he's the fire chief, you know . . . ," Mr. Gideon Pugh said.

"I know. He goes to the Presbyterian Church, right?" Annie said.

"Yes, ma'am. Frank says the fire prob'ly started in the basement."

"But what started it?" Annie asked.

"Frank's got a good eye for fire investigatin', Pastor Ma'am. He'll get out here with his crew later today and go over everything real good. We'll get to the bottom o' this, believe you me."

"I know the church has insurance on the building," Annie said, "and G.P. and I carry a policy on our belongings. Still . . ."

"Don't you fret, Pastor Ma'am, you and Miss Chloe and, uh, the cat can come right on over and stay as long as you like with me and Ma."

"I'll consider that. Thank you very much."

"Least we can do, under the circumstances."

"Speaking of circumstances, Mr. Pugh, I want to ask you something," Annie said.

"Yes, ma'am?"

"I am trying not to be paranoid, but do you think this fire is tied to the threat letter or the dead chickens or . . . ?"

"Pastor Ma'am," he began, and he took a bandana from his overalls pocket and rubbed his neck and arms. He stuffed it back into the pocket and kept his gaze on the parsonage.

"I hate to think it. Ma's been awful wound up about things goin' on around here since you got to town. Nothin' like this ever happened before in these parts."

"But what do *you* think?" she persisted.

"I think we got a serious problem that ain't goin' away, just gittin' worse, practically by the day."

"I agree, and I want to talk more with you and Ma about the problem," Annie said. "But for now, Mr. Pugh, I need to get some valuables out of the house. Do you think Frank would let me go back in—that is, with a firefighter escort?"

"I'll check, but don't count on it." He walked toward the knot of heavy-jacketed volunteers who had turned out.

"Give me your keys. I'm going to move the cars," Chloe offered.

"I don't have the keys," Annie said.

"But your purse is hanging on your shoulder."

"I already looked, and my keys aren't inside my purse. I must have left them on the dining table. I was so intent on getting out of the house with you and Fannie Fay—and the diary—that I forgot the keys."

"Well, I'm going to move my car," Chloe said, heading for the Corvette.

Mr. Gideon Pugh came back with Frank Zellerman.

"Reverend Scovill, I can't let you go back in there right now," Frank said. "There's likely some hot spots in there, plus, in an old building like that . . . how old'd you say it is, Gideon?"

"At least a hundred and forty years old."

"Pshew! Older'n I thought. Like I was saying, with an old house like that we have a lot of unknowns. I can't risk letting you back in there until we're satisfied the fire is out and there is no further danger."

"But my car keys are on the dining table," Annie explained. "I won't be able to move my car or my husband's truck away from the smoke and water. Really, Chief Zellerman, I would very much like to move our vehicles, as well as Hermie's bus that he was kind enough to lend to me. You see how close they are to the house. I fear an explosion."

"Well, that is a problem, I admit," the chief said. "Tell you what, I'll send Orlando and Haninbee in to get 'em. Dining table, you said?"

"Well, probably. I'm not entirely certain. Maybe I should go in myself."

An irritated groan came from his gut. "I don't have time to waste on this. You stay between Orlando and Haninbee at all times. Am I clear?"

"Yes, of course."

The hose crew had nearly completed their work, and Chief Zellerman told them to stand down. He put an outsized slicker and fire hat on Annie, and she traipsed up the stone steps with Julia Haninbee ahead of her and Ellis Orlando behind her.

"Straight ahead, please. The dining room is just beyond the living room," she said to Julia as they went in the front door. Julia turned and took Annie's right hand with her left and shuffled carefully ahead, piercing the damp darkness in front of them with the beam of a large flashlight. Annie tried not to think about the soggy carpet and waterlogged furniture as they crept to the dining room.

"Oh, here they are. Oh, darn!" Annie said as she quickly pulled the keys from her pocket and let them fall on the floor. She pointed down and said, "There they are." Ellis Orlando got in her face and motioned for her to stay put before he bent to retrieve the keys. He jangled them for good measure, put them in a huge pocket of his slicker and pointed back to the front door to direct Annie out of the house.

"Just one more thing," Annie said. Before either chaperone could argue, she went to the upright piano on the north wall of the living room, opened the walnut top and pulled out the garbage bag filled with the supposed remains of Ernie Pargeon.

"That's all, ma'am. Let's go," Julia Haninbee said firmly.

"Certainly," Annie answered. She turned back to speak to Julia, and as she did so she thought she caught a movement on the staircase.

"What's that?" she said, peering over Julia's shoulder to the stairs.

"The chief said to make this quick. Let's move," Ellis ordered.

"I think I see a hand moving over there," Annie said, moving toward the staircase.

"Stop right there, ma'am," Julia said, turning in the darkness to play the light beam toward the stairs. She froze the light. A fallen body lay near the top of the staircase. It was in deep shadow, but Annie could see that the body was that of a woman—a slight woman wearing a T-shirt, jeans . . . and red sandals.

Annie stepped quickly toward the staircase, catching just one glimpse of the fallen woman before Julia said, "Ellis, take Reverend Scovill out of the building and send in the rescue squad. We have another occupant."

As Annie gawped at the figure on the stairs, Ellis moved in to take her hand. She moved like a robot, so distracted was she by what she had just seen.

Annie gave the slicker and hat back to the chief and rejoined Chloe by the mailbox. Mr. Gideon Pugh had gone to speak with the other trustees. Fannie Fay jumped from Chloe's arms onto Annie's shoulders as soon as she approached and sniffed her hair.

"Did you get the keys?" Chloe asked.

Annie felt as if she had just walked away from another universe. She had to force herself back to the present. "Uh . . . yes, as well as . . . Mr. Pargeon."

"But what's all the excitement about? Why are they sending firefighters back into the house?"

"I'll tell you in a minute. First, would you move the Volvo for me? I want to move G.P.'s truck and Old Yeller. I'll join you in the Volvo when I'm done. Okay?"

Fannie Fay was glad to curl herself into a tight ball and go to sleep on the backseat of the Volvo. Annie and Chloe sat in front. They were near the Wilsons' property, where the lineup of vehicles made it look like a drive-in theater.

"They're taking a stretcher into the house!" Chloe said, for she had been careful to park the car so as to secure the best view of the rescuers and their vehicles. A gallery of floodlights had been set up, turning the gray lady into the star of her own horror movie.

Chloe got out of the car long enough to rearrange the bed sheet that covered the seat, then jumped back in. "Who's in there, Annie?"

"When we went back for my keys—and the bones—there was somebody lying on the staircase going up to the second floor. A woman."

"What? I don't understand," Chloe said.

"Neither do I, entirely," Annie said.

Chloe's face grew somber. "Did you hear anything unusual tonight?" she asked.

"Like I told Mr. Pugh, I dreamed of an explosion."

"Maybe you weren't dreaming. Maybe the person they found set the fire . . . or planted a bomb," she said.

Annie thought briefly. "Possibly, but I don't think so."

Annie was about to say more when Chief Zellerman tapped on the windshield. She poked her head out the window, and he said, "Reverend Scovill, can you identify the victim?"

"Victim? I pray she is not dead."

"The paramedics took her in. She was alive when they left. Smoke inhalation. Reason I came over here is we didn't find any ID. Any idea who she is?"

"I couldn't say. Sorry."

"Thanks just the same, Reverend," he said and turned to go. But he looked back over his shoulder and said, "Haninbee reported that you removed property from the house in addition to your keys. I'm curious as to what that is."

"Um . . . just a bag of valuables that has been in my safekeeping." The chief nodded and departed.

"Annie, for God's sake, why'd you tell him that? Couldn't you just tell him about the bones?" Chloe said.

"This isn't the right time," Annie said.

Chloe groaned.

"Forget that," Annie said. "We have to figure out where to stay now that the Misty Blue Room and the USA Room are no longer open for business."

"Didn't you accept an invitation from Mr. Pugh?"

"Not exactly. I'm uncomfortable with the idea of living with any of my parishioners. No privacy . . ."

"Isn't there a Marriott around here?"

"Hardly, but I doubt the church could afford a hotel anyway."

As if on cue, Ma Pugh peered in Annie's window. "Pastor Annie, just follow Gideon and me back to the house. We have two rooms already made up. You and Miss Chloe can stay with us as long as you need to."

Annie hoped Ma Pugh did not hear Chloe's low groan. For once, Annie's feelings matched her sister's. It was time for tact.

"Oh, we could not impose on you," Annie said. "Both of us are picky eaters, and Fannie Fay is a nuisance, and I have calls at all hours and am constantly running in and out of the house."

Ma Pugh chuckled and said, "Pastor, you'd think me and Pa never had six kids high-jinking morning, noon and night and every one of 'em wantin' their own special menu. Why, I can cook up 'most anything spur of the moment. And Pa and I sleep sound as logs on the riverbank. Can't wake us up no matter how hard you try."

"I'm afraid Fannie Fay is terribly spoiled and will natter ceaselessly with your own cat."

"No problem," Mrs. Pugh pronounced. "We'll just send Mister Whiskers to the barn as long as we need to. It's summer and he'll be just fine. He loves it there, chasin' the hens and jumping on the hay. Miss Fannie Fay will have the run of the house," she finished in triumph.

Chloe interrupted. "Oh, Mrs. Pugh, I have terrible allergies," she fabricated effortlessly. "They have been acting up, I regret to report, ever since my arrival. I fear that I must find a room fitted with HEPA filters and non-allergenic bedclothes. But thank you very much for your kind offer."

Chloe's lies were light-years better than Annie's. She sat in awe and turned to hear Mrs. Pugh's response to Chloe's "medical condition."

"Our second girl, Diane, had the same troubles as you. Her bedroom's still got all those gadgets in it. She hasn't been gone but a couple years, you know. We got fiberfill in the comforter, no goose down, and took out the carpet and put in hardwood. I vacuum the curtains and all with a special filter, and there's a special filter on the furnace and on the air conditionin', though we won't need the air conditionin' till August, and of course I done up every sheet and blanket in that room with non-allergic detergent. Let's see, is there anything else?" she asked herself.

That was how Annie and Chloe found themselves being tucked into their beds at six on Sunday morning by Ma Pugh. In one hour Annie would hear the buzzer on the aqua-blue clock-radio and the strains of Three Dog Night's *Joy to the World*.

Death in the Parsonage

"Make ado and have ado." ~~ Proverb

CHAPTER FIFTY-FOUR

Worship attendance Sunday morning was spectacular, given that word of the parsonage fire had made it to the metro page of the *Intelligencer* and therefore been read on the air by every radio station from Charleston to Chester.

Several reporters attended the last few minutes of the service and rushed up to Annie afterward with microphones and cameras. She directed them to Mr. Gideon Pugh and the other trustees, wishing neither to seek the limelight nor to be filmed wearing a dress of Ma Pugh's bought in the era of flounces and flowers.

A grave discussion had been held on the possibility of Annie's gathering some of her own clothes from the parsonage. Her wardrobe was believed by Chief Zellerman to be "plenty wet but not necessarily ruined." But he had safety concerns, and the house was, he reminded everyone several times, the scene of an ongoing investigation. In the interest of convenience, time and safety Annie went with the purple organza from Ma Pugh's closet.

For shoes she wore a pair of Glenn Pugh's sneakers, hand-me-downs that Ma Pugh had salvaged from her donation box. The tennis shoes were the only footwear in the Pugh house besides snow boots and flip-flops that fit

Annie. Chloe had volunteered to go out and buy shoes "that don't make you look like a locker-room vagabond," but Annie thought Ma Pugh would be hurt if the tennis shoes were rejected.

Of course, Chloe had refused to be seen in public in any garments other than her own crisply tailored, carefully selected, closely matched ensembles and stayed behind when Annie left for church in the smelly Volvo. Hermie had already picked up Old Yeller, Ma Pugh told the pastor over breakfast of grits and eggs. Ma had to explain to Annie what grits were, but both grits and explanation stuck on the way down.

Now Annie was seated in her study. Every worshipper had stopped after the service to tell her they were sorry about the fire and would help her any way they could. Annie was grateful but bushed. She was also very anxious about G.P. The Pughs owning no contraption so newfangled as a personal computer, she had e-mailed him from her office before worship. She was disappointed to find no response yet from him and reluctantly headed to the home of her host and hostess.

Lunch at the Pugh house was a six-ring circus. Various children and grandchildren came and went, helping themselves from numerous dishes magically prepared by Ma Pugh between 11:30 a.m. and 12 noon. Annie had no appetite. Chloe ate a thin piece of ham and three slices of cucumber.

Annie went to her room and fretted. She could not sleep. She made numerous calls on her cell phone to check on church matters and to reassure G.P.'s parents again that she was all right. She checked repeatedly, and futilely, for incoming calls. Her laptop was useless without an internet connection.

Around three o'clock Police Chief Ike Henderson called to ask if Annie had any second thoughts about the identity of the burn victim. She didn't think twice before telling him that she believed the woman to be Isabelle Marie Pargeon, long missing daughter of the late Vickie June and Ernie Pargeon.

Ike expressed little surprise at the news. "I thought it might be her," he said cryptically, then hung up.

Restless and anxious, desperately needing rest but distressed by Ike's news that Isabelle remained in serious condition, Annie knocked on Chloe's door.

"I've had no beauty sleep for two nights in a row, and now you have interrupted my nap," Chloe griped. "What's wrong with you, Annie? You should be resting, too."

"I can't sleep. We have to take a field trip."

Chloe grimaced. "In this heat? It had better be to the mall for clothes."

The heat had come slithering back to West Virginia, wilting cornstalks, toasting lawns and inciting cicadas nearly to riot. The parsonage was no more—and hence parsonage air conditioning would never be. The Pughs staunchly held to their August-only air-conditioning philosophy. An electrical brown-out had caused the trustees to declare the church closed to all activities except worship. The mall was the only haven available to Annie and Chloe that had the twin luxuries of cool air and no eavesdroppers.

"Yes, a trip to the mall," Annie said. "Get dressed. Meet me at the Volvo."

As they drove to the mall in Parkersburg, Chloe complained that the car stank. Chloe complained that she was too tired even to shop. Chloe complained that the right stores weren't open Sunday afternoon "in the country."

Annie led Chloe to the Coffee Hut and bought two diet caramel lattes. When they were seated with the cool sweetness lingering on their lips, Annie said, "I want to search the woods behind the parsonage."

"What in God's name for?"

"Isabelle Pargeon's special hiding place."

"Isabelle Pargeon?"

"The girl who wrote the diary."

"You think she's in the woods?"

"No. She's in the hospital. She's the woman who was burned in the fire last night."

"But why was she in the parsonage? Why do you want to scout the forest in this heat? What does this have to do with me?"

"Never mind," Annie said. "You don't have to come. I can manage quite well by myself."

"Bull . . . oney," said she of the pink muck-abouts and satin hiking shirt. "You cannot possibly go on such a foolish errand alone. You'll be eaten by jackals or some other offspring of the wild."

"Not if you fend them off with your Gucci belt. Let's go while there's light."

The woods behind the parsonage were thick and neglected. Some trees were only dead hulls stretching high arms to the summer sky, but the shrubs hugged the earth, covering it like a carpet of briars.

"I thought you said it would be cooler in the evening," Chloe complained. They had been tramping half an hour, Annie leading and Chloe following, without finding a sign of habitation by Isabelle or any other human.

"It is," Annie said. "Didn't you see the big thermometer at the Marathon station? Ninety degrees."

"Ninety degrees with ninety percent humidity. Why, oh why, couldn't I have a sister who likes to take naps and go to the spa?"

"The sauna at the spa is hotter than this," Annie said.

"And the bowels of hell are hotter still," Chloe rejoined. "Besides, you're never going to find it anyway. You have no idea what you're looking for."

"It's the only place I can think of to look. I have to find it."

"Why? Why must you be responsible for everything?"

"Because Isabelle's life and future are at stake. Because her father's body lay buried for years in the basement of the parsonage. Because, intentionally or not, she reached out to me. Because she's alone and hurt. Because nobody except me cares about Isabelle."

"But what do you hope to find in the woods?

"I'd settle for anything that helps me understand what she was doing in the parsonage last night. In her diary she talks about a special hiding place in the woods. She can't have gone far. She was only seven or eight years old."

"I have to rest," Chloe said. They sat on a log. She continued, "You're way ahead of me. I'm still trying to figure out how you know the woman is Isabelle."

"I figured it out. First I met her upstairs in the house last week when I had to go home on an emergency. I found her in the bedroom, and she told me she was there to measure for drapes. But that was a lie. I was so distracted at the time that I let her get away."

"Hm."

"When I got dressed for Ladies' Night Out Friday, I couldn't find my red leather espadrilles."

Chloe was growing impatient. "That makes as much sense as slinking about the trees and . . . the other woodsy things. You still have not indicated how you know the woman is Isabelle Pargeon."

"I know she's Isabelle because I saw a picture of her in Minnie Glendenning's house yesterday. She was much younger in the picture, but those big, brown eyes are unmistakable. And there's one more thing."

"I can't wait to hear."

"The woman in the fire was wearing my red sandals."
Chloe took a deep breath. "Are you sure?"

"Positive."

"So the woman who was found in the burning house is
the same person who wrote the diary, and her name is
Isabelle Pargeon, and she roamed these woods when she
was a child."

"Exactly."

"And you want to help her in some way," Chloe
continued.

"She will come under suspicion in the parsonage fire,
and I . . ."

". . . don't think she set it," Chloe concluded.

"That's right," Annie said. "She was abused horribly as
a child. I know abused children become abusive adults,
but there is a tender and compassionate side of her that I
see in her diary. Biddlebourne did not take good care of
Isabelle Pargeon."

Chloe pulled the Cozumel scarf from her pocket,
folded it carefully and dabbed at a spot over her upper lip.
She arose and crept farther into the trees. Annie followed.
They walked carefully, looking for any sign of human
presence—a tissue, a wrapper, broken twigs. Saplings
switched their ankles and arms, and the mossy earth tried
to swallow their shoes. Annie had Mr. Gideon Pugh's big
barn flashlight, and she snapped it on when dusk turned to
darkness.

They sat on two rocks to catch their breath.

"You are such an idealist," Chloe opined.

"I know I can't make the world right," Annie said.

"Can anybody?"

"God can . . . and is."

"I know you believe that stuff," Chloe said, "but anyone can see the world's a mess. Everything's corrupted. Everything's a lie. Everything's futile."

Annie turned to look at Chloe. "I've never heard you talk that way."

"You think I'm shallow."

"You are not shallow. You are vain," Annie noted.

Living limbs swayed in the wind. Dead ones stiffened. "Why, thank you," Chloe said.

They nibbled on candy corn picked from the Pughs' coffee table.

Chloe said, "Why did you wait so late to start this search? We'll get lost and stumble over vines and lie dying in the deep woods until vultures find our bodies."

"Sister dear, you make everything an adventure," Annie said.

They crept in the back door at the Pugh house shortly before eleven. Ma sat at the kitchen table in the dim glow of a night-light plugged in next to the toaster.

She was reading *The Upper Room* and looked up through the top of her bifocals. Annie and Chloe were filthy and sweaty. Ironically—perhaps justly—Chloe wheezed and sniffled in allergic response to old weedy enemies she'd met in the woods. Annie had a dozen or so insect bites and was scratching furiously.

Ma Pugh didn't say a word. She pointed. Annie and Chloe sat. Ma arose, rummaged in kitchen drawers and set two wet washcloths and a homemade medicine kit on the table. Annie and Chloe wiped with the cloths. Ma swabbed the pastor's insect bites with alcohol and a clear liquid called ZMO. She left the kit on the table, tossed a bag of cottonballs beside it and walked out of the room. At the doorway, without looking back, she said, "Good night, girls. Sleep tight."

Death in the Parsonage

"There are three sides to every story—yours, mine, and all that lie between." ~~ Jody Kern

CHAPTER FIFTY-FIVE

Monday, July 18

Seated with Annie were Mr. Gideon Pugh, present in his capacity as chair of the church board of trustees; Ma Pugh, present in her capacity as chair of the pastoral liaison committee; Ike Henderson, present in his capacity as Biddlebourne police chief and—last and anything but least—the Rev. Burl Stout, superintendent of the church district.

It was potentially helpful, Annie thought as they gathered in her office Monday morning, that Ike's uncle, Phil Avery, was an A-member of the Glory Hallelujah congregation who lived with Ike and Betty Henderson.

Annie had visited the Henderson/Avery home the previous week. The pastor and Betty had enjoyed a chat about Sunday school curriculum and seafood while Ike sat tall in his recliner and tried to keep his gaze off an Indians game on TV. Uncle Phil was at the golf club in Spartansville practicing putts.

On the other hand, Annie thought, it was potentially problematic that she had failed to mention the bones to anyone official, most especially Burl. Burl, of course, had been formally notified of the parsonage fire, and that was the ostensible reason for his presence in her office, but Annie wondered what else he knew.

"Chief Henderson," Burl said, "I am quite distressed by what I have been hearing."

Annie closed her eyes and mourned the loss of her navy-blue suit, white pearl earrings and blue Nikes. Now the high-top tennies were not only ugly and outlandish but also damp and dirty from Sunday's field trip.

Annie gave the superintendent her full attention, as did the others. No one said anything, so Burl continued. "Needless to say, the bishop and I pray for the recovery of the young woman who was injured in the fire, but we are concerned about the possibility it was arson. Chief, what can you report about the cause of the fire?"

"At this point, we have no conclusions, Reverend Stout, although we are conducting a thorough investigation into the fire. All we know so far is that the gas water heater exploded."

"Have you contacted the state fire investigator's office," Burl queried.

"Yes, sir, we have, although I have the highest confidence in our own department," Ike said. "Chief Zellerman of our fire department serves as a teacher for the state, as a matter of fact."

Mr. Gideon Pugh shifted his weight in the chair and cleared his throat. "Mr. Superintendent, Ike here may have his doubts about arson, but I don't."

"May I ask you to explain?" Burl said.

"Pastor's been the target of odd goings-on ever since she came here."

Burl eyed Annie. He lowered his head a bit as if taking upon himself some guilt for this state of affairs. "How's that, Mr. Pugh?" he said quietly.

"I'm surprised the pastor ain't told you herself," he said. Annie did not furnish the pause that ensued, so he continued. "She got a bag o' smashed-up cat guts her first day in the house. Some gad-body left it on the front porch in a store-bought coffee sack, but it was cat guts no matter how it was packaged up, and there was a threat in it, too."

Burl exhibited no surprise upon receiving this information. "Go on," he said.

"Then that letter came tellin' her she had got warned, or some such nasty talk, and not too long after that somebody unloaded a crate or two o' dead chickens in her car . . . ."

"I see." Burl's tone was ominously calm.

"Yes, sir," Ike Henderson pitched in. "My sergeant's been workin' hard to find out who's behind the chicken incident. That was more than a kid's prank, you know. It was deliberate and criminal mischief. And it was darned unusual for Biddlebourne. I'll grant you, the kids'll sometimes pull a slick one with tomatoes or eggs, but this is the first time anyone ever wasted three dozen good chickens like this in the seventeen years I've been with the department."

"Hm," Burl said. He looked at Annie closely. She took that as her cue.

"There is one additional irregularity that must also be dealt with," Annie said. She went to the large bookcase beside the door, pulled the bone bag from behind it and handed it to Ike.

Ike carefully untied the knot in the neck of the sack and peered inside. "These appear to be human remains," he noted. Mr. Gideon Pugh frowned. Burl Stout gazed intently at Annie. Ma Pugh sniffled, and Annie knew it wasn't from allergies.

"Ma, are you all right?" Annie asked.

For an answer, Ma turned to Burl. "Pastor here, she ain't had nothin' but hardship since comin' to Biddlebourne. All that messin' around in her house and the other things . . . and now this fire . . . and a bag of bones!" She took a hanky from her dress pocket and wiped tears from her eyes. The air in the room was heavy with unanswered questions and unspoken accusations.

"Ma," Annie said, but Burl butted in. "Mrs. Pugh, I am aware of Pastor Annie's difficulties, and I promise you that I will do everything in my power to sort this out properly and fairly."

Ma Pugh was not impressed. "Everybody's taken a shine to Pastor Annie. Don't you and that other guy . . . that bishop whatshisname . . . go and put her somewhere else. It's awful hard breakin' in a pastor."

"Now, now, Ma, don't worry," Mr. Gideon Pugh said. He patted her knee. She straightened her back and gave Burl a solid glare.

It was unclear whether the conversational ball was in Burl's court or Ike's. Burl appeared to be waiting for Ike to resume the discussion about the bones Annie had just produced.

"Pastor, what can you tell me about these bones?" Ike said at last.

"Well, you mean like when did I find them?"

"Oh, just for starters," he said with unconcealed sarcasm.

"I dug them up by accident on July third."

"How did you do that?" the chief asked.

"It was quite innocent," Annie said. "I was removing the coal from the coal cellar so that the furnace installers would have a clear work area, and when I swept the floor I saw one bone sticking up. And I got curious and dug up the rest of the bones."

"Why in God's name—uh, excuse me, Pastor—why in the world didn't you bring the bones to the station at that time?"

"It's rather complicated," Annie said.

"I'm not in a hurry," the chief said. Burl's mouth, which had dropped open when the bone bag appeared, remained agape.

"I didn't want to cause undue concern to my husband, G.P. He's with the Air Force Reserve overseas. He was already anxious about . . . about other circumstances in the parsonage. I couldn't bring myself to tell him I'd found a body in the basement." Annie thought she saw Mr. Gideon Pugh suppressing a grin.

"Just how long did you intend to maintain possession of the remains?" Ike asked.

"Until I figured out whose they were and could thus assure G.P. there were no sinister connotations. Nothing for him to worry about. Nothing that would make him slip up and . . . get hurt."

"And did you in fact conduct some kind of investigation?" Ike asked incredulously.

"In a way," Annie said.

"In what way?"

"I looked up some records and asked about a belt buckle and a ring I found with the bones." She was treading perilously close to revealing the roles of Gloriana and Chloe in her subterfuge. Annie closed her mouth and hoped for the best.

"Tell us, please, what you discovered."

"Nothing for sure," Annie said.

"Pastor, there's an inconsistency in your report," Ike said pointedly.

"There is?"

"Yes. A minute ago you said you intended to keep the bones until you identified them, and now you have turned over the bones but say you have not learned whose they are. Which is the truth?"

"Uh, well, I . . . only think I may have figured out whose skeleton it is. It's only a guess, mind you."

"Let's hear your guess," Ike said.

"Chief, I'd really rather not say just yet."

There were sharp intakes of breath in the room. Ma Pugh continued wiping her nose. Mr. Gideon Pugh's face reddened. Burl closed his eyes as if to pray.

Burl must have gotten the help requested, because he spoke up. "Chief, you are in error, I believe. It seems to me that Pastor Scovill has turned the bones in because of the fire. She was properly concerned for them, removed them from the house and turned them over to you as a gesture of good citizenship because of the unusual circumstances. Her action does not constitute any admission of special knowledge. Right, Annie?"

Annie sighed and remembered Great-Grandmother Annie Ido's favorite saying: "Truth seeks no corners."

"Uh . . . partly right," she said.

"I really must insist, Pastor," Ike continued patiently, ignoring Burl's theory. "You see, hanging on to the bones in ignorance of the law is one thing, but knowingly withholding information about an unreported death is another. I'll ask you again. Whose bones are these?" He nodded toward the bag that lay on the berber between him and Annie.

"I can't say." Indeed, Annie believed she could not say more until she knew how Isabelle figured into her father's death. Isabelle lay seriously injured, and possibly dying, at Unified Memorial Hospital. Annie could not bring herself to release information—no, a conjecture—that might further stain the life of a person who could not defend herself. Annie had to know the whole story before she told any of the story. And, she thought, the story might not be hers to tell.

Ike stood and walked to the window. He looked out with his back to the others and said, "Pastor, this will not go well if you do not cooperate with me."

"Sir, what do you mean?" Burl asked.

"I mean," Ike said, "that I will ask the pastor one more time to divulge any and all information she has about the remains, and if she does not, she will face possible charges."

"Annie, tell him what you know," Burl said.

Ha! Burl Stout is sadly mistaken if he thinks he can order me around on this matter. "Burl, I am not in a position to say anything right now," she said.

Now both Burl and Ike seemed agitated. Ike turned back from the window and said to Burl, "Reverend Stout, I'm afraid that we cannot make her talk if she chooses not to. She has rights."

"I'm in the room. You may speak to me, Ike," Annie said. "Are you going to read me my rights?"

"I am, Pastor," he said. And he proceeded to do so, to the acute embarrassment of everyone in the room, particularly Annie.

"You're arresting me!?" she said to the chief.

"I'm sorry, Pastor, but the law is clear on this. I have to go by the book."

Ma Pugh's face dissolved in a flood of new tears. "Now Pastor Annie's got no home but a jail cell," she wailed. "I'm going to go tell the prayer chain about this." She rose and hurried from the room.

Burl spoke. "Chief Henderson, I hasten to remind you that Reverend Scovill is a respected member, a professional member, of the community, and that I and the other officers of the church stand fully behind her integrity. I will vouch for her continued presence in Biddlebourne. You needn't take her in."

"She has refused to divulge information that may be material to a criminal investigation," Ike said flatly. He walked to Annie and said, "Pastor, I'll ask you to accompany me."

Burl made one more valiant attempt to forestall Annie's arrest. "Chief, I remind you that Pastor Scovill has been more victim than perpetrator in Biddlebourne. If anyone is at fault, it is not she. She apparently has been the brunt of cruel vandalism here, possibly including arson, which means that her very life has been threatened. This kind of treatment cannot be tolerated."

"Sir, I mean no disrespect," Ike said, "but you have church matters to deal with. I have police matters to deal with. Besides, if her life is in danger, there's no safer place for her than the station." He said to Annie, "Please come along. I won't use the cuffs."

"I'll be right behind you, Annie. We'll post bail," Burl said.

"Won't be no bail tonight. Judge's gone fishin' to Canada," Ike said.

"Tomorrow morning, then," Burl said.

"Don't know when he'll be back," the chief said. And with that, Ike Henderson followed Annie out the door of her office and escorted her to the cruiser parked in the circular drive in front of the church.

The trustees, with Minnie Glendenning taking charge while Mr. Gideon Pugh tended to business in Annie's office, were deep into a parking-lot meeting over what to do about the parsonage. They gaped when Ike placed her in the backseat of the cruiser.

"I'm just putting you in back for your safety," Ike told Annie. He quickly took his place behind the wheel and started the engine. Annie was relieved when he did not turn on the flashing lights and siren.

"Chief, I haven't heard from my husband yet. I e-mailed him from my office this morning. Will you permit me to use my laptop computer at . . . the jail?"

Ike eyed her in the rear-view mirror. "You think I'm a hard-ass, don't you?" he said.

"I don't know whether you are overzealous in your duties, but I trust that you will be fair. I promise you that there is a very good reason why I can't say more about the bones yet. I believe it will all come to light soon." Annie paused and said, "Do you think I'm a hard-head?"

He nodded wordlessly. Annie couldn't stop herself from laughing.

"Ike, it will be all right," she said.

"Yeah, I'll let you use your computer in the jail. Is that it there in your briefcase?"

"Yes it is," she said. "Thank you, Chief."

"You're welcome."

"What's the woman's condition?"

"Still serious," he said.

"Oh," Annie said. She prayed for Isabelle on the way to jail.

Death in the Parsonage

"Sweet are the uses of adversity."
~~ William Shakespeare

CHAPTER FIFTY-SIX

Law enforcement is a world unto itself. It has its own kings and queens, who wear flowing black robes and wield gavels as their scepters. It has its own militia, identified by their badges and firearms. It has its own language, formed of numbers and letters arranged in cryptic combinations. It has its own architecture, marked by square line and functional design. It also has its own décor, consisting of bare concrete, scuffed tile, metal tables and plastic chairs.

There was little resemblance, however, between a bare-wall cell and the room to which Annie was taken at the Biddlebourne Police Department that Monday morning.

It was a room off Ike Henderson's own office, from which it was separated by a door that he did not lock—or even close—behind him. Although he had Sergeant Boo Dillon fingerprint Annie and list the possessions with which she entered the building, she was allowed to keep her purse, briefcase and cell phone. Nor was she searched, although she voluntarily surrendered her manicure scissors. Neither Boo nor Ike wanted to take the scissors, but they had to relent for the sake of propriety.

"I'm trusting you to stay put in here, Pastor," Ike said as he left the room. She looked around and saw what appeared to be a home away from home for Ike. She supposed there were occasions on which he had to sleep, or at least rest, at the station. The big leather couch on one side of the room looked comfy enough for napping.

The room had a sink, a small refrigerator, a microwave oven and a Sony television set with a VCR player. A coffee table, four guest chairs, a bookcase filled with police manuals and detective mysteries, and a square conference table completed the furnishings. A picture window afforded a generous view of the city park behind the police station, and country art prints on the opposite wall provided another excellent view. Two plants and a grouping of family photos gave the place a touch of home. A door on the west wall led to a bathroom, small but with a compact shower and a complement of blue towels and washcloths.

Annie sat at the conference table and worked. Chloe arrived in about half an hour, followed closely by Shirl.

"I'm not gonna stand for this," Shirl announced as she cleared the doorway. "Ike Henderson will rue the day he put the preacher away!"

"Shirl, he's doing what he thinks is right," Annie said. "I'll be out of here soon enough, as soon as . . . matters are settled. And it's quite comfortable. Look for yourself."

Shirl Burrows took a long, slow gander around the so-called holding cell. "I gotta admit it ain't the Ritz, but it ain't the pits, either, heh heh heh," she said, adding, "First time I been in this room. Ikey's kept it a secret."

"Hmph. Who cares if there's a leather couch? You're in jail!" Chloe wailed.

"Calm down, both of you. It won't kill me to stay here a while. After all, where else do I have to call home?" Annie said.

"Annie, you are impossible!" Chloe shouted. "How can you accept being held here like a common criminal?"

"I doubt common criminals have a private bath with shower, fluffy towels and access to television, internet and a twenty-four-hour telephone. In addition to all that, I can use the time here to my advantage." She stared meaningfully at Chloe.

Chloe sniffed, nevertheless, with disdain. "I shall have to postpone my return to Pittsburgh, you know, since I cannot possibly leave you here alone at the mercy of club-carrying goons."

"Of course you are not postponing your return," Annie said. "You have a show to do. You are the female lead, if I am not mistaken, and a large audience will be quite disappointed if you do not fulfill your responsibility."

"Absolutely not! Are you insane?"

"Whoa. Hold on," Shirl said, jumping into the fray. "Pastor, I'll look in on you three times a day. How's that, Chloe? I'll see to it she gets everything she needs, and more," she said, adding a wink for good measure. Annie wondered whether Shirl intended to smuggle in hooch or hacksaw blades.

"I don't know. I'll think about it overnight," Chloe said.

"But don't you have a rehearsal tomorrow?" Annie asked.

"Yes, but I can miss one rehearsal with little difficulty. They can work on the scenes—though there aren't many—in which I do not appear. Besides, I cannot be seen on stage, even in rehearsal, with my nose and eyes red, which, by the way, is your fault."

Shirl provided a new subject. "Pastor, what do you need us to bring over for you?"

"Are they letting anybody into the parsonage yet?" Annie asked.

"Not so far."

"I guess I'll need basic toiletries and couple of simple outfits—something I can sleep in," Annie said. She handed her bank card to Shirl and jotted her access number on an envelope. "Don't spend more than you have to," she added. "We'll have extra expenses, and I don't know how much insurance will cover."

"Do you need anything from your office?" Chloe asked.

"Not right now. If I think of anything, I can ask Trudy to bring it over."

"What about food?" Shirl asked.

As if on cue, a woman knocked on the doorframe.

"Yes?" Annie said.

"Ma'am, I'm here to take your dinner order," said the gray-haired woman. She wore a pink plaid housedress, and Annie concluded she was not a jail matron.

"It is a bit early," Annie demurred. But her hostess explained. "I'm Mattie Henderson, the chief's mother. He asked me to come over and find out what you want for dinner so's I can go home and cook it and get it back here at five-thirty on the dot."

Annie was dumbfounded by such thoughtful and obviously special attention. Shirl and Chloe clearly were, too, because for many seconds they looked at each other in amazement.

"Really?" Annie said finally.

"Oh, yes, ma'am. Ike said to give you the VIP treatment. Tuna casserole. Fried chicken. Broiled trout. Just name it."

"Mrs. Henderson, I am obliged to you for your graciousness, but I couldn't possibly impose on you in such a way."

"It's no trouble. I do the regular cooking for town guests. That's what my son calls the prisoners. He said to treat you extra-special, and I'm pleased to do so, ma'am."

"Please call me Annie, Mrs. Henderson."

"Well, then, Annie, I'm Mattie, and what would you like for dinner?"

"I'll be happy to have whatever the other . . . town guests are having."

"You're the only one right now."

"The tuna casserole would be fine," Annie ventured.

"Shoot, Annie, that's not much of a challenge. How about broiled trout, rice with vegetables, light garden salad and, oh, say, raspberry cobbler for dessert?" Mattie smiled as she recited an acceptable dinner menu at the Biddlebourne City Jail.

"That would be wonderful."

"Regular or decaf?" Mattie asked.

"Decaf, please."

"Italian, French or thousand island?"

"Italian."

"See you at five-thirty then. 'Bye, ladies."

When Mattie had gone, Shirl laughed and said, "Okay, so I'll come over once a day—at dinner time."

"Seriously, though," Shirl continued, "I heard some scuttlebutt about a garbage bag with skulls in it. Hermie said you gave the chief a skeleton. What's up, Pastor?"

Annie provided Shirl with a sketchy version of the story, for she did not want Shirl, the font of all knowledge in and about Biddlebourne, to connect the dots between the bones and Isabelle's father—if she had not done so already.

"Would you two mind if I checked my e-mail?" Annie asked. "I'm hoping to hear from G.P. He'll have a hundred questions about the fire, and maybe I can communicate with him before dinner."

Shirl looked disappointed. But she said goodbye and promised to return the next day with movies and munchies. Chloe gave Annie a hug and promised to bring several outfits suitable for day and night wear. Annie heard them arguing about colors as they left.

Annie followed Ike's instructions to sign on to the jail's wireless computer connection. When she clicked the message icon on her laptop computer, her heart skipped a few beats because there were two messages from G.P.

She opened the first one. He had received the news of the fire. He was exceedingly thankful that Annie, Chloe and Fannie Fay were all right. He reminded her that their home insurance policy was in the safe deposit box, in case she had forgotten that fact in the confusion. He wanted to know what could be salvaged from the house. He wanted to know if his truck was okay. He wanted her to contact his parents and some of his stateside co-workers to assure them that neither Annie nor he had been injured in the fire no matter what they might see or hear in the news.

In addition, he was worried about her living arrangements. He was worried about the new beds. He was worried about his coin collection. He was worried by the constant stream of "weird stories" about the new Glory Hallelujah pastor he had been hearing through his buddy with the Forty-First. Why again, for instance, was she driving an old school bus around town? In short, what was going on in Biddlebourne, West Virginia?

Annie asked God for strength before she opened his second message, which G.P. had sent three hours after the first. The message, less than an hour old, was brief but powerful. A sob caught in Annie's throat as she read the words: "Special request approved. Coming home. Will contact you ASAP. Love, G.P."

Annie hurried to respond, even though she knew G.P. would already have packed his personal gear and run to a loading bay to await a ride stateside to be with his stubborn, homeless, jailed wife.

"Dearest G.P. I am overjoyed to think of seeing you soon. Please travel carefully. You are in my prayers. Love, your Annie Ido."

She bowed her head in Ike Henderson's side room until the consolation of G.P.'s upcoming arrival had soaked into all the hurting places in her body and spirit. His news gave her a burst of energy and determination. She called G.P.'s parents to tell them the news, then punched in Burl's number.

"Annie, I'm on my way to the jail now," he said when he heard her voice.

"Good. We have some things to talk about."

"Indeed."

"How do you feel about trout and raspberry cobbler for dinner?"

"Quite happily," he said.

"Then I hope you can stay for supper."

"I don't quite understand."

"You will soon."

When Mattie Henderson arrived with dinner, the portions were easily big enough for two. Over fresh trout and trimmings, Annie told Burl about Isabelle Pargeon, the little green diary and the bones in the basement.

"I'm almost positive the woman burned in the fire is Isabelle," she said.

"What makes you think so?"

Annie explained and swore him to secrecy, as she had Chloe.

Burl was perplexed. "I do not see how keeping Miss Pargeon's identity from the authorities will help."

"Don't you see?" Annie responded. "They would automatically think she set the fire—and killed her father to hide the bones forever!"

"Perhaps she did," he said.

"I can't believe that she is responsible for either tragedy," Annie returned. "She's really a gentle person. But she's been so hurt by people and circumstances in Biddlebourne. As much as we can, we shouldn't let her be hurt any more."

"I'm still not following." Burl's eyebrows wrinkled and he tilted his head.

"Isabelle had a horrific childhood. Her alcoholic parents abused her. The school system apparently overlooked her problems. Even the Glory Hallelujah congregation failed her to some degree."

"The church . . . ?"

"By Isabelle's report, Mrs. Pargeon and the children attended the church at some point but were not warmly received.

"Isabelle's only support came from several neighbor women who helped her when things at home became too awful to bear. I think Minnie Glendenning was one of the women who looked out for Isabelle."

"Minnie Glendenning?"

"Yes, Burl, the same woman who has been calling you with all the 'news' from Biddlebourne."

"She is a complex woman. At first she seemed upset that a woman had been posted to Glory Hallelujah, but then she called out of concern for you."

"Really?"

"Yes. She told me about the threats you received, the dead cat, the dead chickens. She thought someone was targeting you. Each time I told her that I trusted your judgment implicitly, and I asked her to do the same."

Annie eyed Burl for a long moment. Finally she nodded.

"I do respect your thinking on these matters," Burl continued, "but it seems your decision to deal with the bones by yourself has taken time away from your pastoral duties. You need to explain your position to your committee chair . . . ."

"Mrs. Pugh."

"Mrs. Pugh, yes. You cannot be absent from your post, let alone jailed during that absence, without making your committee fully apprised of your reasons."

"You're right, of course. I'll talk with Ma."

"And, no matter what you think about those bones, the police will investigate and draw their own conclusions."

"Of course, you're right. If the evidence tells me the bones belong to Ernie Pargeon, I imagine Ike Henderson and Boo Dillon will figure that out, too."

"The bigger question is Miss Pargeon. What do you intend to do if she unfortunately does not recover from her injuries?"

"Burl, I know that I have to tell what I know. But I want to speak with Isabelle first . . . give her a chance to prepare for what might happen."

"What do you think might happen?"

"I don't know what will happen. At best, it could be ascertained that Mr. Pargeon died under circumstances unknown to Isabelle, or at least totally unconnected to her. At worst, I guess, she could be tied to her father's death."

"And what else?" Burl pressed.

"And she could be hurt even more than she already has been. Burl, she's like a small, wounded bird."

"How can you be so clear about her state of mind if, as you say, you have seen her only a few times?"

Annie pulled the little green diary from her purse and told him why she thought it had been written by Isabelle writing as "B.P.," or Belle Pargeon. She handed it to him. "Here. You'll see what I mean."

Burl silently took the diary and spent several minutes leafing through it. "All right, Annie," he said as he handed it back. "I understand your fears about her emotional state. But you simply cannot remain behind bars, so to speak, for long. It is not fair to your congregation."

"I agree," she said.

Annie waited until the cobbler was nearly gone before asking Burl the hardest questions.

"Burl," she said, "do you understand why I did not tell you about the bones when I found them?"

"About that," he said. He took a deep breath. He rested his spoon on his dessert plate. He adjusted his crooked tie to another crooked position.

"Yes?"

"Annie, uh . . ."

"Yes?"

"I suppose we're even."

"What do you mean?"

"I failed to warn you properly of what you would face in the Glory Hallelujah parsonage, and you failed to report the discovery of the bones to me immediately."

"Two wrongs don't make . . . ."

". . . a right. Yes, I know. What I'm saying is that both of us have not communicated as well as we should have, and perhaps we both have learned something."

"Yes," Annie said. "I know I have. And, just for the record, I'm as bewildered as anyone about the threats that I've received. Similar things—but none so drastic— happened in other places, so I just chalked up the notes, the dead cat, the stinking chickens—all of it—to pranksters who would soon tire of their shenanigans. There is too much important work to do at Glory Hallelujah Church for me to allow such things to distract me."

Burl looked out a window a long while. He sighed and turned back to Annie. "I spoke at some length today with Chief Henderson before I came here. He admits his department is at a loss about the threats. He's planning to call in the state police now that this fire has occurred."

"God will help us," Annie said.

"Yes, of course. I hope you know that you can trust me in the future with, ah, sensitive information."

"I promise to be more forthcoming with serious matters. But I have one request."

"What's that?"

"When Minnie Glendenning calls you about church matters, please suggest that she talk with me. I want to deal directly with her issues, not have her think that you will listen to her tattling. When she and I can work together productively, the better off I will be. And the better off the congregation will be."

Burl nodded. "Agreed."

Death in the Parsonage

"Great things are done more through courage than through wisdom." ~~ Proverb

CHAPTER FIFTY-SEVEN

Tuesday, July 19, and Wednesday, July 20

"I'm so sorry, Pastor Annie, but I have to let you know that I won't be able to continue as church secretary after school starts."

Annie switched her cell phone to her other ear. Annie was not totally saddened to hear Trudy's news. Trudy was obviously not cut out to work as a secretary, but the job brought needed income to her family.

Besides, there was another issue. "Trudy, this has nothing to do with . . . our conversations last week, does it?"

"Oh, no, not at all. I'm getting through that, and Mom is, too. It's just that I have to really, really concentrate on my classes next year. I have to plan for my future, and I want to get into a good college."

"Trudy, I understand completely. Of course you must do well in school. It is your top priority. Don't worry about a thing. I'm just happy you can stay on through the summer."

"I really, really appreciate it."

"I'll talk to you soon. Don't worry," Annie said before pressing *end* on her cell phone.

The pastor turned to Chief Henderson, who had been standing in the doorway. It was only nine in the morning, and she had already received a staff resignation, a mail dump from Shirl and the news that Chloe must leave but would try to return for Annie's hearing.

"You okay, Pastor?" Ike asked.

"Yes, Ike, thank you. I slept very well."

In fact, Annie felt so rested she was ready to return to her pastoral duties. "Ike, can't you release me on my own recognizance—or some similar status?"

"Cool your jets, Pastor. I came to say your bail's been posted."

"By whom?"

"Your boss."

"Burl Stout?"

"Yes, ma'am, by him personally."

"But I thought the judge had to set bail."

"Tim Lincoln, that's the judge, did that by phone. Reverend Stout came over this morning with the money, said he couldn't get his check cashed last night 'cause it was so late when he got out of here."

"He posted my bail with his own money?"

"Yes'm. Now get out of here. And here's some more good news. That lady who got burned in the fire has improved some, and they're gonna let her have visitors this evening."

Isabelle felt a jolt of relief. "Oh, thank you, Chief. I'm glad to hear that. And thanks for your hospitality and . . . for facilitating my release."

Ike smiled and said, "Boo'll take you wherever you need to go."

At her office Annie called Burl to thank him for posting her bail. Trudy and air conditioning were absent at the church, of course, because of the continuing power shortage. Annie carried fans from the nursery to her office and worked steadily for several hours. At four-thirty she left to do her biggest task of the day.

The gray lady wore a ribbon of yellow crime tape at her waist. Her crown was blackened, broken, besodden. Like a shameless woman of the night, she winked with her besmudged gables and smiled toothlessly with her gouged-out windows.

On the front porch Annie's begonias drooped pitifully and the door hung on one hinge. The scene inside was worse, with couch and armchairs sooty and stinking, piano ugly with stains and puddled with foul water. The dining table and chairs, the computer workstation, the bookcases, the lamps, the rugs, the carving of the Last Supper, the communion set from her home church, the military awards—all were damaged or ruined.

Annie considered going upstairs to check on the new bed, her grandmothers' quilts, her parents' anniversary portrait and Chloe's things. But the stairway was blocked by fallen plaster and the buckled banister, as well as another sagging strip of plastic police tape.

No matter. Annie turned toward the kitchen and picked her way through the dank mess to the basement door. She took a deep breath, turned the knob and peered down. All the water that had been sprayed onto the house and that hadn't already soaked into the furniture, floors and walls had found its way to the basement. She said a quick prayer, put her left foot on the first step and slowly shifted her weight. The wood held. She descended slowly, testing before each step.

The earthen floor had turned to a quagmire of mud and stagnant water. Flies buzzed eagerly in the near darkness. G.P.'s work boots hung by their laces on her right. She flipped them off the peg and pulled them over the canvas shoes Shirl had brought from the flea market.

Annie slogged to each of the three side rooms, then to the furnace and to the area where the largest pieces of the water heater lay in water. She cast the beam of Mr. Gideon Pugh's flashlight everywhere. Still she didn't see what she hoped to find.

She took an old highchair from its resting place near the electric panel, thankful the panel had been disabled by Frank Kellerman's crew, and stood the chair at the wall behind the furnace. She climbed onto it. The legs squashed noisily into the mud, making a nice anchor. The cheap paneling had warped and begun to disengage from the wall studs behind it. Annie felt behind the paneling inch by inch for about six feet, hoisting the chair into and out of the mud every eighteen inches or so.

Finally, her fingers touched what had to be there. It was a frame of sorts, made of a thin wooden strip. She pulled back the paneling as far as she could. There it was: a door about two feet square, secured with a rusted hook-and-eye latch.

Annie pried at the latch until it gave way and pushed on the door. It opened only a few inches. She moved the chair again, trying to get a look behind the door with the flashlight. She strained her neck, moved the light and saw dusty items in a far corner of the space—a blanket, cookware, a hot plate, canned food and several shoeboxes.

She stood tiptoe on the arms of the highchair but couldn't make herself tall enough to lever her body into the space. She got a pile of soggy newspapers out of the recycling bin and put them under the chair, got back up and, yes, she could lean into the opening just enough to wriggle and hitch her way into the hole.

The space was about four feet high, five feet wide and Annie couldn't tell how long. She saw teen magazines, a stuffed animal, an extension cord and several other items that identified the owner of the hideaway.

The hidey-hole was sad and creepy but, incredibly, not even damp from the dousing of the house. Annie crawled around the hole, playing the light in every direction, until she saw another square plywood door in the low ceiling. There was no latch, no lock of any kind. She pushed. The door gave a little. Something sat on the top side of the door. She shoved hard and the door flew upward, sending whatever had been on it rolling and knocking about loudly.

Annie wrapped the shoeboxes in the blanket and, crouching, carefully poked her head through the opening. She recognized the pantry and stood cautiously. The boxes of pasta, cans of fruit and bags of rice were still stacked neatly on the shelves, but a bucketful of peaches had scattered across the floor. The smell of smoke and wet wood filled her nostrils again.

Death in the Parsonage

"He who looks outside, dreams; he who looks inside, awakens." ~~ Carl Jung

CHAPTER FIFTY-EIGHT

Annie's clergy badge got her past the security guard Tuesday night, but she had to don scrubs and mask to enter Isabelle's sterile room. The nurses confiscated the package that Annie had brought.

Annie entered on tiptoe and peeked around the bed curtain. Isabelle looked like a rag doll made of old-fashioned muslin. Dozens of layers of gauze covered her left arm and leg from toes to thigh. The skin on the left side of her face was dark pink and slightly blistered.

An oxygen mask delivered air to Isabelle, and an intravenous solution dripped into a vein at the crook of her right arm.

The room smelled of unguent, burned flesh and antiseptic.

Annie took a big breath. "Hello, Isabelle. I'm Annie Scovill."

There was no answer, but the patient's right hand lifted from the bed. Annie sat on the vinyl chair next to the bed and carefully took Isabelle's hand.

The nurses had warned Annie that Isabelle had inhaled chemical byproducts of fire, which irritated and possibly singed her respiratory tract. Speech would be difficult for the burn patient.

"Isabelle, I know it's hard for you to talk. I'll just sit here with you if that's okay."

But Isabelle was restless. She moved her right leg and clenched Annie's hand. She swallowed many times and finally whispered, "I've been waiting."

Isabelle relaxed with her hand in Annie's. Within five minutes she was asleep. And so they abided, the patient and the pastor, for nearly twenty-four hours.

Isabelle moaned and coughed, received medications and suffered the indignities of the bedfast. Annie took breaks only for coffee and the restroom.

Police Chief Henderson came by and was told that Isabelle could not yet be interviewed. Shirl arrived with snacks, but Annie couldn't eat in front of Isabelle, whose sore throat kept her from swallowing solids.

Around nightfall Wednesday, just after a cool front slipped in from the west and Biddlebourne's brown-out ended, Isabelle stirred.

"What is it, Isabelle?" Annie asked.

"Thank you . . .very much." Her voice was sand-papery.

"You don't have to speak," Annie said.

Isabelle nodded. Her eyes filled with tears. "I'm worried," she said.

"About getting well? The doctors say you will recover."

"No. About . . ."

"About the things you left in your house?"

Isabelle nodded and choked back a low cry of anguish.

"I'll be right back," Annie said. She returned quickly with a plastic bag. She opened it and pulled out the three ancient shoeboxes. Each was tied with string.

"I believe these belong to you," she said, placing them on the stand beside the bed.

Isabelle's tears flowed.

"And I think this is yours, too," Annie said. She reached into her purse, brought out the little green diary and held it in her open palm. Heaving sobs wracked Isabelle's frame as she grasped the book with her right hand and clutched it to her chest as if it were a lifeline that could rescue her from an ocean of tears.

A nurse rolled a medication cart into the room and wordlessly passed two pills to Isabelle. Annie watched as she swallowed them slowly with water sipped through a straw.

"Isabelle, I'm here to help in any way I can." But Isabelle shook her head.

"Your life has been . . . ." Annie groped for words. A nightmare? A tragedy? An ugly testimony to the protracted failure of school, church and community to detect in Isabelle, Frankie and Sissie the horrific signs of child abuse?

Images of violent mistreatment to innocent children flooded Annie's mind. In the house where she lived—or used to live—unspeakable horrors, maybe even murder, had occurred. Ernie Pargeon surely had died in that house, but Isabelle Pargeon had died there, too, for the soul of the fragile woman lying in this room had just as surely been wounded unto death.

Annie started over. "Your life is a gift from God, Isabelle."

"No," she managed to say. "No. God doesn't care about me."

Annie had sat with parents whose daughter was killed in non-combat military action. She had heard a young wife chastise God for the untimely death of a husband who was not yet into the prime of adulthood. She had seen grandparents standing heart-heavy at the casket of a child who played too hard with drugs. But through all the years and all the tragedies she never had been able to answer their common question: How could God let this happen?

As her own frustration welled inside her the same way Isabelle's was filling her, Annie could do nothing more than weep with Isabelle. She took tissues from her purse and shared them. Tears flowed for many minutes.

In those minutes Annie prayed for wisdom to help Isabelle. Yes, God alone would save Isabelle, but Annie hoped to cooperate in God's work. She believed what she preached, that God willed good for humanity, that God answered prayers, that God conquered death—all kinds of death.

"Open them . . . please," Isabelle said, motioning to the shoeboxes.

"Now?"

Isabelle moved her lips, but no sound came out. Then she nodded, and her intention was clear.

Annie untied the boxes. One held a few photographs— some sepia and some black and white—but all grainy, yellowed, dog-eared. Another held a collection of small leather or rhinestone collars, tiny fuzzy toys and one much-chewed rawhide bone. The last box contained a neat stack of papers and envelopes.

Isabelle pointed to the big blue envelope with the rubber band around it. Annie picked it up. Isabelle nodded again.

Inside the envelope Annie found a small wirebound notebook on which the words *My Story* were printed in a hand that she recognized.

"Read it," Isabelle mouthed.

Annie turned to the first page and began.

This is really how it all stopped. Things were really bad at our house. Both my parents drunk 90 percent of the time. My mom hating Frankie's girlfriend. Hated just about everything. I was thirteen years old, in seventh grade. I remember because my periods started and I didn't know what they were and the gym teacher at school went and got some Kotex for me out of her office and showed me how to use them. I was so embarrassed. Frankie was 16 but he was only in eighth grade on account of flunking all the time. Nobody ever helped him with his homework. He wasn't dumb though.

It was around Valentine's Day and I was in my bedroom. I had cramps. I remember it was Valentine's Day because my dad gave me a valentine gift! Cheap gold earrings, the kind you get for little kids. I couldn't believe it! He never gave me a valentine before. Never gave my mother one either that I know of. Turned out somebody left them on the bus and he didn't turn them in to lost and found. He wasn't allowed to drive, of course, to work or anywhere, because he had so many arrests for drunk driving. Everybody in town knew it, and Boo said if he ever caught my dad anywhere near a car he'd throw him in the clink and let him rot there.

Anyway, it was around Valentine's Day – I guess it was 1990 because that's the year I was in seventh grade – and about seven or eight o'clock in the evening – I was in my room staying out of the way of my mother who was drunk as usual – when I heard a bunch of loud thumps and my dad screaming. I ran downstairs to see what happened. My mom was slamming the basement door closed and locking it – she had a big lock on there that she locked with a key and she kept the key in her bra – and she turned around and said to me, "Your father just went to bed drunk."

I'll never forget it because I didn't believe her and begged her to let me go help him. She wouldn't. She said she had gone to the top of the stairs and saw him lying at the bottom "still breathing." I said I could hear him moaning downstairs. My mother said, "No, he's just blubbering because he's out of whiskey."

I argued and fought with my mother. I was stronger than she was even if I was just a kid. But she had that kind of strength that drunk people have, and I couldn't get the key away from her. She wouldn't help my father or let me help him. Frankie came in from a secret date in the middle of all this and never said a word to either one of us – just went up to his room and slammed the door.

Finally I told my mother okay and went back to my room. But I sneaked out the side door and went to the window on the side of the house over the coal chute and tried to get into the basement that way. But there was snow and ice all around the window. Plus I was cold, really cold. All I had was a thin trench coat. Seems my parents didn't have enough money to buy me a winter coat that year. I cried myself to sleep. See, I worried about my dad, even if he was mean to me. I don't know why. Maybe I thought he would like me better when I grew up. Whatever.

When I got up for school the next morning I felt sick but my mother wouldn't let me stay home from school. I felt worse when I got to school and went to the nurse's office. The nurse called my mother and came back to me and said, "Your mother says you're faking and she won't come to get you." My mother wasn't supposed to drive either but she did all the time and I guess the cops let her get away with it because us kids had to have a way to school and other places sometimes. Trouble was Mom used the car to drive to the liquor store more than anywhere else.

So I had to sit in school all day with a headache and a stomachache. Maybe she was right and I was just "sick"

*in my head from worrying about things at home. Or
maybe it was just the cramps.*

*When I got home from school Mom said my father "ran
away out west with some whore" and we weren't to talk
about him ever again. I told Mom I didn't believe her. She
swatted at me with the snow shovel but missed me and I
ran up to my room. About seven that night she called me
downstairs and told me to cook supper. I didn't say a
word. Just made something for dinner. I don't remember
what.*

*In a while my brother Frankie came in. He acted like
everything was okay. He told me after dinner that he was
going out for basketball. I said it was too late for that, but
he just shook his head and said, "The coach
understands." He was so happy about the basketball that
he volunteered to wash the dinner dishes all by himself.
He never did that. I always had to do the dishes – if
anybody did them. I remember because Frankie hummed
and whistled while he did the dishes. I think it was Little
Brown Jug.*

*After dinner while my mother was in the living room
watching TV I sneaked upstairs to her bedroom to use the
phone. I wanted to call my grandmother or the police. I
sat there and couldn't decide which. Well, my mother
came in to get a bottle of something out of her bedside
table. All hell broke loose. She threw the bottle at me.
Missed me. I was too quick for her! The bottle broke
anyway because it landed on the floor. She picked it up
and came after me with it. I ran out of the house and went
to my girlfriend Julie's place down the road. I don't know
why I didn't tell the neighbors what I thought my mother
had done. I guess I was pretty shook up. I went to their
house so many times before when Mom got drunk that I
guess they just figured she was drunk again.*

Death in the Parsonage

Julie's mother said I could spend the night if it was okay with my mother. She made me call my mom. I couldn't get out of it if I wanted to stay at their house. It was cold and snowing again. I didn't have anywhere else to go. So I called Mom. She told me, "I don't care where you stay, you little sneak." So I stayed that night at their house and went to school the next morning in borrowed clothes. Julie and I were always almost the same size – even shoes! We both wore size nine.

This next part is one of the hardest things that ever happened to me. When I came home from school that day, I was dreading it because no matter how drunk Mom got she always remembered when somebody crossed her. Boy, did she carry a grudge! I was afraid she would be standing behind the door with a knife or a bottle or something. She did that to me a couple of times. Said later it was just a joke. I never believed her. I had to watch my back all the time.

But that wasn't what happened. When I got home there was an ambulance there, which wasn't all that unusual, but this time Mrs. Wilson came over from next door and told me my mom was dying. She said my mom tried to kill herself with a butcher knife but did a bad job of it and she'd had a heart attack on top of the stabbing she'd tried to give herself. I remember walking past the curb and seeing blood mixed with dirty snow from where she threw up blood. My beige trench coat was in the tub soaking in cold water when I got in the house. I had on Julie's last year coat. Seems Mom had my coat on when she started vomiting. What a sight.

Somebody, I don't remember who now, took me and Frankie to the hospital to see Mom. Oh yeah, I almost forgot this. They told me she also had sarosis of the liver. What a nightmare it was to look at my mother. She was swathed all in white and had tubes going in and out of every part of her body. A sight no child should have to look at. I'll never forget it.

Well, for two weeks Mom hovered over death. I didn't go to school the first week and then I went back to school because she hadn't died yet. She was in a coma quite a few days. I would call from school a couple of times a day to see if she was still alive.

Anyway, Frankie and I lived by ourselves in the house all that time Mom was at the hospital. One or two neighbors would bring over casseroles or cookies, but mostly we ate cereal and sandwiches. We found some money in Mom's purse but it was gone pretty quick. Oh yeah. We would order in pizza, it was about $5 every time, so that's why the money went so quick.

Me and Frankie tried to go and stay with our grandmother (our father's mother), but she wouldn't have anything to do with us. She always hated us because we didn't belong to her son. I know that now. She called my mom a whore and a slut and every other filthy name she could think of.

While Mom was in the hospital, I went to the basement again and again to see if I could find any sign of my dad. Nothing. His room was all swept out. Like nobody was ever there.

One evening Mrs. Wilson came over and when she saw what a pigpen the place was (I guess me and Frankie didn't keep it too clean. She said we needed help and she was going to go and call the county. I didn't know exactly who the county was, but I didn't want to be a foster child. The foster kids at school always talked like it wasn't any fun being a foster child.

That same night the basketball coach came to the house and took Frankie home with him. After that for almost a month I only saw Frankie once in a while at school. That was back when we had junior high and

*senior high all together in the same building. He was busy
with basketball practice and games and all. He got new
clothes and the coach's wife gave him a sharp new
haircut. He almost acted like he didn't even know me
when he saw me in school.*

*I was scared to death living in the house by myself but
the county never came to take me away. I guess Mrs.
Wilson forgot to call them. My mother was between life
and death a long time. Finally she came home. I cleaned
the place up real nice for her but she didn't notice. Went
straight to bed. I got up the next morning early and took in
some oatmeal and toast for Mom – that's what she liked if
she didn't drink her breakfast. But she was sound asleep
and I just left it on her dresser. When I got home it was
still there and my mother was still in bed. She asked me
for the hundredth time about Frankie. I told her he was
staying with the coach and his family. She didn't like it
and told me to call the coach to send Frankie home. But I
didn't call. I just went to my room and pretended to be
doing my homework.*

*Well, you'd think my mother was the cleanest person in
the world after she got home from the hospital. Always
before, the house was a mess – clothes laying everywhere,
anywhere somebody dropped them. Sometimes we didn't
get clean clothes for weeks at a time. And dishes would
pile up in the kitchen. Nobody would do them. My mother
never made anybody but me do them, and I didn't always
do them. But after the hospital – wow! My mother made
me do all the cooking and cleaning and laundry. She made
me walk to the grocery store – it was about three miles
away – and walk back with all the groceries. Once there
was more than one trip of bags in my order but Mr.
Wilson came along and gave me a ride.*

Mom never asked again about Frankie. I asked her lots of times about my father but she always told me to shut up, he was in Montana or Utah or somewhere.

All of a sudden my mother was careful about how the house looked! She made me dust! And I vacuumed and washed the windows, too. I also had to take her medicine to her. She'd be real mad if I forgot to give it to her at the right time. She hardly ever got out of bed – mostly to go to the door when her liquor was delivered. See, she had some friends from Claypool who'd bring her jugs of wine and I don't know what else. I asked her once about drinking while she was taking all those medicines, but she told me to mind my own business.

It got so she would get nervous or agitated or something and would get up in the middle of the night and come to my room and scare me. She would throw the door open and yell, "Hey" real loud. It would scare me silly. I started locking my door and she didn't do it any more.

I was tired all the time. Flunking most of my classes. No time to go to Julie's house or anywhere else. Couldn't be on the volleyball team anymore because I didn't have a ride to practice or the games. But Mom started saying the house wasn't clean enough. I had to use Clorox and Ajax and some other stuff I don't remember the name of, and it smelled like the hospital. I was afraid to set anything down because she would pop out of her bedroom long enough to raise hell about a glass on the coffee table or a pair of shoes on the kitchen floor.

I tried to call Frankie at the coach's house but they wouldn't put him on the phone or he wouldn't come to the phone, I don't know which and it didn't matter because I knew he wouldn't come home.

Now I think I know why my mother wanted the house so clean all the time after the hospital. It was because she heard people were calling the county about us and if anyone ever came from the county to the house it would look all neat and clean and they would think everything was okay. But no one from the county ever came that I know of.

My hands were red and chapped from so much cleaning. But at least I had clean clothes. I didn't have nice clothes. I didn't have clothes that fit. But I did have clean clothes. I couldn't visit any of the neighbors anymore either. My mother watched me like a hawk. Afraid I'd tell the neighbors how she was acting. Afraid I'd tell them about the night my dad "went to bed drunk." Afraid I'd complain about doing all the work and getting all the blame for everything that went the least bit wrong.

One day though I did sneak over to my favorite neighbor's house. We had ice cream on the back porch. It was spring. What a good time we had! I didn't tell her anything about my mother or father. I think she knew – or guessed. Anyway, she just asked about me and gave me the most beautiful fan – blue and green with wispy gray patterns – it's silk I think. I don't use it because I'm afraid I'll lose it. But I still have it.

When I got home my mother called me to her room. She complained that she didn't like the soup I had put on the dresser for her. Wanted a hamburger! I made her a hamburger, but she said I took too long and she threw it on the wall and screamed at me something like, "You're nothing but a dirty little bastard. I wish you were dead like your brother Jeffie!" I went to my room. Didn't clean up the kitchen or anything. I cried all night.

In the morning I put on several blouses and two pairs of slacks – even though it was getting warmer. It was May. I put my old stained trench coat, extra underwear, pajamas, four peanut butter sandwiches and the grocery money in my school bag. My mother kept most of the money for booze and cigarettes but she had to give me some to buy medicine and groceries. I lied to her about what things cost so I could save up some cash.

After school that day – oh boy was I nervous in school that day – I walked to the Greyhound terminal in Parkersburg. I don't know how many miles that is, but it's a lot. My feet got blisters on them. I was afraid to take a bus from Biddlebourne because for sure somebody who knew me would see me and report me to the county.

I stopped on the way and bought myself waffles with lots of syrup at the Waffle House. Were they ever good! I still remember them. I drank my first cup of coffee that night. That wasn't good! Very bitter. I accepted a ride from a nice lady I met at the restaurant, but I made her let me out before we got to Parkersburg.

It was after midnight when I got to the bus terminal. Besides the one ticket agent, there were only a couple people there – me and a woman with her little baby. She let me hold the baby a minute. I got a Pepsi out of the machine and waited. I waited all night. When that ticket agent got off work in the morning, a new one came on duty and a bunch of people came into the terminal to go to work I guess. It was pretty crowded. That's when I went and bought my ticket. I looked on the big sign overhead to see which bus was leaving first. It was the bus for Chicago. So that's where I went.

Death in the Parsonage

"It's what you learn after you know it all that counts."
~~ John Wooden

CHAPTER FIFTY-NINE

The story ended there. Isabelle had fallen asleep as Annie read. But when Annie put the notebook beside Isabelle on the bed, she stirred and said, "Don't go yet."

"I mustn't tire you," Annie said. "I'll be back—if that's okay."

"Please. Please come back tomorrow. I want to tell you more," Isabelle said, her voice trailing off as her energy failed.

"Of course," Annie said. But Isabelle was already asleep.

At the Pugh homestead Annie enjoyed a sandwich and salad and reported in detail what had happened to her in the twenty-three days since she had arrived at 1010 Greenbriar Road. Ma Pugh listened carefully, nodding from time to time and wiping her eyes repeatedly.

"Oh, it's all my fault," Ma said at the conclusion of Annie's account.

"What do you mean? I don't understand."

"I'll explain . . . later" was all Ma could be coaxed to say. She rejected Annie's offer to wash the dishes and waved her out of the kitchen with her damp handkerchief. "Shoo, go do your thing," she said with a wan smile.

Back at the church, Annie started Sunday's sermon, titling it "Coming Home," and for several hours studied the Parable of the Prodigal Son. She chose hymns for Sunday, called to check on Isabelle's condition and wrote a note to thank the Wilsons for their assistance the night of the fire. She read letters from vendors hoping to provide materials or equipment for the church addition and responded to each e-mail message that had piled up since Sunday morning. Finally, she read a good chunk of the book of Exodus, a fine story about other people who had lost their way.

She returned to the Pugh homestead around 11:30 p.m., showered and slept through the night—without dreams or nightmares—with a cool breeze blowing in the open windows and riffling the voile curtains.

"No physician like a true friend." ~~ Proverb

CHAPTER SIXTY

Thursday, July 21

"She's been waiting for you," the clerk said when Annie and Minnie arrived at the hospital.

"You go ahead. I'll wait," Minnie said. Annie started to disagree but saw the anxiety on Minnie's face and nodded.

Isabelle smiled, obviously with pain, and lifted a hand toward Annie when she walked into the room. Annie hadn't been asked to wear a gown and a mask this time.

"How are you?" Annie asked.

"I'm feeling a little stronger."

"I'm so glad. I have good news," Annie offered.

"Oh? What?"

"An old friend of yours would like to see you."

"A friend?"

"A friend from your childhood."

"I didn't have any friends . . . ."

"Yes, you did," Annie said gently. She went to the door and nearly bumped into Minnie, who walked past her to the bed.

"Do you recognize me, Belle?" Minnie said.

"Yes. I do. I saw you at Elderdon's last week," Isabelle said. "You didn't talk to me. I thought you were mad at me." Tears and tissues appeared.

"Oh, my beautiful girl," Minnie said, ignoring the bandages and tubes as she lightly hugged Isabelle. "I'm not mad at you! I didn't know it was you!"

"What?"

"You're all grown up now. You've been away nearly fifteen years. Of course I didn't recognize you."

"Really?"

"Yes, yes, yes," Minnie said. "Do you think I could walk past my little chickadee?" Isabelle and Minnie were both crying tears of joy and surprise.

"I'll leave you two to catch up," Annie said. But Isabelle made a stop sign with her good hand. Annie waited until she got control of herself.

"The box. Another blue envelope," Isabelle said.

Annie knew what to do. She retrieved the envelope from the shoebox and found a smaller envelope inside.

"It's from Mom," Isabelle said. Annie stared at it and saw *Isabelle Marie Pargeon* printed on one side with a Seattle address.

"Please read it," Isabelle said hoarsely.

Annie looked at Minnie. Isabelle whispered, "Out loud. Please, Pastor Annie."

Dear Isabelle,

When you was in sixth grade you asked me why I never left Ernie for treating all of us so bad. Well I did try to leave him. Lots of times. I would look at you and Frankie and Sissie sleeping and pack a sack full of clothes and start walking. But pretty soon someone would call Ernie and tell him they saw me walking and he would come after me screaming and threatening. None of the neighbors never reported him. They were afraid of him. I used to go

*to church and pray the police would knock on the door
and take him to jail. But they never did. And so I quit
going to church. God hates a drunk anyhow. When I
would run away he would grab me by the arm and say I
committed adultery and he would take you kids. I knew
that would be a death sentence for Frankie so I stayed. I
don't remember when I started drinking. Ernie beat the
hell out of me every day, and the booze took the edge off
the pain. I didn't let you kids see it all. He'd take his belt
and tie my hands to the bedpost and use his suspenders,
those old blue ones, to whip me. They had big metal clips
and when he got started he couldn't stop. I was sick all the
time from what Ernie did to me. I couldn't go to the doctor
or the drugstore because he threatened to kill me if I let on
to anybody what he did. So I went to Minnie Glendenning
and got herbs for what ailed me. I hate to admit it but I
got pregnant by Ernie when you was about eight years
old. It was a mistake. I couldn't have another child for
Ernie to hurt. So I got some stuff from Minnie that killed
the baby. I'm sorry I killed that baby. But it would have
had a bad life anyhow so I did it a favor I guess. After that
I made Ernie sleep in the basement. Told him I'd tell Boo
D. about everything and prove it with my scars and Ernie
couldn't stop me. He hated me more than ever after that
but he stayed in the basement and I could sleep some
nights, that is when he wasn't hollering up the stairs how
much he loved me. He was a hypocrite and a liar and a
damn fool. He can't hurt any of us anymore. I made damn
sure of that. And you can believe me.*

*Well, enough of that. What I'm writing to tell you,
Isabelle, is something I should have told you from the
start. You and Frankie belong to Vinny Clark. I'm sorry.
Me and Vinny couldn't stay away from each other. Him
married to another woman and me to Ernie was just two
sets of mistakes that we couldn't fix. It was like a disease.*

Ernie's gone, and I don't know if you'll get this letter but I got to try to send you word before I die. I think I'm going to die soon. Nobody comes around the house. Afraid of me. They should have been afraid of Ernie. But I took care of that. Honey, if you want to come back to Biddlebourne, I promise I'll get off the booze and you can live with me and everything will be the way it should have been when you and Frankie and Sissie was little kids. Even if you never want to see me again, if you ever need any help, go to Vinny. He won't deny you. He's promised me that. Honest. I swear. I'm sorry for everything. Please forgive me. I love you, Mom.

Through her tears, Annie gazed at Vickie June Pargeon's letter a long time before she refolded it and tucked it inside the stained envelope.

"Thank you for letting me read your mother's letter," she said.

"She asked me to forgive her. I don't know how I can," Isabelle said. The arm to which the intravenous line was attached jerked to her cheek, and with a clenched fish she began rubbing the tears from her cheek and chin.

"Isabelle, stop!" Annie said, handing her tissues.

"I can't! All my life people only wanted to hurt me. I don't know why. Am I so bad?"

Annie got up and put her arms around Isabelle. Minnie went to the other side of the bed and held Isabelle's hand. The young woman shook and sobbed and spoke the names of the ones who had betrayed her young heart and her young life. "Mommy, Daddy, oh, Mommy . . ."

The nurse must have heard the commotion and came in to see what was happening. But she left when Annie shook her head and asked with her eyes for them to be left alone.

After a long while Isabelle stopped weeping and said, "I'm all right."

"Isabelle."

"What?"

"Do you want to heal?" Annie asked.

"My burns are already getting better."

"No, I mean do you want to heal from the past?"

"More than anything."

"Will you work with me to find a counselor who will help you to untangle your memories and your feelings?"

"Will I have to tell the counselor what happened?"

"Yes."

"Will you be with me?"

"If the counselor thinks it's a good idea, I will go with you to your first session. Okay?" Annie said.

Isabelle sniffled and nodded.

"But I'll be with you as long as you want me to be," Annie said.

"But you just said . . ."

"You and I will work on forgiveness, if that's all right with you, but only when you're ready."

"There are a lot of things in my past. I want to forgive people, but I don't know if people can forgive me. I'm still confused about . . . so much."

"You'll know when the time is right," Annie said.

"How will I know?"

"God will show you."

"God never helped me before."

"Really?" Annie said, and she picked up the diary that lay next to Isabelle on the sheet. "What about this?"

"Did God send you to read my diary?"

"Maybe God caused you to write the diary. Did you ever think of that?"

Isabelle shook her head and closed her eyes.

"I have to go now," Annie said. She looked toward Minnie, who said, "But I'd like to stay if that's okay."
Isabelle nodded.

"Knowledge is power." ~~ Proverb

CHAPTER SIXTY-ONE

Isabelle was gingerly brushing her hair when Annie arrived Thursday evening.

"Belle," Annie said. "It means beautiful. It's your name."

"Yes, it is," Isabelle said. "But I don't feel beautiful. I'm afraid I'll have some permanent scars on my arm, maybe on my leg, too."

"But not on your face?" Annie asked hopefully.

"They don't think so."

"I brought you some things to read." Annie offered Isabelle a small devotional book—topped by a notebook.

"Oh, you found my notebook," Isabelle said. "I wrote such awful things in it about you. Did you read it?"

"I did, but those things don't matter now."

Isabelle drew a deep breath and looked out the window. Neither of them spoke for a while. A crow sat on the ledge looking in.

Then Isabelle said, "I was in the house when you told that other woman . . . Chloe . . . about caring about me. I couldn't believe it."

"I hope you will come to believe it. You matter to a lot of people."

"Do you mean that you forgive me for what I planned, for what you read in my notebook?"

"That is exactly what I mean."

Isabelle opened her eyes and stared at Annie. "Thank you, thank you," she said.

"Isabelle . . ."

"Please sit down, Pastor Annie. I want to tell you the rest of my story. The hospital social worker has been talking to me about it. He said I should start telling my story, that things at home weren't my fault."

"He's right."

"I always felt like I was the one who was wrong. I felt like I was bad because my father and mother treated me bad."

"Isabelle, you weren't the bad one. You never were. I want to tell you my story, too. Okay?"

"Yes."

They talked for more than two hours, Isabelle propped up in bed and Annie sitting in the side chair. The nurse stopped in several times to check Isabelle's intravenous line and give her medication. The nurse smiled at Annie, who sensed the nurse knew Isabelle's recovery depended as much on the words coming out of her mouth as on the drugs dripping into her body.

Isabelle's story was amazing. It was even heroic. Annie told her so and asked her to repeat certain parts of it so she could understand more fully how Isabelle's life had unfolded in the fourteen years between her desperate departure from Biddlebourne and her return to town.

Isabelle spoke of her hopes and dreams, of her desire to start new again in Biddlebourne. Quietly, she admitted that she had once believed Annie Scovill stood squarely in the way of her renewal.

Annie told her about the bones, about finding them in the basement, about frantically hiding them, about suspecting only recently that they were Ernie Pargeon's. Isabelle asked more about the day Annie made her discovery, and she wept quietly as Annie explained how she'd first dug up each bone and later dug up a Pillie Beer buckle and a wedding ring.

"My mother never gave him a ring. He bought one for himself at the five and dime," Isabelle said. "My mother had a wedding ring in her jewelry box. I used to play with it when I was a little girl. But she never wore it. Never once that I saw."

Isabelle's eyelids drooped, and Annie knew it was time to go.

Death in the Parsonage

"Truth may walk through the world unarmed." ~~
Arabic proverb

CHAPTER SIXTY-TWO

Friday, July 22

"You need a raincoat, Pastor?" Chief Henderson asked. He stood in the doorway of Annie's office in his black regulation slicker. Rain had come on the tail of the cool air.

Annie held up her briefcase to show him the striped umbrella snugged in a side strap. "I'm all set."

"Court starts in ten minutes. We gotta go the back way because of, uh, the cameras and all."

"The cameras?" Annie said.

"Yes, ma'am. Channel Four's here, along with Channel Ten and I don't know who all else . . . at least one newspaper besides the *Sentinel.* I shooed 'em away from the police station. Else they'd have followed me here to your office."

Ike couldn't help running a hand through his hair. He had to look good for the cameras, too.

"Ike, I'm sorry for all the disruption caused by this," she said. But he held his hand up and shook his head. "No, Pastor, I'm sorry it had to be this way. I just hope we can get this cleared up today. You know what I mean."

"You mean that you want me to agree in court to answer all your questions about the bones."

"Yeah, I guess so," he said.

"We'll see," Annie said.

As they entered the courthouse, Annie knew everyone was admiring her new blue suit with pearl-gray clerical shirt and navy Naturalizer pumps. But all she heard was questions.

"Reverend Scovill, are you covering up a murder?" someone asked. "Reverend Scovill, Reverend Scovill, over here . . ."

Annie hugged Chloe, Shirl and Gloriana as they joined her and Ike. Shirl smiled, whacked Annie twice on the back and said, "Everything's gonna be all right, heh, heh, heh." Gloriana squeezed Annie's hand, leaving behind a starched, hand-hemmed linen handkerchief.

The courtroom, to Annie's astonishment, was jammed. She wished Sunday morning attendance were as abundant. The entire pastoral liaison committee was present, occupying a whole bench just behind the defendant's table at the front left. Ma Pugh sat on the aisle and gave Annie a pat on the arm as she passed. The church trustees filled the next bench and a half, and behind them were the Power Rangers, who obviously had come to court by way of the Quick Stop, for they all appeared to be chomping bubble gum. Annie wasn't sure who else was present because the chief was already seating her at the table.

Annie was surprised when Chloe, Shirl and Gloriana sat next to her at the table as if they were defendants, too. Annie smiled at them. They smiled back.

They had arrived not a minute too soon. The bailiff bawled, "All rise," and a tanned and fit-looking man swept in on a wave of black serge and Irish Spring. He thunked himself into the big leather seat of authority. A glowing plate on the dais read, "The Honorable Timothy W. Lincoln."

"Sit," he said. Everyone did. The judge addressed a man seated at the table across the aisle. "What's this about, Billy?"

Annie deduced that Billy was the prosecutor. He rose and said, "Your honor, this case is a little unusual."

"Yes, yes," said His Honor. "In what way?"

"Your honor, the defendant in this case, the Reverend Ann Scovill…"

"Annie," she said to Ike, but he just shook his head and shushed her.

". . . is accused of withholding information material to the unreported death of a Biddlebourne citizen, Mr. Ernest Pargeon."

"That good-for-nothing," the judge said. "You got it straight old Ernie's dead once and for all?"

"Yes, Tim, I mean your honor. Reverend Scovill had secreted the aforementioned remains, which the state lab has now determined unquestionably belong to Ernie."

"Can't say anybody's gonna be sorry to hear about it, but I suppose we have to proceed," the judge said. He turned to Annie and said, "Are you the defendant, Reverend Ann Scovill?"

Annie stood. "Annie, your honor."

"Okay. Are you Reverend Annie Scovill?"

"Yes, your honor."

"Have you engaged legal counsel?"

"No, your honor, I have not."

"Do you understand that you are entitled to legal counsel?" he asked.

"Yes, I do. I, uh, waive that right."

"On whose advice?" He stared at Billy the prosecutor.

"Sir, with respect, this is a misunderstanding," Annie said. "I believe that when I explain what happened, the charges against me will be dropped."

"Madam, this is only a preliminary hearing," he said. He turned to the prosecutor and said, "Billy, what do you want to do?"

"Hell, Tim, I didn't know she wouldn't be represented. I guess the people want Reverend Scovill to be bound over to the grand jury."

"What!?" Annie said. "I didn't do anything wrong."

"Madam," Judge Lincoln said, "you will address your remarks to the court, not to the prosecutor. I'll appoint an attorney for you and continue this case until . . ."

Just then the double doors at the back of the courtroom flew open. Actually, they were butted open by the south end of a hospital gurney, upon which lay Miss Isabelle Marie Pargeon. A young man pushed the gurney. Beside him a nurse rolled a stand bearing the intravenous setup that still was attached to Isabelle's arm.

"Order!" the judge shouted. "What's this about? You! State your name and business." He pointed sternly at Isabelle.

Isabelle sat up with difficulty, leaning on her right elbow. "I'm sorry I'm late. We got caught in the rain."

"And?" said His Honor, who seemed to have the patience of a bear burrowing for honey.

"I have some information about Pastor Annie's case—I mean about the bones—I mean about my dad."

"State your name," he commanded.

"Isabelle Marie Pargeon."

Onlookers gasped. A murmur arose across the room like a low tide coming in.

"You know anything about this, Billy?" The prosecutor shook his head and shrugged.

"Young woman, your appearance today is highly irregular," said the judge, and he scratched his bearded chin. The audience, even the Power Rangers, quieted as he cogitated. Annie knew this because the rustling of gum wrappers ceased.

"All right. Approach," the judge said to Billy the prosecutor and to someone on Annie's side of the room. Billy walked briskly to the judge's bench. Annie waited for someone from her side to go forward. Nobody did. Ike looked at her expectantly. Finally, the judge said sternly, "I mean you, Reverend Scovill. Step to the bench."

"Me?" she asked, but Ike nudged Annie forward before the judge had to repeat his invitation to a sidebar. It was Annie's first sidebar. She went up to the grand oaken monument at which Judge Lincoln sat.

The judge spoke to Annie and Billy. "What the hell is going on here? Oh, for God's sake, excuse me, ma'am. I want one of you to explain this to me within the next sixty seconds. Do not further waste the time of this court. It's bad enough I had to end my vacation early for this."

"Your honor," Annie said without looking at Billy, "that woman is Isabelle Pargeon. She's the daughter of Ernie Pargeon. I have been counseling her on . . . matters recently. I have not revealed information about Mr. Pargeon's death out of respect for Miss Pargeon's privacy. I apologize, sincerely, to the court. I don't know why Isabelle is here today, but I think she may want to give information about her father's death. I ask you to hear her out."

"You object to that, Billy?" the judge asked the prosecutor.

"I guess not."

"Very well, then. Step back," the judge said, raising his voice so that all could hear. "The court will hear the comments of Miss Isabelle Pargeon in this matter. Are you prepared to be sworn in, Miss Pargeon?"

"Yes, sir," Isabelle said in her small voice from her gurney. "But I can't stand up yet. May I testify from my bed?"

"This is irregular," he repeated. "However, the court will make allowances for extenuating circumstances. Bailiff, please swear in Miss Pargeon."

Judge Lincoln glared at Annie, then at the prosecutor and said, "The court will question Miss Pargeon. You two sit down."

"The state reserves the right to cross-examine the witness," Billy said.

That statement seemed to rile the judge. "Do you think the court is incapable of fully questioning the witness?" he asked Billy.

"Of course not," Billy said, "but I want . . ."

"All due process will be observed," the judge said. "Bailiff, proceed."

When Isabelle was sworn in, she lay back on her pillow, and the bailiff brought the microphone to the side of the gurney and pulled it to the level of her lips. The judge waited until Isabelle was settled and said, "Miss Pargeon, what is your connection to the matter before the court?"

"It's all about my father's bones."

"Are you speaking of Mr. Ernest Pargeon?"

"Yes, sir."

"Were you present at his death, Miss Pargeon?" the judge inquired.

"I was," she said. A collective intake of breath arose from the onlookers. Then they grew silent. The silence grew so big that the ticking of the wall clock behind the judge sounded like Big Ben.

"When was that?" the judge asked.

"My father died in 1990."

"And this happened where?" he asked.

"At home . . . at 1010 Greenbriar Road, Biddlebourne, West Virginia," she said with a catch in her voice and a heave of her shoulders. Her helper gave her a fistful of tissues. Isabelle wiped her nose and waited for the next question. Annie twisted around toward Isabelle and saw her clutch the sides of her bed. She tried to make eye contact with Isabelle, but the witness was locked in on Judge Lincoln as if he were a grand inquisitor and she his victim in shackles.

"I see," he said. "And how did your father's death occur?"

"He fell down the cellar steps," she said. Another gasp came from the crowd.

"Are you testifying that he died from the fall?" the judge said.

"No . . ."

"Then how did his death occur?"

"He fell down the cellar steps."

"Did your father die from this fall, or did he not?" the judge said. "Yes or no?"

"My father fell down the cellar steps. He was drunk as a skunk."

"And did he die from the fall?" the judge demanded.

"I . . . I don't think so."

"Miss Pargeon, you are trying the court's patience." Annie felt for the judge, but only a little because she thought he was too harsh with Isabelle.

Everyone could see Isabelle gulp, but she responded, "I was never sure. I thought I heard him groan after he fell. I wanted to help him, but Mom said, 'Touch him and I'll get after you with the butcher knife.' She had the door locked. I couldn't get down there to . . . you know . . . go down there and help Daddy."

The judge obviously was taken aback. He looked at the prosecutor, who shook his head and held his hands up in resignation. The judge sighed and plunged ahead. "Miss Pargeon, I must inform you that anything you say may be taken down and held against you. The court has been informed by . . . authorities that you are a person of interest in the fire that happened over at that house last weekend."

Annie was becoming angry, not with Isabelle for her spotty answers but with Judge Lincoln for his mean questioning. Unable to stop herself, she stood and said, "Your honor, she was only a child."

"The court needs no assistance from the defendant either," the judge said.

Annie thought it wise to say no more at that time. So she sat. But Ike stood. What was going on? The police chief cleared his throat and said, "Your honor, may I have a word with the court? Privately?"

"Does it pertain to, of all things, the appearance of Reverend Scovill in this matter today?"

"In a way," said Ike.

Now Ike had gone and made the judge even madder. Annie thought he was about to blow a gasket or short a circuit. But he managed to get control of himself and to say, tightly, "Very well. Court is in recess. For FIVE minutes. Nobody go anywhere. I don't want to have to wait while we collect all the parties again. Miss Pargeon, you're still under oath. Got that?"

"Yes, sir."

The five minutes came and went, but the judge and the chief didn't return to the courtroom. Chloe showed everyone snapshots of her darling Daniella from the California dig. She also had a photo of Bob standing with the coaching staff of some team—the Hornets or the Hellions or some such—from a West Coast league. They talked about lunch, which apparently had been on all their minds.

After more than twenty minutes, the bailiff came into the courtroom and took Isabelle into the judge's chambers. He made Isabelle's crew stay in the courtroom. A half-hour went by. Annie and her group decided on the buffet restaurant so everyone could get what they preferred.

Then the bailiff returned and told Annie and Billy to go see the judge. That made Annie nervous, and she wanted Chloe to go with her, but the bailiff said His Honor wanted ONLY Billy and Annie to come in.

Ike and Isabelle were smiling when Annie got to the judge's chambers. "Reverend Scovill," Judge Lincoln said.

"Yes?"

"Reverend Scovill, all charges against you are dismissed. You are free to go. Please accept the court's apology for any . . . inconvenience of the last several days. And the court thanks you for your service to the people of Biddlebourne."

Astounding! An hour earlier the judge had as much as told Annie to shut up, and now he was apologetic and grateful. Billy the prosecutor looked mystified. Judge Lincoln turned to him and said, "Ike will fill you in. You people are all free to go."

Annie's court experience, little as it was, had been useful. She said "Thank you" to the judge, nodded toward the others and departed. The others saw the wisdom of her exit, for they were right behind her when she turned around to look. They went back to the courtroom, where the bailiff walked to the front and shouted, "Court's over. Everybody go home."

That sat well with everyone but the reporters, who were sorry the case hadn't produced more dramatic results. At first they swarmed around Annie, but after she said, "No comment" three or four times, they moved on to Chief Henderson. Ike slicked his hair and then, as it is said in high places, took questions. His assistant, Stan Neiswonder, stood behind him at attention while Ike spoke.

Burl Stout met Annie at the gate in the front of the room with questions in his eyes and on his lips. "What's going on, Annie? Have you been released?" he said.

"I have. Are you free for lunch?"

"I am."

"The Homestead Buffet—on Dowd Street. Can you meet us there in fifteen minutes?" He nodded and moved toward the rear door, cell phone in hand as he went. Annie went over to thank Isabelle. Minnie Glendenning was handing Isabelle a beautiful bouquet of subtly colored herbs tied with a yellow ribbon. Minnie tucked Isabelle's coverlet around her and said to the nurse, "Let's get our girl back to the hospital. She's had a lot of excitement for one day." Isabelle saw Annie and waved before she allowed herself to be wheeled out. Minnie turned toward Annie for an instant and threw a thumbs-up, and Annie knew that Isabelle was at last in good hands.

They were eight for lunch at the Homestead Buffet— Annie, Shirl, Chloe, Gloriana, Ike, Burl, and Mr. and Mrs. Gideon Pugh. They had barely ordered beverages before Chloe spoke. "So tell me. I can't wait any longer! What happened in the judge's chambers?"

Everyone looked at Annie, but she was officially in the dark, too. She looked at Ike, and everybody else looked at Ike.

"Vinny's boys did it," he stated simply.

"I'm not surprised," Shirl said.

"I have not the slightest notion what you are talking about," Chloe remonstrated. "Please elaborate, if you don't mind."

"Vinny Clark—he runs the hardware store, Miss Chloe—Vinny had his boys set the fire at the parsonage."

"By *his boys*, do you mean the schoolboys who work for him at the store?" Annie asked.

"Only two of them . . . two boys from over Claypool way. You know what they say: 'Nothing good ever comes out of Claypool.' Anyway, Vinny caught the boys stealing lawn mowers from the store. The pair of 'em had been in trouble with the law before and were afraid they'd get sent to juvee—that's juvenile detention, Miss Chloe—if they got caught again. Vinny saw his chance and struck a deal with them. They would do his dirty work, and he wouldn't report their thievery."

"But why would Vinny want to torch the parsonage? That makes no sense," Mr. Gideon Pugh said.

"Oh, it makes sense once you understand that Vinny and Vickie June Pargeon were . . . were . . . an item a long time ago."

"I never heard about that one," Shirl mused.

"Me neither," Ella Mae Pugh said.

"Just the same, they were mixed up with each other for a long time back in the seventies and eighties," the chief said.

"How can you be so sure?" Mr. Gideon Pugh asked.

"Vinny told me so himself," Ike said.

"And you believe him?" Mr. Gideon Pugh persisted.

"Oh, yes. I do believe him because he also told me other things, too."

"What?" Everybody said it at once.

"Vinny told me that he was in the house the night old Ernie fell down the stairs. He and Vickie June had been upstairs, uh, in the bedroom, you know, when old Ernie came home early from work. Had a valentine or some such for Mrs. Pargeon. Busted into the bedroom, and there was Vinny and Vickie June. Ernie told Vinny to get out.

Vinny put on his clothes but went downstairs and hid in the kitchen closet. See, he was afraid Ernie was going to hurt Vickie June."

"For the life of me, I cannot imagine what Vinny Clark would have seen in Vickie June Ransom," Ma Pugh interjected.

"She was a looker back in the day," Mr. Gideon Pugh stated. "You'd see her and Ernie at the county fair and all. Old Ernie had it bad for her."

"Let's get back to Vinny in the closet, please," Chloe said.

"Well, Vinny told me there was a lot of shouting upstairs and cussing and throwing things. He said Ernie came down about fifteen minutes later and sat at the kitchen table drinking by himself for maybe an hour. When Ernie got up from the table, Vinny says, he was blind staggering drunk and yelled some more things up the stairs at Vickie June. She came tearing down the stairs with a lamp base in her hand. Must've jerked it out of the wall cord and all, Vinny figured. Went at Ernie and bashed him a good one smack in the head.

"Ernie was bleeding and staggering and swearing. He got to the basement door and started down the steps but fell almost from the top. Went head over heels from the sound of it, Vinny says. Vinny high-tailed it home then. Never saw old Ernie again, dead or alive. Never asked Vickie June about him, either, though he didn't believe her cock-and-bull story about Ernie runnin' off with a floozy."

"I'm not so sure Vinny wouldn't, uh, adjust the real story to make it Vickie June's fault," Shirl suggested.

"Shirl, Vinny came in on his own after we got the fire investigator's report. Probably heard through the grapevine we knew it was arson. He didn't have to tell us anything. But he came forward anyhow.

"And, when you think about it, there's no way we could prove now that anybody murdered old Ernie. There's just not enough evidence in those bones to prove murder, if murder is what happened. And there sure as heck aren't many clues left in that burned-out house.

"And besides that, we looked at the skull. Wasn't a single sign of trauma there. Maybe somebody bashed him a good one, but that blow probably didn't kill him. Besides, Vinny had another motive for stepping up and telling the truth."

"What?" They all spoke in unison.

"Oh, he realized that Isabelle Pargeon was his own daughter. He was ashamed that he never acknowledged her as his own before. Couldn't, on account of old Ernie takin' such an attitude about it. But when the fire happened and the story got 'round about a young woman bein' in the fire and all, he figured it out. Believe it or not, he wants to make it up to Miss Isabelle."

"Well, I'll be," Ma Pugh said.

"That explains a lot of things," Annie said.

"Like what?" Chloe said.

"Like why Vinny acted . . . differently toward me at the All-American, and why he practically broke into the house while I was there one night last week, and why he questioned me so closely when I bought a pickaxe at the store."

"What'd you buy a pickaxe for?" Ma Pugh asked.

"To check for more bones," Annie said. Ma looked at her with admiration. Annie shrugged and grinned.

Ike spoke. "When Vinny saw those holes you dug up, Pastor, he got real scared. He suspected you dug up Ernie, and it about drove him crazy. That's when he decided to set up the arson.

"And something else. After Vickie June died, he had his boys go into the house and make noises, turn on the lights, stuff like that so's people would think it was haunted."

A second went past before a collective "oh" came from the others at the table.

"What's gonna happen to Vinny's boys who actually did the arson?" Burl asked.

"They'll go to trial. They have rap sheets already, so I figure they'll do some time on this," Ike said.

"Will Vinny go to jail, too?" Gloriana asked.

"It's possible."

"I still don't understand exactly why Vinny wanted to harm me," Annie said.

"It wasn't you. It was the house," Ike said. "He wanted you out of there real bad. See, nobody ever saw hide or hair of old Ernie after that day he took a header down the basement steps. For all Vinny knew, old Ernie was still down there. I s'pect he didn't want anything coming back on his lady love's reputation. Ha. As if she had any reputation left to protect. He was practically beside himself when you bought that pickaxe, ma'am, and that's when he hatched up the fire plan with his boys."

"And he put the cat remains on my doorstep and sent the threat letter and left dead chickens in my car, didn't he?" Annie said.

"Well, ma'am," Ike said, "we got him on the letter and the chickens, or I should say we got the two boys. Fingerprints and all, you know. But we didn't have the cat package to look over for evidence. I guess you got rid of it. Can't say I blame you. Unless the boys confess, we'll never know who put that at your door."

"But why," Annie asked, "did they use animals to scare me?"

Ike swallowed. "Pastor, you probably didn't know it, but there was a news item about you in the *Sentinel* before you came here. It said you loved animals and worked in some kinda animal group, so Vinny figured that was a good and cheap way to scare you."

Gloriana exhaled a low *wow*. "Okay. I get all that," she said, "but why was Isabelle in the house the night of the fire? If she didn't set it, what was she doing there?"

"I can answer that," Annie said. "Isabelle was trying to get upstairs to save Chloe and me."

"What?" Chloe said.

"She told me her story at the hospital," Annie continued. "She asked me to tell people what happened so you would know she didn't set the fire.

"Isabelle came back to Biddlebourne in response to a letter from her mother. Mrs. Pargeon apologized to Isabelle and wanted to start over. But Vickie June died before Isabelle arrived.

"Isabelle was distraught—traumatized, really—by her mother's death because she held hopes of reconciling with her and living with her at the house on Greenbriar Road.

"After Vickie June died, Isabelle did what she had been doing for fourteen years. She hid out. She sneaked into her parents' home. Most of the time she stayed in a hiding place she set up in the basement as a child."

Chloe held up a hand. "Why did she hide? Couldn't she just present her ID and claim the house?"

"Technically, yes, but she was afraid of many things. She was conditioned as a child to think everything was her fault—or her responsibility. She feared that people would find her and punish her for things that weren't even wrong."

"That poor girl," Ma Pugh commented.

"Yes," Annie agreed. "But when Isabelle learned that the family had sold the house to the church, she became even more frightened. She moved out of the house and made camp along Muddy Creek. She kept food and supplies in various hiding places and managed to maintain such a low profile that I don't think anyone in Biddlebourne recognized her."

Ma Pugh and Shirl exchanged looks amazement. "That girl is amazing," Ma Pugh said.

"Especially when you consider that she has amassed considerable savings by working hard, investing her money and imposing self-discipline. She has her income set up to receive only a modest check each month for necessities. She saves the rest.

"She risked her life trying to warn Chloe and me about the fire. She saw what those boys did in the basement and was making her way out of the basement when the water heater exploded. When she realized that Chloe and I had already left the house, she tried to take the stairs back down but was overcome by smoke."

"She saved both our lives—and Fannie Fay's," Chloe said quietly.

"Yes, and she is suffering now because of it."

Chloe nodded, and her eyes shone with tears. "Why would she do that?"

"She heard us talking about her in the basement—you know, when we were down there on our . . . project," Annie said. "She thought of us as her friends. And Isabelle Pargeon has not had many friends in her life. She was so affected by the thought that we cared for her that she had a sort of epiphany. She found the courage to rent an apartment in town and to let herself be seen by the townspeople."

There was silence all around the table. Finally, Chloe said, "She's braver than I would have been."

"Me, too," said Shirl, "but I can't believe I didn't know about any of this. To think that Vinny and Vickie June were messin' around and nobody knew it. That Vickie June was smarter than I thought!"

"I'm still confused. Isabelle left home years ago, right?" Chloe said.

"Yes, and came back to Biddlebourne on and off. Let me fill in some gaps for you."

"That would be very helpful," Chloe said.

Annie continued. "Isabelle ran away from home when she was thirteen, not long after the man she called her father went down to the coal cellar and never came up again. Her mother was hospitalized soon after Ernie's death, and when she returned home she mistreated Isabelle—abused her—more and more. So one day Isabelle packed up and took a bus out of the state."

"So that's what happened," Shirl said. "I knew Vickie June made up that story about Isabelle going to stay with family and all. Vickie June wasn't on speaking terms with ANY of her kin!"

"Where did Isabelle go?" Gloriana asked.

"At first to Chicago, working as a motel maid, and later to other cities."

"That poor little thing. I feel awful guilty about this," Ma Pugh stated.

"Why's that, Ma?" Mr. Gideon Pugh asked.

"Little Isabelle would come to our house—you wouldn't remember, Gideon. You were always out with the herd—and we'd talk and do things together. I knew Old Lady Pargeon was awful hard on her, but I . . . should have looked into it."

"Please don't blame yourself, Ma," Annie said. "Isabelle hid a lot of things that went on in her house out of shame and embarrassment. When she reached out to her neighbors, they helped her in ways that she needed at the moment. Tell me this, though. Did you teach Isabelle how to clean a house?"

"Oh, I didn't think of it like that. We was just doin' things together, vacuuming and dusting and changing beds and such."

"Ma, you taught Isabelle what she needed to know to get her first job. Sure, she was underage, but she was safe and she could clean, and that's what she did. Those skills helped save her."

Ma Pugh sniffled and reached into her handbag for a hanky. Mr. Gideon Pugh put his hand on her arm and said, "Now, Ma, don't take on. I have an idea for you. We'll talk in a bit."

Annie continued. "Isabelle came to Biddlebourne from time to time before Vickie June died, staying in warm weather and leaving in cold weather. She watched her mother from a safe distance and never even spoke to her during those trips. She drew comfort from knowing her mother was still alive."

Nobody asked where Isabelle lived during her sojourns in Biddlebourne, and Annie did not volunteer information about her hiding places.

"Well, I'll be damned!" Shirl exclaimed. She neither apologized for her misspeak nor acknowledged the glower that Ella Mae Pugh bestowed upon her. "So it wasn't Old Lady Pargeon come back from the dead!"

"Shirley!" Ma Pugh said. "What a thing to say!"

"Don't look at me, Ma. Everybody was sayin' it, heh, heh, heh."

"I want to know something else, Chief," Burl said. "Will Isabelle be charged for . . . anything in this matter?"

"No, sir, she will not," Ike said. "She has turned over to me—well, she allowed Pastor Annie to turn over to me—her diary. Everything's in there just like she said it happened. No, sir, she was not at fault in her father's death. No way. And if you folks at the church aren't going to press charges for her breaking and entering . . ."

"Of course not," Annie and Burl chimed. In that moment Annie decided to keep to herself the suspicions about Vickie June Pargeon's use of potentially fatal herbs and potions. For one thing, an investigation could get Minnie into trouble, which would have been very unfair. For another thing, they needed to focus on helping Isabelle heal, not dredge up more ugliness from her past. Now they could let the gossip and innuendo die a natural death. *Ernie and Vickie June, rest in peace—if you can.*

"In which case, Miss Isabelle is free to go about her business as soon as she's well enough to leave the hospital," Ike concluded.

"But there's so much we don't know about Isabelle," Chloe wailed.

"Isabelle gave me permission to share things about her life," Annie said. "She decided that her story must come out—for her own sake and for other reasons. She worked as a motel maid for many years. She'd live in a room at the motel, never buy any clothes except her uniforms, eat at cheap takeout places. She saved a fair amount of money. She assumed the name Isabelle Watkins the day after she left Biddlebourne and eventually managed to get both a Social Security card and a driver's license under that name. If she thought someone was getting close enough to discover her real identity, she would just hop a bus for the next big city. That's why she always lived in big cities. Big cities gave her anonymity as well as a huge supply of potential employers. There were always motels near the bus terminals.

"She didn't have a car until she was nineteen. By the time she was twenty-one she had enough money saved to go to college. She cleaned motel rooms by day and took classes by night. Isabelle Watkins is trained in accounting and clothing construction."

"What about her future?" Gloriana asked. "I dearly hope Isabelle feels she can remain in Biddlebourne."

"She wants to stay and build a new life in Biddlebourne."

"I'm so glad to hear that," Ma Pugh said. "That'll give us a chance to make it up to her—to treat her how she should have been treated from the beginning."

Shirl nodded and said, "But it still looks like you're out of a home, Pastor. You gonna keep your room over at the Pughs?"

"About that parsonage," Mr. Gideon Pugh interrupted. With a wink at Annie, he said, "The trustees has talked. Me and Ma and Pastor Annie has talked. It's all decided. We're gonna build us a new parsonage."

"Hurray!" Chloe shouted, clapping her hands. "I hope there'll be a nice guest room!"

Annie turned to see Burl beaming. "Did you know about this?" she asked him.

"Not exactly, though I recommended that course of action," he said.

"Where will Annie and G.P. live while it's being built?" Gloriana, ever the practical pastor, wanted details.

"Pastor and the mister will park themselves temporarily in our carriage barn. Don't worry, Miss Gloriana. We fixed it all up when our boy Glenn got married. Back in ninety-one, or was it ninety-two, Ma? Glenn, he's been in his own house now, oh, nine or ten years. But Ma's still got the place all decorated up nice. And, anyway, we'll have Pastor Annie in her new parsonage by Christmas!"

Gloriana looked in Annie's direction to confirm this report. Pastor Annie smiled and nodded. They had worked it all out the evening before. Annie laughed and said, "Our bed and G.P.'s desk were already in the carriage barn."

"Oh, Annie, I'm so happy for you," Gloriana said. "You'll have a clean start. But what will the church do with the current parsonage?"

"Why, it goes back to Miss Isabelle, of course," Mr. Gideon Pugh said.

Ma Pugh had seemed impatient while Mr. Gideon Pugh answered Gloriana's queries. Finally, she said, "We also got another surprise for the pastor."

Hm, Annie thought.

"We're giving Pastor Annie a week off so's she and her hubby can have a little vacation together," Ma Pugh said proudly. "With full pay, of course, and in addition to her regular vacation" she added thoughtfully.

"I don't . . . know what to say," Annie stammered. She wanted to say that her work would pile up if she left for a week. She wanted to say that she wanted to stay by Isabelle's side. But she also wanted to say that the events of the last weeks had nearly exhausted her, that her husband was coming home and that nothing would renew her more than time spent with G.P.

"Take the vacation and run," Gloriana advised. They all laughed.

"Uh, Shelby and I hope that you and G.P. will accept our offer to use our cottage on Lake Erie for your little getaway," Burl said.

"How could we refuse?" Annie said. She had been in that cottage. Chintz curtains. Rocking chairs. Windows open to the lake. In short, heaven on earth. And, ironically, heaven on earth without air conditioning.

"While you're gone, the trustees'll just go into the parsonage and carry out anything that can be salvaged. We'll lay it out nice and neat in the front part of the carriage barn—the part where they used to keep the tack," Mr. Gideon Pugh said.

"But won't those things smell like fire?" Chloe asked.

"We'll be real careful, Miss Chloe," he said. "I reckon the mattresses and curtains and all such are ruined, but I think we can save some of the furniture. Pastor Ma'am, we'll throw out everything that's no good anymore, but we'll write it all down and take pictures of it. We'll save everything we can and clean it up real nice. That ought to help when you go to replacing what you lost."

"We are very appreciative, Mr. Pugh," Annie said.

"Call me Gideon," he responded.

"Okay, if you'll call me Annie," she said.

The dessert selection was outstanding at the Homestead Buffet. Even Chloe, to Annie's amazement, ate a cookie.

Before they left the restaurant, Annie made appointments with Burl, Gideon and Ike. When Ike said he would take her in his unmarked car to pick up the Volvo, Chloe, imperious as ever, butted in to say, "I think not, Chief. The car still stinks to high heaven from the chicken episode. Please cause one of your men to drive it over to the Pughs' carriage barn. My sister cannot possibly continue to drive around in that, that stinkmobile!"

"There's Old Yeller," Ma Pugh said.

"No! Absolutely not!" Chloe rejoined. It occurred to Annie that although her sister had her difficult moments, she was quite effective in her own way and that Annie's most prudent course of comment right now would be to make none.

Ma Pugh was cresftallen. Annie would comfort her— later.

"I was thinking that the church could rent a car for my sister to use until she's back from her vacation at the lakeshore," Chloe went on.

Gideon rubbed his chin. Burl scratched his. Ma Pugh snapped her pocketbook shut. "I'm the chairlady of that committee," she said.

"What committee?" Chloe asked.

"The things-the-pastor-needs committee, that's what committee," Ma Pugh said to Chloe, adding, "If you went to church, young lady, you would know how the church runs."

Chloe looked properly put in place. Ma Pugh went on, "I'm the chairlady of THAT committee, and I say this rental can be a compact but not a big sedan. We gotta watch our dollars!"

"Very well, then," Chloe, the transportation agent, agreed. "Please have the car at the carriage barn by eight o'clock this evening. And please remember that my sister does not want to drive around in crazy-colored vehicles."

"Yes, ma'am," Gideon said with a wink to Annie and a pat to Ma Pugh's arm.

Death in the Parsonage

"Marriage halves our griefs, doubles our joys, and quadruples our expenses." ~~ Proverb

CHAPTER SIXTY-THREE

"I told you everything would be okay," Shirl said as she unlocked the Caddie.

Annie tried to get into the backseat, but in a rare display of forbearance Chloe motioned her to the front. Chloe entered the back of the big, white roadmobile and scrunched herself up in order to touch as little of the nicotine-laden upholstery as possible.

"Thanks for the ride," Annie said to Shirl.

"Aw, no problem. Chloe here, she says we got shopping to do. I know where every bargain is anywhere within forty miles of Biddlebourne."

"But I have a lot of work to do if I'm going on vacation," Annie said.

"No, you have shopping to do," Chloe insisted.

"Uh, okay then," Annie said. Shirl stomped the accelerator and burned rubber as they tore out of the Homestead Buffet lot.

"I've wanted to do this for years," Chloe said.

"Do what?" Annie said.

"Help you with your wardrobe. This is wonderful. We have a whole new clean slate to start with. Let's see, we'll need casuals, sports, evening wear and, of course, some good foundation garments, and proper shoes and . . . ."

"I only need a few things," Annie said.

"You need some silk blouses and some fine gabardine slacks—pleated, I'd say—and at least two lightweight jackets, one black and one, oh, I'll decide when I see what they have. Shirl, where are we going first? I want upscale stores with classic collections. Clean lines. Elegant colors. I do not want to see one piece of polyester all day long!"

By now even Shirl knew not to argue with Chloe. They made the rounds all afternoon. Annie tried on more clothes that day than she normally did in a year. Chloe was picky about every seam, every length, every fit. She made one poor saleswoman bring out eight or nine skirts to go with Annie's new nubbly tweed jacket but didn't let her buy any of the skirts. She complained to the manager of the shoe store that NO ONE wanted patent leather anymore and that he could be using valuable shelf space for more promising lines of footwear.

It wasn't enough for Chloe that Annie tried on all those clothes. Chloe selected an outfit that she made Annie wear out of the shop she seemed to like best. It was the tweed jacket with a soft, cream-colored blouse and a complementary skirt that was at least two inches shorter than Annie's usual length. She had to admit, though, that it was a sharp ensemble. Chloe finished it off with a simple gold necklace and gold earrings.

"I never wear earrings," Annie reminded her. "They get in the way when I'm talking on the phone."

"Never mind the phone," Chloe said, and Annie bought the earrings.

On the way out of Belwix's Chloe spotted a cosmetics counter and hauled Annie over to a stool, where she sat while Chloe and the cosmetics lady discussed Annie's complexion and cheekbones. They tried this and that, with Shirl serving as audience and offering additional advice, until they had Annie made up like a grand dame of drama. Annie took one look in the mirror and said, "Way too much! I can't be seen in public like this."

"Perhaps it is more than you're used to," Chloe allowed. They toned down the makeup and gave Annie the mirror again. Annie didn't recognize herself, but she wasn't under a half-inch of cosmetics anymore, so she let the clerk sell her the kit. When they left Belwix's, Annie was one decked-out preacher lady.

"How about some dinner?" Shirl said in the car.

"Okay," Chloe said. That's when Annie started to get suspicious. Chloe had already eaten a meal that day—a big meal. She would not eat another whole meal for at least twenty-four hours.

"I'm hungry, too," Annie said to Shirl. "Where do you have in mind?"

"As it happens, there's a dinner at the church tonight."

"What dinner? How can there be a church dinner that I haven't heard about?"

Chloe, apparently, had caught her earlier mistake and hastened to say, "I suppose I could eat some salad and have some iced tea, but I have to stay away from those church casseroles. They're hard on my hips."

"It's a pig roast. No green salad but plenty of slaw," Shirl said.

"Vinegar or mayonnaise dressing?" Chloe asked.

"Take your pick. And Ma Pugh made some Frisky Granny. I brought the Hanky Panky."

"What's Hanky Panky?" Annie asked.

"Never mind, okay? Let's go," Chloe said.

"Wait a minute," Annie said. "Who planned this pig roast?"

"The committee," Shirl said.

"What committee?"

"The Pig Roast Planning Committee."

"This is the first I've heard of either a pig roast or a pig roast planning committee," Annie said.

"It's a tradition," Shirl supplied.

"It's a tradition that on July twenty-second every year Glory Hallelujah Church holds a pig roast? The Pig Roast Planning Committee did not do a very good job of publicity, I have to say. I do not understand why nobody told me about this earlier."

Annie did realize it was wrong to presume that a pastor knew all, or even most, of what was happening among the congregation on any given day. There had been entire mission projects of which she was unaware until a busload of sweaty missioners returned to the church parking lot. "We had it covered," they would say, and in every single instance she could remember of this go-ahead-and-get-it-done attitude, they did indeed have it covered. This was a healthy thing, healthy for the congregation and healthy for the pastor. Still, she thought that Gideon or Ma Pugh would have let her know about the pig roast because, apparently, it would cancel all other church activities that evening.

"Nah, it ain't that kind of tradition," Shirl said.

Sighing, Annie said, "Well, what kind of tradition is it?"

"The church holds a pig roast every time one of our own comes home from military service. Winter, summer, spring or fall. Doesn't matter. Everybody comes out for the pig roast."

"I'm trying to remember whose son or daughter is in the service," Annie said, opening her day book to scan the member list.

"It's nobody's kid. It's somebody's husband," Shirl said.

"It's for G.P., you ninny!" Chloe shrieked from the back.

"Jig's up," Shirl admitted.

"But how . . .?"

"Never mind how," Shirl said. "We're there." She braked loudly and rolled up the car windows with the button on her armrest.

"How do I look?" Annie said, pulling down the visor mirror. It reflected the image of a middle-aged woman she had never seen. The biggest problem, though, was her hair.

A tap on the car window disturbed Annie's anxious self-examination. A thin, darkly tanned man in uniform stood beside the car. His cap shielded his face from view. She pulled the comb out of a side pocket of her briefcase and began making repairs.

"Annie!" Chloe exclaimed.

"What!?" Annie said.

"That's G.P."

"Is not."

"Is so."

"It must be one of his buddies. The unit has people from all over West Virginia—even from Indiana and Kentucky."

Annie was combing as fast as she could. G.P.'s buddy opened her door and took the comb out of her hand. "You're beautiful just the way you are," he said.

She hadn't recognized her husband's form, but she recognized his voice. He put the comb in his pants pocket and pulled her out of the car with both hands. No more words were necessary. He wrapped his right arm around her waist and planted a big kiss on her. Annie threw her arms around his neck and kissed him right back. Hoots came from across the church lawn—the Power Rangers, she guessed. Chloe and Shirl got out of the car and began walking to the striped picnic tent on the east side of the church lawn.

"How long have you been here?" Annie asked.

"Since this morning. I checked in at the Pughs. I wanted to come to your hearing today, but they convinced me you needed to focus on your court appearance. Gosh, you look great! I hardly recognized you, though!"

"I didn't recognize you," she confessed. "How much weight have you lost?"

"About twenty-five pounds, I suppose. It's okay. The unit doc said I needed to lose it anyway."

"And you're as brown as a coconut!"

"Ah, my lovely. I've been in the sun fourteen hours a day for a long time. What did you expect?"

G.P. was hiding something behind his back. Annie knew most of G.P.'s moves. She thought it might be flowers and didn't want to ruin his surprise.

But when he revealed his surprise, it was not a bouquet of roses. It was a Popsicle. Strawberry. He slowly broke it in two, handed half to Annie, and whispered in her ear, "Happy anniversary, Annie Ido. Wanna go for a walk?"

She accepted the Popsicle and said, "How could you possibly remember that?"

"I remember everything about the summer we met. I thought you were the nicest, smartest, prettiest girl I had ever seen. But you were so shy I was almost afraid to talk to you."

"I was lovesick all summer," she said.

"So was I."

"I don't have anything for you—for our anniversary," Annie said.

"Yes, you do," he said with a big smile.

"G.P.!" Annie said, but she had to laugh. He laughed, too, and the sound of that laughter made the tears that lay waiting begin to slip free. She didn't want to embarrass G.P. in front of the church folks, and she didn't want such an intimate moment to draw public attention. But the tears would not stop. All of the pressures and frustrations and craziness of the last month seemed to be leaking from Annie as G.P. crushed her and the strawberry Popsicle in his arms.

"Annie." G.P. was suddenly serious.

"Annie," he said again.

"What?"

"I'm remembering something else, too." He loosened his arms from her shoulders but held her eyes with his.

Annie's tears slowed. She nodded. "I know," she said. "No secrets. No lying, No whining. No nagging. No sorrow borne alone."

"Annie, why didn't you tell me everything that was happening to you?"

G.P. looked tired . . . and hurt. He swallowed hard. She could see his Adam's apple rise and his jaw tighten above the collar of his blue dress shirt.

"Will you take a ride with me? I think Shirl will let me borrow her car," Annie said.

"A ride? Now?"

"Please. You'll see why."

"Sure, I'll go for a ride with you, but you don't have to borrow Shirl's car. I have the truck here."

"Okay, then. I'll drive. I know the way."

"Not a chance," G.P. said, shaking the keys out of his pants pocket.

"I'll navigate," she corrected. G.P. smiled.

In a few minutes they were at the parsonage.

"Look at her," Annie said.

"Her?"

"The house," Annie said. "She was going to be a beautiful lady again, but look at her now—a burned-out shell."

"Are you sorry?" he asked.

"About the house? Yes, very much. She had almost been redeemed."

"Redeemed? You mean renovated?"

"No. Redeemed. She was a home to child abuse, alcoholism, spouse abuse, maybe even murder. And we were turning her into a place of comfort . . . of shelter . . . our home."

G.P. sat comfortably behind the wheel of the truck. He picked up Annie's left hand and touched it to his lips.

"But it was only wood and plaster and blocks."

"Fixing it up made me feel closer to you, as if I was actually bringing you home by making it into a home."

"It was tough living in the parsonage, wasn't it?" he said.

"There was pounding and fumes and do-overs and workers and problems all the time."

"But you never mentioned those things to me."

"How could I? You were risking your life, living in a tent, sleeping on a bunk, eating in a mess hall. Oh, G.P., I'm sorry I kept secrets from you! Secrets can hurt so much. I've never been as aware of that as I am now. Are you terribly angry with me?"

"Annie, I'm not angry. But I am disappointed. It's not the secrets that bother me. It's that you carried all this by yourself."

"I had a foolish notion that I was protecting you, freeing you from the distraction of worrying about me."

"How long have we been married?" he said.

"Well, more than twenty-five years."

"And do you think that in all those years I might have noticed you told me everything that was going on around you and inside you?"

"Yes, I suppose so."

"And do you think I'd notice if you suddenly stopped telling me all that stuff—what was bothering you and what was making you happy?"

"I see where you're going. Things did get away from me here in Biddlebourne, almost from the beginning. I'll tell you everything. I promise. But I want to hear what you have been through, too. I don't care what the rules are."

"I'll tell you everything I can . . . tonight." Annie opened her mouth to speak but was able only to nod. They embraced like teenage lovers. After a few minutes G.P. said, "Do you think we ought to get back to the party?"

"Definitely, but I want to make one quick stop on the way."

"It must be pretty important."

"It is. I want to visit a man named Franklin Dwayne Cushing. I'll tell you why on the way."

They needn't have worried about any concern at the pig roast for their whereabouts, for Chloe was nicely holding forth in the tent when Annie and G.P. returned. Shirl, they learned later, had asked Chloe to sing a "number or two" from *Guys and Dolls.* Chloe, it was also later reported, had demurred only fleetingly before beginning the show.

Everyone else was clapping, and some were singing along, when Annie and G.P. reached the picnic tent. The pig dripped drops of fat into the stone pit below it, and whoever had been assigned to turn the spit, probably the Power Rangers, had abandoned their jobs and were singing, whistling and hooting as Chloe sang and danced.

"One more time, one more time," the Power Rangers chanted as Chloe finished "A Bushel and a Peck." But

Gideon Pugh held up his hand for quiet and motioned to Annie and G.P. "Come on up here, Annie," he said. "And you too, G.P."

They walked hand forward hand in hand.

"Minnie has something for you," Gideon said. With no further fanfare, Minnie Glendenning stepped up beside them holding an object covered by a flowered bed sheet.

"This is for you both," she said as she whisked the sheet off the surprise.

"Ooh. Aah. Wow," they heard from the crowd. When Annie and G.P. turned together to view the gift, they saw a portrait of 1010 Greenbriar Road. The parsonage was painted gleaming white, and its front door was a brilliant red. A cat sat smiling on the porch railing. Two pairs of tiny wings fluttered near the attic vent. In the driveway stood a beaming couple, side by side: a woman carrying a Bible and a briefcase and a man wearing a military uniform.

Minnie turned to Annie and G.P. and spoke so quietly that only they could hear. "Pastor, I think you might be able to handle Biddlebourne after all." Annie looked at Minnie, who looked back at her squarely. "Thank you, Minnie," Annie whispered.

Aloud, Minnie said, "That's your first parsonage at Glory Hallelujah Church. And the next one will be even better."

"She looks new again," Annie said.

EPILOGUE

"The beginning and the end reach out their hands to each other." ~~ Chinese proverb

The lake shines, reflecting the sun.

The husband runs. With abandon. Still brave, but now barefooted.

The cat lolls. Porch her realm. Seagulls her attendants.

The bag lady is gone. In her grave with her faded clothes, moldy blankets and broken toys.

The sad lady is gone, too. Born anew. Named anew. Found by the brother. Tended by the gardener. Taught by the teacher. Chauffeured by the captain. Embraced by the town.

The preacher rests. Writes. Prays the prayers of the grateful.

~~0~~